THE RIGHT PLACE TO BE

He was going to leave now. Walk out the door. She wanted to stop him but her pride prevented it.

"Anne," Mike said, his hand on the doorknob, "I'm just at the other end of that phone line. Remember that."

She held her breath, waiting for him to leave so she could cry. But he didn't go. He reached out to her, pulled her to him, cradled her against his shoulder. They stood for an instant, not moving, not speaking, content to cling to each other. Mike held her carefully, his hands sheltering her back, his cheek caressing her hair.

She wanted the moment to last forever. She was safe, loved, secure in the shelter of Mike's arms. Then, as she looked up at him and he saw in her eyes what he wanted to see, he gently, carefully kissed her forehead, her cheek, her mouth.

Suddenly, being held wasn't enough, being close wasn't enough. Anne stretched upwards on her toes, arching into his taut body, her arms going around his neck. And their mouths opened to each other, greedy, seeking, savoring the heat and passion that flared between them.

Dear God, it had been so long. . . .

WATCH AS THESE WOMEN LEARN
TO LOVE AGAIN

HELLO LOVE (4094, $4.50/$5.50)
by Joan Shapiro

Family tragedy leaves Barbara Sinclair alone with her success. The fight to gain custody of her young granddaughter brings a confrontation with the determined rancher Sam Douglass. Also widowed, Sam has been caring for Emily alone, guided by his own ideas of childrearing. Barbara challenges his ideas. And that's not all she challenges . . . Long-buried desires surface, then gentle affection. Sam and Barbara cannot ignore the chance to love again.

THE BEST MEDICINE (4220, $4.50/$5.50)
by Janet Lane Walters

Her late husband's expenses push Maggie Carr back to nursing, the career she left almost thirty years ago. The night shift is difficult, but it's harder still to ignore the way handsome Dr. Jason Knight soothes his patients. When she lends a hand to help his daughter, Jason and Maggie grow closer than simply doctor and nurse. Obstacles to romance seem insurmountable, but Maggie knows that love is always the best medicine.

AND BE MY LOVE (4291, $4.50/$5.50)
by Joyce C. Ware

Selflessly catering first to husband, then children, grandchildren, and her aging, though imperious mother, leaves Beth Volmar little time for her own adventures or passions. Then, the handsome archaeologist Karim Donovan arrives and campaigns to widen the boundaries of her narrow life. Beth finds new freedom when Karim insists that she accompany him to Turkey on an archaeological dig . . . and a journey towards loving again.

OVER THE RAINBOW (4032, $4.50/$5.50)
by Marjorie Eatock

Fifty-something, divorced for years, courted by more than one attractive man, and thoroughly enjoying her job with a large insurance company, Marian's sudden restlessness confuses her. She welcomes the chance to travel on business to a small Mississippi town. Full of good humor and words of love, Don Worth makes her feel needed, and not just to assess property damage. Marian takes the risk.

A KISS AT SUNRISE (4260, $4.50/$5.50)
by Charlotte Sherman

Beginning widowhood and retirement, Ruth Nichols has her first taste of freedom. Against the advice of her mother and daughter, Ruth heads for an adventure in the motor home that has sat unused since her husband's death. Long days and lonely campgrounds start to dampen the excitement of traveling alone. That is, until a dapper widower named Jack parks next door and invites her for dinner. On the road, Ruth and Jack find the chance to love again.

SWEETS
TO THE SWEET

JOAN SHAPIRO

ZEBRA BOOKS
KENSINGTON PUBLISHING CORP.

ZEBRA BOOKS are published by

Kensington Publishing Corp.
850 Third Avenue
New York, NY 10022

First Printing: July, 1994

Printed in the United States of America

For Norm, who always encouraged me to go for the dream—and for all the other dreamers who never give up, because they know it's never too late!

And thanks to Ann Wassall for p. 313—remember?

And thank you, Doug: "Mac" and "Mike" are grateful for all you taught me in the Saturday Society at Restaurant Duglass!

Formidable!

"They do not love that do not show their love."

—Shakespeare, *The Two Gentlemen of Verona*

Prologue

Silence. Black silence. Hot, suffocating silence.

Anne lay in that void, unable to see or hear or understand. Then, as the endless seconds crawled past, the initial shock ebbed; fear came to take its place, bringing with it some semblance of rational thought. She was wedged tightly into a tiny space, her arm trapped beneath her and she, in turn, pinned just as solidly beneath something else, something smooth and large and heavy. So unbelievably heavy, pressing her downward, pushing the air out of her lungs.

And the pain. Huge daggers of pain sliced through her skull, rhythmic and unceasing. She wanted to scream but couldn't seem to utter a sound. Couldn't draw enough breath to push sound beyond her throat.

Panic fought loose from the numbing effect of shock, and Anne's skin was bathed in perspiration, cold and clammy. Her heartbeat leapt irregularly and in her stomach lay a heavy knot of fear. Desperation pushed a primal scream to her throat but the panic throttled it to a quiet whimper.

Suddenly, there was a muted crash, the vibrations felt even in this dank hole, as if somewhere far away a heavy weight had collapsed from a great height. And it was something to focus on, something outside of herself. There was still a world out there . . . somewhere. Hot tears scalded their way down her cheeks and, in a way, that was reassuring. She could at least cry. If you were dead, you couldn't cry. So the pain and the tears and the panic told her she was alive.

For how long?

And what in the name of God had happened?

She lay quietly then, through the sick emptiness and the urge to shut off her brain, forcing herself to think.

Last night. They'd gone to dinner, she recalled, a wonderful gypsy restaurant, with flamenco dancers and a man who had played soulful melodies on his guitar. Such a perfect way to spend their twenty-fourth anniversary . . .

Paul! Oh, God, *what had happened to Paul?* She strained to listen, but now all she could hear was the faint drip of water somewhere and, closer, what sounded like the creaking of wood floors, the way a ship sounds on a restless ocean. But there was no ocean. They were . . . she tried to concentrate. Where?

Of course, Mexico City, the Maria Isabella hotel on the Prado until they left for Acapulco—was that today? She swallowed the rising hysteria. Oh God, this wasn't Acapulco. Anne bit her lip until the taste of blood touched her tongue. Think! Concentrate! They'd come back to the room last night, packed up for an early departure, and gone to bed. Yes, that's right! They'd gone to bed. But . . .

She focused . . . desperately: She *must* remember! How long ago had she opened her eyes abruptly, wondering what had woken her? And then the memory was suddenly clear. Lying amidst the soft cool tangle of bedsheets and large comfortable pillows, she had watched, in uncomprehending fascination, the bright bars of sunlight coming through the slits in the window blinds, dancing crazily across the walls, the bedcovers, the floor. She remembered that one last instant when, as if in excruciating slow motion, the ceiling began to come down toward her, and then . . .

"Paul." She couldn't quite control the trembling of her lips and it came out as a grunt, a breathy gasp of sound. She tried again. "Paul!" That was a little better. She stopped, waiting, listening. Was that a sound nearby? *"Paul?"*

"Aaann . . ." So quiet, so low, it was almost lost in the close, dark, airless cavity. She wasn't alone! He was there and he was trying to say her name.

"Paul! Oh, darling, where—?" She couldn't see anything. She knew her eyes were open but. . . . Oh, God, was she blind? No, no, not blind, because even in the darkness she could see gradations of black, and when she closed her eyes there was a change in the seamless dark. With her free hand she tried to reach out and found her fingers tangled in some kind of cloth. The bedsheets! And then her groping fingers suddenly touched a hand, the cool metal circlet of a wedding band. Paul's hand! It felt as cold and damp as she did, but it was his! She squeezed it hard. There was a faint movement in response.

"Oh, Paul, thank God," she gasped. "Are you all right?"

"Anne." His breath was shallow, the words muffled. "I . . . love . . ."

The fingers fell from her hand. Now, except for her own breathing, the silence—and the loneliness—was complete.

One

"Anne, that was my ace! Hey, where are you? You just wasted our last trump." Laura's voice broke through Anne's absentminded fog.

"What? Oh! Oh, Lord, I'm sorry, Laurie!" Anne looked sheepishly at the three other women seated around the bridge table, then lowered her eyes to the cards held in her bloodless fingers. "I don't know what's the matter with me. Damn, I just screwed up our slam, didn't I?"

"Didn't you!" Laura rolled her eyes, then smiled to take the sting out of her words. "Well, I've been playing this crummy game for twenty years and I never made a slam, so why should you?"

"I owe you one." Abashed, Anne finished playing out the hand . . . what was left of it, anyway. She laughed, and two of the women laughed with her. She knew Laura wasn't so easily fooled. "It's a good thing I've got you for a partner, at least you can afford me, so I don't need to feel too guilty." No, only uncomfortable and self-conscious, she mused. A small curl of desperation touched the back of her thoughts, the repressed rush of tears stinging her eyes. It was getting harder and harder to concentrate, to tune in to the people who should have been her comfort, her support. Oh, God, at first she'd thought it was only a matter of time, that she'd get back on track . . . eventually.

"Annie, you're getting worse, not better."

Anne looked up, startled. Was it so obvious?

"You used to be the best bridge player at this table. But lately you . . ." Ruth Gorman stopped, her mouth snapped shut, and she looked from the corner of her eye at the woman on her right.

Laura Garrett shoved the cards into their holder and pushed herself back from the small table. "Anne's just busy thinking about Jerry. With summer vacation coming, it'll be the first time he's been home in months. After all, when your only child leaves for college, the empty nest is kind of scary." Anne was grateful for the change of subject.

"That's right," Jenna Harris chimed in from the opposite seat. "I mean, we've all been through it. Of course, we had younger ones at home. Anne's all alone . . ." Now it was her turn to stop in mid-sentence, her cheeks pink, her eyes stricken. "Oh, honey, I didn't mean . . . it's just that I didn't think . . ."

"Hell, Jenna, you never think," Laura muttered. "Okay, girls, what about some more iced tea? And there's still some cake left if anyone—"

"Come on, stop it now," Anne interrupted firmly. "You don't have to walk on eggs around me. We've known each other too long for this." She looked down at her hands, folded on the table in front of her. "I'm sorry to be such a damn fool." She smiled faintly at the other three women. They'd been friends, because their husbands had been friends, for over twenty years, and they were about as close to her as sisters would have been.

"Oh, Anne," Ruthie said, "it's just a matter of time; don't worry about it. Things will work out." Anne felt the nausea rise in her throat as the clichés tumbled from her friend's lips. If anyone said that to her one more time, she'd heave her lunch in that person's lap!

Anne gritted her teeth and squeezed the offered hand. "Thanks, Ruthie, I'm grateful for the way you put up with me. And now I think I'd better get home—"

"Don't be silly," Laura interrupted. "You're staying for dinner. I hate making salad, anyway, so you can do it. Besides, Jim specifically told me to invite you, and if you're willing, he hinted he wouldn't mind one of those apple pastry things you made for that last dinner party. I've already bought everything you'll need. You can make it here."

Anne wanted only to crawl home and hide, but in the face of Laura's determined assault, she knew she was cornered. Defeated, she stared hard at her friend, who grinned at the precision of her arrangements and rose, putting the cards and scorepads into the drawer of the dining room buffet. It was a beautiful house, with hardwood floors and Oriental rugs, fine furniture that invited and gave comfort as well as beauty, along with some really excellent antique pieces. In every room was evidence that the people who lived there were prosperous enough to afford the best, and had the taste to go along with the checkbook. But more than that, it was a friendly house, which offered welcome. And now Anne accepted that offer, more grateful than she was prepared to admit.

After a flurry of kisses and promises to get

together for lunch in a couple of days, Ruth and Jenna finally drove away, and Anne turned to follow Laura to the kitchen. She was relieved at the departure of the other two. But that was unfair, she thought guiltily. She was truly fond of them. They'd all been so close for twenty years, and yet now she knew the failing was hers more than theirs. They'd gathered around, offering comfort and support, but they could not fill the center of her life, the gaping hole left by Paul's death. In truth, it was easier with Laura alone: There was an undefined, unspoken bond between them; she could let slip the cheerful, well-adjusted mask. Truth could seep out and Anne wasn't uncomfortable with it in front of Laura. Laura Garrett was way beyond the word friend.

"Actually, General," she muttered to her friend's back, "you don't invite, you command." Anne smiled, softening her words, and dragged a large Lucite bowl from one of the cupboards. She knew her way around this kitchen as well as she did her own.

"I wasn't going to give you a chance to say no," Laura said matter-of-factly, handing Anne a knife and a cucumber. "You've done it too often lately and I *know* I'm not that bad a cook." She looked thoughtfully at her friend, then halted in her task of laying out three linen placemats and silverware on the kitchen table. The Garretts had long ago dispensed with the more formal atmosphere of the dining room when they were at home alone or with close friends.

"Annie, I can read you like a book. Usually. But lately that book is closed tight. I know something's wrong, at least more than there should be by now. It's been . . ." She stopped at the stark expression on Anne's face.

"I know exactly how long it's been. And after two years it's time I got myself back together." She said it in a flat, unaccented tone, like one long familiar with the words. She stopped what she was doing, the small paring knife held unnoticed in her right hand and a radish in her left. Her voice was suddenly ragged. "I wish to God I were better at hiding it."

"Hell, your trouble is you're too damn *good* at hiding it!" Laura put the things on the table and walked to her friend. "Annie, do you ever cry? You're so buttoned up and stingy with your emotions, it scares me. Come on, girl, this isn't healthy."

Anne's face was set, blank. "Have you any idea how difficult it is to keep the smile pasted on my face? And yet by now it shouldn't take that much effort. It shouldn't take any effort at all! Hell, the people I spend time with are *friends*, old friends, good friends. I shouldn't still feel this . . . this distance, this separation. . . . I'm beginning to think it's never going to be any different." She leaned over the sink, shoulders slumped. "I didn't mean to dump myself on you. Damn, is that what friendship is . . . never having to say you're fine when you're not?"

"Look," Laura said, refusing to put on the kid gloves, "Jerry's been at Michigan State since September, and with the job he took he's only been home for a few weekends. So, except for winter and spring breaks, you've been rattling around in that house all alone." She stopped abruptly at the involuntary flash of pain in Anne's eyes. "Oh, honey, I'm sorry. It's just that I love you, Anne, and I'm worried about you."

"I know, Laurie, and you don't have to worry. I'm not going to do anything . . . crazy."

"Oh, God, I didn't mean . . . ! Of course, I know you wouldn't . . ." Laura held Anne's icy cold hand for a few seconds and stood quietly, studying the cucumber slices in the bowl. "You're closer to me than anyone on this earth . . . well, maybe except for Jim and the Terrible Tiresome Trio I once gave birth to in some of my weaker moments . . . and there are things you and I talk about I'd never say to him! But, Anne, it's as if there's a door inside your head that's shut, and you refuse to open it and let in the fresh air, even with me! You're not letting yourself heal."

Laura reached into the cupboard for three delicate flowered dinner plates, set them on the table, then turned back to Anne. "You've got to get out more, and I don't mean these bridge games and shopping trips and lunches with the girls." She grimaced. "Even I get a little bored with shopping and hairstyles and bitchy gossip as topics of conversation. And that kind of stuff was never enough for you, even when Paul was alive. I think that's why you were such a good player. You were the only one concentrating on the challenge of the game rather than the girl-talk. But lately you . . . oh, I don't know, you've isolated yourself. You're less involved than ever, as if you're . . . drifting."

"You, my friend, are dangerous," Anne said quietly. "When did you learn to read minds so well?"

"Not minds plural. Just one. Yours, *my friend*. That's the operative word here, kiddo, and don't you forget it." Laura sat down at the table. "Look, Annie, maybe I shouldn't ask, but forty-five is too young to make a permanent retreat from the world. Are you ever going to . . . uh . . . want to go out again?"

"Oh, Lord, Laura, you mean a *date*? I haven't the faintest idea; I've never thought about it." She wanted to avoid this . . . the thought of sitting at a dinner table or in a theater with a man who wasn't Paul. It was an image that frightened and, in some elemental way, offended her. God knows it wasn't a new idea for Laura, who had made vague mention of available males. Indeed, Anne was quite sure that at one time or another the question had been on the minds of all her friends. No one else had actually said it aloud and Anne had thought she might get by a little longer before someone did.

She should have known better. Laura, when she was sure she knew what was best, could hang on and outlast an infinite number of subject changes.

"Annie, there are a couple of men from Jim's plant he'd like to introduce you to. I know them and they're both nice guys. I think you'd—"

"Please, Laura," Anne said firmly, "I know you mean well and I'm sure they're very nice, but I can't handle this . . . not yet." Perhaps not ever. "My God, blind dates at my age!" She tried to smile at the woman beside her. "Laura, you know better than anyone what Paul and I had: the best marriage ever. From high school on he was my first, my only love; he was my best friend. I can't turn off my feelings for him just because he's . . . because he's gone. I wish I could!" She turned away abruptly and the knife clattered as it dropped to the countertop.

"I don't know if I could explain it to you," Anne went on, staring out the window above the sink. "I pray to God you never have to know this feeling! It's like a part of me is broken off, missing, and I don't know where to look for it. I was half of a couple for almost twenty-five years—*twenty-five years*—and I've forgotten how to think like *me!* Paul's been gone two years, and I still can't really believe it will be forever."

Eyes bright and hard, Anne looked at the woman who was so much a part of her, her dearest friend. "Wanna hear something really nuts? I go to the butcher and still buy those little lamb chops he loved so much. Then I cook them and eat them—and I don't even like them! But *he* liked them, and I can't forget that. Isn't that crazy?" The word caught on a note of ragged laughter that descended into a muffled sob. She sank into one of the chairs and rested her elbows on the table, holding her head.

Laura sat beside her, frowning, an expression of worry and concern on her angular face, her arm around her friend's shaking shoulders. "Annie, honey, why have you been keeping this to yourself? Why didn't you tell me? Listen, have you thought about seeing someone . . . a counselor or—?"

"You mean a shrink?" Anne's brittle laugh was filled with self-mockery. "Oh, yes, I've been seeing her for months now." She looked up into startled eyes that she knew as intimately as she knew her own reflection in the mirror. "No, I didn't even tell you. I—I couldn't. Ah, Laura," Anne closed her eyes, "it sounds dumb, but I was too ashamed to say anything. But, by now I guess I'm getting used to it. I suppose," she shrugged, "a person can get used to anything . . . in time. In time," she repeated in a whisper.

"Annie, that's nothing to be ashamed of. My God, if you broke a leg, you wouldn't try to set it yourself. You'd go to an expert, and that's what you've done. Well, good for you! If she can help, that's terrific." Laura smiled. "I'm big enough to admit there are some people who are smarter than I am, even about you!" She grinned. "So, what did she say? That is, if you want to talk about it."

"Oh, sure, after all this time you're suddenly bashful about asking questions? Yeah, right." Anne smiled; she wasn't fooled by Laura's look of wide-eyed innocence. "It's just that I didn't want you to think I was so weak I had to—"

"My God, Anne, don't talk like an ass! Weak. Oh, yeah, that really describes you. Weak! After what you went through? Jeez, anyone else would have been a cringing basket case. But you came through it and you're doing fine."

Anne looked at her. Doing fine. Sure. "That's not what you said before," she reminded Laura.

"Well, yes, but . . ."

"And you were right. As a matter of fact," Anne smiled, "Dr. Friedland's been telling me the same things you have. And I know she's—you're *both* right. I guess my timetable is a little slower than it should be. She said that wasn't so unusual and what I'm feeling now is perfectly normal. It just doesn't feel normal to *me*." She added dryly, "And that's normal, too."

"What did this Dr. Friedland suggest?"

"She said if I'm having trouble . . . adjusting . . . to the empty bed along with the empty nest, that perhaps I need a change of scenery, a time to get back my perspective on my own, away from the familiar . . . to break old habits, I guess. That's what I wanted to tell you. I've been waiting all afternoon to find the right words." Anne slumped down in the hard wooden chair, feet stretched ahead of her, hands jammed into her skirt pockets, her posture strangely defiant. Laura looked at her apprehensively.

Suddenly, Anne grinned. "Oh, don't worry, it's nothing drastic. I haven't joined an ashram or the Peace Corps, though that's not a bad idea, come to think of it. Anyhow, the good doctor suggested I take a trip, get away from the places where Paul and I lived together, the people we were so close to, the whole background of our lives . . . together."

Anne's voice shook, and she bit her lip to keep it steady. "She said I've got to begin to see myself as a person in my own right, capable of doing things alone if I must, accept that and get on with living."

She stopped abruptly. She'd known as soon as she'd heard the doctor say it that it was the right thing to do. To continue living in the same house, seeing the same friends, should have offered her comfort and a sense of security. Instead, she seemed to be stuck on a treadmill, going through a constant replay of times past, unable to move forward.

Here, in Bloomfield Hills, amid the once-comfortable circle of friends and relatives, she would always be perceived—and perceive herself—as what was left of a couple. Poor Anne. Paul's widow. Jerry's lonely mother. She couldn't do that to her son or *herself.* She couldn't, *wouldn't* live out her life like that, with no sense of herself. She had enough pride and self-respect to hate being "poor" *anything.* It was time to accept the fact that Paul was gone. If he'd lived, none of these thoughts would ever have crossed her mind.

But he hadn't lived, and life would never be the same.

"I think maybe, if I take a trip on my own, even a short one, I could begin to function independently. You know what they say about life being a learning experience. So, let's just say I'm past due for this lesson." She sat up, elbows at rest on the table, looking at her folded hands, while Laura made a concerted effort to keep her mouth shut and let Anne give vent to the pent-up emotions that had been building for more than two years.

"Laura, I don't know if it will help, but I've

got to try. I'm so damned tired of crouching in my safe little hidey-hole, living on leftover crumbs from the past. And yet, the old habits die hard. Somehow I can't seem to break the inertia: As soon as I'm with anyone else, I find I'm stuck in a kind of limbo, and I can't break through to see the future. Maybe part of it is living up to the image everyone I know seems to have of me, but it's wearing me out, existing in this permanent state of unease."

She closed her eyes for a moment and suddenly, Laura realized, looked every one of her forty-five years. Even she, her best friend, had not been aware of the toll taken by Anne's struggle to preserve her image.

Slowly, Anne opened her eyes. "Did you ever take any psychology courses in college?" Laura nodded thoughtfully. "Well, remember those rats they had in the maze, reacting automatically to whatever stimuli the professor was using? That's me; I'm trapped like one of those poor rats, in a maze of my own insecurity and grief. And I *hate* it! Maybe off on my own, I can get out of the maze and make some progress at last."

"I think it's a terrific idea! New faces, new scenery . . . and a new perspective, kiddo." Laura sat back, relaxed. "Sounds like you've made some plans already. So, where're you going?"

"Mmm, it's kind of tentative." Between Dr. Friedland and the relentless renewal of spring, the new growth all around her, the sense of rebirth, Anne had known instinctively this was the right move. "Jerry dropped the news that he plans to travel with his friends this summer and . . . well, maybe before he goes I can get a handle on myself. It might help when . . . I mean, the thought of rattling around in that big house all summer, alone and—" Damn, that sounded like poor, pitiful Annie again. "Hell, I don't want my friends setting up a nice little schedule for taking Annie out to air her off." She made a grimace. "I refuse to be a project for one of those 'point of light' awards."

Laura chuckled. "Oh, that'll be the day. I never met the human being who would *dare* feel pity for you!" She put her hand on Anne's. "So, where're you heading?"

"Well, you know how I hate 'sweat weather.' I thought maybe a drive through New England."

"Oh, I'll bet it'll be beautiful! Jim and I have always wanted to do that, though we never thought of summer. We'd always planned to try one of those fall color tours. Hey, didn't you and—"

She and Paul had done that. Anne's thought echoed Laura's. And maybe that's just why she'd chosen it. It would be familiar, with good memories, and yet it would be different enough that those memories wouldn't get in the way of a fresh start. Fall in New England had been magnificent, one of their best memories, that trip. And that was another reason for going now: Fall would have been too painful. But she didn't say it. "Anyway, I think I'll leave as soon as I can make arrangements, maybe the beginning of May."

"Hey, you're really serious about this, aren't you?" Laura laughed, rising to turn on the oven. Thank you, God, she thought. At last, Anne was looking ahead, making plans, something she'd found impossible to do ever since Paul's life had been snatched away so suddenly. As if she knew there was nothing one could really count on and making plans was an exercise in futility. But now here she was, planning and setting goals. Laura's smile was filled with quiet satisfaction at this healthy swing in Anne's outlook.

"So," Laura asked, "how're you going to do it? Oh, listen, I think we've still got last Sunday's *New York Times!* There are lots of tours advertised in the Travel section every week."

"No, I'm going alone. Now don't say it," Anne continued quickly, seeing the sudden dismay on her friend's face. "That's one reason I haven't said anything to you, not until I was sure in my own mind." She looked at Laura, standing at the oven with a casserole in her hands, her mouth open to voice the obvious objections. "Look, I know exactly what you're going to say: I'm a woman who's never traveled alone; I'll have to handle all the arrangements myself, drive strange roads alone; get lodging, eat alone in restaurants, find my way around a map . . . alone. I know all the arguments," Anne stated implacably, "and they're not important."

"What do you mean, not important?" Laura argued. "Honey, you're talking about driving hundreds of miles!"

"*Alone,* that's right."

"Anne, you can be a stubborn mule sometimes. Why in the world can't you do this the easy way?"

"Because I can't afford the easy way anymore, Laura," Anne answered in a low voice. Her friend sat down again at that tone. "I've been trying to live the *easy way* for two years now. Staying in my nice safe home, seeing my nice safe friends, following my nice safe routine . . . and feeling more and more disconnected and helpless and insecure every day. I can't fool myself into using a tour guide to substitute for a husband."

Anne rested her head on her hands. "Oh, God, Laura, I don't want to wind up desperate to get another man just so I can be taken care of. Paul did that, for all our lives, and I loved it—with him. She looked up from hollow eyes. "But I'm *without him* now, and I have to prove to myself that I'm not helpless, that I can survive."

"My friend, if there's one thing I know, it's that you're a survivor." Laura put her hand on Anne's arm and the two women held each other, comfort and friendship and understanding wrapping them together.

After a few moments of silence Anne sat up, still clasping Laura's hand. "I know you'll worry but"—she smiled faintly—"as the old commercial said: 'Please, Mother, I'd rather do it myself.' "

The nice thing about Laura—well, one of many, Anne thought—was that with all her outspoken mouthiness, she also knew when to listen, and when to bite her lips and keep still. After her initial objections, which Anne admitted were perfectly reasonable, Laura had offered only enthusiasm and a welcoming ear to Anne's plans.

Lord, it was hard to believe that she'd done it! Reading until she thought her eyes would pop right out of her head, she'd practically memorized the Triple A roadmap of the route from Michigan, through Canada and New York, then into New England. It had seemed so adventurous, she recalled wryly, the open road and going it alone. Easy to camouflage the fear in the frenzy of packing and goodbyes. But on the long stretches of road, through the quiet miles of solitude alone with her thoughts, it was impossible to escape.

Why had she chosen this particular area to explore? Oh, the easy answers she'd given Laura were valid enough, but she knew what her friend must have thought. Wasn't she merely retracing the trip she and Paul had taken? Wasn't she using this trip as the surrogate for the husband, and friend, and lover she still so sorely missed? And God help her, she *did* miss him, every day, every hour, every night.

Anne tightened her grip on the steering wheel of the Chevy station wagon. Three years old and, after its predeparture tune-up, it ran like a dream. Thank God. She could face the vagaries of life on the road, but breakdowns and tire changes were way down on her list of things to do.

She lowered the window as the car rolled down the two-lane road at its leisurely pace. This was a trip of relaxation. No timetables, no set destinations. No one awaiting her arrival. Her eyes threatened to fill for a moment but she willed the tears away. This was definitely not the time for crying.

Anne breathed deeply of the warm June air flowing through the car. Ah, that tasted marvelous! That ol' devil pollution wouldn't dare raise its head up here in New Hampshire. Lord, she hoped not, though it was probably a vain wish. Human beings seemed to have an infinite capacity for self-destruction.

Funny. That, she supposed, was exactly what she was doing here, hundreds of miles from home . . . searching her own path away from that same self-destructive urge. Oh, not in the literal sense. No matter what, life was too good, the years ahead with Jerry too precious, to remove herself permanently from the scene. No matter what Laura had feared, Anne's state of depression had never gone deep enough for her to be a threat to herself. But, still, she'd been doing a lot of invisible damage, beneath the surface, in her head, where no one could see how weak and afraid she really was.

The sign she'd just passed suddenly caught her attention. She slowed, braked on the empty road, and backed up to make sure of her direction. *Groveton.* She knew it, though it was just a very small place on the map, and to most people not native to these parts it wouldn't have meant anything.

She'd passed Franconia Notch, and even Cannon Mountain, without that gut-wrenching recognition, that instant sense of déjà vu. She and Paul had skied there, ridden the aerial tramway, and gawked at the "Old Man of the Mountains" rock formation . . . how many years ago? A lifetime ago. And yet, it was only when she saw the sign to the little town of Groveton that it had hit her so sharply.

Anne sat there by the side of the lovely little road in the quiet sunlit moments of a dusty June afternoon and, for the first time in a long while, let the tears spill down her cheeks unchecked. *Oh, dear God, how long? How long before I manage to get over this? Will I ever get over this? Everyone tells me it takes time; time will heal it, make it better. How much time? I used to tell Jerry that Mommy would kiss the hurt and make it better,* she thought sadly. But who would do it for her?

It was many minutes later that she dragged the soggy tissue across her eyes and took a deep breath of calming air. "This is no good. Wake up, Annie, before you waste this chance. Remember why you came in the first place, why you had to get away from home for a while." Anne sniffled a couple of times, straightened her spine, and gripped the wheel with new determination. She started the car again and eased back onto the road. At the next intersection, where Highway 3 joined Route 116, the sign pointed to Groveton. She paused for less than a heartbeat, then deliberately turned the other way, a road she'd never been on before, and followed the arrow toward a place called Whitefield.

Two

Ah, Anne thought with satisfaction, *if I wanted to avoid "sweat weather," I've found the perfect place*. She looked around from her seat on the bench and, while the cool, clean breeze of the late June morning ruffled her hair, smiled the smile of a contented woman. As she had for the past three days, she admired the scene and let herself become an avid spectator to the daily activities of Whitefield, New Hampshire. King's Square was an active place this Tuesday morning, the same familiar people taking their usual shortcuts across the cracked and weathered concrete pathway, a group of teenagers chasing each other and a football over the patchy grass, a couple of young mothers pushing strollers and chatting.

She turned her head at the loud pounding that disturbed the serenity of the scene. A bald-headed man of about seventy or so, breathing hard from his exertion, was hammering on a sign. It had come loose from a large maple tree standing beside the gazebo nearby, and announced to all and sundry that the Lions Club would serve pancake breakfasts here, on designated Sunday mornings, June through September.

She sighed. That sounded kind of nice, the image of friends and neighbors gathering to talk and exchange gossip, a festive, familiar, comfortable kind of image, people sharing their joys and sorrows, uncomplicated by anything more than the pursuit of their livelihoods and their familiar activities. Probably just an idealized glossy fantasy, but still. . . . Be nice to be part of that, like being part of an extended family.

Be nice to *let* herself be part of it.

You seem to be drifting, you're less involved than ever. Anne had a vivid recollection of Laura's voice making that observation. She sensed now that it was truer than she'd thought. She *had* drifted away, especially in the past two years, from the friends and interests she'd been part of—or thought she'd been part of— for so long.

Anne sighed deeply and looked around again, reflecting. The inhabitants of these sturdy and comfortable old homes around the square could probably teach her a lot . . . if she'd listen. The houses ringed by their bright green patches of lawn and flowers beneath these ageless trees, and certainly the people living inside them, knew who they were and their particular place in the world. They didn't need guide books or architectural experts to establish legitimacy, nor the false security of conformity to their neighbors to be part of their established order. Ah, yes, Anne thought wryly, the mystique of the independent freethinking New Englander. They were what they were, standing on their own two feet and taking what was dealt, with no complaints and no seeking approval for their actions.

She stretched her legs in front of her, sliding the base of her spine toward the edge of the bench, and contemplated the scene before her. Yes, she sensed the people of this small town knew who they were, in a way her affluent circle back home did not.

Oh, sure, *they* know who *they* are, but who am I? *There's the sixty-four-thousand-dollar question, and after the last two years, it's time for an answer.* Well, by now she'd proven, even without Paul, that she could survive; but life had to be more than mere survival. So, she had to get a life, as Jerry would so neatly put it. All right, but . . . what sort of life would it be?

Suddenly, Anne realized what appealed to

her about the prospect around her: no carbon-copy houses, no regulated uniformity or ubiquitous housing subdivisions, none of the obvious confinement of conformity. She'd bet there wasn't much worry about the approval of neighbors and zoning boards, about what was allowed and appropriate. She thought that she wouldn't mind a little less conformity in her own life. As she'd told Laura, continual worry about maintaining the appropriate facade was a wearisome and exhausting way to live, and especially in the last two years, she'd found herself increasingly impatient with those friends who expected it of her.

All these years she'd been content to be defined in terms of marriage . . . as Paul's wife. Now, more and more often, she found herself driven to define herself in terms of her own person—Anne McClellan. Back home she'd buried herself in a concrete pigeonhole, a coward, she admitted ruefully, though Paul had neither expected nor demanded it: but there'd been a distinct comfort in "fitting in."

She chuckled aloud. Every November, behind the closed curtain of the voting booth, she'd shot off her one meager little cannon of revolt: She'd dared to vote Democratic in the local bastion of Republicans. *Now, how's that for storming the barricades with courageous defiance!* Only now that measly gesture wasn't enough, and her once-comfortable staid little pigeon-hole didn't fit anymore. Back home they'd probably attribute any change to her sudden widowhood, probably think she'd gone "peculiar." And life as the neighborhood eccentric held no charms.

The nice thing about Whitefield, New Hampshire was that no one here would ever judge her, because no one here had known her in her other life.

How strange to think of back home as my "other life."

Funny, Anne mused, stretching and inhaling the clean fragrant air of the summer morning. Somewhere during the past two years she'd begun to mature, to emerge from the cocoon of familiar habits. *So, what will I be when I grow up?* she thought wryly. All this time life had been like a play, and only now was she discovering that she'd been playing a role. But the cast had changed and she was suddenly weary of the familiar part. And yet, although the play was beginning to pall, it was still awfully difficult to rewrite her character.

A sudden shift in the breeze drifted a wisp of her hair across her eyes, breaking the contemplative mood. Anne rose briskly, brushed the dust from her white cotton slacks, and looked around, smiling to herself. One of those plum tarts from Kolchak's Bakery would taste pretty good right now.

She grinned in anticipation. A stop at the small shop and a friendly chat with the sturdy elderly woman who was its owner had become a mid-morning routine in the days since she'd driven into Whitefield. And, since she would probably be leaving tomorrow—after all, there was no valid reason to stay on and she had to start thinking soon about heading home— she'd better take the opportunity to sample the goodies one more time. She'd like to say goodbye to Mrs. Kolchak, anyway.

"Well, hello there, Mrs. McClellan. Just got a fresh tray, right from the oven." The lined face of the woman across the counter was wreathed in a smile as she greeted her newest customer, the flat cheeks pink and damp with perspiration, her thin white hair frizzy from the moist heat. She winced as she set down the large metal baking tray. "Ach, my hands. They are so bad today." She looked down at them, and Anne saw the enlarged and misshapen knuckles.

"What's the trouble? Arthritis?" She'd seen the beginnings of it over the last few years among her friends.

"Yes," Mrs. Kolchak sighed, shaking her head. "My back, too. It's getting so bad I don't know how much longer I can take the weather up here. My daughter out in Santa Fe wants me to move there but"—she looked around and shrugged—"I don't know what I'd do with this place. My husband and I . . . we built it up and it's been good to us. He's been gone a long time now, but I hate the thought of just closing it up. And I don't think I'll have too many offers. Things haven't been that good up here lately. And it's kind of hard work, I guess. Well," she smiled suddenly, "you don't need to hear my problems. Here's your plum tart." She slid it on a paper napkin across the counter to Anne.

Just then the door swung open, and the brightness of the morning was blocked out for a moment by the tall man with the salt-and-pepper hair who was coming through the doorway. He was dressed in the dark blue uniform of the local police department and his eyes were hidden behind dark tinted sunglasses. Anne sidestepped to the other end of the counter, carefully juggling her pastry, leaving Mrs. Kolchak free to greet her customer.

"Ah, Michael, you are late. Here, I've got your usual ready." She smiled brightly at the monument of a man towering over her and bent to retrieve a large white pasteboard box from beneath the counter. "How those boys ever have time to chase criminals I'll never know, they're so busy eating doughnuts."

"Well, if Whitefield's finest ever have to choose between keeping the peace and eating your doughnuts, Mrs. Kolchak, the town's in big trouble. My boys know what's important. They'll go for the doughnuts every time! And"—his grin was wide and warm beneath the thick dark moustache flecked with sprinkles of grey—"*my* appetite isn't so bad, either. As a matter of fact, if my waistband expands any more, the criminals will have to spot me a couple of blocks, otherwise I'll never be able to catch up."

Anne raised her brows and smiled. She'd be happy to reassure him about his physical condition; he looked just fine to her. Absolutely no question about it.

Mrs. Kolchak smiled back brightly at his words, smug in the knowledge that his compliments were well-deserved. Her doughnuts were worth every one of them!

At that moment the beeper hanging from his belt sounded and he quickly handed her the money owed. "Have to get back to the station. See you tomorrow, Mrs. K." He swung around to head for the door and collided with Anne, who'd been standing a couple of feet behind him. "Whoops, sorry. I didn't see—"

"Oh, that's all right," she smiled ruefully, massaging her bruised toes against the back of her other leg, at the same time managing to avoid spilling a crumb. "I shouldn't have been lurking behind you like that." She stepped back out of his path.

"Michael, this is Mrs. McClellan. She's traveling around for a few weeks up here. She's getting to be as good a customer as the Police Department."

He stopped, looking at Anne with curiosity, his eyes flickering over the smart leather shoes, the stylish slacks and silky blouse, the obviously manicured nails with the diamond wedding band still in place on the third finger of her left hand.

"Up from the city, hmm? Spending the summer around here?" His voice was measured and polite, but he looked at her, through her, with a coolness and a kind of instant cynicism that surprised her, as if in those few seconds he'd assessed and labeled and now knew all there was to know about Anne McClellan. She glanced down at herself quickly, checking to see if her appearance had somehow deteriorated in the last few moments. No, she hadn't dribbled plum tart down her blouse and she was no more disreputable now than she'd been when she walked in.

So, what did he see—or think he saw—that he was so sure he wouldn't like? She had taken this journey precisely to escape being relegated to a pigeonhole, and here was this total stranger judging and cataloging before he knew anything about her. To be measured and found wanting so quickly only made Anne more determined to prove how wrong he was . . . whatever he thought!

"Well," she answered, smiling determinedly to fill the heavy silence, "I wasn't planning on staying the entire summer, but Whitefield is a wonderful surprise. I really love it here. I may stay for a few more days." Ten minutes ago she'd been planning to leave.

"And then on to the next place," he said, his cool eyes focusing pointedly on her be-ringed left hand again. "Well, there isn't really a lot for city people to do up here in the sticks, at least not in Whitefield, it's not real exciting." His indifferent glance drifted over her once more, and then he tuned her out with a sense of disinterest and finality, nodded at Mrs. Kolchak, and quickly left the shop.

"Such a nice boy," the older woman said with a fond look after him. Anne stared at her.

"Hmm, *nice* must be in the eye of the beholder." Or he was saving it for a special occasion, and she wasn't it? "Does he just dislike plum tarts, or was it something I said?" she asked, only half jokingly. She was irritated at the sensation that she'd been judged so quickly by a total stranger and found definitely wanting.

"Oh, he doesn't mean anything." Mrs. Kolchak picked up her towel and wiped a crumb from the counter. "I guess he was surprised to think the season is starting this early. It's not personal. He just doesn't much care for tourists in general. He says he likes people who stay put, stay where they belong."

"I see," answered Anne, who didn't really. Where they *belong*? Too bad, really, because except for his unwarranted attitude, she'd felt an inordinate sense of welcome from her first day in this lovely little town. Funny, in a way she felt as if she *did* belong here. "Well, it's lucky everyone doesn't agree with him, or the tourist industry would go down the tubes, fast."

Mrs. Kolchak laughed. "Yes, especially in the fall. The leaf peepers are a big part of our budget up here. We wouldn't want to do without them, that's for sure."

"Leaf peepers? Is that what we are?" She recalled with sharp pleasure the time she and Paul had driven through New Hampshire and Vermont to watch the magnificent explosion of autumn across the green landscape. It had been a glorious sight.

"Oh, it's just our name; we don't mean anything by it," Mrs. Kolchak hurried to mollify her. "We're very proud of our country up here, and most of us like to share it with everyone," she laughed. "Keeps the cash registers jingling and makes the country 'green.' And the season only lasts a few weeks." Just as she turned back to the kitchen, the phone rang.

"Hello, Kolchak's Bakery." She listened a moment and then her features drooped, worry and disappointment on her face, weighing down her shoulders. "No, of course not, Leni. You must stay home, go to bed. Maybe tomorrow . . . ? Oh, I see." She sighed quietly. "Well, it can't be helped. You just stay in bed and listen to the doctor. I'll stop by tonight, when I close. I'll bring some soup. Yes, I know, don't worry. All right, goodbye, dear." She hung up, then stood for a few seconds staring down at the phone, as if she couldn't understand why it had turned on her and given her such bad news.

"Is something wrong?" Anne asked quickly. "Can I do anything?" The usual, the obvious words. One was always so quick to offer, so sure the offer would be refused.

"What?" The woman, her face looking older in the last few seconds, looked at Anne as if surprised to see she was still there. "Oh, no, there's nothing, Mrs. McClellan. That was my sister-in-law. She works here with me but,"— Mrs. Kolchak glanced around with a worried look—"she's in bed with a slipped disk in her back. The doctor said she shouldn't move for a few days, or she'll have to go to the hospital and be put in traction. I don't know what I . . . I haven't arranged for any part-time help yet. School just let out for summer. I don't know . . ." Her words trailed off, and she was again unaware of Anne's presence.

"Uh . . . what needs to be done, Mrs. Kolchak?" Anne spoke abruptly, without thought. But it just seemed the right thing to do. It was clear the older woman needed help: Her hands were giving her such trouble and she was too frail to carry the workload all alone. "I really have nothing important planned for the next few days and I'd love to help out if

I can. Especially if you show me how to make plum tarts." She smiled reassuringly.

"Oh, no, I couldn't ask you to do that! You're—you're a customer, a—" She looked at Anne sharply, and the younger woman was uncomfortably sure that Mrs. Kolchak saw exactly what the big policeman had thought he'd seen. And she felt a surge of annoyance.

"Yes, I know, I'm 'city people.'" Anne's mouth twisted in a wry grin. "Believe me, I've gotten my hands dirty a time or two in my life. And I really don't mind postponing all my *exciting* plans for a while." She grinned persuasively. "Come on, you're the boss. Just hand me an apron and tell me what needs to be done, and I'll try to do it. *That* much I can guarantee: I'll try! Maybe good intentions can make up for inexperience."

She never thought to ask herself about where that road paved with good intentions could lead her.

Anne stretched out on the bed, aware and appreciative, as she'd been the last three nights, of the welcoming comfort of the Spalding Inn's firm mattresses and soft pillows. She was so tired. . . . But it was a good tired, a feeling of quiet satisfaction and achievement. She had done yeoman service these past three days and she was darn proud of herself! She'd learned a lot, and Mrs. Kolchak had been grateful for her help and lavish with praise.

"Ach, but I will miss you, Anne. It was as if God sent you here just when I needed you. I don't know what I'd have done without you." Now that school was out for the summer, she'd been able to make arrangements for some part-time help until her sister-in-law returned.

"I want to thank you, too, Mrs. K. It's the first time in a long while that I can honestly say I've enjoyed every minute of the day."

They'd hugged and kissed, and Anne knew without a doubt how sincere Mrs. Kolchak's fervent thanks were. They'd promised to write and then Anne had left the small bakery for the last time, feeling as if she were leaving a very dear friend. She would never have expected to feel so reluctant to go.

Now she stretched languidly and glanced over at her travel clock. *Lord, I wish I knew where Jerry was. I'd love to talk to him.* She had a sudden need, right now, to connect with home, with her *real* life; she had indeed drifted, and the intervening void was suddenly frightening. But Jerry, backpacking with his friends, was beyond reach and wasn't expected to call her at home for another week.

Home. . . . Yep, it was time, definitely time to head for home. She'd proved what she'd wanted, what she'd *needed* to prove, and in the process she'd learned something very important about herself. So, all in all, this trip had been exactly what she needed.

For some reason, the image of the big rugged policeman flashed through her mind. In a strange way, his words had been right on the mark. She was ready to go back where she belonged.

She clenched her hands tightly together, hot tears suddenly stinging her eyes. Where she belonged.

Oh, God, help me to know where that is!

"Annie! Oh, honey, it's so good to hear your voice! If it hadn't been for those measly two postcards, I'd have had the FBI out after you. You didn't say you were going to be gone for a month!"

"I didn't know it myself, Laura, honestly. And I didn't know how much I missed you!" Anne slumped back on the couch, kicked her shoes off, and moved the phone to her other ear. It was good to hear Laura's voice, and yet it was only this moment that she realized it. All the time she'd been gone, she thought, surprised, she hadn't really missed her dearest friend. Well, perhaps it was just that she'd been so busy coping with her first solo in twenty-five years.

"So, tell me, was the trip as good for you as you expected? Did you get anything straightened out?"

"Well," Anne lay back, feet up, eyes closed, smiling, "as a matter of fact, it *was* good for me, I think. No, I'm sure!" She laughed. "The car was docile, thank God, and I found some great places to stay along the way. Took some marvelous pictures, too."

"I was worried that you'd be lonely."

"I guess I worried about that, too," Anne murmured, twisting the telephone cord around her finger. "But I really wasn't, not after the first day or so. I found I could manage very well." Very well indeed. "You'd have been proud of me!"

She gave a sketchy description of her itinerary to Laura, describing places and scenery and restaurants.

"So where's this Whitefield? You stayed there a lot longer than anyplace else. What was the big attraction?"

"I don't know. It's kind of hard to explain. It's not as if there was anything particularly exciting about it." Not for a big city woman like me. She could almost hear that husky rumbling voice in the cozy bakery. She hadn't seen him again before she'd finally left town, but somehow his obviously harsh judgment of her still rankled, his words had cut deeper than she'd thought.

"Oh, I didn't tell you. There was this fantastic bakery and you'll never believe what happened!" She went on to describe her erstwhile employer and her impromptu job. "Honestly, I was terrific, if I do say so myself."

"God, you have a peculiar way of vacationing! But, I'm not surprised. If anyone could hold her own in a pastry shop, it's you, kiddo. All those lessons you took over the years, all those dinner parties. . . . And those desserts you make! If I can still call you my friend after what you've done to my hips, it's a miracle. And just remember, I expect to sample one of those plum tarts before you forget how to make them."

"Oh, don't worry. Important things I never forget. I know where my priorities lie!" Anne chuckled.

"So," Laura added, "how 'bout coming over for dinner tonight? I'm dying to see you!"

"Oh, Laurie, I'm really bushed. Some other time, okay? I'm heading for a hot shower and bed . . . after I get through this pile of mail they had for me at the post office."

"Yeah, I don't blame you. Oh! Almost forgot. Jerry called a few days ago; since you weren't home, I was second best."

"Where is he? Is he okay? Is he going to call back again soon? What—?"

"Hey," Laura laughed, "one at a time, please. They're in Yosemite Park before they head for San Francisco; he's having a ball; he'll call on Sunday; send money!"

Anne shook her head, grinning. "Nice to know some things never change."

After she'd hung up, she carried her bags up the stairs and got ready for bed. Unpacking could wait until tomorrow.

Tomorrow is the first day of the rest of your life. Yech, now she was resorting to life by cliché. Beneath the fatigue and satisfaction of being once more among familiar possessions, a restless and uneasy feeling swept over her. She should have been happier to be home. There, that was it. She should have been happier . . . more eager for that tomorrow, ready to face the rest of her life with some sense of joy and anticipation, or at least contentment.

And she wasn't.

Her head drooped and she yawned. Fatigue. That's all it was, just plain old exhaustion. After a month on the road, behind the wheel of a car, the excitement of the new and unfamiliar had taken its toll. She just needed a couple of days to get back to normal—whatever that was. *Knock it off, idiot. Go to bed and give it a rest, for God's sake!*

Later, fed and scrubbed, Anne slid gratefully between cool crisp sheets and let her head sink into the welcoming pillows. Lord, had anything ever felt that good! For a few moments she lay quietly, eyes closed, mustering the strength to turn over and try to sleep.

It was only then that she became consciously aware of the silence of the large house. It pressed down on her, pushing against her closed eyelids, filling her ears, a vivid real presence. For the first time in a long while, she felt loneliness gather around her. The house was empty. She was alone, and with a sudden force it hit her: *Jerry will never really live here again.* This summer was the first taste of the future. This moment, now, was the image of all her tomorrows. Alone, in an empty house.

Chilled and afraid, Anne sat up abruptly, all desire for sleep suddenly banished. It was then she noticed again the sizable rubber-banded package of mail she'd picked up at the post office. She reached for it with the quick gratitude of one who finds reprieve from the inevitable. "Damn, now I won't be able to sleep until I look through all this." She'd never been able to leave a telephone unanswered or to refrain from opening presents that she'd discovered ahead of time, either. How often had her mother said it: "Curiosity killed the cat." A-ha, she thought tartly, so *that's* where she'd begun ingesting clichés—at her mother's knee. And, because she always had to have the last word, she'd learned to answer her mother: "Satisfaction brought it back."

"Okay, let's see how much satisfaction I'll feel after I plow through this pile of stuff." Anne punched up the pillows behind her and dumped the heavy packet in her lap, keeping loneliness at bay. It was ten minutes later, surrounded by sorted piles of toss-outs, bills, invitations, and notices, that she finally came to the plain white envelope with the unfamiliar cramped handwriting. And then she saw the postmark: New Hampshire, dated two days before.

She tore it open quickly, looking at the signature first, and grinned.

"Dear Anne. I feel like I've made a new, *good* friend. It was so wonderful the way you pitched in and helped me when I was stuck. Such a wonderful thing for you to do. Well, Leni is okay now, and we're back to normal—for a while. But, I got to tell you, my arthritis is worse than ever, and even in the summer! I just don't know what it will be like when the weather gets bad. I always loved winter, but lately it's harder and harder for me to get around so good. So I think I'll have to close the bakery and move down to Santa Fe, like my daughter keeps telling me. I feel so bad; I will put an ad in the papers around here, but I don't know if anyone will want to buy. But I don't have any choice. Wouldn't it be nice if you lived here? Then *you* could buy it. You'd be real good at this and the customers all liked you. Oh, well, just kidding. We can't change the way things are, can we? Too bad. Anyway, please write me and tell me how the rest of your trip was and if you got home safe and everything is good with you. And your boy, Jerry.

My very best to you, Ilse Kolchak."

Anne laid the letter in her lap, smiling at the almost palpable image of Mrs. Kolchak:

her patient, almost stolid nature; her laughing eyes, now and then shadowed by the pain of her aching joints; the joy of her smile lighting up the thin, worn face. Even at this distance, Anne could feel the deep affection they'd shared so quickly. And Mrs. K's daughter was right: Another northern winter would be terrible for her mother. She'd earned a rest in the warmth and sunshine of Santa Fe.

Well, Anne thought, sliding down under the covers, the lamp left burning on the table beside her, perhaps if she'd lived in Whitefield, she just *might* have taken Mrs. K up on that offer. It had been a lovely week, the best of her trip, for all the hard work and physical effort it had taken. It was a fulfilling diversion and the woman was right, Anne thought with satisfaction: She *had* been good at it. She turned over, pulling the lightweight summer quilt high around her shoulders. Yes, it had been fun, but you can't change the way things are. Mrs. Kolchak was right about that, too.

Or was she?

Anne's fingers clenched the edge of the sheet and quilt, and she felt a sudden fear churn in her stomach. No, it was stupid, illogical . . . irrational! Even a momentary consideration of "what if" was nuts! And she wasn't nuts. Certainly not at this stage of her life, she wasn't. She looked at the glowing lamp beside the bed. Sure, she had her idio-syncracies, but who didn't? A little impulsive, maybe, and perhaps stubborn. Her friends might even say peculiar, but not nuts.

Nah! It was just wishful thinking on Mrs. K's part, a lonely, regretful old lady who didn't want to part with a lifetime's accomplishment. She'd built it and only wanted to see it go on. But wishful thinking was all it was. And, Anne reminded herself, it wasn't even *hers;* it was Ilse Kolchak's!

Defying her utter exhaustion, thoughts raced around Anne's mind, denying sleep for the moment. Well, she probably *could* handle the routine that Ilse Kolchak had followed for so long. After all, at forty-five she was still young enough and strong enough to with-stand the rigors of a full-time job. She could say it with conviction: She'd never been lazy. And, although a few days wasn't a lot to go by, still . . .

No! She burrowed into the pillows, seeking oblivion. She didn't want to have to face a decision like this. And that was utterly stupid. There *was* no decision to make. It was a pre-posterous idea. Who'd even consider a crazy thing like that?

Sleep was a reluctant visitor. Anne tossed

fitfully, waking at frequent intervals during that long night. Running through her mind, intertwined with the memory of Mrs. Kolchak's letter, were Laura's words, a relentless litany repeated over and over: *You seem to be drifting . . . you're less involved than ever. . . .* And Anne had the strangely clear sensation that the tethers to her old life were slowly dissolving. There was, she suddenly realized clearly, nothing, no activity or project, that she was involved in here. Even the friends of twenty-odd years were not the anchor they should have been. *My anchor disappeared in a pile of rubble in Mexico City two years ago.*

One by one the remaining strands of attachment were separating—*you're drifting away, Annie, drifting*—and very soon she'd be left to float loose, free, the momentum already set in motion that was pulling her farther and farther apart from everything that held her to the old Anne McClellan.

Three

Anne sat up, fully awake at only four-thirty on a dark and chilly New Hampshire morning. But what had woken her, broken through the deep, heavy sleep? She looked around, noting the casual disorder in the light of the small lamp she always left burning. After a moment's hesitation, Anne slid off the side of the narrow bed, pulled on her robe, and tiptoed to the door. Cautiously, she peeked into the lighted living room of the small apartment.

No, nothing out there. Yawning, Anne shook her head. Lord, it was bad enough getting up at six o'clock but this was sheer lunacy. She eyed the clock with resentment and shrugged. *Something* had woken her; better check downstairs in the pastry shop.

Quietly, she started down, rubbing the smooth wooden handrail with a proprietary gesture and smiling with self-satisfaction. After all those years spent entertaining Paul's clients, earning the reputation among her friends as a talented baker, and hostessing charity committees and school bake sales, she'd proven the philosophers were right: No experience in life is wasted. And she hadn't taken leave of her senses, either! Her initial indecision long forgotten, she blessed that June day three months ago when she'd called Mrs. Kolchak and, with great trepidation, said yes before the more prudent no could assert itself.

Buying the pastry shop had been an inspired decision and Anne was quite proud of these past three months. True, the character of the little shop had changed, becoming *hers* now. True, it had taken a little while and a lot of concerted effort and patience to win over the longtime customers, who had stubbornly resisted any hint of change. She sighed, smiling ruefully at the memory. But it had worked out. Now the shop was always busy, and she reveled in every chocolate-covered, custard-filled, meringue-layered moment of it! And she hadn't used one cent of the inheritance. That was safely put away for Jerry, and the shop was all hers . . . well, hers and the bank's. But if it weren't for her, "Sweet Expectations" wouldn't exist at all.

And maybe if it weren't for "Sweet Expectations," she wouldn't exist.

Her semi-euphoria lasted until the bottom of the stairs; the sight that met Anne's eyes was her second rude awakening. A sickening jolt of shock, a moment of panicky fear, and then she was just plain angry. Damn! Damn, damn, and double damn!

The stainless steel counter along one side of the large white kitchen was not in the spotless condition she'd left it. Remnants of a desecrated fudge cake gave mute testimony to the fact that *someone* had stopped by for a little late-night dessert! Anne's eyes followed the path from the fudgy leavings to the freezer against the back wall, door open, the uncovered drum of melting French vanilla ice cream dripping onto the blue and white vinyl tile floor, as if the hungry intruder had suddenly changed his mind and made a hasty departure. In the center of the room on a large marble-topped table were the remains of a carefully contrived strawberry torte, a ruined shadow of its once glorious self.

In shock, Anne listened to the silence and, when she knew she was alone, picked her way gingerly through the wreckage of pastry and crumbs littering her path, past mini-hills of whipped cream and spilled milk puddles. She closed the now-almost-useless back door against the cool night air, then headed to the phone. Wryly, she noted the sticker with the police department's phone number, provided by Whitefield's local Welcome Wagon. Anne stared at the mess as she dialed. Some welcome!

"Hello, Officer? I want to report a break-in."

The quiet whisper of the breeze through autumn-crisp aspen leaves, the muted gurgle of the creek rushing over its boulder-strewn bed, were all that disturbed the silent darkness. Mike Novak dipped his head, cupping the flame as he lit the small cigar. The tip glowed, a pinpoint of red, then brightened briefly to a brilliant white, illuminating his drawn face in the darkened patrol car. He relished that first puff, inhaling and enjoying the small pleasure of the smoky tobacco taste on his tongue.

Abruptly, he frowned, cursed, and crushed the glowing embers in the ash tray. Damn! He'd forgotten, for that brief moment, how visible even the smallest flicker of light could be in the unbroken blackness of the night. He'd better be more careful. They'd all worked and waited too long for him to screw up now.

Mike shifted his long legs, easing cramped muscles confined too long in the inadequate space. His watch confirmed his fears: too late. The bastards weren't going to show, not tonight. And he'd been so sure. Well, it would be soon, any day now; he knew he was getting close. He could taste it!

Rotating his stiff neck, Mike stretched, then yawned. Time to knock off and head home for a piece of Caroline's cherry pie and a couple of hours sack time. He thought of Aunt Caroline and smiled. Then he thought of his daughter and he stopped smiling, recalling their conversation at dinner, or at least *her* conversation. As usual, and more frequently in the last two months, he'd forced himself to merely sit and listen while all Helena could talk about was that woman she worked for.

"Mac"! God, he was so tired of the pushy busybody who'd become the prime object of his teenage daughter's admiration; she'd been playing havoc with his life since the first day Helena had started to work for her. But it was only lately that he'd found it so increasingly difficult to restrain his temper at even the mention of her name, and this latest thing was just once too often. This time the interfering troublemaker had gone too far. He'd have to finally make it clear, to her *and* to Helena, just whose guidance and suggestions, whose rules were to be followed. Yes, he was going to have to do something; they definitely had to talk. First he'd have it out with Helena, and then—he heaved a deep sigh, there was no getting around it—tomorrow he'd stop by the bakery. He never called it a pastry shop. It had been a bakery his whole life, and though Mrs. Kolchak was gone, as far as Mike Novak was concerned, it was still a *bakery*.

Tomorrow. Some sleep and then first thing tomorrow . . .

Wearily, he rubbed gritty eyes, massaged the bridge of his nose between thumb and forefinger. He was getting too old for this shit; his back was killing him, his feet were numb, his head ached. God, he was tired! He started the motor and turned up the radio.

It crackled to sudden life, taking indecision out of his hands. He listened to the dispatcher's report of the break-in and burglary and clenched his jaw. He'd never believed in omens, but . . . Mike reached quickly for the radio.

"It's okay, Bo. I'll take the B and E at the pas . . . bakery."

Tomorrow had arrived sooner than he'd planned.

"All right, Mrs. McClellan, is that it?" He looked up at the woman he'd been avoiding for so long, and the sight was unnerving. She wasn't what he'd expected, although he wasn't even sure just what that was. It sure wasn't tousled greying hair and a worn, practical bathrobe. But his view of the world, his sense of ease and control, depended upon things being predictable, conforming to what he expected. The image he'd formed from Helena's conversations these past weeks was at odds with the small, unpretentious, friendly-faced smiling woman before him.

Mike asked his questions quickly, almost perfunctorily. This was a familiar routine and he had other matters on his mind, other business he had to deal with. He'd waited too long, and now that the moment was here he was anxious to get it over with. But he was, first and foremost, a policeman. He was here because it was the scene of a crime; his personal matter was peripheral. "Was that all the damage, out there in the kitchen?"

"To tell you the truth, Chief Novak, it really isn't as bad as I thought when I called. Other than the mess and the broken back door, there isn't much actual damage."

Anne looked at the large man across the table and recalled vividly that day when she'd first seen him. He was as impressive now as then . . . and as cool and aloof. Well, she acknowledged, a person doesn't change his nature with the seasons. This one sure hadn't. She observed wryly that if she should ever see in those hooded dark eyes a flicker of warmth directed her way, she'd start looking for the sun to rise in the west. And that truly still surprised her: She was so close to Helena, she'd assumed she'd be able to call the girl's father her friend, too. And yet, Anne was no closer now to understanding his apparent animosity than she'd been on her first visit to the town so many months ago.

After all, don't I "belong" in Whitefield by now?

But she couldn't fault him professionally, she was grateful to admit. The patrol car, white seal proclaiming the presence of the Whitefield, New Hampshire Police Department, had arrived quickly and she'd given an enthusiastic greeting to the big dark-haired man in the police uniform. Or at least made the attempt.

"Working so closely with Helena, I kind of thought our paths might cross again sooner than this, although I never thought it'd be in the line of duty." At her words, Mike stopped writing and looked up.

Anne recalled clearly the first day Helena Novak had walked into the newly redecorated and reequipped pastry shop, looking for a job. To Anne, up to her elbows in the flour bin, the sight of another pair of willing hands for the bargain price of a dollar above minimum wage had brought instant and profound gratitude. Helena had worked in the shop from that day, and a close friendship had developed between the vivacious fourteen-year-old and her forty-five-year-old employer. Three days a week, after school, and most Saturdays, she filled Anne's hours with cheerful smiles and adolescent gossip and giggles.

Anne often referred to her as "my window on Whitefield," and until this moment she'd looked forward to reestablishing her acquaintance with Helena's father, to meeting the rest of her family. Studying the stern-faced Michael Novak now, Anne marveled at her optimism! The object of her scrutiny was briskly flipping the pages of his notebook as he answered her last remark.

"I was out on another matter, anyway, so I

thought I'd better take this call myself," he said cryptically, for one moment looking decidedly ill at ease.

It was a long time since Anne had allowed herself to depend on someone else. In the years since Paul's death, she'd been busy learning to be self-sufficient and independent, for her own sake as well as for Jerry's. Her son might be in college but he'd needed her as much as she needed him, and they'd found strength in each other during that awful time.

But a sense of relief had rushed over her at the squad car's arrival. How wonderful, even for a short while, to pass a burden onto someone else's shoulders. And a very satisfactory set of shoulders they were, she thought. In fact, they went quite well with the rest of him.

"I've lived in Whitefield about four months now. It's funny we've never run into each other again."

Mike *knew* why they hadn't met. And it had taken some doing, in a town this size, to avoid it as long as he had.

Suddenly, he looked up at her, frowning. "What do you mean, *again?*"

So much for first impressions! Anne smiled wryly to herself. As small as her ego might be, it was still a little disconcerting to realize the lack of impression she'd made on him. She had remembered *him* very clearly. "Well, let's see. If I smear plum tart on my face, would that jog your memory?"

He stared, his expression decidedly peculiar, and he looked as if he regretted opening his mouth. "Uh . . . I don't think I—" By now he was lost.

Anne shook her head quickly. "Sorry, Chief Novak, it's not important. We'd better get back to the break-in. After all, even for us city people, excitement is where you find it."

Like a light snapped on in a dark room, comprehension dawned at last, along with a dull flush of red over his high cheekbones. "You were here with Mrs. Kolchak . . . ?" he said slowly, plucking the elusive fragment of memory from the past.

"Yes, you remembered!" She winked at him to ease his obvious discomfort. "But you know, these last months have helped me appreciate what a nice place this is. Already I feel as if I *belong* here . . . really *belong.*" Anne's smile was contented.

He mumbled something unintelligible and Anne's smile just grew wider. Suddenly, she felt a lot better; she'd been through too much on the way to this point to let this dour man with the angry eyes get under her skin and spoil her new beginning. After all, even the Garden of Eden had its snake.

Oh, come on, Anne, that's a little much, isn't it? The man hasn't really done anything to you, now, has he? Actually, he was here to help her. She drew a deep breath. "Anyway, I just meant I was surprised we hadn't run into each other before this"—she gestured at the mess visible through the door to the kitchen.

Mike had regained his composure and now he looked straight at her, his voice low, cool. "It was never . . . necessary before."

Well! Too bad it was necessary now, Anne thought, startled at his choice of words. She could have gone a lot longer with the status quo, considering his attitude. Although she'd wondered when she'd actually get to meet Helena's parents, until now she hadn't come closer than the snapshot.

"You know, I think you look better with the moustache."

He glanced up again. "Better? How would you . . . I've had a moustache for years, Mrs. McClellan, long before last June."

"Uh . . . right," Anne mumbled. "It's just . . . well, it was the snapshot." The day she'd found Helena's wallet lying open on the counter, the old wrinkled picture had caught her attention. Taken on a sunny afternoon when he and a younger, chubbier Helena were out fishing, the bright summer sun reflected sharply off the water, the glare captured by the lens. The resulting image was overly light, making individual features indistinct.

But the mood, the joyous intangibles of love and happiness, were very clear. He was laughing, trying to untangle her knotted line, and the camera had caught him at the perfect moment—head thrown back, mouth wide with delight, neck and jaw taut with exploding laughter. The small photo was filled with raw vitality, the joyous excitement of a man exulting in a magical moment shared with an adoring and adored child.

Something had stirred in Anne, a queer sense of recognition, and it had nothing to do with their brief encounter the previous June. She'd known that man, with a knowledge that was intuitive. The image in the dog-eared picture of the large, muscular young man and his tiny acolyte, enjoying their day and each other with such uninhibited pleasure, was not easily forgotten. Because they, too, had shared such days, she and Paul and Jerry . . .

She blinked back the tears and turned, gesturing toward the kitchen beyond the door.

"Well, I suppose we'd better get down to business. I guess it's true what they say: 'Man cannot live by bread alone.'" Her laughter was a bit forced in the face of the scowl he aimed at his notebook.

Anne sensed it wasn't merely the greedy felon who'd broken into her shop that had carved that frown between his heavy brows. Deep grooves channeled each side of his mouth, and beneath the luxuriant slash of black moustache, she glimpsed his lower lip caught between even white teeth. The small gesture of uncertainty was the only chink in his formidable armor.

Definitely the strong, silent type . . . and if for some reason he meant to unnerve her with the steady gaze and lengthening silence, the attempt was an unqualified success. "Excuse me a minute, I need some coffee. Want some? I'll be right back."

"No, it isn't neces—"

She disappeared into the kitchen, leaving him openmouthed and alone, his refusal dying on his lips. It seemed inappropriate to accept hospitality from her. Mike rose abruptly and stalked around the cheerful shop, surveying, measuring, judging.

With the soft cream-colored paneling, the chairs around the four tables covered in the dark-blue print repeated at the windows, it was a charming and apparently successful enterprise. Charming. He supposed, for some people, that would be the perfect description of Anne McClellan. But it wasn't her charm that had finally made this meeting so imperative. Still—he gnawed at his lower lip—she wasn't what he'd expected. For one brief moment, he wondered if he could be wrong.

No.

Mike shook his head, annoyed, and resumed his nervous pacing across the blue and white tiles. This indecision was ridiculous. He'd never before doubted his judgment. Life was very comfortable when it was predictable and under control—*his* control. He'd arranged it that way for years and he'd be damned if *she* was going to upset his tidy little apple cart.

Mike turned as Anne pushed through the swinging door and resumed her seat. She carried a tray with steaming glass mugs of coffee and a platter of pastries. She shoved one mug toward him and sipped gratefully from hers.

"Ah, thank God for caffeine!"

Mike knew how she felt. He reached automatically for his, forgetting his intended refusal, ignoring the cream and sugar, as Anne guessed he would. Nothing to soften or dilute the full strong flavor. He cast a dubious glance at the apparently fragile mug dwarfed in his powerful hand.

"Oh, don't worry, Chief Novak, it's stronger than it looks."

Anne offered him a sugar-sticky pecan roll, which he refused. She shrugged, took a healthy bite from her own, and smiled ruefully. "No willpower. And it's too late to beat this body into submission."

Mike thought the body in question looked pretty good. And he was angry with himself for noticing.

He quickly swallowed the hot, bitter brew. "All right, is this all that's been touched?" He didn't *want* to wonder about her or change his opinion. "You didn't mention cash. How much was in the register?"

"As a matter of fact, it was empty. I cleared it after closing. I was going to make a night deposit but I didn't have time. But it's okay, the money's safe. It's upstairs."

"Upstairs?"

"Where I live—upstairs." Anne pointed toward the kitchen and the door to the inside stairway.

"Do you often keep the receipts upstairs overnight?" His eyes were narrowed, his words measured and incredulous.

"Well, now and then. Why? Is that a problem?" Anne frowned, sipping her coffee, thinking he meant the insurance.

"Do you realize how lucky you are he didn't take it into his head to come looking for the money? Whitefield is pretty peaceful, but it's not Utopia." He looked disgusted at such obvious stupidity. "Isn't your life worth more than a few cookies?"

"Oh! Well, I . . . I didn't think—!"

"No, you didn't think." Mike sighed, feeling exhausted right down to his socks.

"Look, it was just kids, out for some kicks. I'm sure they weren't dangerous—"

"Are you an expert on the criminal mind?"

Anne flushed and bit her lip to keep from answering. "No, of course not. But I found this near the door." She reached into her pocket and extended her hand to him, a small object in the center of her palm. It was a round enameled pin with the word *Spartans* written boldly across the center. "It's one of those pins the high school kids wear."

"It could be Helena's."

"No, it was on *top* of the crumbs." She smiled at his surprise. "Agatha Christie taught me everything I know."

His mouth twitched in the face of her persistent good humor. He looked down at his notebook and cleared his throat; he would not allow her to make him like her. "Yes . . . well, as far as catching your thief, I'm afraid this is about all we have to go on."

"Oh, I don't know." For the first time Anne relaxed in her chair. After all, she'd faced worse than *him* in her life and survived. He could put on the *old curmudgeon* act all he wanted; she wasn't fazed by it. After staring death in the face, could Mike Novak be worse? "He's probably got a belly ache, zits, and a case of terminal cavities. It's a good bet his next stop will be the drugstore or the dentist."

Damnit! Mike shook his head, almost smiling. The niggling thought returned: Anne McClellan wasn't what he'd expected. Actually, he wasn't quite sure what he *had* expected. Fishnet hose, maybe, bleached hair and bossy. But not this. No, definitely not this.

Aha! Anne raised her brows. Was that a smile? He quickly averted his face and she thought whimsically of the famous rock formation down at Franconia Notch—the Great Stone Face. Only here he was, sitting in her shop, large as life. She appraised him again. No . . . larger.

But a *smile*, an honest-to-God smile! Just a

small victory, true. But the underdog needs every advantage. And, for some reason, she was sure that's what she was here . . . the underdog. She knew *what*, she just couldn't figure out *why*. And she couldn't figure out the strange expression on his face, either.

Ah, my kingdom for a lipstick and comb!

Well, how stupid. Why would he care? And why should she! Messy hair and bare face were just fine for house calls at the crack of dawn, and it didn't matter a damn how he looked at her, anyway.

Right! Those were *policeman's* eyes, and they were investigating a *burglary*. Anne turned her thoughts deliberately away from the "man" and back to the uniform.

"I'll say this for you: You're one remarkable woman."

Mike's grudging tone contradicted the compliment. Anne wondered again at the latent disapproval she heard, then felt foolish. The ungodly hour, the man's obvious exhaustion . . . that's all it was. Good grief, she was the *victim* here, not the . . . what was his term? . . . oh, yes, the "perpetrator." So what could he possibly have against her? After all, this was her home now; she *belonged*. And the way she looked right now, he couldn't possibly find any trace of "city woman" in her pale naked face and disheveled hair, not at seven A.M., he couldn't!

"Remarkable? Why?" Anne tilted her head quizzically. "I'm probably the most unremarkable woman you'll ever meet."

"I've found that most people awakened at the crack of dawn by a burglar would have dissolved into incoherence by now."

"Ah, well," Anne said loftily, "I choose to think of this as the supreme compliment to my culinary talents." She bowed her head in a regal gesture, then grinned. "As Marie Antoinette said: 'Let 'em eat cake.' As long as it's my cake!"

Mike looked across the table with reluctant approval. She stared right back, imperturbable in her scruffy pink bathrobe, dark hair shot through with random threads of silver still in uncombed chaos. No makeup, and she looked for all the world as calm and comfortable—and charming—as if she entertained policemen at breakfast with accustomed regularity. He thought again of her laughing advice about staking out the pharmacy.

Advice! Mike sat up straight. Hell, that was all he needed, advice from her. That was *precisely* what had compelled him to take this blasted call in the first place!

He gripped the coffee mug and rapped it down on the table with more force than he intended. She'd been right about that: It wasn't as fragile as it looked. Apparently, neither was she. "I think that just about wraps it up." He stood abruptly.

Anne rose with him. "At the very least, this has been an interesting diversion. When they hear about all this, Helena and her friends will really have something to gossip about."

"Helena." He smiled and his expression softened for an instant, then he drew his eyebrows together, something he'd done quite a lot since he arrived at her door. "I know this may not be the best time, but I'd like to talk to you about her."

Something changed in his voice and Anne straightened, alert. "Now, wait a minute! You don't think she's involved in this—!"

"Of course not!" He stared at her. "Don't be absurd."

"Well, you look so suspicious, how should I know what you're thinking?"

"Don't worry." He inhaled deeply. "I'm going to tell you."

Uh-oh. Anne knew, whatever this one-man execution squad had to say, she wasn't going to like it. *I wonder if I'll get a last cigarette and a blindfold?*

"You're going to tell me what?"

"I thought it better to take care of the official business first. I don't like to mix personal and professional matters."

"Personal? You mean Helena?"

"Yes. That's exactly what I mean," he said quietly.

"Uh . . . what about her? She's a great kid, terrific. You must be so proud of her." Babble. He'd reduced her to sheer babble.

"Yes, I am. I think she's turning out quite well, and I'd like her to continue exactly the same way."

"Why . . . uh . . . yes . . . yes, of *course* you would. If I had a daughter, I'd want her to be just like Helena!"

"The fact remains, Mrs. McClellan, she *isn't* your daughter."

Did I miss something here? Anne wondered, puzzled. The accusation in his voice was unmistakable. But what the heck was he accusing her *of*? Anne lifted her chin, trying to outstare him. It's not easy to intimidate when the intimidator is a good eight inches below the eye level of the intimidatee.

"Look, just exactly what are you trying to say, Chief Novak?" What the heck had ruffled his feathers now?

"I'm asking you to please leave Helena's

guidance to me. I don't want, or need, your interference with my daughter."

Anne stared dumbly. Well, the *old curmudgeon* was no act.

"Look, Mrs. McClellan, I'm sorry. I don't mean to be rude, and maybe you didn't realize—" Suddenly aware of how harsh his words sounded, Mike rubbed his forehead tiredly and ran his fingers across his drawn face. "Look, it's *my* word that must be final. All I've heard since she started here is 'Mac' this and 'Mac' that and 'Mac says.' And last night I was informed that no less an authority than 'Mac' told her she should cut her hair and that makeup is definitely acceptable!"

"Oh, for goodness sake! Is that what this is all about?" The light bulb flashed in Anne's brain, the memory of last night crystal clear in her mind. They'd been closing the shop . . .

"Everything's cleaned up, Mac. The whipped cream stuff's in the fridge and the tables are cleared. Anything else?"

"No, honey, I'll finish up." Anne put the last of the New Zealand strawberries back in the cooler, along with the intricate torte she'd just finished. "Go on. I'll do the Meachams' cake in the morning. Their party isn't until tomorrow night."

"Yeah, I know." Helena put the broom back into the small closet at the rear and pulled herself up onto the stainless steel counter across from Anne. "Jennie Meacham told me in school." She reached for one of the lacy florentine cookies lined up in precise rows on a large parchment-lined tray.

"Uh, Mac, I was wondering. Do you think Jennie's pretty?" Her jaws worked methodically to demolish the fragile cookie.

"Well, yes, I guess, kind of. Why do you ask?" Anne glanced at the girl licking buttery crumbs from her fingers.

"Oh, it's just that . . . well, she . . . ever since she started to wear lipstick and all that gunk on her eyes . . . well, I just . . . wondered. Uh, don't you think she's kind of young?"

"Hmm, I don't know. I guess if her mother isn't worried . . ."

"I sure don't have to worry about that."

A strange expression crossed her face and then it was gone. Anne was startled at the subdued sound of Helena's voice; she wasn't sure just what to say in answer to the young girl.

"Uh, well, I guess a little lipstick and gunk

won't hurt her, unless she looks like Bozo the Clown." Anne smiled as she got out the bleach to scrub down the table, glad to see the gleam shining again in the clear blue eyes. "Why did you ask, anyway?"

"No reason, really . . ." Helena examined the scuffed toe of her once-white gym shoe. "Uh, Mac, do you think I'd look okay if I cut my hair real short? Jenny says it would be *rad*. I mean, wouldn't it make me look more . . . uh . . . more . . . you know . . . ?"

"Older?" Anne asked, laughing. "Listen, my sweet, when you're pretty and fourteen, *anything* looks good!" She studied the eager-eyed girl. "Yes, it probably would look cute on you—I assume that's what *rad* means? And, at least with hair, it's not forever. It'll grow in soon enough if you don't like it."

"Yeah! That's just what I—!" The loud honk of a car horn interrupted her words. "Oh, there's my dad. Gotta run. See you tomorrow after school. S'long, Mac. And *thanks!*"

Anne locked the front door behind her, laughing and shaking her head. "Thanks . . . for what?" Through the glass she could see the dark blue Jeep double parked outside, waiting while the girl deposited her books in the back and climbed into the front seat.

Anne tried to study the driver, what she could see of him. Ever since she'd seen the snapshot she'd been curious about him, recalling that one time she'd been in his presence. But Helena's father had proven to be elusive in the extreme.

They hadn't met again, though Whitefield was a small town, and tantalizing glimpses were all she'd had. And, as chatty as Helena was, it was her Aunt Callie she referred to most often. Except for mention of his "do nots" and "no ways," she spoke rarely of her father and never of her mother.

Anne had wondered about it. While his wife seemed to exert little or no influence in behalf of their daughter, *he* seemed to stretch parental vigilance to new boundaries!

And if she'd ever doubted it, Anne thought now, he was being generous with additional proof!

"Yes," Mike was answering wearily, "hair-cut, makeup, among other things. That's exactly what it's about."

"But, don't you see? She only asked what I thought about those things in general, not specifically about her. And I just gave her an honest opinion. I never suggested she do any of those things. If I was in conflict with you in some way, I'm truly sorry. I had no idea—"

"No, as you said before, you 'didn't think.' "

"Now, just a minute—!"

"Look, Mrs. McCl—"

"Oh, *you* may call me Mac!"

He glared at her, then paced off two agitated steps to the door before turning back in one smooth motion, pulling his cap down firmly over his frown. "Mrs. McClellan, I know your type."

"Do you really?"

His tight smile implied he already knew all the answers. He looked cynical as he gestured around them.

"All brand new equipment, isn't it? Brand new *expensive* equipment." You could see it, all right; money was no object. And the large, exceptionally fine diamond rings on the third finger of her left hand—no struggle against adversity here! Probably living off the alimony gouged from a hardworking ex-husband. Wonder how much she'd taken the poor sap for?

"Divorced, or separated maybe, time and money on your hands. 'Wouldn't it be fun to open a little shop?' " Anne flinched. "And when a young girl is impressed with the aura of big city glamour, why, maybe it would be

'fun' to try your hand with her, too!" He
stopped, his voice softening. "Look, I'm asking you now; please don't. I wish I could be
more diplomatic. I don't know how long
you'll be around here before you pick up and
head for greener pastures, but this is our
home—for good. When you leave I don't want
to have to repair the damage." Anne sank
back in her chair as his words washed over
her.

"My daughter works here because she en-
joys it and because jobs aren't that plentiful
for kids her age. If you allow her to continue,
fine, I'll certainly appreciate it. We both
would. But that's all."

Mike saw the raw hurt in her eyes. He
hadn't meant to spew out all his pent-up
frustration that way. Had he overreacted to
Helena's comments last night and the past
few weeks? A man, an honest man—and
Mike Novak was certainly that—a man
trained to examine evidence and to think
logically, could hardly ignore his own motives and behavior.

He knew precisely what was bothering him.

Every time he permitted the truth to filter
to the surface, he felt that twist in the gut
and he reacted with more anger to force it
back down out of sight. Jealous! He was just

plain jealous of the woman's place in his daughter's affections. *Oh, Novak, you dumb sap, you are pathetic!*

Anne was stunned, but her protest was cut short by the jingle of the bell on the front door as it opened to a new arrival.

"Anne, dear, what happened? I saw the police car and I—" The tall, slender, distinguished-looking man stopped as he saw the two people standing stiffly in front of him, toe-to-toe, chin-to-third-button-from-the-top.

"Morning, Novak, what's the trouble here?"

"Gilcrest." Mike barely acknowledged the other man.

"Hi, Elliot." Anne's brief smile of welcome only slightly defrosted the chill in the air. "I had a small break-in this morning and Chief Novak stopped by to make a report—and give me a friendly warning. He's just leaving!" The unfamiliar note of genuine anger returned to her voice.

"A burglary? My God, are you all right? Are you hurt?"

"No, I never saw him. How I wish I had!" It wouldn't be smart to strangle the Chief of Police, but she wished she could get her hands on the thief who was responsible for his presence!

"Yeah, you could have hit him with a cream puff."

Patronizing remarks from the object of her distinctly uncharitable thoughts did nothing to temper her annoyance.

"Are you through with your business here, professional and *otherwise*, Chief Novak?" She pulled open the door with its ill-timed cheerful jingling. If he didn't leave now, she wouldn't be responsible. She might brain *him* with a cream puff . . . with a whole tray of cream puffs! Would that be considered assault with a deadly weapon? Anne clenched her teeth and decided it would be worth it . . . except for the waste of perfectly good cream puffs.

Mike thrust the notebook into his shirt pocket and nodded curtly at the other man. Without looking at Anne, he turned to go.

She couldn't restrain a suicidal impulse for the last word. Anne willed herself back to a semblance of equilibrium and murmured as he passed her. "I'm curious. Are you always so delightful first thing in the morning?"

Mike turned slowly and looked her up and down, his mouth curling in a sardonic imitation of a smile.

"I don't think *you'll* ever have to worry about it."

He closed the door firmly behind him, and the two people staring at it heard the patrol car roar to life. It sped away with an angry screech of rubber on pavement.

Four

As the sound faded, Anne sank into a chair. "Something tells me I'll never get a parking ticket fixed in this town." She looked up, brushing her hair from her weary eyes. "Is he always this pleasant?"

Elliot shrugged, indifferent. He and Mike Novak had lived in Whitefield all their lives, and except for meetings of the town's Selectmen and Chamber of Commerce, they might have existed on different planets. "He seemed angry. What did you say to him?"

"What did *I* say to *him*? Ha! That's a laugh. Boy, if that's how he treats the innocent, he must be hell on the guilty!"

"Now, now, Anne. Here, drink your coffee like a good girl and tell me what happened. I'll take care of everything."

"Elliot . . ." She gritted her teeth. "I'm a grown woman, not a 'good girl.'" Anne closed her eyes for a moment and took a deep breath. "And you don't have to bother . . .

it's all taken care of." She told him about the last couple of hours.

"Everything was fine until he brought up Helena."

"His daughter? What's she got to do with this?" Elliot asked, reaching for a still-warm cruller. He looked with dismay at his now-sticky fingers and Anne quickly handed him a napkin.

"You tell me. She's worked for me all summer, and now a couple of days after school and Saturdays. She's a great kid—wonder who she takes after!" Anne made a face and shook her head. "I know her grades haven't suffered, so he can't be angry about that. But he seems to think I'm trying to exert some kind of nefarious influence over her, interfere with his parental authority. Honestly, it's ridiculous. Since when did 'girl-talk' become subversive?"

Elliot angled his patrician head, a slight frown between his eyes. "Now, now, Anne, you're just overreacting. Let's calm down and not get hysterical."

Anne was not in the least hysterical. It wasn't her "thing"; it never had been—not even in Mexico City. . . . What she was was annoyed. She didn't like being patronized, and with the mood Novak's tirade had left her in, Elliot's timing was abominable. She carried the cups briskly into the kitchen. Mike Novak's hostility had left a sour taste of disappointment. Months of dropped comments from Helena, bits and pieces gleaned from casual and overheard conversation, had gradually distilled an image, an expectation that she somehow knew the man, and now she had to cope with the sudden disappointment: It hadn't been the introduction she'd anticipated; he hadn't been the man she'd imagined.

"Anyway," she drew a deep, calming breath and spoke over her shoulder, "thanks for stopping by." Elliot had followed her into the kitchen. "And you'd better hurry or you'll be late at the bank." She suddenly remembered the hour. "Late? Lord, why are you even up at this time of morning—or is it still night?"

"Ah, well," he smiled, once more showing the warm, pleasant expression with which she was so familiar, "rank has its responsibilities as well as its privileges." His father was president of the bank, a fact Elliot never forgot, nor was anyone else likely to. "I want to work on the books. The auditors are due in a couple of weeks."

"Oh, yes, that's a pretty good reason to drag yourself out of bed." She grinned in sympathy. "Well, you have to get going and I have to mop the floor in here, so . . ."

He looked as if he suddenly smelled something bad. "I don't see why you insist on doing this sort of thing."

"Elliot, Elliot." She shook her head, laughing. "You were born in the wrong century. Honestly!" He was like her mother, sending her off to first grade, all the while walling her in with well-intended warnings and cautions. Then it had been a necessity. Now it was becoming an intrusion. She patted his arm to soften her words and began filling a bucket with hot water.

Elliot stepped back hastily and walked to the outer door, avoiding the coagulating white puddle of ice cream. "By the way, don't forget. Dinner next Friday."

"Of course not. I never forget a free meal, especially with the man who holds the mortgage." Anne felt guilty at her unkind thoughts. After all, even if he did act like a jerk sometimes, he was good company and at least he didn't have hair growing in his ears. And more important, he'd been a friend in her first lonely days here in Whitefield.

"I'll stop by the locksmith and tell him about your door."

"Why, thank you, Elliot." She leaned on the

mop for a moment. "You know, I don't think I've stopped thanking you since that first day in your bank when you approved my loan."

"Don't be silly, Anne. I like helping you. I just wish I could protect you from this sort of thing." He took in the disarray around them.

"Unlike my 'sweet expectations,' I am *not* made of sugar, Elliot. Believe me, I can handle 'this sort of thing.' I really don't need to be protected and cared for."

"Now, now, Anne, that's what I'm here for." He missed, or chose to ignore, her impatient grimace. He bent to place a kiss on her forehead, then closed the door behind him.

An onlooker might have been fooled by the large man's casual posture. The rock-solid body in the rumpled uniform was using all the discipline at its command to maintain the negligent pose.

Mike stood behind the cluttered desk, propped against the window ledge, one hand jammed into his pants pocket, the other wrapped around one of the uncounted cups of coffee that passed his lips each day. This day was no different—only worse.

The report on his desk was the focus of his black thoughts. This latest dumping, last night . . . not a lot, and not enough to do permanent damage, not by itself at least. But the occurrences were escalating—in amount and in frequency. Damn! If they could just find some predictable pattern in the dump sites, something to give them a lead. Mike had had every available man watching last night, even some state troopers having been in on it, and then the damned poison had been dumped up there into the Garland Brook. It was always like that—wherever they *weren't*.

They'd better find the bastards soon, before the damage became irreversible. If that stuff got into the Connecticut River and contaminated the Moore Reservoir. . . . He didn't want to think what damage it could do to the entire New England water supply system. And it was happening on his turf . . . *that's* what rankled!

Mike took another swallow of coffee. He drank too much of the stuff. He knew it. And if he didn't, Aunt Caroline was always happy to remind him. His mouth curved in a fond smile. Sometimes he wondered if he didn't do it to get a rise out of her. He looked back out the window. Was that why he'd acted the way he had this morning? To get a rise out of Anne McClellan?

He'd felt—and hadn't bothered to hide it—distinctly hostile toward her, and he chose to avoid examining his reasons. But he couldn't forget his rudely suggestive last words. What in the name of God had compelled him to answer her that way? He'd sure put his foot in his mouth this time. And the taste was increasingly bitter.

Mike looked through the blinds at the bank across the street. He smiled in spite of himself. Like clockwork, there was Cully Bryant, his youngest deputy, heading over to spend his coffee break with Janine Murray. Though he knew she was a recent graduate of a business school over in Littleton, Mike always pictured Janine still in high school, all pink angora and shy giggles. But Cully was sure hooked on her, and she must be smarter than she appeared if Elliot Gilcrest employed her as his secretary.

The muscle along his jaw contracted. Gilcrest and Anne McClellan. There'd been no hostility between *them!* How did she know Elliot Gilcrest? How *well* did she know him? Hell, who cared! But the irritating thought remained: She didn't belong with that . . . that pretentious bore. Anne McClellan had about as much in common with that pompous self-important peacock as she would have with a cigar-store Indian. The Indian would be better company.

Still, Gilcrest had sounded on pretty familiar terms. "Anne dear!" The words broke the silence in his small office and Mike's fingers tightened abruptly around the heavy mug. He swore as the hot coffee splashed across his hand.

Damn! It was going to be one of those days!

Lord, it had been one of those days!

In five months Anne hadn't welcomed a day's end as she did this one. It had started as badly as anything could and, incredibly, had gotten worse. The dawn encounter with the formidable Michael Novak had tainted the rest of the day beyond salvage.

She was so furious! Cleaning the post-robbery mess this morning, every swipe of the mop was a jab at his unfair judgment. She scrubbed the counters in an inadequate attempt to scrub away the arrogant smirk on his arresting face.

Good grief, that's an awful pun.

But it brought the only real smile to her face all day.

When Helena ran in after school, eager for all the gory details, Anne was hard put to hide her irritation, even with her.

Now, thank heaven, it was only a few minutes after closing when Joe Meacham tapped on the glass and she let him in.

"Wow, that's a beauty!" He handed Anne the money, nodding his enthusiastic approval of the elaborate whipped cream chocolate torte. "This will add a touch of class to the big doings. Sorry I'm so late. Got stuck at the office. Been waitin' long?"

"Oh, no," she reassured him. "In fact, Helena just left a few minutes ago and I had to finish up here, anyhow."

"Helena's gone? I could have given her a lift home."

"Well, you don't have to worry." Anne finished tying the ribbon on top of the large cake box with a vicious yank. "Her father picked her up." The wry twist of her mouth as she stumbled over the word was lost on him.

"Yeah, Caroline Novak runs a tight ship." He laughed, unaware of Anne's sudden stillness. "Death, taxes, and dinner hour at Caroline's table: some things you don't argue with. She's something, all right. Only person I ever saw, man or woman, could make Mike Novak toe the mark. Fine lady!"

Anne winced. Mr. Meacham picked up the large dark blue box with the cream-colored script spelling out "Sweet Expectations." She wished him a happy anniversary and waved good night.

Turning off all but one light, Anne walked slowly to the stairs. A wave of melancholy washed over her as she thought of Joe Meacham and his Connie, their big celebration. She hoped fervently they'd enjoy every minute of it!

Eyes dim with tears, she stumbled on the steps. She had to stop this! Paul was gone. She'd thought she'd accepted that, finally adjusted to it. Yet today she was suddenly assaulted by uneasy flashes of memory. Why now?

The queasy feeling in the pit of her stomach told her. Despite the unpleasantness of their meeting, Mike Novak had struck a responsive chord and she couldn't erase the impression of him etched in her mind, the real one entwined with the anticipated ideal.

Oh, Paul, I miss you so!

But, dear God, for a minute she couldn't recall what he looked like! His plain, dear features faded, for an instant, replaced by a pair of vivid dark eyes, a tanned weathered face, and an exciting mouth shadowed by a thick black moustache.

Now really, Anne. Stop that! After all, she wasn't looking for a man, and if she were, it sure wouldn't be someone else's! She bit her lip and the sudden taste of blood brought her up sharp. "Knock it off, dummy! That's hunger talking!"

Anne flipped the switch as she opened the door and the lamp beside the couch bathed the cozy room in its soft light. Funny how it had become "home" so quickly. Content, Anne rested her hand on the pale oyster fabric of the plump upholstered couch and looked around with unabashed pride. Three months! A remarkably short time for the radical turnaround in her life.

The moment she'd made up her mind to phone Ilse Kolchak, she'd known. The convenient accessible space above for living quarters had turned out to be a serendipitous bonus; it had all fallen into place as if it were, somehow, *meant* to be. She wasn't superstitious, and yet . . .

Anne could still feel the enormous sense of accomplishment she had experienced as each coat of clean fresh paint slid onto the old wood walls, each new table and chair was set in place downstairs, each curtain hung.

The quick evolution from Kolchak's Bakery to Sweet Expectations had been her dream, her creation, and it was really turning into quite a success. Modest, to be sure—she didn't dare tempt the gods' displeasure with gloating—but *oh, Paul, darling, it's a definite success! Your wife is an entrepreneur!*

She looked at the phone on the other end table and her face lit with a sudden impulse. She kicked off her shoes and from memory dialed Brody Hall in East Lansing. It was the middle of dinner hour at Michigan State but maybe . . .

He lifted the receiver. "Yeah?" Jerry asked in a hurried voice.

"Oh, that's some greeting! How come you're not heading for dinner, you old chow hound?"

"Mom! Hi! How's everything going? Hey, what's wrong?"

"My God, you sound like me! Can't I call just because everything's right?" Anne chuckled, happy to hear the familiar sound of her son's voice. "I missed your smiling face and sweaty T-shirts draped over the lamps, so I thought I'd call and say hi."

"I was just gonna grab a bite to eat and then head for the library. Big exam tomorrow.

What's with you? Still communing with nature?" he teased.

He was still dubious about her desire to trade the plush environs of Bloomfield Hills for the chilly mountains of northern New Hampshire. He'd pigeonholed her, too, she thought wryly; he'd never seen this side of his mother, didn't really believe it existed, even now. Anne didn't fully understand it herself. Instinct, not logic, had played the largest part in her decision.

"Yes, I'm disgustingly healthy and productive up here on my mountaintop, but the only nature I've communed with lately has been in the form of a mountain of dirty mixing bowls."

Jerry laughed. "Whatever happened to my quiet, cookie-baking Junior League mother?"

"Booorrrring! Anyway, I *am* still baking."

"Yeah, so how's the cookie store doing?"

"Please! The *pastry shop* is doing just great, thank you. At this rate, my loan will be paid off early."

"Sh . . . er . . . shoot, I don't see why you insisted on taking a loan. I mean, it's not as if there was a shortage of money, Mom."

"I know, dear, but I told you . . . I had to prove to myself I could do it on my own, not with money Dad left." Anne closed her eyes and swallowed. "Jerry, honey, this is the first thing I ever did all by myself. I needed to *know* I could do it."

"You sure did a great job. I mean, to sell the house and move to a completely new place, and to open your own business. Jeez, who'd have believed!"

"Certainly not me!" For a moment Anne wondered if Paul would have believed it. "Honey, I know we talked it all through before, but honestly, you're sure you don't mind that the house is gone? I still feel a little guilty about—"

"Mom, believe me, I don't mind, not if it was the right thing for you. Let's face it, I'm here more than I'd be there, anyway, and wherever you are is home base for me. I'm just glad you're doing something that makes you happy."

"Ah, Jer, I'm beginning to think there's nothing I can't do!"

"Mom?" His voice was suddenly serious. "Are you *really* happy? You're not sorry . . . ?"

"No, dear, I still feel the same—no, better! Honestly, honey, it wasn't a mistake. Somehow, I just feel this is where I belong. When Dad was alive, Bloomfield Hills was home because we were together, a family. But let's face

it. You're grown up. You'll be getting on with
your own life, moving out . . ."

This past summer, instead of coming east,
he'd gotten a job and done weekend backpacking with friends. She knew it was a har-
binger of things to come.

"I can't wait 'til Thanksgiving vacation. I
hope there's some 'old Mom' left under all
that 'new you.' "

"Just try dropping your shoes all over this
apartment and you'll see how much 'old
Mom' is still around, mister!"

"Some things never change." His laughter
was exactly what Anne needed.

"Well, I'll talk to you Sunday night. Is there
anything you want me to send you?"

"Yeah, East Lansing's been hit by a chocolate chip cookie famine. We're starving to
death! Help!"

"You nut!" She shook her head, laughing.
"I'll send the UPS cavalry with a fresh batch
of supplies. Well, guess I'd better let you go.
It's getting late. 'Bye for now. Love you!"

"Love you, too, Mom. Gotta run. 'Bye!"

Six more weeks and she'd be able to see
him, hug him . . . nag him! She grinned.
Mothers were entitled to nag a little. Anne
leaned back into the sofa cushions, still smiling. He always had that effect on her. No

matter what, she was so lucky. He was a good kid, the best, and just talking to him had restored her equilibrium tonight.

Anne looked around with satisfaction at the small corner of the world she now called home. The open spacious room tucked up under the roof was painted and carpeted a pale cream color and furnished with a few light-colored upholstered pieces. Books and newspapers lay scattered across the coffee table, and a partially completed jigsaw puzzle was spread across a bleached pine table in the corner near the kitchen's mini-counter.

Bright and airy for all its limited size, it was very different from the stately house on Vaughan Road in Bloomfield Hills, where they'd lived all those years. Well, of course, it had to be. New person, new start. She was still astonished at the changes she saw in herself.

She turned back to the tiny kitchen and set about making dinner for one.

"Michael, you're late. Anything wrong?"

"Nope, not a thing." Mike smiled, tossed his sheepskin jacket on the rack near the garage door, and bent to give his Aunt Caroline a hug and kiss. He unbuckled the leather belt and slid it and the holster off his still-narrow hips, carefully placing it on the top shelf of the closet.

"Hello, dear." Caroline kissed Helena, then turned back to the stove. "You two get ready, and no dawdling, now, hear?"

Helena followed Mike to the sink in the laundry room. "Okay, Dad . . . give! All the way home you wouldn't say a word."

"Honey, you made up for my silence, believe me!" he teased.

"Well, you said you didn't want to talk business 'til later. Dad, *please*. Everybody's talking about the scam! Any leads?"

Mike dried his face, smiling behind the towel at Helena's version of police procedure and jargon.

"No, not yet. Unless you noticed someone with chocolate under their fingernails? Otherwise we don't have much to go on." Hoping the subject had been exhausted, Mike walked into the living room, sniffing the air with appreciation. "Mmm, meat loaf. Smells great!" He dropped his sizable frame into the well-worn black leather Eames chair near the fireplace and took the newspaper Helena handed him.

"I'm starved. Didn't have much lunch today." Breakfast either, he mused, unless you counted the coffee at Sweet Expectations. The memory he'd been fighting all day was nudged into life, the sweet yeasty perfume of warm bread, the heady aroma of cinnamon and coffee, the stirring indefinable scent of woman. One woman.

Had he thought her charming? No, not charming. A strange, unfamiliar sensation twisted inside him, all heat and desire, then was gone. Mike was badly shaken, and he was annoyed with himself. It had been a long time since he'd been plagued with that problem . . . obviously too long.

He shook out his paper and put on his glasses. And Helena did what she did best. Asked questions. "Mac said you were there this morning, to take the report. How come? Uncle Ed's usually got the early shift."

"Oh, well, remember I was out on that stakeout last night, this toxic waste business, and I just . . ." His words trailed off lamely. All these months he'd deliberately avoided meeting Anne McClellan, delaying, making excuses, though it would have been perfectly normal to go in and introduce himself at any time. Sure, it was irrational, unreasonable, but it had gotten so he couldn't abide even the sound of the woman's name. He'd nodded and smiled, and made appropriate noises when Helena voiced Mac's, latest *obiter dictum*. But his jaw was damned sore from clenching his teeth, and it was a sure bet any mention of her name was good for five to ten points on his blood pressure.

Their meeting this morning had been the match to the fuse, resentment smoldering for so long bursting into flame before he got one foot in her door. Indeed, it began to flare the moment he heard the call on the radio.

"I just figured it was as good a time as any to meet her."

"So, what did you think?"

"What?" His head jerked back to Helena, perched alertly on the sofa cross-legged, elbows resting on her knees, chin propped in her hands. She waited with avid interest for his answer, the sharp blue eyes so like her aunt's missing very little.

"Well, there wasn't much to go on. No money was taken and—"

"Oh, Dad, honestly! What did you think of *Mac*?"

"Oh."

He let the paper drop into his lap. What did he think? Well, to her credit she was certainly a woman who could keep a secret. Obviously, she'd refrained from telling Helena about their strained meeting, otherwise Helena's friendly and cheerful demeanor would be neither friendly nor cheerful! Anne McClellan could keep her own counsel . . . at least sometimes. And she made a darned good cup of coffee.

"She's . . . uh . . . not exactly what I expected." Helena waited. "Frankly, after all the buildup, I didn't know if I'd find Mother Teresa, Ann Landers, or the queen of the Hell's Angels."

Helena sat up straight, eyes wide and mouth open, her feet dropping to the floor in one lithe movement. "But she's not—"

"Look, sweetheart," Mike cut in, a long day's weariness in his voice, fatigue lining his face, "I don't want to criticize. . . . I know how fond you are of her. But if I tell you something, then it's wrong for her to urge you to go against my wishes."

"Dinner, everybody. Let's go!"

Both heads turned, the elder profoundly grateful for the interruption. Dear Caroline, Mike thought wryly. She ran the house with all the authority of a drill sergeant terrorizing a squad of green recruits. But there was nothing she wouldn't do to keep them safe and happy, and Mike was sure women like her didn't exist anymore . . . if they ever had. At best she was the last of the breed, he'd lay odds on that. The two people under her domain were willing subjects to her affectionate tyranny. It was a devotion shared by the three of them, unique and special.

"It's getting cold." Second warning. They'd never had the courage to find out what would happen after a third.

"C'mon, honey. Remember, thou shalt not eat lukewarm meat loaf." Mike tried his foolproof loving-father smile. Her answering frown wasn't what he'd hoped for.

Hands folded in front of her, Caroline sat at one end of the cloth-covered table, presiding over the platters and bowls in regal serenity.

"Cold food won't do much for a hungry belly."

Mike kissed the top of his aunt's grey head as Helena slipped into her chair across from him. "Hot or cold, your meat loaf is a winner, and you know it." Mike made an exaggerated ceremony of shaking out his napkin before he reached for the platter. "Mmm, looks almost as good as it smells."

"Almost?" His aunt raised one eyebrow, a duplicate of his own expression of dry amusement. She'd been parrying his teasing remarks for a good many years.

"Honestly, Daddy"—Helena's earnest voice

and troubled face lent weight to her words—
"I thought you'd really like her."

"Who's 'her'?"

"Mac." Helena's short answer to her aunt
was bleak.

"Mrs. McClellan, down at the pas—the bakery. I met her this morning. There was a B
and E."

"Well, it's about time."

"For a B and E? Why? What have *you* got
against her?"

"Daddy!"

"Michael! Shame on you. I meant it's time
you met her. Helena's worked there so long
I feel as if I know her already."

"Yeah, I know what you mean!" he muttered fervently.

"Oh, Daddy, she's really neat, and she's not
a busybody. Sometimes I ask her opinion and
she tells me, that's all."

Sometimes! "My God, the woman's name
comes up as frequently as crabgrass in July.
But not tonight, please." Mike changed the
subject. "So, how's everything at school?
Shouldn't you get your grades pretty soon?"
He spooned mashed potatoes onto his plate.

"Oh, school's okay." Helena pounced on a
suddenly perceived weakness in his attitude.
"See? You were worried that working would

interfere with my homework, but I'm doing just as good—"

"Well," Caroline corrected with a smile as she passed the gravy dish.

"—well as always. Right from the beginning, Mac told me she wouldn't let me work all those hours if my grades went down."

She missed the spasm of annoyance that crossed Mike's face. Caroline, though, did not. Caroline rarely missed anything.

"And they come out week after next." Helena took the platter from him. "I just have a biology report next Monday."

"Michael, please pass the carrots. And take some first, young man."

"Don't you ever give up, Aunt Caroline?" He grinned, relieved at the safe neutral topic. "You've been pushing carrots at me since 'young man' was a true description," he teased, taking the obligatory spoonful. "And I still had to get glasses last year."

She smiled back, eyes brightening, the lined face suddenly years younger beneath the tightly wound coronet of grey hair. "If you'd ever eaten more than one measly spoonful at a time, you probably wouldn't need them at all." She looked affectionately at Helena. "There are some instances in life, child, when a parent's example ought to be ignored. This is one of them. Although, in your father's case, I'm coming to believe there may be others. Eat your carrots."

She pinned Mike with a thoughtful gaze. No, his reaction to Anne McClellan had not gone unnoticed. Nor had his growing anger. But she shouldn't be surprised. Suddenly, Helena had a new idol. Father and daughter, so close for so long; there was bound to be resentment of the first person to come between them, whether that interference was perceived or actual.

Mike gazed at Helena, realizing anew his child was growing into a stunning beauty, a girl/woman with the awkward coltish grace of her fourteen years and the loveliness that presaged the woman she would become. Thank heavens she had her aunt's capacity for love, her enduring loyalty and strength. God knows, she couldn't have inherited a trace of them from Adrienne!

Caroline knew unerringly the subject of his thoughts. His features always took on that set, grim cast at any memory of his longtime ex-wife. She watched his fist crush the bread he held into crumbs. Helena's resemblance to Adrienne was no deeper than the skin, Michael had very carefully seen to that.

Mike swallowed with difficulty. The food

lost all taste as his thoughts turned backward. Then Helena's words broke through.

"Sunday? What about Sunday?" he asked.

"I just wanted to make sure you don't have anything special planned."

"Uh-uh, nothing really. Might set a load of wood out to dry before winter hits. Hey, if I finish early, how about going out to try for some trout? It's almost the end of the season."

"Oh, gee, I can't, Dad. I have to get some more leaf specimens for my report." There was a guarded look on her face. "And . . . uh . . . Mac once said she'd like to see the hills close up before the snow falls, so I . . . I asked her to come along."

Mike was quite proud of himself: He didn't grit his teeth. What in the name of God was wrong with him? So Helena had a crush on an older woman. So what? Girls went through that all the time, even girls with mothers. Was it so strange for one without a mother? If it didn't bother Caroline, what was his problem?

Caroline was beginning to wonder, too. Over the years Mike had had his share of liaisons with a variety of women, his philosophy, apparently, being "safety in numbers." But they'd never inspired such a visceral reaction. What had happened this morning?

"So, what did you think of Mrs. McClellan, Michael?"

"Why is everyone suddenly so interested in my opinion?"

"My, my, testy, aren't we?"

He ducked his head and took another mouthful of food.

"I understand she's done wonders with her shop. All my friends have said her pastry is marvelous." Caroline waited while a silent moment passed. "I've never gone in there, you know. I guess I thought you might disapprove. Although why I should feel that way I don't know."

Mike was startled. Was he that transparent?

"Yes, dear, your feelings are pretty obvious."

Helena stared from one to the other, her mouth agape. "Gee, Daddy, I never realized you felt that way." She bit her lip and mumbled into her plate, "I kind of thought you'd like Mac."

Not likely! Blondes were his style—tall, curvy, and *temporary* blondes, who knew when to keep their mouths shut, who were out for a little fun, a few laughs, and that's all! At least he knew what to expect of *them*.

Helena was still staring at him; so was Caroline. "Well, don't worry about it, honey. Now that you know how I feel we can just forget it, okay?" He hoped fervently it was okay!

The rest of the evening settled into a familiar routine. An unnaturally quiet and thoughtful Helena went up to do homework, followed soon thereafter by Caroline. He heard his aunt enter Helena's room; where she remained for a long time.

Some time later Mike looked up from his book, startled to see his daughter standing in front of him, the baggy green Dartmouth Tigers T-shirt she used in place of pajamas hugging her narrow shoulders. Her expression was troubled.

"Uh . . . I guess there's something I ought to tell you."

"Why? What's wrong, honey?" He sat up, alert.

"Well . . . uh . . . it's about last night, you know? What Mac said . . . about the haircut and the makeup and boys and . . ."

He almost groaned aloud. Oh shit, not again.

"I mean . . . well, Daddy, it's not exactly what you thought. . . ."

Five

Oh, go away! Anne squirmed deeper into the covers but the intrusive noise persisted. She thrust her hand out to the telephone. *Whatever it is better be worth it!* "Mnnphh . . . 'lo."

"Mrs. McClellan, it's Michael Novak. *Please* don't hang up!"

He needn't have worried. Shock brought her upright and it took only an instant for her to recover.

"Yes, Mr. . . . oh, pardon me, *Chief* Novak. What do you want? I thought you covered the ground pretty well this morning."

"Go ahead, you're entitled." The stilted mumble told Anne how unfamiliar that sort of admission was for him.

"Oh," she yawned widely, "I agree. But why bother! So, what *do* you want?"

"Did I wake you? I didn't stop to think about the time."

"You seem to do a lot of things without

thinking first," she answered dryly. "And yes, you woke me. I start to 'have *fun* with my little shop' at about six-thirty A.M."

"Touché. I deserved that. It's just that it took a while to work up the courage to phone you."

"Courage? You didn't seem to need it this morning."

"Yeah, well, the words come harder when you're wrong."

"Oh?" Anne sat up, leaning against the headboard. "I thought maybe you were intimidated by my cream puffs."

His low chuckle was warm, intimate, and quite possibly the sexiest sound she'd ever heard. Suddenly, Anne flushed at the double meaning he might hear in the innocent remark. She shivered, though the room was warm. Restless and uneasy, she pulled the covers closer.

"Look, I'm sorry I woke you. In fact, I'm— I'm sorry about everything. I had a little talk with my daughter this evening. She . . . uh . . . she told me about your husband. I never knew . . . I mean . . . well, my remarks were way out of line . . ."

"Yes. Look, let's just forget it," she said wearily. "I appreciate your calling to—"

"Well, that wasn't all. You see, Helena also

explained that she, shall we say, *exaggerated* some of your remarks." His voice was quiet, reflective. "I guess she thought if another adult was lined up in her corner, I'd be more impressed with her opinions. Sometimes, it's confusing," he sighed, "raising a teenage girl. She doesn't speak the same language as the rest of us."

His laughter was chagrined and Anne could almost sympathize.

"Anyway, I want to apologize for what I said. It was totally uncalled for. And please, for Helena's sake, don't blame her for this. She didn't deliberately mislead me, I jumped to the wrong conclusion." He sounded disgusted with himself. "She said you might go hiking with her Sunday. I wouldn't want you to back out because of my stupidity."

"Oh, no, I wouldn't let your stupidity spoil anything." Revenge was sweet, Anne thought, content . . . mean but sweet. "I'm just surprised that a policeman *especially* would make assumptions about guilt without proof." The momentary silence was loud, and then she chuckled. "Still, I guess you've groveled enough. I accept your apology. I know only too well what it's like being at the mercy of a teenager."

"You do?" Somehow, despite learning of

Anne's widowhood, Mike hadn't imagined her with her own family. And he didn't know why it should come as such a surprise. She was probably a wonderful mother. He didn't know, either, why he was so sure of that.

"Are you kidding?" she laughed. "My son went from diapers and Little League to bloody noses and bandaged knees—with a few visits to the principal's office in between! Why are you surprised? Oh, yes, of course: My 'aura of big city glamour.'" She heard the strangled "damn" on the other end of the line. "Lord, if you only knew."

Her delightful ripple of husky laughter sent that twist through him again, the same restless sensation he'd felt in her shop that morning. Mike closed his eyes and pictured her, warm and drowsy, lying in a tumbled nest of sheets and pillows, wearing. . . . Would she be wearing anything at all? Suddenly, his body felt full, tight. He ached with a strange, urgent kind of empty wanting and the receiver trembled in his hand.

". . . glamour! If you could see me now!"

"Yes."

The quiet intensity of the single word stunned them both into silence. Without thought, Anne hastily pulled the covers up to her neck, cheeks burning. She was confused, ridden with feelings she'd almost forgotten. For so long she'd been wife and mother, friend and neighbor, and the once-familiar language of innocent flirtation had been put into cold storage, grown rusty from disuse. But that's just where this conversation had drifted, perilously close to flirtatious innuendo. She wasn't prepared for that, she wasn't comfortable with it, with those sensations his hoarse whisper had aroused. For that one moment, despite what her mind told her, her body remembered . . . remembered what it felt like to be totally and completely and excitingly alive.

No! She had no business having these feelings. And he had no business inspiring them! And—oh, God!—how would his *wife* feel to have her husband talking that way? *How dare he!*

"It's very late, Chief Novak, and I don't imagine Caroline—*that is her name, isn't it?*—would be thrilled with this conversation, do you? *Good night!*"

She slammed the phone down as hard as she could and reached instinctively for Paul's picture in the crystal frame on the bedside table. Clutching it to her chest like a shield, Anne huddled under the covers, until fitful sleep finally returned.

Mike stared at the buzzing phone in his hand, his sudden surprising arousal ebbing now. Slowly, he replaced the receiver, perplexed at her sudden fury. What in the world was wrong with the woman? Why should Aunt Caroline give a damn what he said, no matter how stupid? he admitted wryly.

Hell's bells, no wonder girls were so incomprehensible sometimes. They were practicing to be women!

Mmmm, heaven! Anne inhaled deeply, with gusto. What could compare to the crisp, clean air of early autumn, the smell and sight of vibrant glowing foliage, the sharp purity and tang of cool mountain air tasting faintly of burning leaves?

Anne had learned, the hard way, to search out and find all there was to be had in every precious day. Pensive, she zipped her light jacket over the cotton turtleneck. How foolish she'd once been, how foolish they'd both been, she and Paul, assuming the stream of years would be unending, to be taken for granted and wasted without thought. In that instant, all those lost years were suddenly too painfully fresh and vivid.

She shrugged off the grey shroud of might-have-been. This was a new day, and this one would not be wasted.

Anne loved this season, the crowning achievement of nature's feverish summer schedule. As magnificent as Michigan's fall had been, with its glorious jewel tones, the annual ever-new explosion of glowing autumn colors, these high, dry granite mountains of New Hampshire, offered the senses a feast Anne thought might be equaled no other place on earth.

Or is it because I'm different now? Her perceptions had altered, along with the rest of her life. "Ah, what the hell, Annie. Stop analyzing and agonizing. Enjoy . . . no questions."

She looked at her watch and chuckled. "Damn, I told Helena I'd be there at ten. Mother was right all those years ago. I probably *will* be late for my own funeral."

Funeral. The grin wavered for an instant. She'd *almost* reached the point where words and images didn't need to be chosen quite so carefully. Almost, but not quite. Well, no one said it would be easy. *But we're getting there, kiddo, we are definitely getting there.*

Anne buckled the red helmet, tied the light nylon fanny pack around her waist—noticing ruefully that the fanny in question was a little more prominent than it used to be—and mounted the gleaming little red and silver Honda. Her gesture to adventure and excitement. *As if a new business, a new town, and a new mortgage weren't enough adventure and excitement!* Well, hell, life didn't have to begin at forty. It could begin at any time, even close to fifty . . . whenever!

She kicked sharply into starting gear, the quiet motor hardly noticeable in the Sunday somnolence, and moved at a sedate pace through the town, waving and smiling at people who were now part of the familiar fabric of her daily life. She increased speed when she approached the outskirts of Whitefield.

Nothing but a beautiful day ahead and time to enjoy it—Anne swerved, then righted herself and the bike—unless you hit a pothole. Regrettably, in life, there were always potholes.

Good grief, how appropriate. The Sunday Sermonette!

The pull of the airstream as she skimmed north along Route 3 was an excitement Anne hadn't yet outgrown. When Jerry came east for the holidays she'd let him try the bike, without the maternal worry over city traffic to distract her. He'd love it! After he stopped laughing at the sight of his mother in her helmet and fanny pack.

The road twisted and climbed, and soon she spotted the house Helena had described. It sprawled above a heavily wooded ravine that slashed across the bulky foothills of the Presidential Range to the northeast. Anne pulled up atop a small rise in the road just before it dipped down to pass the long curving driveway.

She breathed a deep sigh of admiration. It was a gem of a house, mounted in a glorious setting of uncultivated shrubbery, lovingly protected by the lacy yellow-gold of white birch and the unique scarlet splash of sumac. The side facing her might have begun as the ubiquitous simple A-frame, but it had taken on a life of its own amid the granite magnificence of its setting.

The pointed thrust of a dark shingled roof echoed the upward reach of far mountain peaks, and natural stone slab walls and weathered silvery wood reflected the familiar provincial architecture of the northeast. The huge expanse of windows, rather than shutting out the extremes of weather, so much a fact of life in these parts, opened to embrace them. The structure seemed to have evolved from its environment, a pleasing perfect blend of New England's comfortable tradition and New Hampshire's stubborn individualism.

It surprised her. Her perception of its tight-lipped judgmental owner didn't jibe with the impression of warmth and welcome she felt at the first sight of his home. And yet, how accurate was her initial judgment? That odd late-night phone call . . . it couldn't have been easy for him to apologize. She'd bet a bundle it didn't happen often! But then, he had to go and spoil it with that out-of-bounds remark.

For a moment Anne frowned, wondering. Had she perhaps overreacted, reading into it more than he'd intended? Probably, she admitted wryly. After all, she might make Cub Scout leader, possibly neighborhood "cookie lady." But definitely not femme fatale material, not on her best day! And that dawn meeting had been a long way from her best.

Come on, just forget it! *He* probably had—she could only hope. Anne wheeled down to the drive, a sharp turn bringing bike and rider to an abrupt halt at the side of the house.

The cough of the motor died and the parti-colored autumn foliage rustled dryly in the gentle breeze. She hung the helmet from the handlebar and, fingers combing through short silver-shot dark hair, strolled toward the back of the house, where a steady thwack-thwack was the only evidence of activity.

Anne glanced at her watch. Fifteen minutes late. She was surprised Helena wasn't patrolling the road looking for her. Too bad she wasn't. Then Anne wouldn't have to worry about meeting *him* again—him and his wife, the elusive Caroline. Damn, she felt guilty . . . and she hadn't *done* anything!

Except, perhaps, to imagine a little, her conscience prodded her. Well, what the heck, she comforted herself, even a President of the United States had once "lusted in his heart"! And anyway, she thought primly, it *wasn't* lust, not really.

Cold comfort, indeed.

Any hope she might have had of avoiding the formidable head of the household died a quick death as she rounded the corner and glimpsed the uncompromisingly male figure at the other end of the terrace that extended the length of the house. Fortunately, his back was turned and he was unaware of her, the sound of her approach hidden by the noise and his total absorption in the job at hand.

Anne saw the flash of metal as sunlight glinted off the large ax blade that he swung high over his head, then back down with measured but lethal intent. He was splitting a good-sized stack of logs piled in an attached shed. Anne smiled to herself for a moment.

Back home most men of her acquaintance would need to be shown which end of the ax was the working end. Fireplaces were usually filled with gas jets and fake logs, and if the real thing was in evidence, you could be sure the wood had been cut by someone else.

She looked more closely now at the back of the man in question. Despite the slight chill of early autumn, he'd stripped off his T-shirt, which lay abandoned on the stack of logs beside him. Wow, the thought flashed through Anne's head, if he's responsible for a whole New Hampshire winter's worth of firewood, it's no wonder he's got shoulders like that!

Yes, and I'm sure his wife appreciates them, too!

With a resolute squaring of her own shoulders, Anne advanced toward Mike. The moss-covered pebbled path rendered her steps almost soundless.

As she saw his profile, she was struck by a thought: This was a happy man. Gone was the tense, hard anger she'd seen at their first meeting. This man was at peace—with himself and his world. His features were relaxed, at ease, and he was simply enjoying the physical release this ordinary homely chore afforded him.

Mike swung the ax with deceptive ease, driving the sharp blade into the hard wood as effortlessly as she would draw a hot knife through butter. The constant rhythmic shift and pull of muscles, still beautifully formed beneath the taut skin though there was no mistaking the mark of years and age on his body, held Anne's admiring gaze. In her world, the one that still provided most of her daily references, one didn't come across the unclothed human figure, not often, unless a pool or a beach figured prominently in the background. But this particular partially unclothed human form was very much in evidence, right here, right now. He filled her eyes and her senses with the living vital energy of his presence.

In his uniform Mike had been formidable. But in bare skin the sight was devastating! His dark hair, more unruly than the other morning, was wet, matted with sweat, the silver streaks more evident today, his skin slick and damp with physical effort.

And suddenly, Anne felt slightly sick with shame at her own thoughts, as unbidden as they might be. Generations of propriety and virtue stood vigilant guard against that momentary surge of rebellious hormones.

Still, she stared, unable to break the tenuous connection. Fortunately, the closing of the screen door and footsteps clicking across the stone terrace did it for her.

"Michael, did you—Ah, you must be Mrs. McClellan." The tall, spare grey-haired woman, holding a plaid shirt in one hand and a threaded needle in the other, stopped on the second step and smiled warmly at Anne.

At her first words, the rhythmic thud of the ax ceased abruptly. Mike swung around to find Anne, her cheeks flushed with embarrassment at having been caught gawking.

He lowered the ax, wiping the sweat from his forehead with the back of his large, calloused hand. Mike wondered how long she'd been standing there. Something in her wide dark eyes, the alert tension of her body, told him more than Anne could have known. Body language was familiar territory for a well-trained police officer—and for a normal healthy male. Mike Novak was both.

The older woman was speaking and Anne's eyes darted nervously to her, away from Mike's disturbing smile. "Been looking forward to meetin' you, my dear." She slipped the shirt over her arm and, with an expression of welcome on her lined face, extended a wrinkled but still firm hand.

Mike walked to her and put his arm around the woman's narrow shoulders, a wide grin slanted across his mouth. His moustache twitched. A cat with a trapped mouse would have looked less dangerous than he did at that moment.

"Oh, that's right, you two haven't met. Well, let me introduce you," he drawled. "Anne McClellan, this is my aunt, Miss Novak. Of course, everyone around here calls her Caroline."

Anne stood there, gaping dumbly at the other two. "Caroline. *This* is . . . Caroline?"

That lady, the object of all this bewilderment, was feeling a bit disconcerted herself. "Yes, well, now that we've got that settled . . ." Caroline's smile softened her words. She took Anne's hand in hers again, giving their flustered visitor time to recover her poise, which seemed to have disappeared abruptly.

"It's a pleasure to meet you, my dear. Helena is so very fond of you. And not many people on the dark side of thirty could fit that description. Not without benefit of a guitar and sound amplifier," she added dryly. "Wait, I'll go get her. And Michael, mind your manners. Put on your shirt." She pumped Anne's hand once more, then went to fetch her great-niece.

Anne turned reluctantly to Mike, who stood leaning against the terrace wall, arms folded, waiting patiently, that damnable smile on his attractive mouth. He raised his brows with an annoyingly smug air of superiority.

"Speaking of jumping to conclusions . . ."

"I . . . well, naturally I thought . . . uh . . . Caroline was your wife, and I assumed—"

"Tsk, tsk," Mike shook his head. "I assure you I have no wife, and a very wise person recently warned me not to . . . let's see, how did she put it? Oh, yes, not to 'make assumptions about guilt without proof.' "

"Will you please stop quoting me to me," Anne mumbled. She closed her eyes, annoyed with herself, and fumbled in her pocket for her sunglasses, thankful for something to hide behind. Because she found it increasingly difficult to take her eyes off him. "Couldn't be satisfied with your pound of flesh . . ."

A particularly bad choice of words, she thought ruefully. Flesh. Lord, the man was a visual magnet. She'd never been particularly susceptible to the lure of the male physique. Before. It certainly held no mystery for a woman married so many years, who'd borne and raised a son. But what woman wouldn't be enthralled with the smooth, supple play of muscle, bone, and skin, whether hefting the heavy ax or, as now, poised quietly, at rest?

The sunlight glinted on his dark weathered skin. A sheen of moisture glazed his face and his body, and Anne saw a droplet of sweat slide slowly down his neck, hesitate for a moment in the hollow of his collarbone, then begin to inch its crystalline way down the center of his chest and the solid conformation of muscle, and her eyes followed to the low-slung worn and faded sweatpants clinging to his legs.

Anne's tongue darted out to moisten suddenly dry lips. She felt uncomfortably warm, her cotton shirt clinging to her clammy skin. With all this cool, clear, crisp New Hampshire air, she had to pick now to forget how to breathe? Damnit, lungs, do your stuff! She pulled in a shaky breath. Well, thank heavens at least her lungs, despite her heart and pulse, still responded to reason. Oh shit, she was too old for this!

"Excuse me," he smiled into Anne's wide-eyed stare, "I never buck Aunt Caro's orders." He reached for the crumpled white shirt and pulled it smoothly down, for which Anne was profoundly grateful. "And now I really have to get back to work."

Oh God! Anne could feel the blush of humiliation spread across her throat and face. He was laughing at her! The miserable, no-good, arrogant son of a bitch . . . he was *laughing at her!*

Anne made a stab at dignity. "I was just . . . just . . ." What the hell was she *just*? ". . . trying to remember if I'd brought my lunch." Oh, wonderful. Sure, he'd fall for that!

"Ah, yes, you did look a little . . . hungry."

"Don't be crude, Chief Novak!"

"Sorry." He looked properly chastised. "Still jumping to those conclusions. But then," he winked, "neither of us seems to have a monopoly on that, do we . . . Anne?"

A humbled Anne rolled her eyes skyward. "What can I say . . . Chief Novak?"

"Mike."

"What?"

"You can say Mike. My name is Mike," he teased. "Why don't you try it? It's easier after the first time." He had a stubborn wish to hear his name on her lips.

"Mike." Anne said it slowly, carefully, drawing it out, rolling it on her tongue, enjoying the taste of it. Then, catching herself, she shrugged sheepishly. "It seems bad manners and quick judgments can be found anywhere! It's a wonder there are no broken bones, with all this conclusion jumping."

He laughed aloud, eyes crinkling, head thrown back. And for a moment she saw once more the man in the photograph, that instant of uninhibited pleasure, the open unguarded expression of enjoyment, and she felt an answering flood of joy within herself. In that moment she warmed to him, the uncomfortable sensations of the past few minutes dissipating, feeling the beginnings of what might become a real bond of friendship.

"Hi, Mac!" Helena slammed through the screen door and leaped over the three steps to land beside Anne with a jarring thud. "Aunt Cally said you were here. I'm ready, let's go! S'long, Dad." She threw a kiss at him as he lazily balanced the ax in his hand, gaze fixed on Anne. Helena bounced toward the edge of the ravine, where a small path angled off into the brush clinging to the steep hillside behind the house. Anne followed more sedately in her energetic wake.

Just then Caroline, framed in the doorway, called after them and they looked back. "When you two get back, Anne, I hope you'll stay for Sunday supper."

Helena nodded enthusiastic agreement. Mike approached them, seconding the invitation. "Of course you'll stay." His assured voice, disturbingly close to Anne's left ear, cut confidently through her automatic demurral. "It's time we got to know each other better. And by then I'm sure you'll be . . . hungry." He winked. "You look like a lady with a healthy appetite."

The withering look she aimed at him would have frozen a lesser man. Oh, she'd *kill* him if she got her hands on him!

At the thought of her hands on him she turned, hurrying to follow in Helena's footsteps, away from the house . . . away from the man.

Six

"Have mercy, please! Not another mouthful," Anne begged, laughing.

She'd fallen on her dinner like the survivor of a recent famine. Not by word or glance or the flicker of an eyelid had Mike shown he recalled their earlier exchange. But now he looked down at his plate and smiled to himself, proving how strong were both his patience and his memory.

Anne pushed the plate away decisively and tried to ignore his disturbing presence. It was like ignoring a redwood tree in the garden. "Caroline, that was marvelous! I never knew roast chicken could taste so good. Between my feet and my stomach, I may never move again!"

"Helena worked you pretty hard today, hmm?" Mike's eyes crinkled in a smile of understanding. She'd been running *him* ragged for years.

"Well, I was expecting an easy stroll in the

countryside. I'm a little out of shape for mountain climbing."

"Oh, Mac, those weren't mountains. I mean, if you want *mountains*—!" Helena dismissed Anne's alibis. "Those are just little hills. And I needed some really good trees."

"Strange, the 'good trees' never grow on level ground . . . only where an acrobatic mountain goat can barely get at them."

"Or a determined fourteen-year-old biology student," Caroline added dryly. "She forgets to push her off button every now and then."

Helena merely grinned at their good-natured laughter as she rose from the table.

"Well, guess I'll get this stuff out of here so we can have dessert," she said with an eager look at the casserole resting on the sideboard. During dinner it had cooled to an edible temperature, and the dining room was now permeated with the comforting sweet-spicy incense of apples and butter and cinnamon.

Anne gazed after the girl as she disappeared through the kitchen door. "You were right," she smiled at Mike. "You *have* done a nice job raising her." He had not elaborated further on the absence of a wife on the scene and Anne wouldn't ask Helena, but at this moment she was intensely curious.

He smiled, pleased. "The lion's share of the

credit goes to the boss here." He reached over and squeezed his aunt's hand, then leaned back as Helena returned, put a wrought iron trivet on the table, and set a steaming coffeepot on top.

"The way to her heart is definitely via her stomach," Mike stage-whispered as she fell into her chair without wasting a motion, reaching for a plate before her rear hit the seat.

"Pity Helena doesn't move that fast for stewed figs," Caroline observed dryly, the smile in her eyes softening the tart words.

Mike grinned at Anne. "Actually, Helena forces herself to eat this, just to salve Caroline's feelings."

"Here, Anne, try some apple grunt."

"Apple . . . *grunt?*" She laughed with delight. "What in the world is apple grunt?"

"Just our Yankee version of cobbler."

Anne took the plate Caroline handed her, along with the small pitcher of heavy cream. "Mmmm," she closed her eyes, smiling, savoring the first forkful. "You can call it anything you like as long as it tastes like this!" She chewed and swallowed with utter bliss.

Caroline shrugged modestly, pleased nonetheless. "Just an old standby . . . been doin' it for years. The secret is a healthy jolt of applejack," she laughed.

"Don't let her fool you," Mike confided. "She makes it for special occasions." He lifted the coffee cup to his lips, swallowed, and smiled at Anne. "And you're a very special occasion."

Hell of a time for a hot flash, Anne thought, ignoring the real reason for the heat that washed over her at his words, his gaze. Ignoring her own sudden confusion, Anne took refuge in scraping her dish clean, sliding her tongue across her lower lip to savor the last moist crumb.

Watching her, Mike's throat went dry and for a single instant his cup shook in his hand. He managed to remember where he was before his strange reaction became noticeable to the others and concentrated on picking up his napkin from the floor, carefully arranging it in his lap.

"I admit it, Caroline," Anne continued, desperate to fill what sounded like a huge void of silence around the table, "I couldn't do as well as this if I stood at the stove for the rest of my life." She made a concerted effort to narrow her circle of conversation to Caroline, ignoring Mike. Or trying.

"She's a nice girl, Michael." Caroline smiled, patting Anne's hand, and looked at her nephew. He was gazing thoughtfully at the nice girl.

"Well, thanks," Anne smiled determinedly back at Caroline, "although the 'girl' disappeared long ago, as my aching body keeps telling me."

"Oh, that's just Aunt Cally, Mac," Helena mumbled through an apple-filled mouth. "She still calls Daddy 'young man' . . . at least when she scolds him."

Anne choked. The thought of anyone "scolding" the tough sample of masculinity sitting across from her, especially this frail old woman, was so patently absurd that Anne chuckled incredulously and found her equilibrium miraculously restored. And then the room filled with their laughter joining hers. Comfortable, Anne felt as if she'd been sharing the joys of this family for a long, long time.

"What the heck, Aunt Caroline!" Mike pushed himself up from the table. "Let's live a little. Leave the dishes and come sit in the living room a while. I'll help you with 'em later, while Helena's doing her homework." He steered them all out of the dining room and down the hall.

Mike settled his large frame in his favorite chair next to the crackling log fire. Unusually content, Anne leaned back into a corner of the sofa, Helena cross-legged at the other end, near Mike's chair.

Caroline, across from Mike, began to rock back and forth. "So, tell me, Anne, how did you happen to settle in Whitefield?"

Good old Caroline, Mike smiled to himself. He'd been meaning to get around to it, and here she was taking care of it for him, as she'd done so often in the last fourteen years. Listening intently for Anne's answer, he lowered his head while he lit one of his thin cigars.

Anne glanced at him, sensing his concentration on her words. "Well, it's hard to say. I lived in Michigan most of my life, in and around Detroit. But about two years ago my— my husband . . . my husband died, and I—" Anne swallowed, shrugging. "I wanted to get away for a while. When my son started college last fall, it seemed a good time." She spoke with very little inflection, hurrying past an uncomfortable subject.

Mike was at least as uncomfortable as she, recalling his hasty misjudgment. Anne offered no embellishments to the bare outline, which of course did nothing to discourage Caroline.

"But why here?" Caroline wondered. "We're rather off the beaten tourist path, except for the annual fall rush of leaf peepers, of course."

"Oh, Paul and I vacationed near here a

couple of times, skiing down at Cannon Mountain, and one year we were two of those leaf peepers. I remember we drove along the . . . I think it was called the Kancamagus Trail and up to Lost Nation Road near Groveton. We loved it. It was very beautiful, and I guess I just wanted to see it again." She cleared her throat and blinked quickly. "Anyway, I drove into Whitefield by chance and fell in love with it." A smile of genuine delight brightened her face.

"So, you came to visit and just stayed on?"

"Not exactly," Anne chuckled, and explained about her impromptu employment with Ilse Kolchak the previous spring, the letter, the consideration she'd given this decision. "So, you see, I'm not *quite* as impetuous as all that."

Or hadn't been before. Anne's expression turned thoughtful. She spread her fingers on her knee, tracing a pulled thread in the denim, recalling the past year and that strange wrenching impulse to turn from the known to the unknown. She frowned. Change was good, but perhaps . . .

Mike saw it immediately. For a brief moment she looked . . . trapped. Without examining his strange urge to protectiveness, he gave her a way out. "Well, I have to agree with your choice. I love it here, and I've never seen a more beautiful place. By the way, how did you enjoy the scenery today?" His eyes stayed on Anne but he spoke to his daughter. "Where did you take her, babe?"

"We didn't go far. . . ." Anne groaned in disagreement. "Oh, Mac," Helena teased, "we weren't more than a mile from here."

"And all of it uphill!"

"Well, yeah, but that's where all—"

"—the good trees are. I know, I know!"

Mike and Caroline grinned broadly at each other. "I don't know, babe," he gestured at Anne's sadly dilapidated gym shoes, the small scrapes on her arms, the abrasions showing white on the darker denim of her jeans. "Looks like you had her hiking through caves!"

Anne kept the smile pasted to her mouth. It took a lot of effort but it worked. They didn't notice anything. If only he hadn't mentioned the cave. The smile stretched until she thought her jaw would break, her nails puncturing grooves into her damp clenched palms.

She'd felt so stupid! She'd tried, made more of an effort than anyone could know, and yet she hadn't been able to set one foot inside the small, dark, dank cavern. An implacable icy panic and the image of Paul's lifeless face had held her frozen, blocking her way. Anne wondered how Helena could have been fooled. Anyone could have seen, certainly an alert intelligent and very observant fourteen-year-old.

"Gee, it's funny you mentioned caves, Daddy. Mac, what happened to you when—"

"Oh my gosh, look at the time!" Anne abruptly interrupted. "I've really got to get home. I have to be up at six, and my alarm clock already has it in for me." She hurried to her feet, surreptitiously wiping her palms against her jeans. "Helena, my sweet, thanks for a great day. As soon as I heal, maybe we can do it again! No, honestly, I'm just kidding. I did love it!" She laughed, hugging the girl, then turned to Caroline.

"I can't begin to thank you for tonight. It was wonderful." She held Caroline's hand for a moment. "I'm so glad we've finally met."

Caroline leaned forward and touched her dry lips to Anne's cheek. "Helena talks about you so much, I feel I've known you as long as she has. Please feel free to come over any time, to visit—or to talk. I mean that."

Anne knew she did. Caroline Novak was not a woman for meaningless words. "If you'll promise to come in for a cup of coffee when-

ever you're in town." They nodded in understanding.

"Good night, Mike. It was nice meeting
you . . . this time." Anne smiled and turned
to go. "I'll be seeing you—"

"Well, for the next ten minutes, at least."
Mike had hefted himself from his chair and
walked down the short hall to the back door.

"Why? What—?"

"Come on, I'll drive you home," he said,
returning and pulling on his jacket.

"But I have my bike—"

"You think I'd let you ride that thing on
these roads after dark?"

Let her? She stared straight at him. "Well,
I seemed to manage well enough coming out
here."

"Anne, he's quite right," Caroline interjected, touching her arm lightly. "There are
no lights on the roads and they can be
treacherous in the dark."

"Hey," Mike's grin teased, "let me do my
macho act and drive you home. Caroline
would skin me alive if I let you ride that toy
bike. Do it as a favor to me."

"But I—" The three stubborn faces in front
of her stilled Anne's protest. She wasn't crazy
about being alone with him for the ride, but
actually, it was kind of nice to have someone

worry about her, to act so protective, after all this time.

Mike stowed the bike in the back of the Jeep, eased smoothly out onto the road, and headed slowly toward town. "Buckle your seat belt," he said.

Amused, she did as she'd been told. "You're a cautious man, hmm?"

"Always." *And try to remember that*, he warned himself.

Anne settled back in the comfortable silence, the fleeting strain and distress she'd felt in the living room already vanished. She felt slightly foolish and was grateful no one had noticed.

She'd have been less relaxed if she could have read Mike's mind. When he got back home, he'd have to ask Helena a little more about the afternoon. *Something* had happened—at least to Anne. But for now he leaned back, one elbow propped on the door, the other hand resting lightly on the wheel as the dark shapes of night flowed past the moving car. Helena might tell him what had happened to Anne, but who the hell would tell him what was happening to him? Whatever it was, he decided suddenly, it might be better to stop it, right now. He glanced at Anne, his cynical smile shadowed by the dark brush of his moustache.

"Do you do that to everyone?"

"What? Do I do what to everyone?" She looked over at him.

"Charm them that way."

It didn't sound like a compliment.

"I don't think I've ever seen Caroline won over that quickly, not by anyone. She's a hard case."

Must run in the family, Anne thought.

"It's not so easy to earn her approval. And I know damn well she doesn't bestow kisses freely. Yeah, I'd say you've made a friend in Caroline. And her friendship isn't easily come by." Mike's dark brows were raised in grudging respect and then his jaw tensed for an instant. "Even ol' prudent and practical Gilcrest fell all over himself for you the other day. You seem to have the entire town of Whitefield eating out of your hand."

"Not quite," Anne answered dryly. "You've managed to resist my fatal charm." She folded her arms and looked away from him. "I'll have to try more 'eye of newt' next time."

Mike chuckled. "No one in his right mind could mistake you for one of Macbeth's witches." His mouth twisted in a wolfish grin as he looked over at her, dark curls brushing the back of her neck, the lovely full mouth, the maturely voluptuous body. "Uh-uh."

"Thanks—I think." Anne stared out the side windows, deliberately away from him. She was suddenly acutely uncomfortable in the close interior.

They drove for a few more moments before Mike broke the strained silence. "Look, I'm sorry. I didn't mean it to sound like the third degree." In the dark she sensed he shook his head. "It's just . . . there's something about you, Anne McClellan, something—"

"Believe me, there's nothing. What you see is what you get."

"Yes, that's what I mean. Too damned good to be true."

"Are you deliberately speaking in riddles? I don't understand you."

"My sentiments exactly."

"Honestly," Anne sighed, exasperated. "What is it with you? What's to understand? You always assume I have devious ulterior motives. Can't a person just be what they appear to be?"

"Rarely."

He pulled up in front of her shop, the lighted windows of the apartment above throwing a pattern of bright squares across the sidewalk. Anne turned toward him.

"You really are a cynic, aren't you?"

Mike's mouth twisted. "I'm a cop, a realist. I see things as they are, not as they should be or as I'd like them to be. I don't fool myself with fairy tales about 'happily ever after.' "

"What in the world produced such a jaundiced viewpoint? I'd have thought life up here is idyllic. A lovely quiet town, crime not exactly a major problem. Everyone here seems to love you. . . ."

"Oh? Have you checked with everyone?"

Anne hoped it was dark enough to hide the blush. "Stop avoiding the subject. You know what I mean. You have a good life, friends and family, a lovely daughter anyone would be proud to—"

"No, not *anyone.*" His words were very quiet.

"And I . . . what?"

"Come off it, Anne, don't tell me you haven't been wondering about my . . . about Helena's mother. Didn't you check on her, too?"

"Now, look here, I may have a lot of faults—yes, I *do* have faults—but nosiness isn't among them. Whatever else you may believe, I don't pry and I don't gossip!"

"Touché." He ducked his head, then suddenly reached for her hand. It was small and warm, and it felt perfect tucked into his. "Did it again, didn't I? Open mouth, insert foot. Guess I'm still too touchy about some things."

Damn! he thought. Adrienne hadn't stayed around for long, but the damage she'd done had lasted a lot longer than the marriage.

"Thirteen years. Even Pavlov's dog wouldn't react to the bell after that long," he muttered.

Anne was stunned at the pain in his words. He looked so strong, so imposing. Somehow one forgot that even Mike Novak could bleed.

He quickly dropped her hand and put his back on the wheel. "You see, even I'm susceptible to your charms. Forewarned but still not forearmed." He frowned, an oddly quizzical smile on his mouth. "I'd better get your bike out and get out of here before you have me spilling my whole dull life story."

Anne was quite sure nothing about him could be dull. Her hand still tingled from his brief clasp. He radiated excitement and sex appeal like heat from an old furnace. *Sex appeal.* My, my, she shook her head. Her calm, prosaic thought processes were suddenly so vivid and fanciful. She wasn't about to dig too deep for reasons, either.

Mike hauled the gleaming red bike out onto the sidewalk, as if it were no heavier than the ax he'd been using earlier, and followed Anne around to the small garage behind the building. She opened the door and he put it inside next to the sleek black body of an elegant sportscar.

"Ah, yes, the famous Porsche 944 Helèna keeps talking about." He looked her up and down. "What a contradiction you are. To look at you I wouldn't have thought 'Porsche.' "

"That's not very complimentary."

"No, it just means there's a lot to you I haven't seen yet."

Anne sighed. "Well, you're probably right. This was my big gesture when I decided to move. Down deep I'm more 'old Chevy station wagon.' "

Mike grinned. "What did you say before? 'What you see is what you get.' I don't think so. There's more to you than one might think, isn't there?"

"Haven't you learned yet that I don't like to be pigeonholed?"

Mike leaned against the open garage door, one hand in his pocket. He lifted the other to Anne's shoulder, the weight of it satisfyingly heavy. She felt uncomfortably warm. He brushed his hand over her flushed cheek and she almost stepped back.

"Oh, I'm not jumping to any conclusions. I'll take my time." The hair at the base of Anne's neck stood up.

He cupped her chin for a moment and she expelled a sharp breath. "Yep, have to give this a lot of thought." His quiet words gave the moment a strange air of intimacy. "I was wrong once; wouldn't want it to happen again. Doesn't look good, the Chief of Police making such errors of judgment—bad for the old image."

"I'd never tell," Anne murmured. "You can trust me."

Mike's eyes glittered in the faint light. He dropped his hand, straightening abruptly, and Anne stepped back, startled. His eyes were dark, his mouth curled in a tight smile. "No thanks. I'm not real big on trust, Anne. It's an old trap; I don't depend on anyone and I don't expect too much from anyone. Safer that way. No disappointments, no unpleasant surprises."

Anne slid under the covers in her dimly lit bedroom, recalling Mike's words. He hid himself so carefully. Always on guard, making sure not too much of the real man was exposed. She'd had a few tantalizing glimpses tonight, but then that inner censor snapped shut and, once more, the surface man, wary and careful, was all she saw.

No disappointments, no unpleasant surprises.

And not many pleasant ones, either. Anne frowned, her lips curved in a sad smile as she drifted into sleep. Poor Mike Novak. And she was probably the only person in town who would describe him that way.

Seven

"Jeez, Ed, what'd you do here? The desk is so neat I can't find a damn thing!"

Ed Pritchard heaved his ponderous bulk from the chair with surprising speed, entering Mike's office before another roar could rattle the windowpanes. T.G.I.F., he thought. It had been one hell of a week with the "grizzly" in here, growling around the office.

"Hey, Mike, I only threw out the garbage. Half the stuff was outdated memos and announcements, and the rest was stale doughnuts and cigar ashes and mildewed french fries. You been bitchin' 'bout the mess for a week." He stuck his hands in his pockets and stared blandly at the crack in the ceiling. "Along with everything else."

Mike glared at his deputy, a fearsome expression guaranteed to wither any living thing within twenty feet. But Ed didn't wither easily. Having survived twenty-three years on the force, the last thirteen with Mike, he knew how to avoid treacherous ground.

"You got new shoes, mebbe?"

Mike stared at him. "What're you talking about?"

"Well, you been actin' so testy I thought you might be breakin' in a pair of tight new shoes. Either that, or you're horny."

Mike tried out his usually trusty squint-eyed stare, but his laugh broke through at the truth of Ed's words. He shrugged at his always-genial deputy, wondering for an instant how close to the mark Ed might have come. But he dismissed the thought almost before it appeared.

"Yeah, you're right. I've had . . . a couple of things on my mind lately." He settled back in his chair behind the exemplary surface of the desk, his voice trailing off as he swiveled about to stare out the window facing the bank across the street.

Ed stood, watching thoughtfully as Mike's attention wandered. A speculative gleam lit the deputy's brown eyes. He began to probe, carefully.

"By the way, Mike, I ought to be mad at you."

Mike swiveled around to face him. "Why?"

"Well, all week you been bringin' in these

doughnuts and pastries and stuff, and Sylvie's got me on this diet and she's 'bout ready to skin me alive. Now, how'm I supposed to diet with all that good stuff around here?" Every morning for the last five days, the inevitable dark blue and cream box had been present beside the coffeepot when Ed reported in. He recognized it, having stopped at Sweet Expectations himself more than a few times. The new owner was real nice, a good-lookin' woman, to be sure. He'd never have thought she was Mike's type. . . . Ed looked closer at his preoccupied chief and smirked. Hmmm!

Mike sat motionless, deep in thought, unaware he was the subject of this interested appraisal, unaware of almost everything, in fact. Ed was right about his temper lately. And it would be foolish to pretend he didn't know the reason for it. Mike knew quite well what—or who—that reason was. He'd been drinking her coffee and eating her pastries for a week now, ever since that night he'd taken her home after Sunday supper.

His feelings, when he'd abruptly left Anne at her door, had been badly tangled. He'd wanted to avoid thinking of her, but every morning he found himself parking outside her shop, his sudden gifts of goodies to his office staff the excuse. Anne McClellan made him damn itchy, and he was afraid to start scratching. She scared him and his temper showed it.

He took a deep breath. Damn! This was insanity. What business did she have taking up residence in his mind this way? He sat up, looking quickly from the window and back to his work. If he needed a little female companionship, one fast phone call was all it would take. It was Friday; he'd give Honey a call, ask her out for dinner. Hadn't seen her in a while, anyway. *She* never confused amusement with emotion. Just a good dinner, enjoyable conversation, maybe a movie. No strings attached, or even implied, which was just what he needed. Anne McClellan definitely came with "strings." Entanglements he didn't need or want.

Mike slapped his hand decisively on the desk. "Okay, Ed, let's get to work. Where's the bad news from the O.W.M. on the pollution level?" The New Hampshire Office of Waste Management had begun sending daily reports a month ago.

"You're right about that, Mike . . . bad news. It came on the fax this morning. They tested farther upstream this time and the level's up again; seems like it happened about two days ago. Looks like they're close to pinpointing the site, though. They figure it's someplace right near here, maybe Johns Bog Brook."

"That close?" Mike stared at the official document, frowning. "Well, I shouldn't be surprised. They've been moving steadily west across the state. The lab said it's mostly suspended sediment from paper mills, and Berlin isn't that far."

Both men glanced at the large state map on the wall, the row of colored pins cutting a steady line across the top third of the roughly triangular shape of New Hampshire. "Look here, the first reports were from around Berlin—Jericho and Mill Brook—then Garland Brook. They keep moving west, toward the Connecticut." Mike's frown was worried. "Let me see that report." He took it from Ed's hand. "Sure, the last time was the Caroll Stream, and now this; it's too damn close for comfort. I swear I'm gonna get this son of a bitch if it's the last thing I do! He's been smart so far and lucky . . . always where we aren't. But . . ."

Mike studied the report, then rose and walked to the detail map on the wall. "He seems to know just where he can get in close to the river, where he won't be seen. Now, if he follows the same pattern, he'll . . ." Mike moved his finger up the blue line on the map, a feeder of the Connecticut River system running the length of the New Hampshire/Vermont border. He put a colored pin just southeast of the town where the latest report indicated the most recent chemical dumping.

Ed peered over Mike's shoulder and watched his finger move a little farther upstream from the last pin. It stopped, moved on, then came back and deliberately tapped the isolated inlet shown there on Johns Bog Brook.

"If I'm right . . ." Mike spun around so fast Ed had to jump to get out of his way. "C'mon, Ed, let's go. I want to find this last spot and see if he left us something we can use." He grabbed his jacket and headed for the door, a red-faced Ed Pritchard hurrying in his wake.

Anne followed the hostess to the small table set for two. The Friday night crowd was just beginning to thicken so they hadn't had to wait for their reservation, which was just as Elliot had planned it. She sighed. He was tied closer to set routine than anyone she'd left behind in Bloomfield Hills. Well, rigidity was a state of individual mind, not geography.

She slid into the chair Elliot held for her now and smiled as he seated himself opposite. The table sat before a large window that opened on an expanse of lawn sloping toward a glass-smooth pond, just beginning to stiffen under the icy New England winter. The candles in the comfortably cozy room reflected cheerfully off the dark glass, giving the scene a festive air of welcome.

"I do like this place. It's so warm and friendly." The Spalding Inn managed to blend country warmth with city elegance, and maintain an ambiance of genuine comfort and sophistication all at the same time. "And I'm starving."

Elliot flipped open the heavy embossed menu with an efficient gesture. "Yes, I've noticed you have a healthy appetite." He looked at her with an indulgent smile, then applied himself to the selection of their dinner.

Anne bit her lip, chagrined. Funny, the words were the same. From Elliot they were patronizing, even slightly disapproving. But on Mike Novak's lips they'd been playful and teasing. And she knew, cheeks suddenly burning, while she resented the one she'd secretly enjoyed the other. She had a prescient feeling this would be the last time she and Elliot faced each other across a dining table.

She buried her head in the menu, ashamed of her thoughts. Which was ridiculous. Elliot was observant and astute, but he wasn't clair-voyant. To her relief the waiter appeared to take their order, but as he moved away Anne looked up and gasped quietly. Perhaps *she* was the clairvoyant.

With the image of him still fresh in her mind, Anne blinked; for a moment she thought she'd conjured him from her thoughts. Mike, the real Mike, had materialized at the entrance to the restaurant. It was a true testament to her self-control that Anne stifled her surprise . . . and pleasure.

She'd seen him in uniform, and even in his impressive semi-bare skin. He was no less im-pressive now, thick silver-speckled dark hair tamed for the occasion, the well-tailored suit draped beautifully over his body. His shoul-ders and chest, while a little too thick and solid for a male model, still would not have looked totally out of place on the cover of *G.Q.* How about *Playgirl,* she thought self-de-risively. Even across the large room his air of authority, restrained though it might be, was unmistakable, his presence riveting. Or was it only to her? For a heartbeat, the distance be-tween them disappeared and she felt a wave of heat rush through her veins. The menu trembled in her hand, a shiver skittering across her spine.

Then she noticed his companion. There was no doubt at all that *she* was real, Anne wryly acknowledged. Anne watched, not realizing a frown had appeared between her alert dark eyes.

The woman's dress fit her beautiful body as if it were made of spray paint—bright yellow spray paint! With the color of her hair and the dress, she looked as if a golden spotlight were shining on her. The better to see your cleavage, my dear!

Oh, Annie, Annie, do you hear yourself? Shouldn't she be too old for this sort of thing? She closed her eyes, resting her forehead on her hand. Maybe there were no more tables available. Maybe a sudden police emergency would hasten their departure. Maybe the blonde's teeth would fall out. Anne wearily opened her eyes but the blonde's faultless smile was still in place.

Mike met her eyes across the spacious room, a lifted eyebrow suggesting surprise at Anne's and Elliot's presence. He nodded once in acknowledgment, an appraising half-smile on his lips, and with his deliberate prowl ambled toward them, blonde still in hand. They arrived just behind the waiter and his laden tray.

"Hello, Elliot, Mac. Nice to see you." *Nice*

wasn't quite the word for it, Mike thought, even as the words came from his mouth.

"Evening, Mike." Elliot eyed the two newcomers with surprise and just the slightest hint of annoyance. "Never seen you here before."

"Oh, I get over here now and then," Mike shrugged. They wouldn't even have been there now if Helena hadn't casually mentioned Anne's phone call from Elliot that afternoon. So Mike wasn't quite the believer in coincidence he professed to be. But that was privileged information he'd have admitted to no one.

"Why don't you introduce us," Anne suggested sweetly.

The warm expression in Mike's eyes belied his cool smile. "Honey, this is Anne McClellan . . . or would you prefer Mac?" he asked easily. "And of course Elliot you know. Mac this is Honey."

Oh, I'll just bet you are, Anne thought.

"How do you do?" Honey's voice was surprisingly soft and modulated, the accent faintly suggestive of Boston. Her handshake was firm, her smile warm and ingratiating.

"So nice to meet you," Anne said insincerely as Elliot half rose and gave a perfunctory nod.

Honey smiled pleasantly at the couple, and

then her mouth curved into an engaging smile and she winked. "I like your dress."

Anne looked again and realized, startled, they were wearing the same dress. She knew when she got home she would burn *hers*. Her nice chic, understated basic black elegance faded into ignominious obscurity beside Honey's mellow yellow. *Her* V-neck seemed to point nowhere, while Honey's led the way to vast and voluptuous treasures. Anne felt, with a sinking feeling, she *looked* like a "Mac." And Honey definitely looked like . . . honey.

There had been times, over the years, when Anne had been less than satisfied with what she'd considered her overabundant curves. But right now she felt like an overstuffed mattress. The fit of that dress on Honey gave new meaning to the term "surface tension." All in all, with her superstructure so precariously cantilevered, Honey was an engineering marvel.

Anne didn't examine the cause of her unreasonable reaction. The young woman was surprisingly friendly and composed in the face of the less than congenial atmosphere at the table, and there was truly no reason on earth for Anne's irrational reaction. She knew she'd regret it later. But this was now and Anne only wished he—*they*—would go away.

She bit her lip and her eyes held a distant expression as she nodded goodbye.

Mike's expression was amused for a moment, and then it assumed a dark intensity that would surely have melted Anne's reserve if she hadn't made herself turn away from him and reach for her spoon. The couple said their goodbyes and followed the maitre d' to their own table.

Anne forced herself to swallow her cream of broccoli soup and pay attention to Elliot. All of a sudden his company was becoming unendurable, and his continuing conversation showed he was as insulated from her distress as he was from Honey's glorious charms. It seemed to be Mike who held his interest.

"I don't understand him," Elliot mused, looking after the retreating pair. "There was certainly no lack of suitable women who would have made an excellent mother for his daughter. I understand his wife came from a very fine family, good background. A lot of money."

Elliot seemed to feel those two things were automatic companions, Anne mused. While that was evidently where his interests lay, she'd have loved to learn more of the unknown ex-Mrs. Novak. But not from Elliot. She couldn't bring herself to scrabble around for bits and pieces of gossip to allay her curiosity. It was a perverse sense of loyalty to Mike, though why it had blossomed so unexpectedly she didn't understand. But it stilled Anne's questions about his past.

While the waiter served the main course, Anne looked at Elliot, curious. "I don't agree that a person should marry merely to provide a 'suitable' parent for a child." She thought of Jerry; but he was a grown, almost-adult young man. Helena had been an infant. Anne leaned back, toying with her fork and the suddenly unwanted food. "Actually, Helena's a wonderful, sweet, loving child, so it seems Mike and Caroline have succeeded beautifully on their own, without having to bring in a substitute from the bench."

He had the grace to look uncomfortable. "Still, Anne, one ought never to lose sight of one's options. In terms of practicality, it would have been the expedient move. After all, Helena was only an infant when he came back here, and Caroline was rather advanced in years even then."

Elliot knew more about them than he'd cared to admit. "Back? From where?" The question rushed out before she could stop herself. "I somehow thought he'd lived his whole life here." Anne kept her voice casual . . . with some effort.

"Oh, no, he was gone for a few years after he graduated from Yale Law School." Anne stared, startled. "Lived in New York, I think." Elliot shrugged, disinterested now. "I'm not really sure. I told you, we're not close." His expression showed quite clearly he preferred it that way.

"How is that? It's such a small town and you're almost the same age."

"Anne dear, he went to White Mountains Regional High School. I went to Exeter."

And as far as he was concerned, Anne realized, that said it all. Up here, Gilcrests, like Cabots, obviously spoke to God—certainly not to Novaks. Not if they could avoid it. And then only rarely.

"Yes, I see." Had that slightly smug expression, that condescension in his voice, always been there? Why hadn't it ever bothered her before? Why did it bother her so much now? She was increasingly disturbed, all at once, at being included in Elliot's "thee and me" air of superiority. In that moment Anne knew she'd never again be able to tolerate Elliot's attitudes with such unquestioning equanimity. Elliot was a bore, and an arrogant, snobbish bore at that. The combination was suddenly intolerable.

Restless and uncomfortable, Anne tried— and failed—to ignore the couple across the room. But each time she allowed her eyes to stray, she found that dark gaze pinned on her.

Anne had forgotten that another pair of eyes might also be interested. Elliot's speculative look rested on her for a few seconds as comprehension dawned and he recognized where her attention lay. His expression froze for less than an instant and then he spoke, quietly and smoothly, with no outward sign that he was even aware of Mike Novak's presence in the room. "So, what have you been doing with yourself lately?" She jumped at the sound of Elliot's voice. "With the auditors coming in, I haven't had much free time." He reached across the table to take her hand, his eyes cool, assessing. "Did you miss me?"

Quickly, she disengaged her hand and picked up a fork. "Well, I haven't had much time, either." Actually, she hadn't missed him at all. For a moment she smiled, recalling Mike's daily appearance at her shop, the jokes, the small talk, the growing friendship that had developed so spontaneously and unexpectedly between them. "I've been awfully busy in the shop. By the end of the day, I'm exhausted."

"Now, now, Anne, you shouldn't work so hard. I warned you that work is too much for you." He leaned back, folding his hands on the table. "Not to mention how it looks."

"Elliot, I don't give a damn about how it looks; there's nothing demeaning about honest work. For heaven's sake, we've been over this ground before. Drop it, please." And if he said *now, now* one more time, she'd . . . she'd mess his hair!

"Certainly," he muttered stiffly. "It's just that you need to relax and get out more."

"As a matter of fact, I had a wonderful day out last Sunday. Helena took me on a nice long hike, out along Johns Bog Brook—isn't that a wonderful name?—just past the most beautiful little sandy cove. You know, I never associated New Hampshire with secluded beaches."

He looked up, startled, eyebrows raised in consternation. "I didn't realize you liked mountain climbing."

"Helena assured me," Anne answered with a chuckle, "they weren't 'real' mountains." Her animated smile was enthusiastic. "It's such beautiful country, rugged and yet so very lovely at the same time. Not really intimidating, just . . . peaceful, almost hypnotic. We ate lunch on a ledge outside a cave above the water, and we could see for miles."

"I wish you wouldn't go up there." His white face and worried frown surprised her.

"Why, Elliot, how sweet of you to be so concerned, but it really wasn't dangerous."

"But it sounds very isolated. Does Helena go there often?"

"Oh, don't worry, she knows every inch blindfolded. It's her favorite place. You know, teenage girls are just like anyone else. Sometimes they need a place to be alone in." He looked unconvinced.

"Honestly, Elliot, there's nothing to worry about." Still, his concern was rather endearing though, as usual, overly protective. She reached over to pat his hand in reassurance. His skin was cold and clammy. Anne's eyes widened. "Elliot, is something wrong? Are you ill?" His pallor, the beads of perspiration, were themselves the answer to her question.

"I . . . I'm sorry, Anne, but I think we'd better go. I should know better than to eat crabmeat. It doesn't agree with me."

"Of course we'll go! Drop me off and go straight home, and get right into bed." He really did look awful. It wasn't very nice of her to feel grateful for his sudden illness, but she was relieved the evening was ending so early. They made a hurried exit from the restaurant, Anne deliberately avoiding any glance at the only table she was interested in.

Mike noted their hasty passage, Anne's departure leaving a sudden void he couldn't explain. He took a long, deep swallow, almost draining the glass of its scotch and water. He wouldn't examine the reasons; he only knew the amusement was gone from the game.

And suddenly he couldn't go on with it. "Honey? I just remembered something I have to finish down at the office. Would you mind if I took you straight home after dinner?"

"Don't be silly, Mike, we've been friends far too long for that. Just give me a rain check."

"Well, I did promise to take you dancing. . . ."

"Believe me, dinner at the Spalding Inn makes up for a lot! My alternative was Taco Bell; does that tell you anything?"

He squeezed the hand she offered, but while she quickly finished her meal, he cast another look at the table the other couple had deserted, the muscles along his jaw tensing perceptibly. Swallowing the last sip of her wine, Honey watched him.

"Is she new in town? How come I haven't seen her before?"

"What? Who?"

The blond head tilted to one side, a knowledgeable smile on her shiny red mouth. "Don't recite pronouns to me; *I'm* the English teacher here, remember?" She winked and leaned back in her chair. "You know very well who. Come on, Mike, give! I've never seen that look on your face before."

"Oh, she's Helena's boss. Runs the new pastry shop down on King's Square. Helena likes her."

"*Helena* likes her." He didn't say anything else and Honey's smile grew wider. "Ah so. Well, it's about time." He stared at her quizzically. "You know, Mike, I've enjoyed all the good times we've had and I want you to know I'll always think of you with a great deal of affection."

"What are you talking about? Are you going someplace?"

"No. But I think you are." She looked pointedly at the other table. "We've had fun and I treasure our friendship, but I think you're right: We'd better make it an early evening. Your heart's not in it." Her blue eyes sparkled with good humor. "You might as well forget the rain check, too."

He just stared at her. She was, always had been, level with him. They went back a long way and they'd had some damned good times together; that was all either of them had ever wanted or expected. But now he was angry with himself, because all at once it was no longer good enough. A week ago they would have enjoyed each other on those very simple, very basic, very limited terms, and they could both have counted the evening a success.

But somewhere he had crossed a line, a narrow and all-but-invisible boundary, and even Honey was aware of it. He couldn't go back, but neither was he quite ready to chance the path if he went forward. Mike didn't like being unsure. And so he was angry. At Honey, because for him what she was was all she was. At himself, because what *he* was was suddenly not merely alone but lonely. He'd never been lonely in his life, and the bleakness of the feeling depressed him now.

He dropped some bills on top of the check and followed Honey from the restaurant.

On his third pass around the square, Mike pulled the car into the curb and turned off the motor. The cool, silent dark was a welcome contrast to the currents swirling in his brain. Damn! He clenched his fists around the steering wheel in a fresh spurt of anger. He didn't like this new, unknown Mike Novak—indecisive, out of control. He could have been sharing some nice cool jazz with a nice warm blonde!

But here he sat, like a moonstruck cow-eyed teenager dreaming about the girl next door. No, not true. That was no girl up there. Anne McClellan was all woman.

Some evening it had turned out to be, he mused, taking one of his small cigars from his pocket. Mike stared up at the bright squares of light above the bakery windows, the flickering match briefly illuminating his thoughtful eyes as he inhaled deeply. He'd been so sure he would prove to himself—and her—how unchanged his life still was, how free and uninvolved. He'd deliberately flaunted Honey, proving to Anne his undomesticated status. As if she cared! All he'd accomplished was concrete proof that something *had* changed . . . radically. Otherwise why would he have shied away from spending the rest of the evening with Honey? But seeing Anne with that supercilious asshole Elliot Gilcrest . . .

Mike sat up, his head swiveling to look around him.

Gilcrest's car was nowhere in sight. He exhaled a long breath of relief, then leaned back once more. He had some thinking to do and he might as well do it here. He looked again at her bright windows, then up at the moon, partially obscured by the swirling smoke. Mike frowned. It wasn't smoke; grey cloud masses were scudding across the dark sky. A storm was coming, and fast.

Wonder if their sleazy friend would try a dump with the weather acting up? The roads down to the creek bed could be treacherous even under the best conditions. Probably safe for tonight.

Far off a deep rumble of thunder reverberated down the valley. It was followed by another, even louder, and then a strange heavy silence. On the horizon thin slivers of lightning skittered across the black sky, like stick figures caught in a crazed electrical dance on the distant mountaintops.

In that instant the heavens split open like a fragile eggshell, the silence shattered by one deafening crack of explosive thunder. A blinding white incandescence poured through the jagged tear, the brightness blazing for one brief moment, then receding, leaving the crash of the bolt ringing in his ears.

Mike got out of his car, his skin tingling strangely, and stood looking in every direction to see if anything had been hit. The darkness told him nothing. And then he realized the darkness told him everything. Because it was absolute; a power line was down somewhere. He reached into the car for the radio mike.

"Vince, Mike here. What's going on? Is the power out all over town? Over."

"Yeah, Chief, the transformer down at the junction was hit. Whole town's dark. We've got the auxiliary generator on here."

"How about the hospital and the fire station?"

"No, they've got their generators going, too. I can see from here."

"Okay, get some extra uniforms on the streets. I want coverage, just in case. I'll be there soon."

"Will do. Don't rush, everything's under control. Oh, say hi to Honey for me, Chief. See ya. Out."

Man, oh man, news sure travels fast around here. Mike smiled to himself for a moment at the town grapevine's efficient news delivery. Tsk, tsk, didn't they know that Honey was home already?

He looked back once more at the now-darkened windows of Anne's apartment. An eerie silence blanketed the street and the faint acrid smell of sulphur hung in the air; the blackness was total. Hmm, strange. No flashlight, not even the flicker of a candle. He hesitated, then impatiently ground the cigar under his foot, pulled his own light from its clip on the dash, and quickly crossed the street. He ran up the old wooden stairs at the side of the building.

There was no answer to his repeated knocking. He bit his lip, worried, then tried to peer through the window. Nothing.

"Anne? Anne, it's Mike. Open up. *Anne!* What's wrong?"

Still no answer, not a sound. He knocked again, louder this time. "Damn!" What if she'd gone to Gilcrest's? He didn't want to think about it.

Minutes passed, the silence broken only by the noise of his continued pounding on the door. And then he heard a crash, the sound of glass breaking . . . and again, silence. Alarmed, he stood back, raised his foot, and kicked at the door. It flew back against the inner wall with a crash and he stepped through into the dark interior.

"Anne! Anne, where are you? I know you're—*Son of a—!*" Mike banged his leg against an unseen kitchen cupboard. He stopped, rubbing his knee for a moment, and in that instant he heard it, strange muffled panting, a hoarse stertorous gasp so low he almost missed it. He switched on the flashlight. Now if that didn't show how screwed up he was. . . . He'd forgotten he had it! He shook his head and walked into the large living room area.

At first he saw nothing unusual; the furniture all seemed to be in place and undisturbed. But somewhere he heard that trapped-animal breathing, and then a small sob. He swung the beam of light in the direction of the sound and it caught her, squeezed into the corner, hands stretched out and flattened against the walls on either side, the shattered lamp on the floor beside her. She didn't move and she didn't speak. She couldn't see him because her eyes were shut tight, her mouth open in a silent scream. Mike could almost smell the stark terror in that room, could see it in the way she held her body motionless. He moved quickly to her.

"Anne? Anne, it's me, Mike. Please, open your eyes. Talk to me! Annie, my God, *what is it?*"

Eight

In the beam of light Anne's face was dead white, hair clinging damply to her forehead and the back of her neck. Mike stooped to set the flashlight at their feet and touched one of her hands, warming her cold, stiff fingers in his. He put his other hand on Anne's head, stroking her hair gently to ease the grip of her terror.

"Shh, shh, it's okay. Everything's okay, I'm here. It's all right, Annie, take it easy." She moaned, a low-pitched formless note of despair, and he felt her taut fingers loosen before she slowly sagged away from the wall into his arms. Mike held her, her limp body trembling violently with the sudden release of tension. He pulled her close, cradling her in the strength of his embrace, grateful he was there to give comfort. He felt the cold sweat on her body, still shaken by diminishing shudders.

"Anne, listen to me. Anne! Where are the candles?" He spoke slowly, carefully. "The power's out all over town and I don't know how long it'll be off. Have you any candles?" He led her to the couch, murmuring quietly as if to a frightened child, all the time stroking her hair, her hands. "Atta girl, just sit here. Everything's going to be all right."

He moved to pick up the flashlight left on the floor but she held on to him, clutching his hand in wordless protest, eyes still squeezed tightly shut.

Mike was worried. He was not a man easily cowed by fear, but her reaction frightened him. She was almost catatonic with terror. It wasn't until she blinked a couple of times and finally looked at him, really seeing him, that he felt the release of his own fear.

"M—Mike? What are you . . . ? Wh—what happened?" Anne took a shaky breath and touched her damp forehead with a still-trembling hand. "That . . . that explosion, the lights went off so suddenly. I was . . ." She stopped, her thoughts a long way off for a moment. His quiet voice brought her back.

"It wasn't an explosion, Anne. It was lightning. Took out the main transformer. I . . . I was passing by when it happened, so I stopped in to make sure you were all right." What if he hadn't been here? What would have happened to her, alone in the dark?

The dark.

He remembered clearly the night of her Sunday outing with Helena. He'd left Anne at her door and, when he returned home, made his daughter tell him in detail about the afternoon hike.

"It was only when Mac and I got to the cave," Helena had explained. "It's just a little hollow in the hillside, really, right above that sharp curve in the creek. Anyway, I wanted to show it to her and suddenly her face got all white and, you know, kind of . . . funny, and she just stopped in the opening and wouldn't move. Then, finally, she blinked and backed out and sort of, you know, laughed and said it was too beautiful a day to be cooped up in such a dark, gloomy place. So we sat down under a tree outside and ate our lunch. And after that everything was fine."

Mike could still remember Helena's puzzled expression when she told him. He'd shared it. But he was beginning to understand now. "Annie, how about some coffee? Oops, forgot. No electricity."

"There's to—m—mato j—juice in the fridge." She could almost smile at the grimace on his face. "I see this beggar's a chooser." Her voice was tremulous but at least she was attempting a joke.

Mike's laugh was perhaps a shade too hearty, showing his relief at her recovery. "Okay, just a minute, I'll bring it to you." He rose, taking the flashlight with him, and her composure crumpled. She jumped up, clutching his arm.

"No."

"God, Annie, I'm sorry! I didn't realize . . ."

Mike put his arm around her, to calm her, to comfort her. But, strangely, it was he who was comforted, by the way she felt in his arms, by the scent of her perfume, by the sweet softness of her body under the thin fabric of the dress, by the way she filled an emptiness he'd only recently discovered.

There was an excitement in the touch of her hair against his cheek, his hand sliding down the soft curve of her back. She clung to him, so close her body and his were an extension of each other. He felt tight, taut, the blood arrowing through his veins in a hot flood of arousal. The hand at her waist bit into the fabric and the soft flesh beneath, pulling her even closer, close enough so nothing could hide his reaction to her.

Even as Anne tensed to instinctively pull away, Mike bent toward her upturned face. Tilting her head, he touched his lips to her cheek, her eyelids and, before he could stop himself, her mouth. The sweet warmth of her lips tasted of promise and desire, and he pressed her even closer to his body, the hot flare of excitement touching every part of him.

Yet it was a strangely gentle kiss, even tender, and Mike was surprised at the rush of new emotions inundating him. He wasn't sure he could have broken away from her just then.

For one moment Anne clung to him as if he were the only steady thing in a crazily tilting universe. All the known landmarks suddenly disappeared and all that was left was the two of them. The touch of Mike's mouth, his hands, his body pressing so intimately against the length of hers, caused a fiery heat to surge through her veins and she felt as if the sun were burning in her breast. Here was life, and warmth, and excitement; everything the world should be, could be, and hadn't been for so very long—until this moment.

Anne pulled back, violently twisting from his arms, her quick, heavy breath loud in the silence. Her response had shocked her, frightening her almost as much as the terrifying moments in the sudden blackness of the night.

It had shocked Mike, too. But not quite as

much as his own body's response to her. What had happened to him? Confusion about himself was one thing on which Mike Novak never wasted time. And yet this woman had confused and disoriented him from the moment he'd set eyes on her. He shook his head; he had to get hold of himself.

Mike looked down at Anne's upturned face, the naked expression of shame, the unnatural glitter of her dark eyes, quickly hidden behind lowered lashes. Behind her their shadows, entwined, slanted across the dark wall in the beam of the forgotten flashlight on the floor. But for that solitary slash of light, they were suspended in a black spatial void, separated from the reality of the world by the unreality of this moment.

Mike stepped back abruptly. This moment *was* unreal. He'd better remember that. Anne was not herself, unnerved as she was by the sudden blackout, assaulted by her hidden terrors. Never would she be as vulnerable as she was now, and he felt an awful shame at how close he'd come to taking advantage of her. It would be all too easy to mistake the heightened emotion of the moment for genuine feeling. A very bad mistake, one neither of them would be able to forget or forgive. Not ever. Mike swallowed the sudden tightness in his throat and bent to pick up the flashlight.

Anne stood very still, willing her self-control to return, not knowing how to face him, what to say. The evening's events had been harrowing, to say the least, but her unforgivable reaction to him was disgraceful. She'd embarrassed him, humiliated herself. Mike had offered sympathy, compassion. Nothing more. Her cheeks burned. It couldn't be anything more. She didn't want anything more.

It was a few seconds before Mike trusted himself to speak. "Come on, we'll go forage together. I'll pour the juice, you get the candles." He knew, without question, she'd have candles. She wouldn't chance darkness without that security.

Soon the room was filled with the glow of the many candles Anne set out. The golden light chased darkness into the corners and they sat together on the couch, drinking the still-cold juice. Mike was glad to have something so innocuous to fill his hands, otherwise . . .

"Let's see if the phones are okay. I ought to check in with the station, anyway."

"Oh, of course! I'm sorry, Mike, you have more important things to take care of. G . . . go ahead. I'll be fine, just fine!"

A smile trembled on her lips as she re-assured herself of that. She was still coming to grips with this latest manifestation of the "new Anne McClellan," this stranger who had very nearly kicked over the traces in the arms of a man she hardly knew. She didn't recognize herself anymore and it worried her. Yes, she'd been caught in the old terror, surprised by its fierce strength, even now. But could that explain it? Was that excuse enough? Hardly, she admitted silently, reluctantly.

She'd thought she could handle her fears, thought she was prepared for anything. Anything but Mike Novak. And her own wildfire emotions. She could hardly face him. She repeated her words, needing a reassurance she didn't really feel. "Honestly, I'll be just fine. Go on, Mike."

He didn't believe her for one second. "Oh, they can struggle along for a while without me, I'm afraid." Mike smiled with false calm as he dialed headquarters. "Vince? How's it going? Good. Who's on the street? Tom and Ed—oh, he came back in?—okay. How long 'til the transformer's repaired? Well, that's a break! And no reports of any trouble? All right, I'll be down soon. Yeah, I know you're doing fine without me." He winked at Anne, huddled tightly into the sofa. "That's what I'm afraid of." He spoke a few more instructions quietly into the phone and hung up.

"If they ever realize how well they can manage without me, I'll be out of a job."

"Huh?" She looked at him, then quickly away. "Oh, I seriously doubt that. Paul—Paul used to say that's the mark of a very good executive, when his staff can handle a crisis without him. It shows how valuable he really is."

"Paul?" He sat down next to Anne, careful to keep a few inches between them. He didn't want to remember how perfect she felt in his arms.

"Paul is—was—my hu . . . husband." She had that strange tight look around her mouth again. The hand holding her glass jerked violently.

"Anne?" he asked quietly. "What is it? Why don't you tell me about it?"

"Tell you? Tell you what? There's *nothing,* really—nothing!"

He waited, then took her glass from her, placing it along with his own on the table, and reached for her cold hand. Fingers entwined, they sat in peaceful silence a few seconds, until her breathing slowed and she sat back quietly.

"Look, I don't want to pry—"

"Then don't!"

"Anne, I know what hysteria is, and you were about as close as you could come without actually going over the edge. Now, that's not 'nothing.'" He put one finger under her chin and turned her face toward his. "I've seen you in a crisis situation, remember? You're one cool lady, and if a B and E by the Cookie Monster didn't bother you, I figure it would take a lot more than a simple lights-out to upset you this much. It must be a pretty heavy load to tote by yourself. Wouldn't you feel better getting it off your chest? Sometimes that's all it takes to get rid of something that's eating away at you." He pressed her hand. "You know, Anne, everyone's afraid of something."

She closed her eyes, and a single tear slipped from beneath the dark lashes. Something inside Mike twisted and he hurt for her pain, feeling its stab deep within himself.

Anne sighed, a shaky breath torn from the depths of her soul. "I thought if I ignored it, didn't think about it, it would just . . . just go away. In fact, I thought it had. It's been so long and I tried . . . I tried so damned hard." Exhaustion lay in every word.

Mike slid his arm around her shoulder and held her tight. "Why don't you try talking? It might help."

"I don't know . . . I thought I'd licked it, but now I wonder if it's ever going to be any different."

"Anne, stop that." He waited a moment, inhaling softly. "Was it the darkness?" She was very still, her skin chalky white in the flickering light. "Have you always been afraid of it?"

"No, of course not. Just since Paul—" Her voice stopped, and they heard the sound of a cold wind soughing through the trees around the square.

"So . . . why don't you tell me about Paul, Anne." Mike's voice was gentle, his words quiet, and he clasped her hand firmly.

He had to strain to hear, her voice was so low, so hesitant. "We—we were on a trip to Mexico . . . Mexico City. It was going to be a second honeymoon." She stopped, taking a deep breath. "We were having such a wonderful time, and we had reservations in Acapulco that night. Only, we never . . ." She swallowed and clenched her chattering teeth, holding her head rigid, reclaiming her cool dignity before she continued.

"Before we could get up that morning, we were literally thrown out of bed; there was this terrible shaking and the whole hotel seemed to vibrate under us. Then, all of a sudden, the floor just . . . dropped away and we . . ." She dropped her head into her hand, shaking it back and forth.

"Okay, Annie, relax a minute now. That's right." Mike kept stroking her hand, remembering the news reports. The devastation had been unbelievable all through Mexico's densely populated capital. He waited until Anne stopped trembling.

"I suppose I lost consciousness. When I finally came to, I couldn't move. I was pinned down under what felt like a mountain of rubble. Later I found that's what it was. I remember how quiet it was—such a terrible silence, like the end of the world. As if no one else was left anywhere. And dark, so black . . ." She shuddered again and slumped back into the sofa cushions, head back, eyes closed. Her face was ashen in the soft light.

Anne was quiet for so long Mike wondered if she were going to finish. Then suddenly she spoke again.

"After a while I heard something, someone moaning, and I—I realized it was Paul, next to me. God, we were still holding hands! I figured it was a miracle we were both alive and I was so grateful! He tried to talk but he couldn't. I held his hand—that's all I could do. I couldn't see or move. And then . . ."

she stopped. "Then he squeezed my hand, and he—he just . . . he—he died."

Anne slumped, as if the last shred of willpower had dissolved with her final words, and Mike cradled her to him, holding her, unable to offer anything but that small comfort. In a flat, whispered monotone, she finished telling the nightmare memory.

"They told me later we were only down there a few hours, Paul and I," her voice rose, "only a few hours, *and there was nothing I could do.*" Her words poured out in a gathering flood of hysteria. "Oh, God, he was my husband, Mike, the dearest, sweetest man in the world . . . and I couldn't do anything to help him!"

Moments passed, the silence absolute but for the hissing of the candlewicks as the flames consumed them, the soft sound of melted wax plopping to the surface below. He was reluctant to break the silence, and so he merely held her close until the shaking stopped and she was quiet again, sharing her anguish. Mike knew there were no words to ease the horror she'd been through, the suffering and pain, the devastating loss.

It was Anne who moved first. In the stillness, Mike's heart thudded loudly in her ear and she remembered where she was. She pushed herself away from his arms and sat up stiffly, awkwardly smoothing her hair, her skirt.

"Sorry, I really lost it there, didn't I? I didn't mean to let go . . ." She stopped, shaking her head self-consciously. "Well, you have to admit, you asked for it." She made a not-quite-successful attempt to smile, stubborn pride reenforcing her battered willpower.

Mike straightened, running his fingers through his hair, conscious of how much her story had affected him. He took a deep breath. "I'm glad you told me."

Though still pale, Anne's cheeks had lost their stark pasty look. Her breathing, too, was close to normal now. "Look, I'm sorry I put you through all this, but I'm sure I'll be fine now. The blackout just took me by surprise. You don't have to baby-sit me anymore." She stared down at her hands, willing them to be still. "I'm very grateful you happened by, Mike. I owe you more than I can say." She took a deep breath, squaring her shoulders.

Suddenly, her thoughts veered back to the present with a healthy instinct and she looked straight at him, eager for any other focus beside her fear and memories. "By the way, what are you doing around here, anyway? I thought you'd be settled in for an evening with . . . uh . . . what's her name? Honey?''

Mike chuckled quietly, relieved. He could deal with this kind of reaction. "Actually, it's Harriet, but not many people use it."

"No, she's a lot more Honey than Harriet," Anne mumbled.

"Oh, there's more to Honey than meets the eye."

My Lord, how *could* there be? Anne wondered waspishly, then felt ashamed of her mean thoughts. She didn't know anything about the woman save what she looked like. Anne felt uncomfortably akin to Elliot Gilcrest at that moment.

"Is she from Whitefield? I don't believe I've seen her around." Anne wondered at the perversity that made her prolong this conversation. "I gather you're old friends." She stood, collecting the empty glasses, and turned toward the kitchen, feigning a casual disinterest that didn't fool Mike for a moment.

He followed close on her heels, admiring the way she moved inside the knit dress, taunting himself with visions that had no business taking up space in his imagination. She was small and vulnerable and appealing, and he couldn't take his eyes off her, remembering all too clearly how she had felt in his arms. At some point she'd taken off her shoes and her silver-specked hair was mussed, disarranged from the more careful style she'd worn at dinner, inviting his fingers to comb through the soft waves. He preferred it this way. He jammed his fists deep into his pockets before instinct became action.

"Oh, yeah, I've known Honey quite a while, I guess. We're . . . good friends." His smile was devilish in the flickering candlelight.

"Obviously." Anne could see the knowledge of her feelings in his eyes, embarrassed that she was so appallingly transparent. She lashed out sarcastically.

"What happened? It looked like nothing short of paint remover would scrape her off you."

She turned away abruptly, furious at herself for allowing the words to escape. She sounded so bitchy. Trouble was, she *felt* bitchy!

Anne turned on the water to rinse the glasses. "Sorry, none of my business. I guess I was wrong. I am nosy, aren't I?"

"Interested sounds nicer, I admit. And as you told me once, you're *not* perfect, after all—thank God!" He grinned with a lightness he hadn't felt since he'd first seen her sitting across the dinner table from Elliot.

With a rueful smile on her face, Anne

stood staring down into the water swirling around the drain. Her mind must look like that, she thought wryly, all her vaunted rationality disappearing like the water. She drew a deep breath.

"Well, Mike, I guess you've done your good deed for the night. I do appreciate it, but you'd better get over to your office. They probably need you by now." She didn't say anything about her own need. She didn't have the nerve to explore that particular avenue just now.

Mike would have been all right, might have gotten away with mouthing a few polite words, his pride and ego and heart intact, if only she hadn't looked at him at that precise moment, a bleak, lonely expression; refusing to surrender to fear, too proud to ask for help. His heart lurched and he reached for her, instinct stronger than reason.

"Anne? I'm just at the other end of that phone line, any time you want me. Remember that." He turned her to him, pulling her into the shelter of his embrace. She filled his arms, and he cradled her against his shoulder. They stood for that instant, not moving, not speaking, content to cling to each other. Mike held her carefully, his hands sheltering her back, his cheek caressing her hair. He thought he might stay there forever, holding her, coming alive the moment he touched her again.

Neither of them knew quite why or how they sensed that comfort and security weren't enough, or when that blurred into a wilder emotion. They only knew the instant when he stared down at her, seeing in her eyes what he wanted to see, and gently, carefully, kissed her forehead, her cheek, her mouth.

Anne met his kiss, returning it eagerly, searching and tasting, open to savor everything, suddenly greedy for all he could offer. She was safe here in the secure shelter of Mike's arms. For a moment she pulled back, drawing a ragged breath, looking up at him and seeing nothing but the shadowed planes of his strong face, hearing nothing but the loud drumming of her own heartbeat in her ears.

Anne hadn't planned it, hadn't known she wanted it. But suddenly she was absolutely sure this was the right place to be . . . held securely in a pair of hard, strong, gentle arms.

Mike Novak's arms.

And suddenly being held wasn't enough, being close wasn't enough. And she wasn't sure what would be enough. Hesitant, unsure, Anne reached up, pushing trembling fingers through the thick crinkly grey-flecked black hair, sliding her hands down the back of his neck. She touched the curve of his ear and his muffled groan spurred further exploration. His jaw was granite-hard, in contrast to the scratchy-soft moustache shading his mouth.

His mouth, that same mouth that had been so grim and unyielding in anger and remembered pain, now the source of such indescribable pleasure. Heedless, Anne stretched upwards on her toes, arching into his taut body.

Mike wasn't prepared for the hot rush of desire that pounded through his bloodstream, battering past all his good intentions, his noble resolve. Forgotten. All forgotten in the heat and excitement of this moment, in the delight of her mouth, her body.

Anne's arms wound around his neck and their mouths opened to each other, greedy, seeking, savoring the heat and passion that flared between them.

He tore his mouth away, groaning. "Oh God, Anne, don't. I can't . . ."

But he could. Her eyes were closed, her head thrown back, and he lowered his mouth to nuzzle her exposed throat, gently touching with his tongue, delighting in the salty-sweet taste of her. His hands slid down to her waist, then up, up, fingers splayed, thumbs caressing the softness beneath her breasts. A sharp gasp escaped Anne and Mike pressed his palms over the hard tips that beaded beneath his touch, enthralled with the response she couldn't hide, any more than he could hide his reaction to her. He was painfully aware of his arousal.

After that first stunning shock, Anne didn't draw away. She trembled and pushed closer to his caress, eager for each exquisite pleasure. She hadn't known how far she'd retreated from life, from the admission that living was more than eating and sleeping and working. Life was feeling the blood rush through her veins with this bubbling excitement; breathing air that tasted of sparkling wine; knowing the world offered a myriad of delights if you only wanted to reach out and take them. Dear God, it had been so long.

She felt a slight shudder along his spine as he pulled her closer, drawing her into the cradle of his thighs, the hard thrust of his masculinity. Her unsure hands slid down his broad back, warm and hard and solid beneath her searching fingers. There was a special excitement, knowing he was as lost as she in the discovery of the magic between them. But this wasn't a moment for thought. It was for feeling, for exploring sensations and emotions that had lain dormant, forgotten all this time since Paul . . .

Paul!

Mike knew immediately. Her mouth stilled, her body stiffened, pulled back slightly. She lowered her hands and her head, turned away, and stepped back from the edge.

"No, Mike, please. This isn't . . . this isn't what I want. I shouldn't have. Please forget this happened. I'm sorry." Anne turned abruptly and Mike's hands dropped awkwardly to his sides. He watched her walk stiffly into the other room and stand looking down at her hands, twisting and turning the ring on the third finger of her left hand. The large stone glittered coldly in the guttering candlelight. She seemed mesmerized by the sight, excluding everything else but the ring.

"It's been a long night, Mike. I think you'd better go now." Her voice broke and Anne didn't even look at him as he came toward her. She was as rigid as a pillar of New Hampshire granite, and just as unyielding.

It was painfully obvious she neither wanted to see nor hear any more from Michael Novak. And how could he blame her. But he couldn't leave with this awful silence between them.

"Anne, please believe me, I didn't mean for

hat to happen. I know it was unforgivable, but it just . . ."

She wasn't listening. Mike looked at her for a moment, a frustrated expression on his face. She had shut him out. Shaking his head, he turned and walked slowly to the door, wanting to explain, knowing it would do no good.

For a long time, he didn't count the minutes, Mike sat in his car at the curb below her windows, unable just yet to leave her behind. He lit one of his cigars and sat, impatiently drumming his fingers on the wheel.

He'd learned a lot tonight, he thought ruefully. About Anne, certainly. And about himself. Oh, yes, he'd learned about himself. He was grateful for that, at least. Well, wasn't he?

And Anne. . . . It helped to know . . . to know what? The terrors in her mind? They could be understood, perhaps even exorcised. But what about her love for her lost husband, her marriage? Knowing all that didn't help anything, did it? It only made everything worse. How the hell could he compete with a dead man?

Compete? He leaned his head against the back of the seat and blew a circle of smoke into the darkness, taunting himself. When did he cross the line from observer to competitor? And for what? For Anne?

For Anne's love?

Ah shit! At this stage of his life, who *needed* this?

A thoroughly shaken Michael Novak drove quickly away from the dark and silent street in front of the dark and silent building.

Nine

"*Monday, Monday, I'm so glad you are here . . .*" Anne hummed along with the Mamas and Papas, whose voices on the oldies radio station were a comforting sound from younger days. Actually, they weren't all that comforting; in fact, she decided abruptly, they lied like a rug.

There wasn't much *glad* in her view of this particular Monday. Gloomy Monday. Blue Monday. Yeah, much more like it. After that catastrophic Friday night, the starkly gloomy Saturday, and a depressingly introspective and lonely Sunday, how good could she expect Monday to be?

It was almost with relief that she heard the sound of the bell over the shop door. Anne sighed and turned to take care of her next customer, breaking into a spontaneous grin.

"Caroline! How nice to see you. You just stopping by, or can you stay for a cup of coffee?" Anne came from behind the counter, wiping her hands on her apron, and took

Caroline's hand in hers, a smile of welcome on her face.

"Well, this is partly business and partly pleasure," the older woman answered cheerfully. "Anne, I must say, this place is looking wonderful. I'm afraid Ilse let it begin to run down toward the end. I suppose what with her arthritis and all, she just couldn't keep up with everything that needed doing. Now you, on the other hand, have young blood."

"Oh, sure, young blood." Anne grimaced, massaging her lower spine for a moment, and leaned back against the glass display case. "Caroline, I know now Einstein was right: Everything is relative. *You* may consider this blood young, but most mornings and every evening, I could give you a good argument!" Then she smiled and shrugged wryly. "Ah, well, no one put a gun to my head. I'm the one who looked in the mirror and said 'thou shalt bake.' Guess I just like to complain"— she looked around proudly—"almost as much as I love this place."

She pulled out a chair at one of the small tables and gestured for Caroline to sit. "Listen, set a spell, and I'll get us some coffee; I need a jolt to my battery." She was back in a few seconds and sat down opposite her visitor, who had slipped off her coat and set her purse, shopping bag, and gloves beside her chair.

"So, you said business and pleasure." Anne took a long swallow from the steaming cup, settled back in her chair, and looked inquiringly at Caroline. "I hope this is the pleasure. Now, what's the business?"

"Mmmm, good coffee, Anne." Caroline swallowed slowly, savoring, then settled back in her chair. "Well, you know next week is Helena's fifteenth birthday. We—Michael and I—are giving her a little party and I was wondering if you could make the cake for her?"

"Oh, I'd love to! She mentioned the date once, and I was going to ask you if there's anything in particular she wants."

"I'm the last person to know what a fifteen-year-old girl would want," Caroline observed tartly. "I probably wouldn't approve, anyway. But you see her and her friends here all the time. If you don't have any ideas . . . well, Lord, I don't know who would." She nibbled a healthy piece of the almond coffee cake Anne had set down with the mugs, then took her pencil and checked off an item on the list she'd drawn from her sweater pocket. "If I don't write it down and check it off, I don't remember my own name. Now, Anne, how much will the cake be? And don't argue," she admonished briskly, forestalling Anne's protest. "I said this is business. I don't want something for nothing. I'm going to pay you for it."

"Don't be ridiculous, Caroline. It's not for nothing. I feel as if she's almost family"—she put her hand on the older, more wrinkled one—"and I'm so glad there's something I can do for her birthday and for you. She, and now you, have really made me feel welcome in Whitefield."

She realized for an instant that Mike's name was conspicuous by its absence, that she was making a concerted effort to separate him from the other two in her thoughts. And of course it wasn't working. And why had she thought it would? Even the glass mug in Caroline's hand reminded her vividly of that first time, the predawn interlude in her shop after the break-in, Mike sitting in the same seat, perhaps drinking from the same mug, staring at her with those incredible eyes. . . .

She forced herself to concentrate only on the present, swiping away faint beads of perspiration with the small paper napkin. The hot coffee she'd just swallowed, or maybe the heat from the ovens, or *something* was making her very warm.

"Of course, it will have to be chocolate, for

Helena. You think I should make it in the shape of a lipstick tube? That would really be appropriate," Anne chuckled.

"Ah, yes, Michael would surely appreciate that," Caroline nodded with a grimace. She was well aware of her stubborn nephew's blind spot where Helena was concerned. He'd have kept her forever a child, if he could, and he associated Helena's burgeoning maturity with Anne's influence. That it would have burgeoned without any help from anyone never crossed his mind. She sipped from her cup and watched Anne from beneath lowered eyes, and was rewarded with the flash of recognition on the younger woman's face. Yes, obviously she recalled Michael's pronouncements and ultimatums regarding his daughter. Anne's cheeks were flushed . . . and *not* from the heat of the ovens, either.

"Yes, well, you're probably right. I suppose a more traditional cake would be in order," Anne said briskly. "So, what day do you want it for?"

"Oh, Lord, my head." Caroline shook it. "Didn't I tell you? Michael and I are calling all her friends to come for a sleep-over next Friday night. Only Helena doesn't know. It . . . it's a surprise party. Isn't that grand?" Caroline's smile was wide now, her eyes gleaming with enthusiasm. "Oh, I'm so excited. I haven't been to a surprise party in years! When you pass seventy," she observed dryly, "people are understandably reluctant to subject you to strenuous surprises!"

"What a terrific idea! She'll *love* it," Anne exclaimed, leaning over the table toward Caroline. "What can I do to help? Do you have to decorate the house? And how will you keep her in the dark? That kid's the nosiest thing on two feet. Always has to know everything that's going on."

"Yes. Imagine living in the same house with her!" Caroline shook her head and laughed. "Michael's going to take us to a fancy restaurant for dinner over in Lincoln, or maybe the Kimball Hill Inn. We figure it will take some time to go back and forth, and while we're gone her friends can get the house ready."

"I volunteer, too," Anne said eagerly. "I'd love to help."

Caroline chuckled. "All offers gratefully accepted. How are you at blowing up balloons? By the time we get home everything will be ready, and then they'll have their ice cream and your cake." Caroline beamed, happy with the logistics she'd arranged with such painstaking labor . . . truly a labor of love.

"Well, my lungs can't compare with a fifteen-year-old's, but as I said, you can have anything else," Anne grinned. "It sounds great, Caroline. They'll have a ball! By the way, a little hint from the voice of experience: I always found with my son Jerry and his friends, no matter how much they'd packed away at dinner, they were always ready for more later in the evening. And from what I've seen, teenage girls aren't that different from boys, not in the food department. A few pizzas might go over big with them. Do you think you need to plan anything else for the rest of the evening?"

"Well, Michael thought they might like to rent a video." Caroline smiled and shook her head. "My heavens, when I reached my fifteenth birthday we didn't have money for movies, and we were thrilled to the ground just to have a scratchy little radio!" She sighed, "You know, Anne, I look around and find myself in the middle of a whole new world."

She shook her head in renewed wonder, and Anne found herself agreeing more wholeheartedly than Caroline's observation warranted. She knew what that was like, all right—waking up and finding yourself in a strange place in your life, and it *was* just like a new world. It had happened to her after Paul . . . well, after he died.

There, she could say it—*died*—and time kept right on passing, she kept right on breathing. Life went on and nothing was forever. Things changed and it was a new world, maybe not better or worse . . . just different. And in its way the sense of change in her life struck her as sharply after two years as it did Caroline after seventy-two. She patted one of the gnarled hands in understanding. "Ah, Caroline, everything changes, and if we didn't keep moving, we'd get swept under by the flood. That's what I admire about you: You're rooted in what *was* but you're always facing ahead to what's *coming*."

"Ah, me." Strangely flustered, her cheeks unaccustomedly flushed, Caroline wasn't comfortable with such blatant compliments. She took a deep breath and drained the last of her coffee before rising briskly to her feet. "I sometimes wonder why what's coming always requires so much more energy than what was."

"When you find *that* answer, parents everywhere will award you the Nobel Prize . . . and a year's supply of vitamins!"

The door closed behind Caroline to the

sound of their laughter and Anne headed for the kitchen with a broad smile on her face. Monday was looking better already. It had been so nice to chat with Caroline, especially in view of the tension-filled minutes she'd had this morning waiting to see if Mike would come for his usual Monday order of doughnuts.

He hadn't and she'd been relieved. *Sure. And how do you spell relief? D–I–S–A–P–P–O–I–N–T–E–D, that's how. No one else is reading your mind, dummy, so you can at least admit it to yourself. You were hoping he'd come in and things would miraculously be as they were before*—before that fearful lightning bolt had sent her over the edge, into Mike's arms. She'd spent all of Sunday psyching herself up to the point where now she wanted to face him, finally, get it over with, put it behind them. Get back to normal.

And, as she'd been asking herself for what seemed forever, just what was "normal"?

"Hey, Annie, you in there?"

"Louise, is that you? Just a minute." Anne spun around, retracing her steps to the counter. Louise Rowen, her neighbor from the card and gift shop three doors down, was studying the contents of the display case as if her life depended on her final decision.

"Sorry, Lou, didn't hear the bell. Daydreaming, I guess. Anyway, I think I'll pass on our coffee break. Caroline Novak was just here, so I've already had my caffeine ration for the day. God knows what unspeakable things'll happen if I have any more."

"Well, honey, I'll have a cup anyway, and you can come watch me inhale a few hundred calories. Although making me do that all alone is not what I'd call an act of friendship."

Anne chuckled at the often-repeated complaint from the woman who, from the day the doors opened on Sweet Expectations, had made sure Anne knew she was sincerely welcomed in the neighborhood. Not everyone in town was that enthusiastic about a newcomer, especially a lone woman taking over an established business from an owner who was a known and accepted commodity. Whitefield, New Hampshire hadn't quite made up its collective mind about Anne McClellan. *Yea-ah, well, we'll see, we'll see.*

Lou had pitched in and helped, as if they'd been friends for years, and Anne sometimes wondered what her first six months might have been like if Louise and her quiet, thoughtful husband Carl hadn't been the kind of people they were. Lou's ruddy, plain features and overstuffed body wouldn't have won any contests, but in her company for ten minutes, that observation faded away forever. She was a genuinely warm, giving, beautiful human being—to her friends. Make an enemy of Lou Rowen at your peril, Anne thought with amusement. She had a memory older than dirt for a wrong done to her or to anyone she considered a friend. *Oh, Laurie would love Lou!* Anne thought with a smile.

Now, frowning in concentration, Louise finally pointed to the plump iced cinnamon rolls, huge pillows of sweet dough generously dusted with cinnamon and studded with rum-soaked raisins, sugary white frosting dripping down the sides. They were as large as a salad plate and Anne could hardly keep them in stock past noon. Today Louise's choice left only one more in the case.

"Oh, well"—Anne eyed its lonely splendor for a moment, then surrendered to her baser instincts—"maybe I'll join you and finish this one. It doesn't look nice to display just one," she rationalized. "And after all, I didn't eat anything else this morning, not even with Caroline." Her teeth sank into the sweet, moist dough and she thoroughly relished the wonderful taste of her own creation. Mmm, these *were* damned good! And she could always walk a mile this evening to burn up the calories. Yeah, sure.

"So, how's Caroline doing these days?" Louise mumbled around the cinnamon dough. "I haven't seen her in a dog's age."

"Ah, she's terrific, isn't she?" Anne smiled, her eyes bright with the image of Caroline. "She'd be perfect for that *Reader's Digest* thing . . . you know, 'the most unforgettable character I ever met.' She really is, at least for me. She kind of sits back and looks at all the foolishness going on around her and shakes her head, and waits until someone is smart enough to ask *her* for the answers to life's puzzles. Then she quietly sorts through the tangles and unties the knots and, voila, all of a sudden order out of chaos. And even if that's too simplistic, it's just how she makes me feel." Anne grinned, then took another large bite of cellulite-in-the-rough.

"You make her sound like some guru or something," Lou grinned. "And if there was ever anyone who is definitely 'of this world,' it's Caroline Novak." She wiped crumbs and frosting from her mouth, then took a gulp of coffee. "But, one thing's for sure: Mike was real lucky she was around when he needed her. I raised my two kids and I know how tough it had to be for a sixty-year-old spinster to suddenly be in charge of bringing up baby. Especially after living on her own down in Concord all those years."

"Oh? I thought she'd always lived here."

"Nah, she was a teacher, went down there to work, and never came back. Not until Mike's father died. She stayed on and then later he showed up here with the baby."

"Didn't he—?" Anne suddenly remembered that Lou, while becoming a good friend in the last few months, was, first and foremost, thrilled with a good juicy bit of gossip, preferably *new* gossip. In a town as small as this, gossip would rank high on the list of hobbies; no need to feed her habit. Too much interest in Novaks—*any Novaks*—on the part of "the new woman" was not good to display within hearing distance of Lou's supersensitive antenna.

Louise popped the last piece of the bun into her mouth and picked up stray crumbs from the plate with her finger, smiling with satisfaction. "Now, that's a great way to start a day . . . with a sugar high. Won't do much for my hips but . . . well, you can't have everything." She looked down at her endowment from Mother Nature. " 'Course, it'd be nice to have *something.*"

"Don't complain. You feel good and Carl seems perfectly happy with a well-endowed woman." Anne started to smile, then had a sudden flash of recall: Honey, beside Mike, standing in the doorway of the Spalding Inn dining room. Ah, yes, speaking of well-endowed . . . !

Damn! This morning she couldn't seem to do anything to avoid all these reminders of Mike, and now Honey had arrived on the scene, too. A plague on both your houses . . . you, Mike Novak, and your "Honey-bunny"! Grrrr!

"Hey, Annie, what's eating you? All of a sudden you look like you're ready to chew nails. You can't envy my endowment that much!" Louise grinned at her friend and pulled her jacket back on, preparing to leave for her own shop. "Something bothering you?"

"What?" She focused again on Lou. "Oh. Oh, no. No, it's just . . . well, Caroline asked me to do a birthday cake for Helena's party next week and—" She stared at Louise in dismay. "Damn! It's supposed to be a surprise. Lou, don't you dare say anything to anyone, please! I don't want to spoil it for Helena."

Well, Anne realized, at least she'd managed to change the subject and cover that momentary slip into anger and memory . . . and Mike, she thought wearily. Lord, she seemed to have a knack for finding friends who could practically read her thoughts. First Laura in Michigan and now Louise in New Hampshire; they had an awful lot in common, she thought wryly. Either she was as transparent as cellophane or she attracted mind readers like flies to . . . Honey.

Damn!

"I won't even mention the party, promise. My lips are sealed, except when I come in here for coffee or at the next meal, whichever comes first." Lou grinned, reaching for the doorknob. At that moment it swung open sharply and she found herself face to face with Mike, who stopped short on the threshold, startled by the unexpected encounter.

"Morning, Lou. I . . . uh . . . I just came for some doughnuts for the . . . uh . . . crew at the station."

Head tilted thoughtfully to one side, Louise studied him for a moment, wondering just why he should feel it necessary to give her unasked for and unwarranted explanations. Mike was not usually generous with small talk and just now he looked decidedly ill at ease. She glanced back at Anne and found that exact expression frozen on her face, too. Hmm, how *very* interesting!

"Yeah, Mike, the stuff in here is really

great!" She winked at Anne, grinned at Mike and, zipping her jacket, walked jauntily out into the street. Yep, *very, very* interesting.

"Well, hi there, Mike. I didn't think I'd see you this morning. You're late." Anne smiled, an utterly casual, friendly, unconcerned smile, a smile she'd have given any customer who came through the door. Only the death grip she had on the tray in her hands would have given her away, that and the sudden lurch in her stomach that threatened to heave the recently consumed cinnamon bun.

The momentary feeling disappeared quickly, *as do most aberrations,* she admonished herself. *And don't forget that.* That's what Friday night had been, of course, and she immediately filed it under *"A* for aberration," not to be removed from her mental files again—ever. If she wanted to make her life in Whitefield—and she knew she did—then it would be far better for all concerned if she and Mike could be easy in each other's company . . . neighbors, friendly acquaintances, even friends.

"So, what'll it be . . . the usual, or do you want to try something different?"

"Uh, yeah, I guess," Mike muttered. A helluva note, standing here tongue-tied and nervous at this stage of his life. For Helena's sake, for his own peace of mind he'd better get past this stumbling block named Anne McClellan, and fast. And why should that be such a problem? Look at her standing there, smiling at him, so easy, so unconcerned. Had the other night really been so unimportant to her? A spasm of anger shot through him. He'd been making himself crazy for nothing. Hell, if she'd forgotten it so quickly, then so would he. Who did she think she was anyway, making a mess of his nice comfortable life!

Anne noted the sudden darkening of his features, the tight lips; his face was a storm warning, and automatically she braced herself. "You want a dozen assorted?"

"Yes."

Well, words were flowing like honey—like *molasses*—around here this morning. "Caroline was in a while ago. We had coffee and she told me about the party. It sounds great. I told her I'd help out." Anne kept the bland smile pasted on her mouth while she slipped the pastries into the blue box. "I was wondering what I could get for Helena. I'd like it to be something special and—"

"We're used to the simple life up here; make it something smaller than a Porsche!"

Sarcasm etched every word in acid and Anne almost dropped the box in her hands. She stared. What the hell was eating him?

"Excuse me? Would you like to tell me what's your problem all of a sudden?"

He made his voice steady, even. "I'm sorry, Anne, but you have to admit you're used to affluence in your life, material things. I just don't want Helena spoiled by money, by a preoccupation with things. It's bad enough with some of her friends, and teenage girls are impressionable and—"

"Mike, what you know about teenage girls—and *me*, for that matter—could fit on the head of a pin, with room left over for the Declaration of Independence!" He'd never seen her temper but he sure saw it now.

"Damn you! All I asked is what she'd like for her birthday. I'm not planning on buying her soul!"

Shit. As usual with her, he seemed to have put his foot in his mouth! God, he was so tired of being *wrong*. "Look, I'm sorry. I just thought—"

"Well, you just thought wrong!"

He shook his head, an odd little smile flickering across his mouth.

"I'm going to tell you a few facts of life, Chief Michael Novak, facts of *my* life. I may have some money now—when Paul died he left me comfortable and secure. And that's what *you* see. Well, *Chief Novak*, Paul and I were a long time getting to this point, I can assure you. What the hell do you know about sitting down with the checkbook and figuring out whose turn it was to get paid that week? And when we finally scraped and saved and borrowed to start our own business, being afraid to answer the phone because it might be the bank telling us we were overdrawn. Not allowing myself to buy one item at the supermarket unless I had a discount coupon, literally counting pennies for *everything*. To this day I can't stand the sight of macaroni and cheese, and I know about a hundred and ten ways to stretch a pound of hamburger meat to make a meal for three people, with leftovers! I can thin out a pot of soup to last for days, because that's all there is in the refrigerator, and I—"

Mike moved closer to the counter and took her hand in his, not allowing her to pull free when she struggled with him for a moment. "Anne, please. I—I'm sorry." Again. "I didn't mean to . . . to . . . hell, every time I open my mouth, I seem to jump to some lousy conclusions. At least with you." He held her hand between his, smoothing the skin, taking pleasure in her warmth. Her hand was warm but her expression wasn't. Neither were her words.

"It's a dangerous exercise—jumping to conclusions. You find out the hard way that things . . . people . . . aren't always as they appear. If I'm going to be judged, then judge me fairly. That's all I ask, but I won't accept less."

"Fair enough. That's the least you should expect." Her cheeks were flushed with anger, her eyes bright with an adrenaline high. She looked wonderful! "I think the trouble was, I walked in here ready to be angry with you and . . . well, I guess it showed."

She had to smile at that. "Understatement of the year. Now, would you mind telling me why? Did I do something . . . else?" Anne teased and felt the immediate ebb of the angry tide. It was a relief to let it go.

He sighed, shaking his head. "No. It was guilt, pure and simple. Saturday night—"

She stiffened for a moment. "You don't have to feel guilty about anything, Mike. You didn't do anything I didn't let you do. I'm the one who should apologize."

"At least you're back to Mike," he said gently. "Well, I still feel responsible, but now that we've both apologized for whatever, let's try to forget it." Fat chance, his libido was telling him. He dropped her hand quickly.

Anne heard the words with some regret. It

was what she'd wanted him to say, of course, but it was too bad it came so easily. *Oh, you want him to agonize a little more, to suffer?* Yes, as a matter of fact, she did!

But all she said was, "Okay with me. Friends?" He grinned and they shook on it. If they released each other's hands a trifle slowly, neither was ready to acknowledge that fact.

"Caroline was telling me about your plans for Helena's birthday. Sounds terrific. Aside from the cake, if there's anything else I can do, just tell me."

"Listen, if I can keep it from Helena, *I'll* be the one who's surprised. We haven't made much of a fuss so far and it's driving her crazy. Hey! You're probably just the person to ask. Got any suggestions for a present?"

"You, too? I just asked Caroline the same thing. She didn't have an answer. I was wondering, what's she getting?"

Mike's smile grew mellow, a tenderness showing that he reserved for very few people. "Ah, Caroline's giving Helena a watch." He said it with such emotion, Anne felt mystified at the importance he seemed to place on the gift.

"Is it an unusual kind of watch?" she wondered aloud.

"Yeah, you could say that." He leaned against the glass display case, hands thrust into his pockets. "Caroline was living in Concord when the war began—World War II," he explained to Anne's puzzled expression. She nodded in understanding. "She fell in love with the principal of the school where she taught. They were going to be married but"—he shook his head and shrugged—"he was killed at Anzio. She never really got over it, never loved another man. Anyway, he gave her a watch when they became engaged; it was to be until he could come home and afford to buy a ring. She's treasured it all these years, and now she said she wants Helena to have it because it should go to someone she loves."

There was a moment of silence. Anne swallowed, her throat thick with sudden tears, and put her hand on Mike's arm. "Thank you for telling me that, Mike. How lovely, and I can't think of a more meaningful gift for Helena. I know she'll love it."

"Yeah, I think she will. She's got a really sentimental streak, that kid, though no one's supposed to know. It's not 'cool'!" They smiled at one another in understanding and then Mike stood up straight, pulling his heavy uniform jacket into place. "Well, I've been trying to come up with something, too, been wracking my brain, and I guess you were right. I really don't know what teenage girls like."

"Easy . . . teenage boys. But," Anne leaned on the counter, head tilted in thought, "since you won't give her one of those, let's try to think of something else. Hmmm, something to do with rock music? I know, I know," she chuckled at his horrified expression, "but this too shall pass, believe it. Oh, wait!" Her eyes widened, and she turned and hurried into the kitchen, coming back before he could react. "Here, in yesterday's paper—I keep them here for the customers to read over coffee. Anyway, she and Jennie were giggling and drooling over . . . now, where is that . . . yes! Here, there's a concert down in Concord they were talking about. You know, a group 'to die for.'" He grimaced and rolled his eyes. "Yeah, well, you and I aren't fifteen. What do we know?" They chuckled together and then she looked back at the paper. "Now, if you really want to be a hero, maybe you can get some tickets to this. How's that for a great idea? 'Oh, Anne, you're terrific!'" She grinned at him in triumph. "That's the best thing I can think of—and it costs a lot less than a Porsche."

"Touché. But, you know, I have a feeling you've come up with a great suggestion. I wonder if . . ." He frowned, deep in thought, then smiled again. "I think I just may have an idea. I'll let you know how it works out. And thanks again . . . Madame Guru. I'm beginning to think you're the only link between Helena's teen years and my sanity."

He grinned, and Anne felt a surge of pleasure at the way his face lit up, buoyant and joyous. For the moment they shared that happiness. It was an instant of intimacy, that sharing, and they looked at each other for a long moment before Mike cleared his throat and stepped back a pace, and Anne handed him the now-filled box and quickly put his money into the cash register. But the moment was there between them, clear and remembered, though neither would speak of it.

Mike left hurriedly, and it was some indication of his distress that he hardly noticed the man who stood outside the shop window.

For a moment his eyes followed Mike as he drove away, then he turned back, looking inside with a steady gaze fastened on Anne as she disappeared into the kitchen. Disappointment in her judgment and resentment at the perceived insult in her obvious preference showed for a moment on his handsome face. Then Elliot Gilcrest turned away, continuing on to the bank, his face expressionless, his eyes dark in thought.

Ten

"The Dead Weasels! Oh, Dad, they're awesome! I can't believe it! How'd you get them? The Dead Weasels! They're only giving one concert and it sold out in two hours!" Her surprise birthday party now attaining the heights of perfection, Helena was jumping up and down with excitement at the four small pieces of cardboard, the passport to Utopia, that Mike had just put into her hands.

"You can be sure I wasn't at the head of the line," he answered tartly, tremendously pleased that the gift had turned out to be exactly right. He looked over his shoulder at Anne, standing and grinning beside Caroline. Another thank you he owed her. Her suggestion for the perfect gift had been right on the mark. "The Dead Weasels," he'd gaped when she showed him the ad. "God, whatever happened to names like The Four Aces or the Ames Brothers?"

With a sympathetic laugh, Anne had comforted him. "At least The Beach Boys and Johnny Mathis are still around. Some things do last!"

"Where'd you get them, Dad? Wow, they'll *die* when they find out at school. The Dead Weasels," she repeated, awestruck.

"I have a couple of friends down in Concord who owed me a favor. After all," he grinned, "what's more important than the Dead Weasels?" And a daughter's smile.

"And *four* tickets!" Helena, Jennie, and Diane Kelso were practically incapable of coherent speech by now, so excited were they at the forthcoming concert and the prospect of being among the privileged thousands of screaming and adoring weasel worshippers.

"Oh, wow, Mr. Novak, you're the greatest!"

"Yeah, awesome!"

"Where's Sandy? She'll . . . like . . . *die*. I can't wait to show her!" Helena peered around the room. The rest of the churning crowd of teenage bodies populating the living room were once more utterly uninterested in anything besides the music blaring from the large boom-box sitting on the mantel.

Caroline whispered in Anne's ear, "I'm glad I gave her my gift earlier. It could never compete with *The Dead Rats.*"

"Weasels!" Anne admonished with a grin.

"Weasels. I stand humbly corrected," Caroline agreed, smiling indulgently at Helena who, having found the fourth member of the inseparable quartet, Sandy Larkin, was reliving the excitement of the concert tickets all over again.

A rapturous Helena turned back to her beaming father and threw herself at him to give him one more hug. He squeezed back and kissed her soundly on the forehead. The sparkle of light on gold caught his eye and he picked up Helena's hand to admire once more the beautiful watch circling her left wrist. Its antique design of gold and enameled flowers set with chips of lapis lazuli flashed and sparkled in the bright light with every movement of her arm.

"You know, honey, this is the beginning of a family heirloom. It's very precious to Aunt Caro, that's why she gave it to you. You're very precious to us, too." He had to fight to keep his voice light, to keep the tears from his eyes. She'd never forgive him if he embarrassed her in front of her friends. And nothing was more embarrassing to the teenage psyche than genuine, heartfelt, adult—especially parental adult—emotions. Reaction to the music of Weasels didn't even come close.

"I really do love it, Dad. It's hot!" Helena held out the designated arm for the admiration of the immediate vicinity and then swung back to Caroline, throwing her arms around her neck. "Thank you, Aunt Cally, I love it! I'll take real good care of it, promise," she whispered in her ear, then kissed her thin cheek.

"And thank you, Dad! This is the best birthday ever!" It was only when they were in public, Mike had noticed with amusement, that "Daddy" reverted to "Dad."

"Well, Michael, you must be relieved to give her something that doesn't have moving parts," Caroline said, smiling as Helena carefully buttoned the priceless tickets into her pocket.

"Yeah, Dad, next year's the Big One—number sixteen! Hey, I saw this real neat used car the other day," Helena teased, "totally rad. Mmm . . . vrooom, vrooom!"

Mike rolled his eyes toward the ceiling, thereby giving her and her friends a good laugh at his expression. The looks they gave each other said it all: Parents, with their strange sense of humor, are kind of dumb, but they mean well so we have to humor them.

Just then someone turned up the stereo

even higher for the dancing, immediately distracting the younger generation from any further dealings with the older. Anne linked her arm in Mike's. "You know what I learned a long time ago? Teenagers are God's punishment for enjoying sex."

His mouth stretched in a grimace and he shook his head. "I have a feeling that next year at this time I'll be a sadder but wiser man. *She's* going to be behind the wheel of a car? No, I don't think I can—"

"Mike, Mike," Anne shook her head slowly, "you can't escape it. Right after lipstick comes dead weasels, then car keys, followed closely by—" she paused dramatically, "boys. *Dates."* His frown was forbidding. She chuckled. "And in your case, apoplectic fits."

Still laughing, Anne shrugged and turned to follow Caroline into the kitchen to replenish the chip and dip supply. She turned back to him. "By the way, don't you think it's a little inhibiting, even intimidating, for Helena's father *and* the Chief of Police to be smack in the middle of this party? Come on, Mike, give us the pleasure of your company and give the kids a break."

Smiling, Mike followed, seeking refuge in the only teenage-free, relatively quiet area in the house. At the door he turned for one affectionate last look at the crowded room, seeking out his daughter's tumbled dark hair and his happy, proud smile dissolved into a thoughtful frown. In seconds it assumed truly momentous proportions. On the kitchen threshold he stood dead in his tracks, eyes hard and cold, expression stormy.

"Mike, will you hand me . . . Mike? My God, what's wrong!" Anne stood beside the sink, staring at him, the bowl in her hand forgotten. "You look ready to commit murder."

"Close," he muttered, his hand holding the door open, his eyes still on the scene in the other room. "If he touches her, I'll . . ." The muttered threat remained unfinished.

Anne and Caroline both looked at him, at each other, then back at Mike. "What are you talking about, Michael?" Caroline asked quickly, walking to him. "If *who* touches her?" There was no question as to the "her"; only Helena would rate that kind of reaction from Mike. "Michael!" She had to shake his arm to regain his attention.

He hadn't taken his eyes off the gyrating teenagers. Anne moved to his other side to take a peek, too, then she sighed deeply, tugged his hand, and managed to pull him into the kitchen.

"Come on, Mike, dancing isn't a sin, is

it? What's so terrible about Helena dancing with . . . a *boy!*" She tried to erase his thunderous expression with some humor, but knew immediately it hadn't worked.

"It's not funny, Anne!" He swung around to her. "That kid is trouble . . . and I can't figure out what the hell he's doing here, anyway! Who invited him?"

"I did, Michael," Caroline answered briskly, chin up, ready for an argument. "Sandra Larkin is Helena's friend and her brother Jamie is only a couple of years older; he knows all these children. Their family seem like nice people . . . even if they don't have any money." Her tone was acerbic, matching the annoyance on her face.

"Damn it, Caroline, I don't give a shit"—she raised her eyebrows—"a *darn* how much money they have—or don't have. You know that's not—" He looked at her, then back at the closed door. "I just don't want Helena mixed up with him."

"Uh, Mike," Anne said hesitantly, "they're just kids. And they're dancing, in the middle of a crowd in *your own house*, for goodness sake. Where's the harm?"

"The *harm* is right out there. That kid, Jamie Larkin, is the *harm*. He's—he's—he's trouble, I can smell it."

"You're repeating yourself, Mike," Anne said, also frowning now. "Explain. What exactly do you mean by *trouble*? Did he do something? Has your department had a problem with him?"

"No," Mike muttered, opening and closing his fists as he moved restlessly around the white and yellow checked vinyl floor. "But that's probably only because he's lucky and smart . . . too smart. And frankly, I won't be surprised when something does happen. It's written all over him, like an accident waiting to happen."

Anne and Caroline stared at each other, puzzled. When it came to his official duties, Mike was the most careful of men, fair and non-judgmental. But of course, right now he wasn't the Chief of Police. He was Helena's father, and that was enough to make all the difference in Mike's eyes.

"Oh, sit down, Michael!" Caroline ordered. "Here, count to ten and have some coffee."

He almost smiled at that. It was Caroline who was always warning him that he drank too much coffee. Now she poured him a mug and he concentrated on her actions, trying for a few moments to avoid thinking of what was happening in the next room. He took a sip, swallowing with a grimace. Damn! She was still force-feeding him decaf.

Anne sat down beside him and sipped from her own cup. "What is it that's so bad about Jamie Larkin? I see him all the time in my shop and he seems like a good kid. Kind of quiet, doesn't talk very much, but he works hard and—"

"What do you mean, works hard? For *you?*" Mike stared at her.

"Well . . . yes, for me. Helena told me how bad things are for them. Their father has a bad back and his workman's comp is being held up for some reason, so he can't work and there's no money. Their mother does house cleaning when it's available, and I feel so bad for them, I try to give Jamie some work now and then, when he's not working over at the gas station—sweeping out and stocking supplies in the cooler and storage room. Some dishwashing sometimes, too."

"Was he working for you when you had the break-in?"

She stared, her eyes narrowing with irritation. "Yes, he was, and that doesn't make one bit of difference! It just so happens I gave him a key—"

Mike slammed his fist on the table in

astonishment and anger. "A *key!* Why didn't you just hand him your checkbook!"

"I *trust* him. Oh, I forgot, you don't believe in that word, do you? Well, that's your problem, not mine! Yes, I gave him a *key*, so he can come in before I open and do the floor and the dishes. It's a convenience, for both of us. So, you see, Jamie wouldn't need to break down my door to pig out on pastry. A, he has a key, and B, he can have any of that pastry any time he wants it, the same as Helena or I. There's always leftover stuff in the cooler."

Anne paused abruptly, took a deep breath, and deliberately willed herself to feel calm . . . or at least she tried. "Which is exactly what I told him when he started working at the shop, and which is precisely why it seems perfectly natural when I give him bread and stuff to take home; I've told him it's left over and would be thrown out anyway so he might as well have it. If he thought it was . . . God forbid . . . charity, he'd throw it in my face. That's why I knew you were wrong, even if there was no other evidence. He's tough, that kid, and proud, and he takes nothing for nothing."

Mike rewarded her with a chastened expression and shrugged in surrender. "Okay, Anne, maybe you're right, but I hope you understand I had to ask." Then he shook his head, looking hard at the door again. "But I still don't like him," he muttered.

"But *why?* For heaven's sake, you're being unreasonable!"

"I think I know why," Caroline interjected in a soft, thoughtful voice. The other two looked up at her, suddenly remembering she was there; she'd been utterly silent during Mike's accusation and Anne's defense.

"Does he remind you of someone you know?" When he looked at her without comprehension, she continued. "He's *you,* isn't he, Michael? You look at him and see yourself—an angry, hurt, determined, and proud young boy. He's hard, at least on the surface, just like you were, and he doesn't seem the type to care what happens to anyone who gets in his way. He resents being an outsider, being poor, having people point to his father and make mean remarks about drinking—no, in *his* case, it's probably being lazy or shiftless, isn't it?"

Caroline took a deep breath, head tilted to one side as she gazed at the darkened window above the sink, looking back rather than out. "You look at Jamie and see yourself, what you once were, sullen and resentful and ambitious, and you don't like it or trust it, or him." She turned then and looked across the room at Mike, who hadn't taken his cold eyes off her, almost mesmerized by her words. "I think Anne's right, Michael. Helena's fine with Jamie . . . as safe as she would be with you." Caroline took a deep breath. "Because he's a lot more like you than you realize."

"Knock it off, Aunt Caroline. You don't know what the hel—you don't know what you're talking about!"

She looked at him over the tops of her glasses, smiled slightly, and raised her eyebrows, not bothering to argue.

The room was quiet for a few moments, as quiet as the loud rhythmic musical beat from the next room would allow. Until her name was mentioned, Anne had thought that Caroline, and perhaps Mike, too, had forgotten she was there. Distinctly uncomfortable, she wished there were some way she could disappear. Mike, had he been given the choice, certainly wouldn't have wanted her as witness to Caroline's revealing words. He was a private man, and in this room too much of his inner self had been laid bare, truths he obviously hadn't wanted revealed. Perhaps even to himself.

The mood was abruptly broken when the door was thrown open and Helena burst into the kitchen holding out an empty bowl. "We're out of chips and we need some cold soda—" She stopped short and looked at the three people frozen in their positions. "What gives? Something wrong?" She searched her father's face, then Anne's. "Hey, what's the matter with you guys? This is a party! Aunt Callie?" She turned to her aunt. "You okay?" she asked, beginning to look worried.

Well, Anne thought resignedly, Caroline had already included her in the conversation as a dissenting, and interfering, voice. In for a penny, in for a pound. He could only kill her once. Before Mike could say something he would definitely regret, Anne jammed her foot down hard on his toes and laid a forcefully restraining hand on his arm.

"Yes, dear, everything's fine," Caroline answered into the waiting pause. "This is the senior citizen department, here; we don't have your energy level. So have pity."

Anne laughed, pressing ever more firmly on Mike's foot, white-knuckling his arm. "Yes, we needed some R and R—resting and recharging, batteries that is." She grinned at the three girls in the doorway and, feeling it was safe for the moment, rose from the table and handed them the needed supplies. "Here, Jennie, take the rest of the dip."

"Helena, you and Sandy can take these bottles," Caroline added. "They should be cold enough. Say, where's Diane?"

"Oh, she's dancing with my brother," Sandy piped up, before she stuffed a handful of chips into her chubby cheeks.

The two women exchanged quick glances, and Mike managed to keep his mouth stretched in what might pass for a smile. At least, Anne thought gratefully, he was silent. The two women shepherded the girls back to the party with new fuel for their perpetual motion machines.

Relative silence descended on the kitchen again, and as if she'd heard nothing unusual in the recent exchange, Anne rose and took Caroline's hand. "I think it's time for me to head home. No," she turned to Mike, stopping his automatic offer to drive her, "I drove myself tonight—in a *car*, thank you—and I don't want to take you away from the big doings."

"Yeah," he said acidly, looking again at the closed door. "Big doings." His expression said there'd better not be too many *big doings* going on in that living room. Lights on, feet on the floor. Or else.

"Ah, Michael, you'd think you were the first father to bristle with the protective urge. Puberty comes to us all, girls *and* boys, no matter how parents fight it." Caroline was amused and tolerant. Poor boy, it was difficult facing *these* facts of his life: Daddy's little girl would never be completely Daddy's again.

"Yeah, well, I'm not so old that I can't still remember what teenage boys are like when they're around teenage girls." He sounded so hopeless and helpless, Anne couldn't restrain the quick laugh that bubbled up. He looked at her and she stifled it quickly.

"Sure," he said with resignation, "what do you know? You *raised* one of them." He said it as if he'd just discovered some strange new species and was still very wary of its possibilities.

Anne watched the play of emotion flickering across his face, the puzzlement and worry, and she could almost feel his frustration and sense of ineptitude in dealing with the rush of time. She could so easily allow herself to put her arms around him, comfort him, try to coax a smile from beneath that dark slash of moustache, kiss away the anxiety.

She shoved her hands deep in her pockets. Just as well she was leaving . . . in her own car. She had planned more carefully than she'd ever want to admit—it was a telling fact that it had been that important to her—to eliminate the possibility of further cozy little *tête-à-têtes* between her and Mike Novak in any setting that could, by any stretch of either of their imaginations, be described as intimate. Although nothing could be more intimate than Caroline's inadvertent revelations this evening.

But not alone again. Not ever, if she were smart. Being near him in a crowd was disturbing enough—she felt the emotional rush even now. Who knew what her newly unpredictable self would allow to happen if they were alone? No, thank you!

After this little scene tonight, do you really think he wants to get any more intimate with Mrs. Know-it-all? Not! No, she thought, not likely. And why did that probability seem so bleak?

Her thought was borne out with his perfunctory polite protest. "Are you sure you'll be all right?"

"I'll be just fine, Mike. Haven't you ever heard of women's lib?" She grinned. "See you in town, and thanks, Caroline, for letting me help out." The two women hugged each other and Anne looked around quickly for her jacket, anxious now to be gone. "It's been a great evening!" Well, maybe *great* wasn't the auspicious word to use just now. "It was a lot of . . . fun."

Mmmm. Fun. Well, part of it, anyway. And

part of it had been informative. Damn, maybe
more than she'd have wished. That unexpected
and poignant insight into the boy Mike had
once been had left her disturbed, unsettled . . .
and deep down inside aching for him, for the
childhood he'd never had a chance to enjoy.
She had a feeling she wasn't going to forget
Caroline's remarks very quickly. From the expression still hanging around the edges of his
face, in his eyes, neither would Mike.

"Well, the least I can do is walk you to
your car." A subdued Mike Novak took her
coat from the hook next to his near the back
door and helped her on with it. Together
they walked out to the driveway where her
Porsche was parked.

"That was nice of the kids . . . no one
boxed me in. I can make a fast escape." She'd
meant it as a joke, but she suddenly realized
there was more truth than humor in the
words. Perhaps Mike heard that, too.

"I hope what Caroline said before didn't
drive you away." He looked back at the house.
"I mean . . . well, I'm sure it was embarrassing for you to be dragged into the middle of
a family discussion."

For an instant Anne recalled her words to
Caroline, that they all seemed like "family,"
and she almost smiled at the irony. But the

greater irony lay in Mike's words. Was he *apologizing* to her? Good God, she'd thought he would kick her keester out the door after Caroline's holding her up as a reference for Jamie Larkin. After all, Mike had made no secret of his dislike for anyone interfering in his decisions, most especially those concerning Helena. And most especially when the "anyone" was *her.*

"Look, Mike," she chuckled, "believe me, I'm at an age where the memory is the first to go. By the time I get home, I'm afraid anything I heard tonight will be forgotten."

"Yeah . . . well, I could see you were uncomfortable." He shook his head, half smiling. "Shit, Caroline sure knows how to push my buttons, doesn't she?"

"Lord, we all have people who can do that, Mike. My son, Jerry, is a button expert, and Laura—she's a friend back in Michigan—she's another one. At least Caroline has the decency and reticence to hold it to a minimum."

"Anyone who knows Caroline Novak knows she keeps all her words to a minimum! Except around me, of course." He grinned then and she was inexpressibly relieved. "I suppose I should be grateful she does it so rarely. Thank God for small favors, and don't ever tell her I said that or my life will be impossible around here." They laughed together then, and the evening's tension drifted away on the chilly night breeze.

"Well, I'm off for home. I really did have a great time." She flopped her hand back and forth and made a face, then winked at him. "No, I mean it, Mike; it was fun. You can count yourself a big success after this. Every parent in town will probably hate you."

"Why, what'd I do?" he asked, startled.

Anne grinned. "Think Dead Weasels. Listen, it's tough to keep up with someone who's been dubbed awesome by a teenager. As a matter of fact, I recall being on the receiving end of that feeling myself not too long ago." Her smile was understandably self-satisfied and he looked appropriately chastened.

"Go on back inside, Mike, it's getting cold out here." He'd left the jacket of his grey tweed suit inside and now stood with his hands in his pants pockets, his tie hanging loose against the white broadcloth shirt. As far as she was concerned, Anne realized, cold was the last thing *she* felt! Which was exactly why her earlier resolution made so much sense . . . and why at this very moment the fact that she was ignoring it made so little! She yanked open the car door.

Mike held it while she buckled up. He

looked away, up at the almost cloudless sky, breathing deeply of the cold, sharp air. "You can almost feel winter coming in. I wonder if Helena will hold me to my promise?" he mused, staring up at the three-quarter moon, streaked with shreds of low-flying clouds.

"What promise?" Anne, fumbling with the ignition key, looked up at him for a moment.

"I promised her one last fishing trip. And if we don't do it tomorrow, we won't do it. It's getting cold fast."

"Well, knowing her memory, you'd better haul out the fishing rods and the heavy sweaters. She shows no mercy, that one," Anne laughed, envying his jaunt into the wilds of New Hampshire not one little bit. "Have fun . . . better you than me." Her Sunday would be spent curled up on the couch with the *New York Times* crossword puzzle, a cup of hot coffee, and a warm Danish. Yeeaaah!

"Now, go on back and enjoy the party. And, Mike . . . ?" She put her hand on his arm for just a second. "Enjoy Helena, too. At the risk of being dubbed Madame Busybody again, she's a good kid. You know that and I know it . . . and down deep in her teenage subconscious, Helena knows it, too. She'll never do anything to hurt you. You just have to keep things in perspective; us parents have to do a lot of that! After all, they're only kids. Let them enjoy the fun of *being* kids."

More than I ever could. The words were written across his face, in his dark steady eyes, a sense of sadness, a sense of regret for things undone, untasted.

The moment passed and he looked down at Anne. "You once told me you didn't pry. I guess you meant it. That . . . that business before, with Caroline and . . . Jamie, and . . . well, someday I'll tell you all about it. I suppose you have a ri—" He stopped just as the motor purred to life, then he shut his mouth abruptly. "Drive carefully," he said quickly, slammed the door shut, and stepped away from the car.

He watched her back down the drive, a sense of astonished clarity washing over him. *Anne was right.* Jeez, was she *always* right? But he knew in his heart it was Anne, her calming influence, her insight and wisdom, that had helped him keep his cool when he might have caused a scene and ruined Helena's evening, and perhaps a lot more. His foot was too large to fit comfortably in his mouth.

A cold gust of wind made him shiver, and as he saw her taillights disappear around a curve in the road, his last words came rushing back into his mind. He recalled very clearly what he'd almost said: "You have a right to know." A *right?* A right to *what?* To know him? To be close to him?

God, that's what he wanted, all right, what he'd wanted for a long time, wasn't it? To be close to her, to feel her close to him; to touch her, to drag his fingers through that silver-speckled mop-top; to feel her strength and softness, the womanliness of that body of hers; to find the inner secret of her warmth, her concern, her comfort; to kiss her again and again; to finally know all there was to know about Anne McClellan.

He stared down the moon-silvered road and felt cold deep into his bones. It would take a lifetime to know Anne McClellan.

A lifetime.

Eleven

"Aw, c'mon Mac, it'll be fun . . . honest!"

Anne looked at the telephone and pictured a breathless, impulsive Helena at the other end. And was Mike there with her? Fun. She wondered if she'd ever again think of Mike Novak and a feeling as innocent and simple as fun in the same breath.

"I really think your dad would enjoy it more with just the two of you."

"Naah, he'd like you to come along. Me, too! After all, it's my birthday weekend." Suddenly, the sound was muffled, as if she'd put her hand over the receiver and was speaking to someone else. Anne rolled her eyes. *Someone else.* Well, why couldn't it be Caroline? Hell, she knew why: Because it had to be Mike; that's just the way fate arranged things. Then Helena came back on the line. "Wasn't last night great?" Anne was certain she could hear Helena grinning.

"I'm sure glad you guys like each other. I wanted you to be friends."

"Uh . . . well, sure, we are, honey, but—"

Helena's motor was in no danger of running down and she kept cajoling. "You're all caught up with the baking, the bread dough's already in the fridge, and there aren't any special orders 'til the end of next week, so you have nothing to do today!" she summed up triumphantly.

"Oh, sure, except for laundry and housework and just plain sitting." No, Anne decided, this mustn't go on another second. She could feel her resolve weakening. "Oh, listen, Helena," she lied glibly, quickly, "I have something on the stove and I think it's burning. Got to run. But thanks for asking me to go with you. 'Bye, honey!" She dropped the receiver into its cradle like a hot rock.

"Friends. She wants us to be friends." *Friends* was, perhaps, going too far, Anne thought wryly. Of course, Helena wasn't aware of the after-dinner agenda she and Mike had shared the night of that big storm. Or the current between them last night or all the days between. *Well, kiddo, maybe it was a one-way current!* After all, it *had* been a while since that night, and exaggeration thrived on memory; hadn't she herself noted recently that the memory was the first to go?

And yet . . . the still-vivid image of that night, when she let herself think about it, continued to make her uncomfortable. A woman her age, showing such disgraceful lack of restraint! And letting Mike think . . . well, God only knew what Mike had thought.

There was a word—an ugly word—for a woman who acted that way, leading a man on. But she hadn't meant to. . . . She thought suddenly of Paul. It was hard to let go of twenty years of fealty. And they'd been such wonderful years! Paul, her friend, her lover, the man with whom she'd conceived and brought forth a son . . . Paul, her husband, who'd shared a dream for a lifetime.

Tears welled and she dashed them away with the back of her hand. The dream was over, the lifetime cut brutally short, and the beloved father, her friend and lover, gone in the blink of fate's eye. He'd gone, and he'd left her behind. At the beginning there were days she had missed him so it was a palpable agony to push her way through the leaden hours. Thank God those days had passed now, though they were not forgotten.

And yet, Anne knew, if he could have spoken, if he could have come back even for one moment, he would have told her to get on with living. Paul McClellan had lived his life with verve and gusto and pleasure; he hadn't been the kind of man to believe in *suttee*. He would never have asked it of her, so why was she asking it of herself? Anne sighed quietly. Just when she figured she'd beaten all possible fears to the ground—*bang*—along came one more out of left field.

You ninny, that's it, isn't it? That's what you're afraid of, aren't you, to be just Anne McClellan, out there on your own, in charge of your own life? She'd been so used to being Paul's wife she still hadn't gotten beyond being Paul's widow.

Well, even if it was being forced on her, perhaps it was time! Time to stop clinging so desperately to Paul, time to get used to being who she was, time to begin to consciously define her life in terms of what *Anne* felt, what *Anne* needed.

She sniffled away the last of the tears and took a deep breath, feeling suddenly light, free, eager . . . and alive! She snatched up the phone again, before she thought better of it, and dialed.

"Helena? Hi, it's me. Listen, I thought about today and I've changed my mind. Is it too late?" Some perverse imp inside her wished it were!

"Oh, Mac, that's great! No, there's plenty of time. We're still getting ready. Just a minute." The line was silent for a moment, then Helena was back. "Daddy said we'll pick you up in half an hour. Okay?"

"Uh . . . sure, okay." So, Mike would be in the driver's seat, and no emergency escape available this time, damnit! "Should I bring anything, wear anything special?"

"Jeans, and a warm sweater and jacket . . . and don't forget your long johns! We'll bring waders." That muffled mumble again, then, "You got any of those brownies?"

Anne chuckled, "I'll scrounge up something." And what were waders? They sounded suspiciously related to water and getting *wet*. Didn't one fish lazing idly under trees while a line dangled into the water, unattended? Well, she'd find out soon enough. No sense sounding any more ignorant than she already did. "Is your Aunt Caroline going, too?" Ah, foolish hope.

"No, she used to go fishing with us, but she says the damp air and the walk down to the river are too much for her arthritis. The closest she gets now is tying flies for Daddy."

Anne couldn't begin to imagine the fastidious, reserved Caroline Novak doing something as disgusting as that sounded.

"I'm real glad you're coming," Helena bubbled on. "It's probably the last time we'll get to go this year. It'll be fun!"

Anne laid the receiver gently in its cradle. Like pulling teeth, an afternoon with Mike would be fun.

What the hell was she getting into here? Deeper and deeper. When had Indiana Jones climbed inside her skin?

Annie, my girl, it started the minute you wrote that letter to Ilse Kolchak. That's where you laid it on the line and cut the cord.

"As if you're drifting away."

Anne jumped and looked over her shoulder. "Laura?" *Well, that's crazy, for sure. I'm all alone and now I'm beginning to hear voices. If there's one thing I don't need now, it's that.*

Then she grinned. But what a great idea! That was precisely what she did need . . . to get in touch with Laura, with reality, with common sense. Anne glanced at her watch. Well, no matter, she'd make time for this. She sensed it was very important that she did.

Drumming her fingers impatiently on the table, Anne waited for the phone to be picked up out in Bloomfield Hills, Michigan. "Laura? Hi! It's me, Anne!"

"As if I wouldn't know you. . . . You kidding? That'll be the day! Oh, Annie, it's so great to hear your voice! Lord, I miss you! You're lucky I'm even speaking to you, now that I think of it. How could you go away and leave me!" she wailed across the miles. "I miss you! But I'm so glad you called. I forgive you, anyway. Funny, Jim and I were just talking about you . . . well, kind of. I mean, we were thinking about driving through New England, the color change and everything, you know? And we thought maybe next week. . . . Oh, listen to me! You called and I'm doing all the talking. So, what's up? I'm dying to hear about everything. Why'd you call?"

"Well, Laura, cat got your tongue?" Anne laughed. "Anyway, I'm glad you stopped for air! Honestly, you never talked that much when I lived a mile away. You've changed." *Ah, yes, haven't we all!*

"No, not really. I'm still rotten at bridge and I still have circles under my eyes like Frisbies. But I'm lonesome for you, Annie. Why couldn't you move to Florida like everyone else our age? At least I'd see you once in a while when we go down in the winter. But, my God, *New Hampshire!*"

"Honestly, Laura, it's still in the continental U.S., you know. You don't even need a passport!" Anne shook her head, smiling at her friend's skewed sense of geography. "And it happens to be absolutely beautiful up here, so there. The people are terrific—well, most of them—and the pastry shop's doing so well I can't really believe it! Yeah, things are going great."

"You sound so good, Anne." Laura's voice was quieter, thoughtful. "You did the right thing, didn't you, honey? That really is the place for you now, isn't it?"

"Oh, Laura," Anne said with certainty, "it is. I can finally say I *belong* here; even Mike would have to admit it."

"Mike?" Laura snapped to attention. "Who's this Mike? Have you known him long? What does he—?"

"Hold it, Sherlock. He's the Chief of Police and—"

"Police?" Laura yelled. "Did something happen?"

"Laura, for heaven's sake," Anne laughed, "nothing happened, except for that little break-in I told you about. Other than that, nothing. Remember, his daughter works for me so we . . . uh . . . we get to see each other now and then."

"Now and then. Hmm." There was speculation and much imagination in that "hmm." No one knew Anne like Laura knew Anne. And the antenna was at full extension now.

"So, anything you want to tell me? What's he like? What's he *look* like? You two been—?"

"Oh, come on, Laura, I'm just a little too old and creaky to play Juliet, and he's not my idea of Romeo." Well, that might be open to debate.

No!

"Anyway, we're just . . . friends."

"Uh-huh, friends. Close friends?"

"Laura!"

"Well, you're not telling me anything, so I have to ask. So, is he married? What's he like?"

"No, he's not married, and he's . . . he's . . . well, he's tall, and he's got dark hair, a little grey, and a moustache. . . ."

"Oh, God, Rhett Butler!"

"Fiddle-dee-dee, Laura! No, he's not Rhett Butler—and I sure as hell am not Scarlett O'Hara. Hell, my waist isn't within spitting distance of eighteen inches, not even my thighs! And I wouldn't be caught dead wearing drapes out to dinner!"

"Damnit, Anne," Laura managed, when she stopped laughing, "You really aren't going to tell me anything, are you?"

"Nope."

"Well, sweetie, that tells me a lot! So there!"

"Oh, I should have known better than to call you."

"Yeah, why did you call, anyway? It's nine-fifteen on Sunday morning, and since I'm usually still sleeping and you're glued to your TV watching your dream man Charles Kuralt, tell me what's so urgent that you called? TV broken or is something wrong?"

"Oh, Laura, I'm sorry. I—I just forgot it was so early." Sounded lame, even to her, Anne thought. "I . . . well, I'm supposed to go fishing and—"

"You're *what*? Wait, let me shake the sleep out of my ears. Uh . . . did you say *fishing*? No, I must have heard wrong. You couldn't—"

"Yes, Laura," Anne interrupted with a quiet chuckle, "I said the *F* word. I think that's why I called: I hoped you'd talk me out of it, or at least come up with a good excuse to beg off."

"Well, who're you going with? I mean, she, he, or it must have the powers of persuasion of an angel. I'd love to meet this—" Her words stopped abruptly, then she asked in a soft, guileless voice, "Uh . . . Anne, you going fishing with this Mike?"

"Helena's going, too," Anne answered quickly, her tone more defensive than she wanted to admit.

"Mmm-hmm."

"And just what does that 'mmm-hmm' mean?" Anne demanded.

"Why, nothing, Anne. Nothing at all."

Silence hung on the line between them, *at Sunday long-distance rates, yet,* Anne thought irrelevantly. "Oh, all right, Laura. I admit it, I called because I—" she sighed heavily, "I don't know what to do. I think I'm scared."

"You? Scared? Come on, who're you kidding, Wonder Woman? You're not scared of anything, and you know it."

"So much for your intuition. I'm scared shitless."

Laura's words were measured. "If you are, it's because there's more going on here than catching a fish. And if it's upsetting you like this, then that's exactly why you can't back out. You know that. You knew it before you dialed the phone, didn't you? If you're asking what I think, all I can say is go for it, Annie. Don't throw away the chance if it comes along, not before you know for sure. Anyone who gets to you that deep and that fast, well . . ."

She didn't have to say any more, because Anne knew the answer already. Had probably always known. And if she ran away from the answer to this question, she'd never rest easy again, never be sure if she could trust her judgment. And she had to know that; it's what all her decisions in the past year had been leading up to. There are no sure things, but to win anything you have to take a chance. *Take a chance*. She sighed again. "Yeah, you smart ass. You always know everything, don't you?"

"Well, no, not *everything*," Laura chuckled with false modesty, "but I know you, honey, and I trust you. So, trust yourself. Like I said . . . go for it. The oracle has spoken!"

"Oh, you nut! But," Anne's voice was warm with affection, "thank you, friend—for everything."

"C'mon. I didn't do anything, Anne, you know that. I only said what you already knew. After all, everyone likes proof that their decisions are right. Go, have fun, and don't do anything I wouldn't do—no, forget that. Do *everything* I wouldn't do! But just remember, I get to be the bridesmaid!" A sharp click ended the conversation.

Anne hung up with a look of longing at the untouched crossword puzzle and pen, the coffee heating in the kitchen. Just an hour ago life was so simple. Now she was going to spend a day in Mike Novak's company, and she couldn't blame it on the persuasive talents of a budding fifteen-year-old lawyer or even a very good, though possibly imprudent and

misguided, dear old friend. She had only herself to blame.

God, what an awful thing to have to admit
to yourself.

The icy cognac-colored water swirled around
her legs. Anne was filled with expectations of
frozen blood and wet feet, not quite trusting
the ungainly rib-high boots Helena had resur-
rected from the depths of the Novak garage.
They hung in baggy disarray from wide loose
straps over her shoulders. Well, at least one of
her questions was answered: Now she knew
what waders were. A less attractive outfit she
couldn't begin to imagine.

"I must be nuts." Her muttered words were
whisked away in the chill breeze blowing
down from the direction of the Whites.
"What sane person would voluntarily subject
herself to this?"

She tightened her grip on the soft cork
handle of the bamboo rod, careful to avoid
the shiny metal reel. Anne knew she had to
be careful of anything with moving parts; the
rod itself was bad enough. It stuck out from
her body at an ungainly angle, and she
couldn't have held on tighter if she'd been

with the Flying Wallendas clutching a balancing pole fifty feet above the ground.

"Stop gritting your teeth, Annie. And ease up on your grip. That thing's too expensive to replace if you snap it in half. Remember, trout fishing isn't a contact sport and you're not out hunting Jaws."

"Okay, but Helena promised me this would be fun." Anne looked with longing at the grassy bank beneath a large oak tree, then gestured down at her baggy sweatshirt, commandeered from Jerry's discards. Five faded words were plastered across her chest: *Are we having fun yet?* "Well, are we?"

Helena giggled and Mike rolled his eyes, an unexpected laugh welling up. "Yeah, can't you tell?" But, damn, he meant it! The memory of that night after the storm in her apartment, their parting, had held cold comfort and little promise. And even last night, when she'd left the birthday party, he'd have given odds she wouldn't come with them today. He'd been noticeably impatient on the way to pick her up. He'd never felt *quite* that eager to catch a fish before.

Anne relaxed at last, her hands loosening on the long fishing rod. "Is anyone going to fill me in? I mean, is there a secret handshake or an initiation ceremony or something? I feel like such a dumbbell. Someone *please* tell me what to do! All the way out here, you two were talking in code, for heaven's sake—tippets and roll casts and loop control—and I'm still waiting to find out what nail knots are. Although I'm not sure I ever want to know about caddis flies . . . yuck! I'm warning you, Mike, no matter what Caroline does, I refuse to do anything disgusting with any insects."

They both looked at her, obviously mystified.

"Well, Helena, you said Caroline used to come with you and she did something awful with bugs and . . ."

Father and daughter stared at her expression of sheer revulsion, then burst into loud laughter as Anne's words trailed off uncertainly into the late morning sunlight. Mike grinned while Helena collapsed onto the September-brittle grass of the riverbank, swallowing an onslaught of giggles. Puzzled and vaguely embarrassed, Anne waited impatiently for them to snap out of it. Mike finally rearranged his grinning mouth and cleared his throat, then splashed carefully closer to her and put a hand on hers. It lingered there a moment before he reluctantly forced himself to move it.

"Sorry, Annie, couldn't help it." Beneath the

velvet slash of moustache he bit his lip, dark eyes sparkling with delight. "Guess I'd better explain. You see, you don't fish for trout with bait. Helena must have been talking about tying flies." He smiled at her shuddery nod. "They're not real flies," he reassured her gently, "they're *artificial* lures made out of bits of fur and feathers. Caroline's a whiz, when her fingers aren't bothering her too much. She's been doing it since she and my father were kids."

"Like I said, I don't speak 'fishing.' I hate to admit this, Mike, but I've only gone fishing once in my whole life, and then I used salami for bait instead of"—she grimaced—"worms."

His eyes crinkled in amusement. "I wonder if fish suffer from heartburn?"

"Better than me suffering from heaving stomach!" She peered down into the water, strangely grateful not to see anything live in the vicinity of her feet. "Did your father take you fishing here when you were small?"

"Yeah," Mike smiled sadly, then his eyes grew cold for a moment. "He used to, before . . ."

"Daddy? I'm gonna start now. It gets dark early, remember?"

As always, Mike thought gratefully, Helena was an instant antidote to dark memories.

"Yes, honey, poor feeble ol' Dad can still manage to remember some things."

"Ha, ha. Droll, very droll." Eagerly, Helena grabbed a businesslike rod from the assorted equipment lying on the bank and stepped off into the swirling river flood.

"What kind of rods do you two use? They're not like this bamboo thing you gave me."

"No, these are graphite. I guess you could say graphite is state of the art but . . . well, bamboo is tradition." He said it with affection and nostalgia in his voice. "Actually, the bamboo is mine, but I think it'll be easier for you to control 'til you get the hang of it."

"There speaks the eternal optimist!"

"If faith can move mountains, it sure as hell can move a fishing line."

Anne nodded, unconvinced but still glad she'd allowed herself to give in and join them for this day.

A slight frown creased Mike's forehead as he turned toward the bank. He moved to the sandy verge between water and land, bending to pick up something lying half hidden beneath a fallen branch.

"What's that?" Anne asked. Mutely, he held out his hand. Lying in his palm was a small trout, in death its iridescent silvery scales dull and almost colorless.

"Is that something to worry about?" Anne was puzzled by the suddenly serious expression on his face.

"I'm . . . not sure." Mike walked a few more feet downstream. "Wait here, I'll be back in a minute." He walked on, peering down at the bank as he went. She saw him stoop again, a motion he repeated once more before he turned and retraced his steps.

"I don't know. . . . Too big a fish kill to be accounted for by natural attrition. Something else killed them, and I'm afraid I know what it was." He shook his head, anger and worry plain on his face.

"What is it, Mike? You look positively ominous." But Anne couldn't erase his grim expression.

"We've been after some dumpers lately."

"Dumpers?"

"Illicit toxic waste disposal, if you want the technical term. There's been a rash of toxic dumping in the last few weeks and it's beginning to affect the water system in the whole area. In fact, that night you called in your burglary, I was on a stakeout over at Caroll Creek." He looked down at his hand, still holding the first fish he'd found. "We didn't know they'd come this far."

"But"—she gestured at the pristine look of

the scene around them—"it looks so beautiful, so peaceful. You wouldn't think—"

"See there?" He pointed to the shore, where the undergrowth grew heavy to the water's edge. "Look closely, you can see the brush and grass on the edge of the bank, where it's dead. And that's not from the cold. It's only in a couple of spots, where it comes in contact with the water."

"Does that mean we can't fish here?" Anne gazed around them, at the beauty that only a few moments ago she'd thought so inviolate.

"No, it's all right now. Mother Nature does a pretty good job cleaning up after herself— and us. From the looks of these fish and plants, the damage was done some time ago. Not enough to cause widespread effects, but enough to leave the evidence." He shook his head again. "All because some greedy, no-good son of a—" The sharp succinct expletives were quickly bitten off. Mike shrugged. "Well, we'll get him; I just hope it's soon enough."

He went quickly to the tackle box lying on shore and, emptying a plastic bag of its extra reel, proceeded to fill it with three of the dead fish and a sample of the withered flora from beside the river. In a small plastic vial that had held a fishing lure, he scooped up some of the water. "I'll get the State Police tox lab down in Concord to analyze these, just to make sure."

He stood staring down at the closed tackle box a moment longer, then turned and smiled at Anne, quickly lightening the somber mood. "Sorry about that, but it makes me so damned mad. The balance of nature is fragile and we should pass all this on, not carelessly spoil what we've been given. We're . . . well, at least we *should* be . . . caretakers." He looked away, down toward where Helena, biting her lip in concentration, was patiently waiting a strike. "I always figure being out here is a kind of gentle reminder . . . at least it's usually gentler than today."

Suddenly, he turned back to her, shrugged, and shook his head. "Well! Professor Novak's lecture is over for today. Sorry, Anne, don't look so serious. I promise I didn't forget what we're here for. Come on, now that I have a captive audience, let's start lesson one."

Her eye couldn't follow, so quickly did Mike move. His fishing line hissed through the air, fluttering like a leaf to the water's surface, barely disturbing the smooth rush of the swollen current.

"Okay, now you try." He stepped back, ducking just in time to avoid the lethal swing of her arm back over her head. "Whoa, there! The idea is to get the hook into the *water.*"

"Oh, Lord, I'm sorry, Mike. When you did it, it looked so easy. But the pole and line just didn't go where I aimed them."

"That's okay. Now that you understand the wrong way, let's see if you can get it right."

He came closer, tucking his own rod into the back of his belt, and put his hands over hers. They both stopped for a moment, each enjoying the remembered touch of the other. The warmth of his fingers in the icy air was a gentle shock to her senses, not at all unpleasant. The pressure of his body behind her, cradling hers protectively, brought a breathless feeling of comfort and sensuous warmth. For a fleeting instant his arms tightened around her, the heat he generated seeping through her clothing, even through the heavy rubberized canvas of the waders, into her blood, erasing the dampness and chill. Any other discomfort seemed far away and definitely worthwhile.

It would have been so easy to forget where they were or why they were here.

A yell from downstream where Helena was grappling with her suddenly bent rod and taut line broke Anne's momentary distraction.

"She's got something! Oh, Mike, look! It's a *fish!*"

"No kidding—a fish! How 'bout that!" He stepped back quickly, chuckling, and Anne laughed at herself, hearing the foolish excitement in her voice, knowing as he didn't that it was not all due to Helena's catch.

"Daddy, Mac, look at him; he's humongous! I think I . . . oh, darn!" The sudden limpness of the line, the rod snapping back to its natural state, were evidence of the wily trout's wealth of experience. It had slipped the hook and vanished beneath the foaming water, where it would live to grapple on other days with other fishermen and other hooks.

"Well, babe, if nothing else, trout fishing teaches you patience. Don't forget, it doesn't come quick or easy, but when it happens, it's worth the wait."

"An ideal to live by," Anne murmured, looking at him quizzically, as Helena turned away to go on with her search for a more careless trout. "I never realized fishing was such a philosophical pastime. I figured it was just another excuse for the good ol' boys to get together for beer drinking and challenges, like a game . . . you know, a 'guy' thing, man against nature, all that macho stuff."

"Well, I suppose it is for some, but I think

people who enjoy trout fishing are a different breed."

"Different? How?" Anne was enthralled with this chance to see what lay beneath the surface of the Michael Novak he allowed to be visible.

"It's a solitary sport." He glanced over at Helena. "Even when you're not alone you're . . . alone. There's a kind of . . . I don't know . . . a thoughtful dimension, between the world of fish and water and the larger world, and that outer one somehow becomes less important."

Anne studied him, then looked around, aware now of the sharp clarity, the scent of moist leaves and dark earth, the crisp smell of autumn. "Trout live in nice places. Is that what you mean, that fishing is about just . . . being there?"

Mike nodded, smiling. He scooped up a handful of water, letting it flow between his outstretched fingers and trickle back to the passing current. "That's why I get so pissed off when someone comes along and spoils it, deliberately, the ones who don't give a damn!"

They shared an unbroken silence for a few moments, punctuated only by the splash of water on the rocks along the shore and the quiet sound of an occasional bird brushing through the branches above their heads.

"Thank you, Mike. Thank you very much."

He started and turned his head to her. "For what?"

"Oh, for all this," she glanced around them. "For letting me see, showing me . . ."

He flushed and shook his head. "Come on, it's getting late. Pretty soon it'll be time for lunch, and I still owe you that lesson." He came close again and lifted her arm, angling the rod back over her shoulder, careful now to keep some space between their bodies. It was too easy to give in to the feelings he always had when he was close to her, too easy to forget her attachment to her late husband, to forget his own resolve and what the past had taught him. . . .

"Now, hold the rod firmly and keep your upper arm relaxed, elbow in."

Anne tried again.

"No, Annie, remember: You're fly-fishing, not crocheting!"

"Chauvinist!" She frowned in concentration, vainly trying to understand what she was doing wrong. By now he must truly regret allowing her in the car, she mused, no less giving up his treasured handmade resin-impregnated Orvis bamboo magic wand! But he was as patient and sweet-tempered as an altar boy. She wondered when the other shoe would fall!

She made one more attempt.

"Ah, nice! You did it!"

Anne felt a rush of pride. She'd done it! Only, what was *it* and how had she done *it*? If she ever found that out, she could bask in the sunshine of success.

"Now, can you do it again?"

He certainly had an uncanny knack for reading her mind. Well, shoot, self-confidence was the first step to success, wasn't it? Did he think she couldn't even learn to put a hook in water without being led by the hand every step of the way? She decided, considering the last twenty minutes, the question was better left unanswered.

"Well, of course I can! I—"

"Hey, Dad, is it time to eat yet? I'm starving!"

Anne gave fervent silent thanks for Helena's bottomless appetite. Saved by the bell—or the bologna, as the case might be. "Yes, that's a great idea, Mike. I'm kind of hungry, too."

"Let's not go into that now. I think we've covered that ground before." His crinkly eyes and wide grin spoke volumes. Obviously, *his* memory was just fine, thanks! Anne wondered if you could strangle a smart ass with fishing line.

Twelve

After a lunch of Caroline's cold broiled chicken, hot coffee, and Anne's contribution of chocolate brownies, they sat on the bank just talking, the occasional silences restful and pleasant. At least *their* silence was restful. Helena had brought a small transistor and headphones, and she now sat beneath the tree, her entire body keeping time with an invisible rock group banging out their dubious rhythms in her ears and her head, leaving Mike and Anne in blissful ignorance of Helena's chosen entertainment.

It was a good, comfortable time, shared by people at ease and happy with each other's company. Even the weather cooperated. The sun shone through the fir trees and the flame- and gold-covered branches of the aspen and maples, dappling the dry grass bank with shifting patterns of light and shade. After they'd packed away the last of their picnic, Anne sat propped against a tree trunk while

Mike began to get his gear together again for another try in the stream. He nudged Helena's bottom with his toe and jerked a thumb toward the river. She nodded back and rose, stowing the transistor in with the rest of the gear.

"Okay, Daddy, I'm going, I'm going!" And within seconds she was headed for midstream, still singing softly, moving in the familiar rhythm of the song she'd been listening to.

Mike smiled with love, then turned back to Anne.

"I know I'm repeating myself, Mike, but . . . thank you."

He looked at her, content to enjoy the picture she made in her faded jeans and baggy sweatshirt, her cheeks pink from the crisp fall air, her grey-frosted hair unkempt and wind-tossed, her eyes bright and glowing. Then he roused himself. "Don't thank me . . . you haven't caught anything yet," he teased. He felt marvelous, more relaxed and at peace with himself than he had in a long time.

"Ah, you ain't seen nothin' yet, as the man said." She smiled companionably at him, then looked around at the trees . . . at the swift-flowing river . . . at Helena already back at her spot a few yards away. "But I just wanted to thank you for a beautiful day. I can't tell you what this has meant to me. I feel better out here than I have for . . . well, for years, maybe. I can't explain it, but it's like I've come together out here. Like I'm becoming whole again. Ah," she stood up then, brushing off the seat of her pants, "I guess that sounds dumb or crazy. Anyway, I'm having a great time today, thanks to you two. I really appreciate it."

"Me, too, Anne." He looked steadily at her, all thoughts of fishing forgotten. "Me, too."

They stared at each other far longer than they knew, and it was Anne who looked away first. Because she knew if she hadn't, he'd have seen all the things that had been hidden, that she'd hidden from herself, that were still too new to bear the light of his gaze. Not now, not yet. She wasn't ready, and she wondered if there would ever be a day when she was. But she knew right now was too soon.

"Well," he inhaled deeply, turning away, "I think it's time to try one more time. I don't like to admit a fish is smarter than I am," he laughed. Laughter was always a convenient way to evade the deeper, more troubling emotions, the ones that demanded decisions, that raised questions when you had no answers. But he was running out of laughter, and excuses, and time. He felt it slipping away at an ever-increasing rate and he didn't know what he was going to do when it came to an end.

"Do you remember what you learned this morning?"

She raised her brows. "Yes, the memory doesn't go *that* fast, you know. I think I can still dredge up some recall. This is a rod, that's a fly, and you are a smart-ass macho know-it-all! Have I got it all right?" she asked sweetly.

His yelp of laughter was loud enough to make Helena look up for a moment. "Yeah, I think you have," he said at last. "Oh, yeah, you've got it, all right. And I assume you understand all about fishing, too."

"Of course," she smiled back, "I understand perfectly, thank you." She raised her eyebrows, expressing surprise that he could doubt it.

"Good!" Her omniscient fishing guru grinned. "Remember to keep your elbow in and stick to the inside curve of the river." He turned around and splashed away to try his own luck, then turned back for one more admonition. "Try that spot over there under those bushes. By the way, if you fall down and your waders fill up, don't panic.

Let the river take you downstream until you hit a shallow spot." He didn't hear her snarl over the sound of the water or see her aggrieved look. He was too busy trying to keep his laughter to himself.

Anne watched through narrowed eyes as he checked his own rod and ran his fingers over the end of the hook, checking something on the barb. In reluctant admiration, she marveled at the quiet grace of his rolling, arching upstream cast. The far end of the line drifted delicately and accurately to a spot behind a fallen log. An inquisitive trout poked its nose into the air for a fraction of a second, then shrewdly dipped beneath the water and disappeared from view, leaving Mike's line bobbing aimlessly on the surface.

No matter. He remained relaxed, waiting patiently, his feet in their ungainly waders planted firmly on the river bottom. A man who had all the time in the world and meant to enjoy every second of it. She envied his air of self-possession and serenity.

Well, she could stand here admiring him for the rest of the afternoon, or she could put to use the lessons he'd taught her. How difficult could this really be? A couple of more tries and she'd have it down pat. She'd show him! This was Anne Ruth Jerome

McClellan he was dealing with, and by God, she could catch any fish this river, and Michael Novak, could throw at her!

Anne tried to imitate the angle of his shoulder, the bend of the arm, the grace, as she cast her nylon filament, *with the No. 12 Adams attached,* as she'd been duly informed, out over the riffling water.

Splash . . . and nothing. Hmmm. All right, once more.

Splash . . . and nothing. Hell's bells, was even Mike Novak worth this? She tried, with arguable success, to hold on to the thought that patience was its own reward.

Oh, yes, this was fun.

And then, on the fifth try . . . victory! Her trout rose suddenly, majestically, from the quieter water beneath the overhanging branches, fins silhouetted against the white froth and the descending sun's golden reflection. He arced above the surface for an instant, in a graceful aquatic ballet, to hover over the hook. Then both feathered fly and fish disappeared beneath the water. There was a tremendous tug on the end of the line, almost jerking the rod from her unsuspecting hands. Anne pulled back, yelling without thought. Mike, and then Helena, splashed to her side as she struggled to control the tautly bowed rod and the fish attached to the other end of it.

"Easy, gently now. Start to reel him in. Play him slowly, Annie, slowly." Mike's calm murmur was in direct contrast to Helena, who was squealing and jumping up and down with excitement, as much as her hip boots permitted.

"Ah, he's a beauty!" Mike pulled out a large net as Anne's line disappeared back into the reel, and the fish was drawn closer and closer to them.

She stared down at the beautiful steelhead trout, ungracious and defiant in its defeat. Caught in the net Mike held, its tail churned and splashed with a magnificent rebellion, fighting capture to the end.

"Mike, he's so huge!" Her eyes were riveted on the fish and it seemed to look back, proud courage in its unblinking stare. Slowly, Anne let out her breath and swallowed.

"Uh . . . look, Mike, I have to tell you . . . I don't think I could ever eat anything I've been in a staring contest with. I . . . I'm sorry, but . . . could we please let him go?"

Mike's smile lit his eyes before he bent over and gently eased the hook from the wide mouth of the still-struggling trout. Then he handed Anne the handle of the net and she tipped it gently to one side. With a disdainful flip of its iridescent tail, it rejoined the teeming life of the river and swam gracefully away.

"Mike, I just couldn't kill him; he fought so hard. And I felt like a *murderer!* He was looking right at me. It just didn't seem right . . ."

"Annie, don't apologize." He put his arm around her shoulder and squeezed for a moment. "I thought you understood. . . . That's what the surgical pliers are for. Remember when I showed you how to press down the barbs? We never keep what we catch. I suppose it's a kind of hand-to-hand combat: You learn too much respect for your adversary to destroy him needlessly. Now someone else'll have a chance to catch him, too."

"You're a nice man, Michael Novak."

"You're not so bad yourself, Annie."

"Oh, jeez, you're both wonderful," Helena mimicked, making a face.

Anne laughed self-consciously. "Well, I thought, for a minute there, I was loony, bonding with a fish." They grinned at each other. "I suppose I'd feel differently about it in the nice civilized confines of a restaurant, surrounded by lemons and butter and dill sauce. But here on his home ground I . . . I just . . ." She blinked suspiciously moist eyes and cleared her throat. "Well, why are we just standing here? Let's get going. We're wasting time and I want to try again!"

Father and daughter smiled at each other with smug superiority at the easy conversion of this new disciple. Anne moved away from the shore, kneeling down awkwardly in the water to grope for the end of her line, checking on the condition of the fly. "I swear, I'm beginning to feel as if I actually belong out here in the middle of a river. I mean, surrounded by it, really a part of it . . . !"

Literally. The relatives of the fish she'd so generously released didn't return the good feeling; another large trout brushed her thigh, energetically splashing her full in the face, which was on level with his agile tail. Startled, she fell back into the water and the frigid stream suddenly began to cascade in a freezing waterfall right over the top of her waders.

"Oh, damn, that's *cold!*"

She tried frantically to rise but the icy water sought its own level inside her waders. "Hey, Mike, *help!*"

Anne was immobilized, thrown off balance by the force of the current. The cold was numbing and she toppled sideways, losing her grip on the rod as she fell. Mike grabbed for it, tossing it on shore as he came quickly toward her. Flailing helplessly in the swift flow of water, Anne remembered his earlier warning and forced herself to stop struggling. *Don't panic. The water's shallow.* In seconds, her rear came to rest at the nearby curve of the riverbank, sliding and bumping along the sandy bottom, none the worse for the intermittent stones and debris it encountered along the way.

Mike splashed up to her only seconds later. "Anne! You all right? What happened?" He assured himself of her safety, then permitted the grin to spread across his face.

"I'm fine! Just dis—g—g—gusted with myself. I didn't realize I w—was in deep water. God, how clumsy can I be!" She looked up at him, annoyance and humiliation on her face. The icy water swirled around her shoulders, splashing up into her face every few seconds. "I can't believe I let that happen!"

"Oh, you're not the first, and you won't be the last. It's a common hazard, along with insect bites and hooks stuck in your skin." Still laughing and shaking his head Mike reached down to help her to her feet. "No, don't try it yourself. There's too much water in the boots to manage alone. For once just relax and let someone else help you!"

Anne knew he was right and she let him

pull her upright. He put his arms around her and held her tightly, as if it were the most natural thing in the world. And as far as she was concerned, it was. Even worms and flies—real flies—would have been worth it if this were her reward.

"Aaaaah-choooo!" Her nose was pressed into his shoulder and the sneeze was muffled, but that didn't conceal the force of it.

"Oh, damn, you're freezing! Helena, quick, run up to the car and bring down the blanket from the back seat." She was already on the way. "And my jacket, too!" he shouted after her.

"Aaaaah-choooo! Oh, Mike, I'm so sorry." Through loudly chattering teeth, Anne tried to apologize. "I've r—ruined your last chance to go f—f—fishing this . . . aaah-chooo! . . . year!" She huddled small inside her soaked clothing, trying not to let the cold wet cloth touch her frozen skin, trying not to move at all. If she were completely immobile, maybe she wouldn't feel the cold quite so much. Dear God, she'd never been so cold in her life!

"Believe me, Anne, I've fished enough in my life so I won't miss it. As long as you're okay!" His voice was filled with intensity as he stared down at her, and she knew it was true. She trembled and Mike couldn't be sure it was from the cold alone. He bent to kiss a droplet of water pearled on the tip of her eyelashes; gently, his mouth moved to her lips. She shivered violently, uncontrollably, and he lifted his head.

"Oh, God, I'm a real horse's ass! I've got to get you out of here!" Pushing aside the loose shoulder straps, Mike lifted her right out of the still-filled waders and half carried her to the shore. After managing to kick off his own boots he sat down, his back braced against the trunk of a heavy old aspen, and pulled her close, cradling her against the shelter of his chest.

"No, don't . . . I'm getting you all wet!"

"Forget it. Just help me a minute, Anne." He began to pull her sodden sweatshirt over her head.

"D—don't, Mike. I'm f—*freezing!*"

"I know, that's why you have to get this off. It's sure not doing you any good!" He started to unbutton the wool shirt she wore beneath her sweatshirt.

"Now, just a minute, mister! What do you think . . . aaahh-chooo! . . . you're d—d—do-ing?" She tried vainly to push away his hands.

"I'm trying to thaw out an icicle! What the hell do you think I'm doing?" He peeled the soaked shirt off her arms, skin bluish-white and goose-bumped in the fading sunlight. "Take my word for it, the way you look right now isn't arousing my hormones!"

"You silver-tongued devil you!" Despite her grey-blue pallor, Anne's eyes flashed for a moment.

Mike removed his down fishing vest, then quickly peeled off his own heavy sweater and pulled it over her head. He wrapped the vest around her and pulled her icy body close into the heat of his own. Ah, well, he smiled to himself, so he'd lied. His body was making him painfully aware of that. Bedraggled, frozen, wet hair plastered to her head and her face, all color gone from her cheeks, lips bloodless—but she was certainly capable of arousing *him!*

"Mike, you'll be too cold. All you've got on now is that thin T-shirt! I c—can't let you do that—"

"Oh, yes you can." Mike tightened his embrace and Anne stopped struggling, giving in and enjoying the intimacy, despite the chill that seemed to have infiltrated her very bones. Even if she'd been offered an electric blanket just then, she very much doubted she'd have moved. He'd pulled her out of the river, up on shore, and now she was in his arms—and still in deep water!

He rubbed his cheek over the top of her head, tucked there into the spot just beneath his chin, all the time massaging her arms with his big hands, waiting impatiently for Helena to return yet selfishly wanting this secluded intimacy to last. Unable to stop himself, he slid his hands under the vest and the sweater.

"Mmm, Mike, that's nice." Her mouth was pressed against his throat and her breath touched his skin, warming him. For a few seconds she rested in his arms, trying to still the continuing shudders wracking her frame. She remembered vividly the other time he'd held her this way. "This is getting to be a habit," Anne whispered through still-chattering teeth.

"A very nice one, too!" He pulled her even closer, rocking her in his arms, bending to kiss her closed eyelids. The tiny spidery veins beneath the fragile skin showed pale blue against her milky colored flesh. His tongue darted out to follow the delicate tracery.

Anne sighed and wriggled closer. Her body was enclosed in a solid block of ice, yet deep inside she was burning, a white-hot glow spreading through her veins. "I th—think I'm beginning to f—feel . . . aaah-chooo! . . . a little w—warmer."

"Yeah, me, too!" God, he was going to burn up, right here beside this icy river! He moved his hands up the length of her spine beneath the sweater and her shudders were slower now, her skin perhaps marginally warmer, or at least less cold. His fingers spanned her waist and slipped down, peeling away the clinging thermal underwear and jeans. No, better wait for Helena and the blanket.

"We . . . we really ought to get your jeans off, too." His breath was labored, his voice shaky.

"Mmm, s—subtlety is not y—your strong suit . . . aaah-chooo!"

"Don't you know this is the recommended treatment for hypothermia? I'm doing this for your own good." The warm breath of his whisper curled around her ear and she held on to him even more tightly, small delicious shivers radiating through her body.

"Medicinal p—purposes only, hmmm?"

He closed his eyes, nodding.

"Mmmm," she sighed softly, "if I believed that, I'd be in the market for swampland in Florida." But she didn't move from his arms. Her head rested against his chest and the accelerated, steady drum of his heartbeat was hypnotically reassuring. Between it and the gentle caress of his fingers, Anne drifted, with occasional wracking shudders, in a misty netherworld of dreams and desire.

In seconds the sound of Helena crashing through the underbrush at breakneck speed broke their reverie. "Hey, Dad, here's the blanket and your jacket." They had just enough time to sit upright and move a few inches apart, before she skidded to a stop beside them.

"Are you okay, Mac? Boy, you're a mess! You must be *frozen!*"

"Ah, thanks a lot, I really needed that!" Anne grinned ruefully and reached for the blanket Helena held out to her. "Mike, put on your jacket or you'll freeze to death."

Helena looked at her father, noticing that his sweater was now worn by Anne. Then she spied Anne's soaked clothing nearby and grinned slyly at the two adults busily ignoring each other. "Gee, you were smart to take off your clothes. You could get frostbite or something." She didn't even try to hide her glee. "It's a good thing Daddy was here to help. He knows all about survival in the woods and all that stuff." The grin spread wider across her mouth. Fifteen was not so dumb, it said. Fifteen knew a few things that a parent might not realize!

"Uh . . . yes, your d—dad was very . . .

uh . . . helpful." Anne ducked her head and wrapped herself tightly in the large blanket, shivering anew without the warm shelter of Mike's arms to ward off the cold.

"Anne, pull off your jeans, quick. Your legs must feel like popsicles by now." He swung around immediately. "And you, young lady, you can get those waders out of the water and collect the fishing gear." His stern look quieted Helena's mouth before she could utter any more observations. But her laughing eyes and gleeful expression said it all.

Her cheeks flaming despite the cold, Anne clutched the blanket close to her and turned away. Under its protection, she wriggled awkwardly from the clutches of the clinging denim, first removing her waterlogged socks and shoes. Hopping on one foot, then the other, she huddled within the protective folds of her improvised tent. She was profoundly grateful to hear Mike's next words.

"Okay, let's get back to the car and head for home. We've had as much fun as we can stand for today, don't you think?" He smiled benignly and winked broadly at Helena. Laden with the lion's share of their equipment, she began to trudge up the trail to the car, followed closely behind by a barefoot

Anne, Mike, and his burden of three pairs of hip boots.

Anne stumbled and he reached out with his free hand to steady her, grasping her shoulder through the coarse woolen fabric. Mike smoothed the matted hair back from her brow, letting his hand linger on her neck, his fingers gliding across the delicate flesh. He felt her subtle shiver beneath his touch, felt his own answering reaction. He dipped his fingers under the edge of the blanket, circling the arch of her neck, idly following the line of her throat, then farther, along the smooth ridge of collarbone. He felt the rush of her pulse beneath his fingers, a sudden sharp intake of breath, and gently pulled his hand back. But his arm remained around her shoulder all the way up the path to the parking spot. Well, she *might* need his help, with that clumsy blanket wrapped around her.

Without any prompting, Helena scooted into the back of the car and Mike helped Anne into the front seat, as close as he could get her beside him. He turned on the motor, got the heater going full blast, and then stowed the rest of their gear before he climbed behind the wheel. As they pulled out on the trail to the main road, Mike was already speaking to his office on the radio. "Tell the State boys to get over toward the top of the Caroll . . . see if they can find any place where a heavy truck has been down near the water. It wouldn't be too recent, but they might find some tire tracks, footprints. We haven't had rain lately, so there might still be something. It's a longshot, but . . . oh, tell them I'm bringing in some specimens for their lab."

He replaced the mike and looked over at Anne. "You sure are waterlogged. Caroline will have my head for this, you know." He shook his head ruefully. "And she'll be right."

"That's silly. If I'm a klutz, it's not your fault!" She reached from beneath the woolen folds and patted his knee. Before she could move it away, he rested his right hand on top of hers, effectively keeping it just where he wanted it. Anne looked at him but he was carefully staring straight ahead at the shadowy road. She settled back contentedly, the solid contour of his thigh under her palm. It felt very good, embarrassingly good. "Don't worry, Mike. I'll protect you from Caroline."

A loud whoop of laughter emanated from the back seat. "Daddy, want me to vouch for you, too? If I know Aunt Cally, you'll need all the help you can get!" She slid down on her spine, lounging across the width of the seat, feet resting on the opposite window.

Mike grinned and headed the car southwest on Route 116, back toward Whitefield. It was a short drive, but Anne's hand resting warmly on his leg, her fingers taunting him with their intermittent caresses, made the distance an eternity. Her wandering fingers made the Chief of Police come dangerously close to climbing a tree with his Jeep.

Less than forty minutes later, they were within sight of the house, its brightly lit windows signaling Caroline's welcome. Instead of passing the drive, Mike turned in. "Helena, I'm dropping you off to get started on your homework. Tell Aunt Caroline not to wait dinner for me. I want to take Anne home and make sure she doesn't get pneumonia."

"But, Daddy, I haven't any home—" He caught Helena's eye in the rearview mirror and his hard stare squelched the rest of her protest. She quickly climbed down to the driveway. "Oh, right! I forgot the . . . uh . . . the book report! Yeah, I have to do a book report." She leaned in the open door for a moment and kissed Anne on the cheek. "I hope you had a good time, even if—" She gestured at the heap of sodden clothing lying at Anne's feet. "Remember, you were the only one who caught anything!"

"I had the most wonderful day I can remember in a long time, sweetheart. I'll go home and get into some warm clothes, and I'll be fine. Don't worry." Anne waved a small salute as Helena disappeared through the front door.

She and Mike were well on their way before Anne said anything. She wriggled closer to his side, the steady blast of the heater dissipating the last of her chill. "Why, Mike, I think it's just *wonderful* how conscientious you are about Helena's 'homework.'" Anne looked up and batted her eyelashes at him.

Mike chuckled, tucking her hand into his and holding it close to his chest. He rubbed his thumb over and around her fingers and felt them warm beneath his touch.

"It's not Helena's homework I'm thinking of, it's ours."

Thirteen

Beyond the thud of the closing door, the apartment stood silent, waiting. The faint light of the bedroom lamp coming through the door exaggerated the late afternoon shadows of the living room. Automatically, Anne's hand reached for the light switch. Mike stopped her.

"No, Annie, you don't need it. Not now. Not tonight." Somehow he was very sure she had to face this night without any reminders of the past.

Anne wanted to reach out, to touch his cheek but, suddenly shy, kept her hand clenched in the fold of the blanket. In the twilight of early evening, his features were hazy, indistinct. "I . . . I'm not sure what happens next."

"Aren't you?" Mike's husky whisper clouded her feelings with unnamed impulses, forgotten sensations, and his steady gaze held her fast. He put his hand under her chin, rough fingers tracing a feathery caress over her cheek, her hair, his thumb stroking the ridge of her brow.

"Uh, would you like something to drink? Coffee? Or some wine, or . . ." Anne found it strangely difficult to draw a breath. His touch, she thought dreamily, seemed to have that effect on her. "Damn," she muttered, staring down at her feet. "You'd think at my age, I'd be ready with all the glib words."

"You only need one word, Anne, the right word."

Her shaky knees ready to collapse, Anne walked unsteadily to the couch. The ride home had been quiet, a comfortable silence between them at first. But the closer they got to town, the greater grew her worry. What if this was a mistake?

Mike stood where he was a moment longer, barely able to make out Anne's figure huddled on the couch. Deliberately, he opened his fists, jammed down into his pockets, willing himself to listen, to understand. His mind counseled rational behavior. His libido, on the other hand . . . well, his mind and his body were not quite in sync at this point.

"What's wrong, Anne?" His voice was calm, not betraying the tension beneath the surface.

"Mike, it seems so fast."

He didn't need to see her face to know what was written there. Indecision, doubt. Guilt. "Anne, we're two mature, experienced adults. . . ."

"That's it! I'm not! I'm not experienced at all!" She rose from the couch, eluding his outstretched hand, and walked restlessly back and forth, kicking the twisted blanket from her ankles. "When I married Paul I was a virgin. Can you believe it? The last of the species in captivity, I think!" She shrugged. "We were married over twenty years, Mike, and he was the only man I ever . . . ever . . . since he died . . ." Anne's voice cracked, then went on, wry, self-mocking. "God, this is embarrassing! Well, I'm sure you get the picture." She sank down again on the cushions, huddled in the blanket's folds, feet tucked under her. She lay her head against the back of the couch, eyes closed. All in all it had been an exhausting day.

And the day wasn't over. Mike lowered himself carefully into a chair facing her. They had to clear this up, but it was not a time to push her, either physically or verbally.

"Anne, what are you afraid of?" he asked quietly. "Is it Paul? Are you afraid you're being unfaithful?" The thought startled him. He'd never been fortunate enough to know that kind of love and devotion between a husband and wife. Mike chewed on his lip. Lucky guy! Paul McClellan had been dead and buried for over two years, his life cut short by a tragic whim of nature, and yet Mike felt a gut-wrenching stab of envy for this man he had never met and would never know. What must it have been like to have the love of a woman given so completely and unreservedly?

A palpable tension stretched between them, and Mike found himself straining to keep from leaping up and pulling her into his arms, forcing her to forget everything, every*one*, but him.

Now just hold it, Novak. What do you really want from all this, anyway? Right now, he was afraid to find out. Afraid to find out he might have been wrong . . . about her, about himself. He'd made a conscious effort to avoid permanency in his life as far as women were concerned. He had been convinced for a long time that it was an illusion, one he didn't need or want. The principles of a lifetime were shattering under his feet. Perhaps she was right, perhaps it was too fast.

"No, it's not guilt," she answered his last words quietly. "I thought about this a great deal when . . . when . . ." She flushed, remembering the night of the big blackout.

"Oh, I've missed Paul, that's true. But I think I've accepted reality. I'm not clutching at the past, Mike, believe me. He would have been the last man in the world to expect me to stop living. He was a man who thoroughly enjoyed life, and I think he loved me too much to want me to leap on the funeral pyre."

Mike listened intently to Anne's halting voice.

"It's hard to put into words. I've been thinking about this for some time now, you and I, and—" Anne was suddenly aware of how that sounded. Embarrassed, she sputtered, "I mean, I thought about what *could* happen *if* we . . . that is, if you . . ."

"I understand, Anne. You're not the only one who's been thinking." Thinking? Sometimes, lately, he'd wondered if his brain had permanently relocated south of his belt buckle.

"It's been a very long time for me, and I just don't want to . . . uh . . . disappoint you. It's different for you. You're used to . . . to . . . you know," she ended lamely.

"What the hell do you think I am? Some minor league Don Juan?"

"Oh, God, Mike, there's nothing minor league about you!"

Without thought, he rose, pulling her from

the sanctuary of the enveloping sofa cushions. "Ah, Annie, Annie, I sure as hell would like to know where you got the idea I'm Whitefield's resident Casanova." His chuckle was low, husky. "I assure you, I have neither the time, the inclination, nor the stamina to fill that role!"

She frowned, skeptical.

"Well, but I thought—"

"I *know* what you thought!"

She closed her eyes, blushing, no words on hand to answer him.

He pulled her closer into his embrace, stroking her back through the rough cloth, marveling at the sense of completion he experienced with her body nestled against his. His cheek rested on her head and the soft curls tickled his nose. It was a pleasantly disturbing sensation.

"Still jumping to conclusions, I notice." *You ass. Of course she's jumping—you're the one who pushed her!* He remembered Honey and almost groaned aloud. "Guess there's something about me that inspires it, hmm?"

"Yes, there's . . . something about you, all right . . ." Her throaty murmur floated between them, the air almost shimmering with urgent unspoken thoughts. Anne tilted her head to stare up into his face, clearer now because he was so close. Mike's hands still clasped her arms, crushing the coarse cloth. He drew her closer until her head rested on his chest, his labored breathing visible through the thin cotton T-shirt he had on under his jacket. She remembered she still wore his sweater.

"I'd better get out of your things."

She stopped abruptly and they stared at each other.

There are moments in life when all things are suddenly clear, as the quiet water of a lake on a summer afternoon or the cloudless sky of a spring morning. In the gloomy dusk of a chilly autumn day, Anne and Mike found that moment.

Slowly, Mike lowered his head. Consumed by a hunger, a need that cut deep and sharp, his mouth touched her parted lips. He felt the soft caress of her breath, moist and warm, and he couldn't get enough of the taste, the scent, the feel of her under his hands, his mouth. He pulled her still closer and lifted her inches from the floor, sliding her slowly up along his taut body, torturing himself with the feel of her against his arousal. Aching with want, he moved his hips against hers, unable to resist now that she was so close, calling forth an answering flare of desire, before he let her slowly back down to the floor.

Throbbing through her veins, a rush of sensation inundated all fear and reason. She burned, dear God, how she burned! Anne yearned to wrap her arms around him, banish every obstacle, postpone all the qualms until some other time, until tomorrow. Tomorrow was soon enough to question and worry and doubt. Now, this moment, this was all she wanted.

Anne struggled to free herself from the enveloping folds of the blanket, to hold him, to touch his face, his hair, his cheek. She shifted beneath Mike's hands, and the blanket pooled around their feet. In seconds, his heavy wool sweater followed.

With a blind, unquenchable need, he drew her nearer again and for once Anne was grateful for the darkness. How would her body look to him? she wondered. She had a vivid recollection of Honey standing tall and firm and slender beside Mike; Anne could never again look as firm and lithe and lovely as the younger woman. Too many years, *too many cinnamon buns and brownies,* she admitted ruefully, not to mention a child and the force of gravity. Better to imagine, in the dark, than to see and be disillusioned. At least for a while she could forget comparisons, forget the years . . . forget everything but here, now.

Over the thin fabric that confined her breasts, Mike's fingers skimmed lightly, just brushing the soft swells rising above the lacy edge, dry now from her body's heat. *And that's a lot of heat,* she thought and gasped, arcing toward him, her body instinctively seeking his touch.

Lovingly, he caressed her, and now every part of her body ached for more. His too-gentle fingertips were maddening, and Anne was totally enraptured, beyond time or place or caring. Desire—sudden, unheralded, irresistible— swept away every thought or hesitation.

"Ahh, Mike, I . . . I want . . ."

"What? Say it, Anne," he groaned. "Tell me this is right. Tell me . . ."

"Yes, oh, yes, Mike! Yes!" Her hand on his rough cheek, she kissed him, sliding her mouth across his, hot, open, ravenous for the taste of his kiss. He still carried the faint scent of autumn air, trees, and the river, all mingled with his own special smell, coffee and tobacco and *Mike,* and Anne breathed it in, giddy with an excitement she couldn't recall feeling for a long time.

She pulled back slightly, her hands still caressing his neck, his jaw, skidding urgently across his shoulders and chest, then down to his waist. The thin cotton of Mike's shirt offered no resistance, and she quickly dragged it up and over his head.

That first warm touch of her hands on his skin drove Mike on. He groaned when Anne's fingers danced lightly across his chest, lighting small fires along his nerve endings that would not be quenched until . . .

"No fair," he whispered in her ear as she trembled in his arms. "My turn." Mike fumbled with the clasp of her bra, and it was gone. When his tongue touched one tiny rigid crest, Anne thought she'd burst from the waiting, the wanting. She'd loved Paul, but she'd never wanted him with such hunger, such need. She wanted to touch Mike, to learn his body, to feel the heat and strength of him; it was no longer enough to hold him and be held, to kiss him and be kissed. A gnawing emptiness consumed her, and fear and caution were forgotten.

"Mike? Mike, I . . . . Now, Mike, please!"

"Yes! God, yes, Anne!" He slid his hands over her hips, dragging the cotton panties down, caressing her thighs, the length of her legs, here and there pressing his hot open mouth to the cool skin. Anne felt her bones dissolve. She sank to her knees, Mike's body as close to her, as much a part of her, as her own skin.

His hands moved across Anne's trembling body, and she marveled at the myriad sensations that shook her. Like coming to life in the center of a wondrous kaleidoscope, color and light and pleasure and so many things she'd never even suspected. And where his hands moved, his mouth followed.

She shivered. Her hands, no longer needing any conscious thought from her, slipped down Mike's spine to rest on the belt riding low on his hips. With a wanton teasing that was new to her, Anne's fingers slowly eased beneath the leather and denim, moving languorously, the edge of her nails scraping gently over his flesh, and she felt the spasm of his reaction when her hand finally rested on the fabric stretched taut below his belly.

He groaned aloud, afraid she would stop.

Anne fumbled with the buckle and then the zipper. But he didn't help her. She was glad. She needed to know this was her choice, her need fulfilled by her own desire. The room was still, save for the quiet slur of their quickened breathing, the raspy sound of the zipper.

Anne's touch burned on Mike's skin. As one they moved, still embracing, mouths fused in a hot, moist, furious kiss. They knelt facing each other and Anne lay back, her arms reaching up to pull him down to her. The air was chill on her skin where his body's heat had been only seconds before. "Come here," she whispered. "It's cold down here alone."

"Oh, Annie, *cold* isn't exactly the word I'd use!" he moaned. He had quickly discarded what remained of his clothing and now he lay beside her, his leg caressing the length of hers, before he suddenly whispered a short curse. "Wait, Anne. I just remembered . . . before we . . . uh . . . go any further, I've got to get . . . something . . ." He reached behind her, struggling to get hold of his jeans, all the time unwilling to let her go completely. "Ah, there it is." He found the pocket, then turned away for a moment, the small latex circlet almost hidden in his hand.

"Mike," she chuckled, more reassured than she'd thought, "I'm glad you were so thoughtful, but on the other hand, no one wants to be considered a sure thing."

"Hell," he turned back to her again, "if you knew how nervous I was after you called back this morning, and how I debated over taking it with me, you wouldn't worry about being taken for granted, believe me!"

Mike could only make out the dim outline of her form in the sparse light filtering through the window from the square outside and from the lamp in the other room. But it was enough. He touched her throat, kissed her mouth, and followed his hand with his lips. Anne shuddered as he gently fondled first one, then the other breast, cherishing each, tenderly worrying the rigid tips between his teeth, then bathing each in the warmth of his tongue. She arched and he filled his mouth with her.

"M . . . Mike, oh, oh God . . ." She couldn't have begun to imagine the sensations bursting upon her at this moment. There were no words in her world, in any world, to do justice to this feeling.

"I swear, Michael Novak," she sighed, her voice ragged, urgent, "if you don't stop fooling around and get down to business, I'll . . . *oh!*"

And the kaleidoscope shifted.

"You'll . . . mmmm, God, you're sweet, Annie . . . ! You'll what?"

Anne could almost hear the smile in his whisper. She was smiling, too.

"Oh, Mike, I think I'll probably do most anything you want!" she sighed softly. When he moved inside her, as gentle as a spring breeze, she was filled with an exquisite feeling of joy.

A tender smile on his mouth that Anne couldn't see, he rested his head on her forehead, willing himself to quietly absorb every last bit of pleasure in the moment, his flesh joined to hers, resting within hers. Their faces touched and Mike felt the gentle tickle of her eyelashes against his cheek. Resting his weight on his elbows, their hands clasped tightly, fingers entwined, he exerted all his strength to control his body for just a few seconds more; he wanted this to last. But his body would not be patient for long. He gazed down, trying to watch her face as he began to move, slowly, rhythmically. But he couldn't see her features, and then it didn't matter. They were both caught in the ancient pulse, the joining of man and woman that was eternal promise, eternal fulfillment.

Anne gasped aloud once as Mike moved and then she began to move with him, faster, faster, every nerve and cell and muscle in her body part of their union. The seconds skimmed past in one timeless exquisite blur, her hot supple skin slipping against the coarser texture of his. Passion and joy, lust and tenderness, swirled together in a rainbow blur, and then the kaleidoscope burst in a glimmering shower, melting deliciously around them into lazy, peaceful darkness.

"Wow, Novak! You think you could patent that?"

One elbow resting on the plush carpet, Mike lifted his head slowly, straining to see her face, a grin widening his mouth. "Almost as much fun as landing a trout, hmm?"

Anne nodded and held him tighter. But a worm of unease crept into her thoughts for an instant. This fish was no keeper, either. He might appear to rest in the net for a moment, an illusion that could bring her transient pleasure, but he was destined to return to his freedom.

Strange. She had wondered what it would be like if they ever made love, but she'd never thought any further. Just as well. She had the feeling that considering a future involving Mike Novak would not bear much thought. Fortunately, the darkness veiled her expression. She wondered what it would have told him.

The next moment she was grinning to herself. The muffled sibilance of his steady breath in her ear told her she needn't have worried. Mike wouldn't have noticed anything. He was asleep.

She lay beneath him, his cheek resting on hers, his steady breathing a gentle drift of air in her ear, his heartbeat thudding above her own in comfortable cadence. The cool air hadn't stolen any of the warmth from his body, and though asleep, he still held her secure in his strong arms.

Even with the heavy weight of his body, Anne was filled with a sudden buoyant lightness. After all, permanent attachments had been the farthest thing from her mind. And, she shrugged mentally, perspective once more in place, *that's* what she should have remembered from the beginning: She and Mike were not carving permanent niches in each other's lives.

Anne felt a wry grin lift her lips. It was certainly a radical shift in her moral perspective, but her disapproving ancestors could be reassured it was only a temporary fall from grace. Mike couldn't be expected to indefinitely be an item on her social calendar. He'd move on. But however long their relationship lasted, at least she'd proven she was a healthy, normal woman; her ego could be comfortable with the fact that she was still desirable enough to attract, even momentarily, a man like Mike Novak. Better to be the flavor of the month than to stay untouched in the freezer forever!

She rested content in his embrace for a few more moments, then carefully eased out from under him. Anne pulled the discarded blanket across the floor and gently covered his bare back, her fingers straying for an instant in a tender caress down the length of his spine, seeing in the near-darkness with her hands his power and strength at rest now, remembering how he felt inside her.

Knock it off, Annie, my girl! She pulled back sharply, shaking her head at the images she had called forth. Standing, she wondered which she needed more—a good hot shower or a good cold one.

She stood and turned to the bedroom, and only then did the blackness of the room penetrate her consciousness, and it was the sound of Mike's even breathing, the mass of his body beside her, that kept the sudden rush of panic at bay. The blackness was not complete or unrelieved, and that was what she held on to. She could see . . . something. Not much, but something.

For a while he had banished the fear, but it was an old and faithful companion and it returned quickly. She clamped her teeth shut and stumbled to the bedroom, relief flooding her at the sight of the lighted lamp unobstructed and in clear view. Still shaking, she walked quickly to the bathroom door, stopping for a moment at the sight of her naked body in the full-length mirror.

Well, not so great, but on the other hand not as bad as it might have been. Although she did look as if she were smuggling cottage cheese in her thighs!

It was the muffled sound of rushing water that roused Mike from his dreamless sleep. Groggy at first, he couldn't recall where he was or why he was lying on the floor. Then, in a rush, it came back and he smiled to himself. For a moment he had the impulse to join her in the shower, but he stayed where he was. He knew instinctively Anne wouldn't want that. The intimacy they'd shared had not dissolved all barriers. She would still reserve to herself some of them. And for him, too, barriers remained. One night, one woman, would not erase them all. Although, perhaps, it was a beginning.

The thought startled him, disturbing him. Mike sat up abruptly, the coarse wool blanket settling around his hips unnoticed, and groped for his discarded pants and the slim packet of small cigars. He exhaled a circle of smoke as he leaned back against the couch, one arm resting on an upraised knee.

Barriers. Now that was something to consider. He realized how many had already fallen by the wayside since he'd met Anne McClellan. A dangerous lady, he mused wryly. He recalled vividly that first early morning meeting. The minute he'd driven up to her shop, seen her silhouetted in the doorway, the soft curves of her body limned in the bright light of the kitchen, it had hit him like a fist in the stomach, involuntarily, unexpectedly.

And the disturbing sensation still pervaded his body, a sensual catalyst battering at self-restraint. Until tonight. When she held him, answering his kiss with a fire to match his own, he'd known it was useless to search for self-control. It had disappeared as quickly as the trout had disappeared back into the river this afternoon. And he was left with questions.

Recalling how she'd come to life in his arms, how she'd responded to his kisses, his touch, he felt a stirring in his body all over again. *Damn! Novak . . . you've got big trouble.*

He was still shaking his head when Anne came back into the room, wrapped in the silk caftan she'd been saving in the back of her closet for "someday." Serious or not, future or not, there was still a matter of pride, more important now, perhaps, as she closed in on fifty. She wanted to look good for Mike Novak.

The moon had risen above the trees in the park below. A single shaft bathed his head in silvery light, tracing the outline of his upper body in iridescence against the window beyond. Anne stood frozen in the doorway, taken with the unreality of the picture before her. The room glowed with an indirect luminosity, and Mike at its center. She pushed away the notion—it was a trick of light and whimsy. Talk about getting older! She'd never been subject to fits of fancy before. Surely she wasn't going to begin now.

Only the whisper of silk rustling around her legs alerted Mike to her presence. She knelt beside him, her hand on his, their eyes level. It was hard to read her expression and he feared, in that instant, he would see blame on her face.

"Remember me?" she asked quietly. The gentle pressure of her hand on his eased Mike's worry and the relief he felt was overwhelming.

He welcomed her back with a broad smile and, before she could resist pulled her across his lap, cradling her against his body. "Mmm, you smell nice!" He buried his face in her hair, inhaling the scent of soap and shampoo and clean-scrubbed skin.

"A definite improvement on 'eau de trout,' wouldn't you say?"

"Mmm, yeah, I would definitely say!" He held her, quiet and unmoving save for his lips nibbling around her ear, the tender spot just behind it, his tongue making slow, delicate forays into the dips and curves of the sensitized flesh. God, he loved to feel her respond like that in his arms!

"That's . . . mmm, don't stop . . . that's so nice," she sighed. He stroked the curve of her spine through the gossamer silk, tracing every inch up the length of her back, then down again, a caress she found hypnotically delicious. She snuggled farther into his embrace, her voice muffled against his chest, and smiled when he shivered at the touch of her lips moving on his skin.

"Now, of course, we're supposed to light cigarettes and feel smug," he mumbled against her hair.

"Oh, Mike, what a shame I don't smoke," she purred innocently. "Does that mean there's nothing else to do?" He knew she was smiling—he could hear it in her voice—a lazy, dreamy smile, and even the imagining sent a shaft of heat through his body.

"We can innovate," he drawled, kissing the hollow at the base of her throat. "I notice you're very good at . . . innovating."

"Thanks . . . I think." She trailed a finger lazily across his chest, drawing a delicate pattern over his shoulder and down his arm.

Suddenly, he shifted pulling her up straighter on his lap. "Sit here, like this. I want to look at you." The night cast shadows across her face, but he could still see the glint of moonlight in the dark pools of her eyes, her slightly parted lips, the damp curls drying into a silver-lit gamin mop around her head. He positioned her so she was sitting atop his thighs, her knees on either side, imprisoning him. It was a captivity he had no desire to escape.

He reached out and placed one hand on her breast, softly unconfined beneath the loose fabric. "You are a beautiful woman. . . ."

"Beautiful! Come on, Mike, you don't have to—"

"I know I don't *have to*." He caressed her through the silk. "You heard me . . . *beautiful*."

"Mike, I'm almost fifty years old—a very well-upholstered fifty, I'm afraid—and even when I was twenty, Miss America didn't have to worry about me!"

"Anne"—he looked straight into her eyes,

forcing her to look back at him—"you're a *woman*. Look, at fifty-three, believe me, I'm not looking for a skinny, plastic-perfect Barbie doll. You're flesh and blood"—he sank his fingers into the softness of her hips—"and very nice flesh and blood! And as far as I'm concerned, every bit of it is terrific." He teased her nipple, visible through the silk, with his tongue, and the moist spot showed dark against the paler fabric. "Just remember, Annie, the only one who wants bones is a dog! As for me . . ." He settled her more firmly in his lap and she was left with no doubts about what *he* wanted.

"Okay," she breathed softly, "I'm a believer." Bolder now than she would have believed possible, she moved, rubbing against him, feeling his hard arousal through wool and silk.

He closed his eyes, head back, the words almost strangling in his throat. "Annie, stop wiggling around. Please!"

"I'm not wiggling. I'm writhing with passion. Jeez, you ain't got no romance in your soul!"

"I'll give you writhing with passion—"

"Oh, I hope so. I sincerely hope so!"

Mike slid his hands to Anne's shoulders, pulling her closer to his mouth. His kiss was relentless, consuming, the fire building suddenly, urgently, in his blood.

Anne tasted the sudden saltiness of her own blood and didn't care. He invaded every inch of her body, every cell, every atom and thought, and she would drown in desire before she would end his kiss. Unbearable heat was licking at her nerve endings, her body alight with the fire of a thousand suns; he must see it shining through her skin, her eyes, must be blinded by it!

"I . . . oh God, don't move for a moment, Anne!" Mike held her away for an instant, his breath harsh and labored. He fumbled with the slippery silk, finally pulling it over her head and freeing her of it. "I want to look at you."

His whisper held her still as he cupped her breasts, gently running his fingers across the nipples gleaming pale silver in the dim translucent light. His soft butterfly touch almost sent her past the edge of restraint. Anne was held in a kind of lassitude, barely swaying. Her body seemed to hold itself still, subtly following his hands where they moved in gentle exploration. Her breasts needed his touch, her shoulders arched as his hands moved across them and down her spine. Her thighs trembled as his hands stroked tender paths across the delicate inner surface of the warm flesh, and the languid dreamy spell held her.

Mike was drifting in the same languorous haze, content for now to learn all the textures and undulations of her body. She didn't quite believe yet what a desirable woman she was. But he knew it! God, his body was certainly making him aware of it!

His hands slid along the lush curve of her bottom and her hips. Suddenly, he felt her stiffen, holding herself very still, as his hands rested on the dark tangle of curls at the delta of her thighs. The pulse of her arousal beat against his palm and she waited, almost afraid to move, caught between dream and reality.

She groaned, then moved convulsively against his hand, head thrown back in abandon, loosed from a world of reality by the magic of his caresses. His thumbs gentled the rigid nub at her core, stroking her until she knew she would burst into flames. And she wanted to burn! Every cell, every nerve end in her body, was connected to this one spot and to his touch. He fondled her until the rippling explosions coursed through her rigid body with the force of a lightning bolt, and the stars finally burst behind her closed eyes.

Anne sagged across his chest, her arms

wrapped around his neck. It was minutes before she could find the strength to speak or move, and then she held back from the truth she was beginning to sense, hiding behind easy flippant words.

"Oh, Novak, you are a man of many surprises. Whatever that was, it registered at least a nine and a half on the Richter Scale!" She sighed contentedly, feeling newfound courage. "Too bad it had to end."

"I'm sure glad you feel that way." He was painfully aware of how much self-control he'd been exercising. Watching the beautiful arousal showing nakedly on her face right there before him had helped him hold back. But it had been painful. He felt the hard swelling of his own body. It was still painful, an exquisite torment he couldn't stand much longer. He moved slightly beneath her.

Slowly, Anne raised her head and gazed down at his face, the faint sheen of perspiration glistening in the faint light. "Thank you for . . . for that." His restraint had cost him, yet he'd been totally unselfish in the giving of pleasure. It was one more part of the real man she knew lived inside Michael Novak's skin, and she treasured it.

She put her hands on his shoulders and bent to kiss him. It was not a gentle kiss. Her mouth slid across his, voracious, seeking, giving. She ran her tongue over the uneven ridge of his teeth and across the harder flesh of his palate. Their tongues flirted and caressed, touching, then touching again. She sank her teeth gently into his lower lip, then moved her tongue over the soft flesh. His body shuddered beneath her.

"Mmm, you're slightly overdressed for the occasion, aren't you?" Anne sat up on her knees and pushed the blanket away from his thighs. "That's a lot better, isn't it?" Her murmur was soft, almost a whisper.

His body shone iridescent in the dim light and her hands slid across his broad chest, raking through the crisp mat of hair. When she touched one rigid nipple, he tensed, groaning. Anne stroked the sensitive spot again, sculpting him with her hands, giving pleasure for pleasure. He felt so good!

She bent to kiss him again. If her hands aroused him past anything he'd ever thought possible, her mouth drove him quietly wild. She strung a hot path of small biting kisses across his belly, her tongue laving the dimple of his navel. It was almost impossible for Mike to hold back, but the delirium of sensation she was creating was spiraling higher

and higher, and he wanted it to go on forever.

Anne trailed her fingers lightly across his
belly, and his body jerked beneath her.

"Oh, God . . . talk about . . . writhing with
. . . passion," he gasped, reaching up for her.
"Now, Anne. Now!"

Without taking time to think about it, she
leaned over him, bracing herself on his shoulders, then rose and set herself down again,
on him, around him. An explosive sigh burst
from his mouth and he was caught in a mael-
strom of sensation as he moved within her
body.

Anne moved with him, clutching his shoulders. Somehow, she was aware of every part
of her body, every sensation, every sense mag-
nified. She felt the heat of him lancing upward and outward, spreading in undulating
waves of shimmering light, and then she
knew one blinding moment of pure joy. The
sensation swelled into a tapestry of stars and
light and beauty, and then it burst, bringing
them full circle back to the warm haven of
each other's arms.

Fourteen

Night cloaked two sleeping figures still locked in close embrace.

Mike opened his eyes, this time needing only a few seconds to orient himself. His left shoulder was wedged painfully against the edge of the couch, and for an instant he wondered where the hell he was. Then the scent of Anne's hair teased him to full consciousness and he smiled, content. He felt at joy and at peace with himself for the first time in a long while, and he folded Anne closer to him.

Contentment. Mike thought of the word again. That particular feeling was an important part of his reaction to this woman he held in his arms.

He placed a gentle kiss on the top of her head, tasting the soft caress of her tousled hair. Anne brought the whole spectrum of his emotions into play. She could evoke his laughter as well as his concern. He'd felt lust and tenderness, and he'd lost the ability to recognize where one stopped and the other began. It had always been so easy for him to mark the boundary lines, containing his feelings for other women within the limits he chose to set. But Anne McClellan refused to stay where he assumed she belonged. Her lovely presence was becoming an important factor in his life, in his thoughts. And he felt powerless to stop it.

She turned slightly, a quiet sigh parting her lips, and nuzzled against his shoulder. Mike swallowed with some difficulty and moved his mouth just behind her ear, the soft, steady rhythm of her breathing quickening at his touch.

"Don't I know you? You taste familiar." Her husky murmur ruffled against his skin. Her arms around his waist tightened, then rested easy again. Anne looked up at him through still-sleepy eyes, remembering everything. In the faint spill of light from beyond the bedroom door, she studied his face, so important to her now, as a lost traveler studies a road map, looking for the way home.

"Ah . . . if you'd like another taste to make sure . . . ?"

"Oh, I'm sure!" Sadly, she was. She would treasure this night always, cherish the mem-

ory through many empty nights. But that's all
they could have, all it would ever be—a memory. Because in that split second her thoughts
had shown her truth, when and where she
least expected it. This night with Mike had
been wondrous, magical, a breaking free from
the bonds of reality. But it was a reality that
had retreated, not disappeared. It was and
would always be *her* reality.

She was too set in the pattern of her life
to break it so drastically at this late date, not
even in the face of what she felt for Mike
Novak. And she should have known! The casual roll in the hay, the one-night stand, was
not for her. She was no Puritan and she
would never judge right or wrong for someone else. But for her—no good.

And she wouldn't even be here now if her
heart hadn't known all along what her mind
had refused to recognize. Mike Novak meant
a lot more than just tonight and satisfying
sex. Well, more than satisfying! But Mike was
not a man for tomorrows. He'd never promised or even hinted at more than "now."
That's what he'd offered, that's what she'd
accepted.

How could she have known it wouldn't be
enough?

But she mustn't allow her facade to slip.

Not now, not here. Later, when she was alone. But not in front of him. He would be uncomfortable, and their relationship—whatever it was or might turn out to be, even if *friendship* were the only word to describe it—would end before it ever got beyond beginning. Anne sat up slowly, easing away until she felt air on her bare skin instead of the warmth of his body.

"I think I'm too old for this. My back is killing me." The light touch. Whatever else she said or did, the light touch was the thing. "Isn't this what mattresses and box springs are for? Ooohhhh," she winced, moving to sit beside him, her back resting against the sofa.

"Mmm, now that's one of your better ideas." Before she could protest, he rose quickly, pulling her with him. Maybe he could still move quickly; she had to be dragged!

"Oh, please, have pity. In the age of the physically fit, I seem to be physically *mis*-fit!" *Don't think. Don't think! Keep it light!*

"You couldn't prove it by me. I thought you were very . . . fit." His grin shone even in the dim room. "Now, where do you hide the bedroom?"

"Wait a minute, Tarzan." She knelt stiffly to pick up her hastily shed caftan. "Ouch!" She put a hand to her lower back. "All I can say is, for a man of your age, you're pretty spry."

"Spry! *Spry?*" He swatted her lightly on her behind, and with a wink, she took his hand and led him toward the door.

"Oh." He stopped. "Well, maybe it's a good thing we didn't make it this far." He laughed, and she began to laugh with him when she saw the expression on his face. The room had been furnished by a widow, one with no plans to be merry. "I've heard of sleeping single in a double bed, but there's no way on God's green earth we could have slept double in *that.*"

"Novak, I have absolute faith in you. Somehow, someway, you would have come up with something."

"Is that a pun?" He hugged her, the grin widening at her blush. "Listen, by now I almost think I *could* accomplish anything. Damn, twice in one hour. Who says men begin to decline after fifty?" He sounded inordinately pleased with himself, smiling down at her. "Do you have any idea how wonderful it is to see a grown woman blush in this day and age?" He looked back at the narrow bed and then suddenly his eyes darkened. He stared, a tad too long, his eyes fastened on the picture standing beside the lamp. Even from here, even in the dim light, he knew whose picture it was.

"I guess it's just as well we stayed in the other room." For a moment he was annoyed, disappointed. And it was worse because he knew he had no right to any of those feelings. Who the hell was he to expect her to turn her back completely on the past? Had he? But he was profoundly grateful their beautiful night had not been spoiled by Paul McClellan's presence in the room with them.

Quickly, he kissed her cheek and walked toward the bathroom. He needed some time alone to get his act together.

Anne stared at the closed door, listening to the sound of water splashing in the shower. Then, purposefully, she walked to the table and picked up the ornate frame, staring for some moments at the smiling clear-eyed man in the photograph. It wasn't signed, it was just . . . Paul. Paul as he'd always been, as he'd always be in her memory.

Anne drew a deep breath. But that's what he was, a memory. A beautiful, important, beloved memory, but a memory nonetheless. She'd passed beyond the time in her life where memories alone could keep her warm at night or provide a reason for living.

Well, she'd made the choice and she would

have to go on. Alone, without Paul. She closed her eyes, resting her forehead on the top of the frame. Perhaps without Mike, too. But if that were the only way, so be it. Anne had tested her strength, and she knew it would support her now, as it had in the dark days after the funeral. Accepting this new-found feeling of love for Michael Novak was not easy; accepting his lack of it for her would be harder still. But it would come, and it had to begin now.

The man in the photo smiled up at her with approval. Anne opened the drawer and slipped the picture inside. She and Mike could still have the rest of this one magical night.

When Mike emerged a few seconds later, he was surprised to find Anne waiting for him, propped against two plumped-up pillows, the sheet modestly covering her still-unclothed body, the soft light spilling into the shadowed corners of the room. He walked slowly across the room and stood by the bed.

So, the picture was gone. He frowned, wondering what it meant. Wondering why his heart leapt with elation in that split second.

"Come on in out of the cold." She patted the space next to her.

"Are you kidding? I'd need a shoehorn." He eyed the minuscule space warily.

"Oh?" She grinned archly. "I never thought you would give up so quickly. Aren't you up to the challenge?"

He raised his eyebrows. Then, pulling aside the sheet and nodding with satisfaction, he dropped the bath towel from around his waist and lowered himself carefully to lie on top of her. "Mmm, good fit, and right on top of the problem!"

"And definitely *up* to the challenge." They both started to laugh and it was only the sudden noise of the telephone ringing that stopped their mutual enjoyment. Anne squirmed over to the phone, and Mike wiggled his brows to show how enjoyable her maneuver was. While she twisted to get the receiver, he did a little squirming of his own and she began to giggle. "Hello, who . . . shh, stop! Uh . . . who is it?"

Her eyes widened and she abruptly bit her lip. Mike stilled instantly. "Jerry! How are you, honey?" Her cheeks were bright pink and she looked at him helplessly, then back at the phone. "Uh . . . no, nothing is . . . wrong. I . . . uh . . . I was just out of breath from . . . from coming up the stairs!"

Mike almost choked and she tried to kick

him in the shin. She missed. "Why are you calling so early, dear?" She turned to stare at the small bedside clock. "My God, it's after eleven!" She shook her head resignedly. "Well, yes, I meant to call you, but I . . . I got busy with . . . with someone—*something* else. No, honestly, everything's fine!"

Mike nodded vigorously in agreement and she punched him in the shoulder. "Ouch! That hurt." His hoarse whisper was louder than he'd meant it to be.

"What? Oh . . . well, yes, Jerry, he's—it's Chief Novak, of the Whitefield Police. No, dear, nothing's wrong. Honestly, I'm fine. He . . . he just stopped by to check on the back door. You know, after the break-in and all . . ."

Anne lay there, trapped by Mike's unyielding body, desperately trying to sound unruffled for Jerry's benefit. Mike blew in her ear. She asked about Jerry's studies. Mike kissed her neck. She choked and asked about schoolwork again. "I asked you? Oh! Uh . . . what . . . what did you say?"

A stern warning look settled Mike down and she quickly finished her conversation. Promising to call Jerry the following week, Anne carefully replaced the receiver. "I could kill you! That was my *son!*"

"I know, and I'm sorry." He really was.

Mike couldn't understand the perverse impulse that had wanted to make his presence known to the boy.

"You seem to have a nice relationship."

"That we do," Anne chuckled, slipping her arms around his neck. "Why, sometimes I actually get the feeling he's glad I'm his mother. Of course, it helps that I've been in training for years to be the perfect woman. I mean, what else do I need for the title? I bake good brownies, I make great coffee, I screw around"—she wriggled a little closer, although the size of the bed made that almost unnecessary—"and my son even likes me." Anne grinned.

Mike didn't.

"Lucky kid."

Anne waited, quite still, struck by the odd note in his voice, but when he didn't say anything else, she tried to act as if nothing had changed. But it had. That small cool moment, the flash of bleak regret in his voice, had suddenly changed everything. He still rested atop her, leaning on his forearms, his body nestled against hers, skin to warm skin, comforting and exciting and increasingly dear, and they couldn't have been more intimate. Yet Anne felt they were separated by something almost impenetrable.

"What's he like?" Mike asked abruptly, looking down into her eyes. "Does he look like his father?" *Good God, Novak, you can't leave it alone, can you?*

"Yes, very much so." Anne smiled reflexively, thinking of Jerry and even of Paul. Somehow, now, she could speak of Paul with fondness, without the pain.

"You loved him very much, didn't you?" He could say it now, as long as the eyes in the photograph were locked away. Maybe it was because she seemed to accept reality with a calm assurance he hadn't seen before. "Didn't you ever disagree, fight?"

"In twenty years, are you kidding? I may be the perfect woman, but I'm not a saint! And, believe me, neither was Paul," she said dryly. "But at least we were smart enough to talk more than we yelled. And more important, we were smart enough to *listen*. It's funny, but now I can't even remember what we argued about. Oh," she grinned, "yes, ink spots."

"You argued about The Ink Spots?" Mike looked down at her quizzically.

"No, you fool. *Ink* spots. On the sheets." He still looked puzzled. "I like to do the *Times* crossword puzzle before I go to sleep at night. I always fall asleep with the pen in my hand." She shrugged. "Ink spots."

"You do the crossword puzzle with a *pen*? Boy, talk about the perfect woman!"

For a few moments they smiled into each other's eyes, then Mike's expression sobered. "You had a good marriage, didn't you?"

"Yes," Anne murmured, her steady gaze unwavering, "it was a very good twenty-four years."

"Twenty-four years . . ." He closed his eyes for a moment and shook his head. "I didn't think those kinds of marriages existed anymore." His smile twisted. "When people stay together that long these days, it's usually from inertia."

"Oh, Novak, you are a hard case, aren't you? But, really, it's no secret." Her expression was very calm. "It was love and friendship . . . and trust."

"Trust." He gazed down into her quiet eyes, then in one well-oiled motion Mike rolled over and sat up on the edge of the bed. He braced his hands on his knees and looked down at the floor, then stood and walked to the window to stare out into the darkness.

When he didn't speak Anne broke the strained silence. "You have a real hard time with that word, don't you? Why is it so hard to believe? If there were no trust, there wouldn't have been *any* years, no less twenty-four. You can't build a life with someone you can't trust."

"No, you certainly can't." His tone was distant now. Then he inhaled deeply. "Well, it's pretty late; guess I'd better get going." He wheeled around and walked into the other room. Startled, Anne followed, wrapping the sheet around her, suddenly uncomfortable in her nakedness. He was zipping up his jeans.

"It's not really fair, is it, Mike?"

"Fair?" He looked up at her, shrugging. "Well, Anne, a lot of things in life aren't fair. What exactly did you have in mind?" He pulled his T-shirt over his head.

"You know an awful lot about me but I really know very little about you." She tried to sound casual. There was more than enough tension in the room already. "Remember what you told me once? If something bothers you, sometimes talking about it helps. You were right, you know. It does."

He stared at her for what seemed an eternity, the brittle silence stretching between them. And the barrier she'd sensed so strongly weakened. It was still there, but perhaps a bit weaker.

"Well, I don't think there's that much to tell. It's no big deal, really." He pulled on his socks, then found his shoes and put them on, too. "I suppose you're talking about my wife—my ex-wife—aren't you?" His features grew very still. "You want to know about her? Okay, why not?" He shrugged and leaned back, as if her concern and interest in his past were the least interesting things she could have on her mind.

"Adrienne was a beauty . . . I mean, a real crowd-stopper. And I guess you could say she was kind of a party girl. She liked the good life and good times. And, to tell you the truth, now that I look back, I really can't blame her. . . . I did, too, back then. She was really just a kid when we married and that kind of life was all she ever knew; it's what she had when I met her. Why should she ever have expected to settle for less? But I'll say this much for her: She never lied or pretended to be anything other than what she was. It was my fault, I suppose. What she was was exactly what I wanted." He lit one of his cigars, unable to conceal the slight shaking of his hand.

Anne listened in silence, not sure what to say, not sure there was anything *to* say. He rose and walked to the window, puffing once on his cigar.

"You're right. I haven't told you much about my life, have I? Well, let's see . . . I went to law school at Yale." He said it without pride, without emphasis, and when he glanced at her, her stare brought a grim smile to his mouth. "I guess you didn't know that." Well, she'd told him she didn't pry.

"Or, maybe I should go back farther than that. I worked my way through Dartmouth, had a part-time job with the campus police dispatcher, my first experience working with the police," he said with irony. "I actually enjoyed it more than I'd expected, but of course Dartmouth was only my first step; Yale was the big time, the real beginning of the dream."

He closed his eyes for a moment, remembering. "To get away from here forever . . . to be rich . . . to make something of myself. And I did it. I left Whitefield behind and I never looked back." His voice was pensive. "Strange, now, to remember how much I hated this place."

"But I thought you loved it here!" Anne hadn't meant to interrupt. "I can understand wanting excitement, success, wider horizons.

But why would you hate a beautiful place like this?"

He looked at her with a bitter smile, just short of a sneer. "Not so beautiful to me. I was always just the Novak kid. 'That Novak kid, he's no better than he ought to be. What can you expect? The father's the town drunk and the mother's the town whore!' "

Anne sat on the edge of the couch, silent, fists clenched inside the folds of the sheet, waiting. She watched the curl of smoke from his nostrils as it dissipated in the still air. Better than watching the raw pain etched on his face.

"You know, it's funny, I can still remember her. And she was no beauty. But even if it was dime store perfume, she always smelled nice. Not like my father. He usually smelled like a distillery." Mike shrugged and flicked some ashes through the slightly open window. "Well, why not? What the hell else did he have? At least he knew the bottle was all his; he didn't have to share it with every other man in town. And when you're blind drunk you can escape . . . for a while."

Anne winced and caught her lips between her teeth. Mike's face was so still, so cold . . . utterly devoid of emotion. This was costing him a lot, she knew. How long had he kept it inside himself? She almost wished she'd never asked him to tell her.

He went on, as if he'd forgotten she was there. "One day she got on the Concord bus with a guy who'd been working with one of the lumbering crews in the area and"—he snapped his fingers—"like that, she was gone. God only knows where she met him or how long they'd been planning it. Or whatever happened to her." His tone of voice was merely conversational, a recitation of simple fact. "We never heard from her again. And as rotten as she was, I guess Pa still loved her, in his way. It didn't take him long to get down to some serious drinking. Fortunately for him, he died quickly once he put his mind to it."

Anne swallowed and, with some difficulty, managed to speak. "Couldn't Caroline help?"

"I didn't even know her until she came home for Pa's funeral. He'd driven her away years before and she'd been teaching school down in Manchester." His eyes softened instantly. "When she found out my mother . . ." the word dripped with sarcasm, "was . . . gone, she decided to stay up here with me. We hit it off almost from the moment we met. And I thank God for Aunt Callie. She was my stability, my rock . . . my *family*. If it hadn't been for Caroline . . ." He stopped, still caught in the past.

Anne rose and went to him. She put her hand on his arm.

"Parents are people, too, Mike. They can be weak and selfish and stupid . . . and cruel. But most aren't like that. Look at you. You're a loving, devoted father, and Helena adores you."

He looked at her now, his smile cool in the moonlight. "Yes, Anne. Of course you're right." Gently, he lifted her hand off his arm. The message was clear: He wanted no understanding compassionate companion just now. And he'd have walked straight out the door if he thought she harbored any pity for the child he'd been. The last thing Mike Novak would ever tolerate was pity. It was too cheap an emotion for a man like him, for the man he'd become at such great cost to the man he might have been.

He walked back to the chair he'd sat in earlier and sprawled, fingers tented across his chest. "So, what else do you want to know?"

"I told you once, Mike, I don't pry. If you don't want to tell me any more, don't. It's your business." *Not mine.* She was overcome with a deep sadness. *Never mine.*

Anne reached abruptly for the lamp and

turned it on full. Light returned them suddenly to the world they had left behind only a few hours ago.

Mike blinked in the sudden flood of light, quickly reassembling the mask he'd let slip in the darkness. "Ah, what the hell," he said wearily. "It's no big secret, not around here, anyway. All old news, and they've probably forgotten most of it by now." He tilted his head and looked straight at her. "Haven't you wondered what happened to my . . . to Helena's mother?"

"Adrienne. Well, yes, once in a while, I thought—"

"Of course you did. Women always do."

Well, that put her in her place, didn't it. How pleasant to be lumped so cavalierly with "women." "I'm me, Mike, not your narrow-minded image of most women!"

"No," he murmured thoughtfully, "you're not, are you?" He shook off that thought and sat up. "Did you know you're looking at the embodiment of the American dream?" He smiled coolly at her stare. "Work hard, live clean, and good things happen. And it's true. I worked very hard and lived very clean—so that I could prove to Whitefield the Novaks weren't all trash.

"I did have to wait a while. . . . They

drafted me first and I got shipped to Nam. But I figured, what the hell? It was a chance to be a hero first, before I went for the gold. And if I didn't make it, no big loss to anyone. Well, maybe Caroline, but that's all." He took another deep drag on the glowing cigar. "Shit, some kids have to learn the hard way! Almost got my ass shot off a few times . . . but it looked great on my resume later! I had *proof* for everyone—from Whitefield, New Hampshire to Burton Stanley Marshall and Park Avenue—that the Novak kid *was* a damn sight better than he ought to be."

Anne leaned back and tucked her feet under her, forcing herself to listen to the quiet horror of his words. She understood the importance of this moment, despite a sudden perverse desire to stop him before he went any further.

"Who's Burton Stanley Marshall?"

"Old B.S. Ah, you have no idea how appropriate that was." Mike's smile was unpleasant. "He recruited me at Yale. Talk about dreams coming true: He was it. The rich boss with the megabucks, and his beautiful daughter came with the deal, too. Yeah, everyone has his price, all right. She was mine, and she was a pretty good piece of ass for the money." Anne winced at the deliberate coarse-

ness of his words. She had a feeling he'd
done it for her benefit alone—to shock her,
to put her at a distance.

"We got married pretty quickly, too quickly
I realize now. I should have known. . . . He
called her his princess, and no one ever told
her princesses grow up and get pregnant," he
said wryly, hands clasped behind his head,
staring up at the ceiling.

"Poor Adrienne. Now I can look back and
even feel sorry for her. She was a child in a
woman's body and nobody'd ever prepared
her for reality. My God, how she hated being
pregnant. Every second of every day of every
week she hated it. Hated me, too, I guess.
She'd have had an abortion in a minute if
she hadn't been afraid of what I'd do." He
stopped, rubbing his exhausted face with his
hands.

"Hell," he grimaced, "that was the worst
nine months of my life, too. Nam was a picnic
in the woods by comparison. But"—he stopped
and quite suddenly his face lit up with a
glowing smile—"when Helena was born it . . .
hell, it was a whole new beginning for me. I
knew I could stand anything, even life with
Adrienne and her father, if I had that little
girl to come home to every night. The nurse
we hired probably didn't even know what

Adrienne looked like; I don't think she ever saw her. But I used to rush home at night just so I could feed Helena her last bottle and put her to bed."

Anne marveled at the expression on his face as he spoke of that time and Helena. The softness, the tenderness, were wondrous to behold. She had to blink back the sudden tears stinging her eyes. Mike was quiet for so long she wondered if he were finished.

Finally, even he heard the silence and looked over at her, a cynical smile twisting his mouth. "I know exactly what you're thinking: How did I wind up as chief of a two-bit police department like this, with such a plush situation and those high-powered legal credentials?"

She had, in fact, been wondering something very much along those lines.

"It's kind of ironic. I have my esteemed father-in-law to thank for the best move I ever made in my life." For a moment his face was hard, cold. "God, I can't stand being grateful to that bastard for anything." Then he shook his head ruefully.

Anne didn't know what to say to that; it didn't seem to require any words from her.

"Between old B.S. and Maurice Atherton, it wasn't difficult, believe me." Her expression must have shown she was lost, because he quickly explained. "Atherton was his old friend and a very valuable client—we're talking mucho big bucks here, you understand—and they wanted me to defend his son on a drunk driving charge." His expression went curiously blank. "They didn't have to twist my arm very hard, either. And I did a very good job of it, too."

He rose slowly, walked back to the window, and stared across the square at the illuminated steeple of the church. "Too damn good. Two months later Junior was back in jail again, only this time it wasn't D.W.I. It was manslaughter. He ran a red light and killed a pedestrian."

He threw the cigar forcefully out the window and swung around to face Anne. "And I could take all the credit for that one, couldn't I? I mean, *I was the one who'd put him behind that wheel.* I went home that night and I was so sick I threw up my guts. Sick with all of it—B.S. and the Athertons of the world and the lawyers like me . . . the two-bit whores who took a fine profession and made it a dirty word!"

He stopped abruptly, staring down, then after a few seconds of silence took a deep breath. His next words were quiet, thoughtful. "That's when I took a long hard look at myself . . . and Helena. I could see her, when she grew up, becoming another Adrienne or a spoiled rotten 'Junior.' Wasn't it Oscar Wilde who said it, something about knowing the price of everything and the value of nothing?" Mike rested his head against the glass for a few seconds.

"It was crazy, but I can remember thinking about Whitefield for the first time in years. Even when Caroline and I wrote each other, I never gave much thought to the town, never asked her about it. But right then it looked awfully good to me. You know, I've wondered about it now and then; all those years when I was a child, I'm not so sure the humiliation I felt wasn't in my own mind. I couldn't really recall anyone ever snubbing me or calling me names; no one had ever actually been unkind. I began to see that a lot of my resentment was toward what I *imagined* people were saying. I had more self-hatred than anything anyone else ever felt toward me."

Mike sighed and closed his eyes for a moment. "And I just wanted to come home. I never wanted to see the inside of a courtroom again." His tone was unutterably sad, poignant. He sighed and stretched his shoulders, rubbing the back of his neck.

"Well, Adrienne was a bit put out, to say

the least, when I told her what I wanted to do. I should have known. I guess Freud would say I did. Anyway, she just laughed in my face. She didn't say a word, just kept on laughing. That's when I knew, *really* knew, it was all over. I think I was relieved. I know she was. It was 'goodbye, good luck, and don't bother to write.' Boy, I never saw her move so fast. Thank God I slowed her down long enough to sign the custody agreement." He laughed suddenly, an ugly mirthless sound. "Adrienne would have been horrified to know how much resemblance she had to my loving whore of a mother!"

The ticking of a clock was the only sound to disturb the silence for long minutes. Anne pulled the sheet tighter around her shoulders, feeling the chill in the air for the first time.

"Mike, I—I'm so sorry. Thank you for telling me. It explains . . . well, I think I understand now—"

"Do you? Well, maybe you do. You seem to be a very understanding lady." He suddenly stood up, gathering his sweater and jacket from the floor near the couch. He stared down at them in his hand, recalling the day, the night. His mouth was set and he turned stiffly. He'd wavered, but no more. She had to understand once and for all where he stood. He wasn't going to repeat his mistakes again. He wasn't going to destroy himself over a woman . . . as his father had done, as he'd almost done with Adrienne. Not Mike Novak.

"You were curious. Can't say I blame you. You're so close to Helena and Caroline, and . . . well, you were entitled to know." The unspoken words hung in the air: *after tonight*. Mike made a curiously vague gesture to the air and walked to the door. "I think I'd better say good night. It's late and we both have early hours, so . . ."

"Uh, yes, of course." His departure was so abrupt Anne was unprepared. After the wonderful way it had begun, she hadn't quite expected the night to end like this. "I'll . . . will I see you soon?" Damn, how did you ask a man if he wanted to see you again? Liberated or not, it just wasn't her style.

"It's a small town; of course we'll see each other." At her empty gaze, the long silence, he stopped in the open doorway. "Look, Anne, I like you very much. You're a wonderful woman." *Wonderful. Such a pale word for what she aroused in him. All the dreams and tomorrows. . . . But he didn't believe in tomorrows, did he?* He went on, his voice cool, his words very rational.

"But I don't want any ties. I've had them before, and obviously they aren't as permanent as one would hope. So why look for the disappointment? I've arranged my life the way I like it and I'm not ready to change. You deserve—" For a moment his voice caught. He took a deep breath. "You deserve someone who wants permanency, ties. Someone who believes in that trust you have such faith in. I wish . . ." *I wish . . . oh, God, how I wish.* Mike looked away, out into the blackness of the night. "That just isn't me."

She heard his steps echo as he walked down the stairs, heard the car as it pulled away from the curb, heard her heart beating furiously in her chest. It was a long time before the hot tears began to slide down her cheeks, and it was a very long time before they stopped.

Fifteen

King's Square was filled with what looked like the entire population of Whitefield, New Hampshire. Two Sundays a month, from June to October, the Lions' Club pancake breakfast always pulled a big crowd. Everyone—at least everyone minus this one, Anne thought wearily—enjoyed the chance to see everyone else all in one place at one time. For a dedicated gossip, it was like dying and going to heaven.

"Here's the cake I promised you, George. I already cut it in squares for you." The oversized commercial pan Anne carried thumped heavily as she set it down on the long paper-covered table. She waved to the small man in the large white apron who, mercifully, didn't get close enough to offer the comment she'd heard too often this past week about how peaked, pale, and under-the-weather she looked and was everything all right and did she enjoy the fishing and . . .

Resolutely, Anne squared her shoulders and

turned to survey the scene with all the eagerness of Sydney Carton going to meet Madame Defarge. It didn't help her mood that an almost carnival gaiety pervaded the crowd. The still-green grass and the almost-garish fall colors splashed across the foliage were a beautiful backdrop to the festive atmosphere. The air was deliciously redolent of coffee, maple syrup, and the faint wisp of woodsmoke. But the only positive note Anne could think of was that it was the last of these breakfasts for the year. No more facing observant neighbors' eyes en masse. Hibernation was coming. Hallelujah.

Through the milling crowd Anne spotted Caroline in quiet conversation with Betty Hamilton, the owner of the Yarn Barn, and wearily she began to make her way in their direction. In good conscience she couldn't just ignore Caroline, although at this particular juncture it was a definite temptation. Thank goodness Mike was not in evidence at least. Just then Helena appeared at her side, scarfing down a buttermilk biscuit, syrup dripping off her fingers.

"Hi, Mac! Just get here?"

Anne hugged the girl. "Yeah, I had to wait for the apple coffee cake to finish baking. I think Mr. Bailiss had given up on me." She'd put off the baking until the last possible minute, not wanting to be in King's Square this Sunday morning. She kept remembering last Sunday morning, getting ready to go fishing.

And last Sunday night.

Mike's final words had burned themselves into her brain, replaying a constant litany all week. Fortunately, Anne's summer tan hadn't yet worn away and even Helena didn't notice the sudden flare of color the memory brought to her cheeks. For which she was grateful, because just then Anne looked over at Caroline again . . . and saw Mike standing beside her. As if her glance were palpable, he looked up at that moment.

For a fraction of a heartbeat they stared into each other's eyes over the heads of people they'd completely forgotten. Anne's heart slammed against her chest and air was suddenly hard to come by. All the hurt, all the frustration, was erased on the instant, and before she could think about it, she felt a joyous smile tug at her lips. But it died prematurely when, after one nod, he turned and walked away in the opposite direction, saving her another dose of humiliation. Somehow her feet managed to continue functioning, if nothing else did.

So much for the old "we can still be friends" gambit.

"Hello, Anne dear. How've you been?" Caroline pressed her cheek to Anne's.

She knew Caroline well enough by now. Caroline was asking more than that.

"Oh, I've been better," Anne answered wryly.

She shivered inside her heavy turtleneck sweater, feeling chilled in the brisk fall morning and unutterably weary all of a sudden, and she longed for the quiet solitude of her own company. Cheerfulness demanded too much effort, more than she could summon at the moment. As soon as it was decently plausible, she would make some excuse to leave.

"My, you're beginning to sound like a native," Caroline observed tartly. "I could say the same about Michael."

"Yes . . . well, don't, please. Uh, Helena, I think someone's waving at you. I'm positive he isn't waving at me!"

Helena looked up, and her eyes grew large for a moment. Then she barely lifted a hand and turned back to Anne.

"That's Josh Cappello!" Her whisper tailed off into a squeal. "He's in White Mountain High! His father's one of Dad's men. But he . . . oh, wow, he's coming over here. Mac, he's coming *here!* Do I have any lipstick on? Is my hair—? Oh, jeez, he. . . . Hi, Josh! Uh, how're ya doin'?"

The tall, gangly boy with the unruly blond hair lifted his hand in a casual salute. "Hi, Helena, Miss Novak."

"Good morning, Joshua. This is Mrs. Mc-Clellan. Anne, Joshua Cappello."

Anne smiled and held out her hand, surprised at the boy's sudden pallor. Then he turned red and swallowed twice. He took her hand and pumped it up and down a couple of times, then quickly dropped it. "Yeah, you have that bakery where Helena works, don't you? Uh . . . you've got some great stuff!"

"Why, thank you, Josh." There could be no greater testimonial than from a teenage boy with a healthy appetite. "I'm flattered. I don't believe I've seen you in the shop. If you like fresh apple cake, go see Mr. Bailiss. I just brought it over."

"Did you bring any of that strawberry whipped cream stuff? That's really awesome."

"No, not for a couple of months. Sorry. Strawberries aren't in season now, and anyway, whipped cream and bugs-in-the-park are a bad combination. But the apple's pretty good, honestly."

"Uh, Helena, wanna go get some? There's a bunch of us gonna hang out over there by the gazebo."

Ignoring the fact that she was crammed to

the brim with buttermilk biscuits, Helena nodded her head happily and they headed for the long tables laden with food.

"What happened? I thought it was Jamie Larkin who was so awesome?"

"Ah, Anne," Caroline observed tartly, "even I know the fickleness of the teenage girl. You should listen to them more carefully when they're in the shop. If you want a lesson in the wayward heart, take a look at Jennie Meacham, the femme fatale of Coos County! One day that girl will be in the Guinness Book of Records for discarded boyfriends, mark my words! And, since Helena's a perfectly normal young girl, Josh needn't prepare to stay on top of the heap for long. His days are numbered!"

Anne laughed, the first full-fledged flash of pleasure she'd enjoyed in days. "Speaking of Jamie"—she glanced around at the crowd— "I don't see him or Sandra here today. I guess he's home nursing his broken heart. And as for Josh . . . well, I don't know, Caroline. From the look on Helena's face, I think he may last a while. He is kind of cute, isn't he? Or should I say he's a 'hunk'? And is he 'totally awesome' or 'really rad'? I'm not sure what's *in* this week," Anne chuckled as she and Caroline watched Helena's bright yellow sweater and Josh's faded blue sweatshirt disappear into the crowd.

"I believe Helena would describe you as totally awesome. She thinks you're one step below Mother Theresa since Michael allowed her to wear lipstick." Caroline fastened the top button of her bulky sweater and turned back to Anne, smiling thoughtfully. "She's positive you're responsible for his sudden change of heart. And she's right, you know."

"Well, don't expect any more sudden changes. Personally, I've had more than enough of those recently, and I'm pretty well bankrupt in the influence department."

"Hmm."

Caroline was not one to waste words. She'd witnessed firsthand the state of Mike's misery this past week and had surmised, quite correctly, the cause. And that cause, standing beside her, didn't look any better right now than he did.

"My dear, in this life I've come to the conclusion that the greatest asset one can cultivate is patience." And with that cryptic statement, Caroline patted Anne's hand, smiled sagely, and went to sit down at one of the many long tables that had been set up on the grass, joining her friends in gossip and knitting. Anne stared after her, a skeptical look on her face.

Sure, patience. Easy for you to say, Caroline. You've had years to learn about Mike Novak. I've had a couple of weeks.

And that's all I'll ever have.

And why would I want any more? she wondered. He made his feelings clear. I'd have to be a first-class masochist to give him another chance.

Which, of course, he's already made clear he doesn't want, anyway.

The threat of sudden tears made Anne turn abruptly and hurry toward the sidewalk, away from the crowd, the interested eyes, away from . . .

"Hello, Anne. It's been quite a while, hasn't it? I hoped you'd be here today."

"Oh, hi, Elliot, I didn't see you. I mean," she added lamely, "it's so crowded." Not only hadn't she seen him in her path, he'd been almost invisible to her lately. Since Mike. . . . No, she had to stop this. And now was as good a time as any. Anne forced a smile and turned her full attention on Elliot. He was leaning against one of the tables, sipping coffee from a heavy white china mug. Even in a sweater and informal slacks, he looked as studied as if he were behind his desk in the bank.

"It's not as good as yours," he lifted the mug to her before he took another sip.

"Why, thank you. You haven't stopped by lately. I've missed you." Oh, Anne, if he believes that, you can start selling swampland in Florida. "Where've you been keeping yourself?"

"Ah, I might ask you the same." He didn't quite succeed in sounding as casual as he wished nor in erasing the sullen cast of his face. That Anne had called off their last two dinner dates and cut short a recent phone conversation was bad enough. But to find that at the same time she'd been enjoying the company of Mike Novak in preference to his had, in Elliot's eyes, made her apparent defection intolerable.

He put the coffee on the table and took her hand, pulling her gently but inexorably toward a couple of chairs beside them. "Sit down. I'll get you something to drink." He walked off, stopping frequently along the way to shake hands and exchange words with everyone in his path. Anne watched him, because it was safer than letting her eyes wander over the rest of the crowd. Mike had to be here, somewhere, and she didn't want to allow herself to be aware of him. So instead, she concentrated on Elliot.

He's working the crowd like a politician on the trail of an untapped vote, she observed wryly. It wasn't Elliot's normal style and she wondered at it fleetingly. Maybe she'd been wrong about him; she'd certainly been wrong about other things.

At last he reached the large coffee urns and filled a mug for her, returning in the same manner and the same pace at which he'd gone. Anne had no polite way of taking her leave, and that was just fine with Elliot. He read her expression without strain and didn't care one whit how uncomfortable she might feel. He wanted his due. And here, right now, was as good a time as any.

How dare she humiliate him the way she had, in front of the whole town! Everyone knew, had known, how it was with them. How he'd *thought* it was with them. To be thrown over for someone like Mike Novak. . . . No, oh no, the bitch wasn't getting away with it. And this was a perfect opportunity, not to be missed.

He sat beside her and ostentatiously draped his arm over her shoulder. Short of an outright confrontation, Anne had no choice but to stay where she was, apparently at ease and enjoying his proximity. Grateful for something to do, she held the hot mug and warmed her cold fingers before taking a sip. Well, fine, let Mike Novak see that he wasn't the only pebble on her beach, the only fish in her ocean, the. . . . She quickly gulped the hot coffee and focused on Elliot.

His smile was fixed in place as he looked over Anne's shoulder to greet a couple strolling past. "Hello, Margaret, Simon. Wonderful day, isn't it?" They nodded cheerfully and exchanged a few words of greeting before waving goodbye to Anne and moving on. Elliot turned back to her, looking quite pleased with himself. "I've been meaning to drop in to the shop but my schedule's been very full lately." He almost preened, and the gleam in his eyes was a close runner-up to his teeth. "There's been some talk—nothing official yet, mind you—but still, some folks around here think I might be a good bet to run for Congress from this district."

Anne almost choked on her coffee. The accuracy of her recent thoughts startled her but Elliot didn't seem to notice, so preoccupied was he with smiling jovially at anyone who was within hailing distance. He sat up straighter, adjusting his shirt collar unnecessarily—it was always in perfect order—and looked around complacently, the lord of the manor surveying his fief.

Anne, that's mean. He was your friend from the beginning and he's never done anything to deserve that. He's not perfect, but are you? At least Elliot seemed to *like* her. She held on to that thought.

"That's wonderful, Elliot. I never knew you had an interest in politics." Actually, now that she considered it, he'd probably thrive in the public spotlight.

"Frankly, Anne, I'm not sure I'd really want to get involved in the bureaucratic wrangling of Washington, but if the people around here really think I can be of service . . ." He shrugged, a confident smile on his mouth. "Of course, my family does have connections who might be helpful to our area. And after Congress, who knows where it might lead." He shrugged, smiling and waving at someone across the square.

Then he looked directly at her and Anne cut in hastily. Wherever it led, she was not going down the path with him. If he harbored any thoughts in that direction—and she feared he did—she'd have to stop it now. "I'm sure you'll do a fine job in Washington if you decide to run. I wish you all the luck in the world." She rose swiftly from the rickety folding wooden chair and he followed. "I really have to get back to the shop and get a couple of things out of the way, but it's been good talking to you, and good luck with your campaign."

Even Elliot understood the finality in her words. When she leaned forward to kiss him goodbye on the cheek, he turned his head with deliberate calculation, and in full view of half the town, she found herself kissing him full on the lips.

Before she could show surprise or displeasure, he patted her arm in a purely friendly gesture and firmly pushed her away from him. To anyone watching, it would look exactly as he wished it to look: Anne had kissed him and he had turned away her affections. They would think the choice *his,* not *hers.* A small victory, but he savored it.

"So long, Elliot." With a quick flash of insight, Anne understood his enjoyment of the petty triumph and she was annoyed at the way this whole morning was turning out. She did not enjoy being manipulated. Elliot smiled serenely, patted her hand again and, shaking his head, turned to stalk more wild votes. Anne quickly continued on her way.

Across the patch of grass behind them, Mike was an unwilling witness to the scene they played out, pain gnawing at his gut, jealousy rising in his throat. And what right had he to any of those feelings? He'd told her exactly how he felt, hadn't he? Dog in the manger wasn't exactly the most flattering description, but it fit. Uncomfortably well. He didn't want her—he'd certainly made that clear—but he didn't want anyone else to have her, either. That the anyone else could possibly be Elliot Gilcrest was just a little added salt to his self-inflicted wounds. The kiss was about all he could take. Frustrated, Mike kicked a few newly fallen autumn leaves out of his path and walked away.

Waving halfheartedly to Ed and Sylvie Pritchard across the way, Anne tried to thread her way through the throng, not wanting to have to stop and make conversation with Mike's deputy, of all people. In truth, she hoped to avoid speaking with anyone. But it was destined to be a losing effort. Much as she'd have liked to, she couldn't ignore all the greetings from people who'd become her friends and neighbors in the last few months. They'd welcomed her warmly, helping to make both her new life and new business successful. If her life were to put down permanent roots in this lovely town, she couldn't, wouldn't, cut them off now.

And she did want new roots here, she realized. Despite Mike Novak, despite the discomfort of seeing him constantly, she knew she wouldn't, couldn't, cut and run. If she were going to prove to herself that she could indeed stand on these two legs of hers, steady and firm, it would have to be here, now. Because if she caved in at this first appearance of trouble, then she would never again be sure of her newly developed independence and strength. And they were too important to discard that easily.

She caught a glimpse of Helena and Josh in the midst of a larger group of kids, sprawled along the benches and the steps of the neat white gazebo on the edge of the grass. Josh turned around and saw Anne looking his way. His face flushed noticeably even at that distance and his mouth opened dumbly for a moment, before he turned his head jerkily in the other direction. Boy, she really had some effect on him. *Well, Mike, is he mesmerized by the glamorous older woman, too? My, my, I'm just reeking with fatal attraction!* To be brutally honest, kiddo, it's probably the strawberry torte.

Anne stopped suddenly, in mid-stride, eyes widening with a flash of revelation. She took a deep breath and walked purposefully toward the scattered group of teenagers.

She smiled at them, waved at Helena, and touched Josh lightly on the arm. "Josh, could I talk to you a minute? There's something I meant to ask you." Anne edged away from the group, gesturing for Helena to stay.

"Uh, yeah, Mrs. McClellan. So what did you want to . . . ?" His question trailed off weakly when he saw the steady gaze she aimed at him. He coughed, looking away, shuffling his feet in the dry leaves. He waited, growing more obviously uncomfortable by the second.

"Well, Josh," Anne said quietly, "I think I have something that belongs to you. It's back at the shop." When he stared dumbly at her, she continued. "Your Spartan pin. I believe you dropped it the night you . . . uh . . . stopped in for cake and ice cream." He paled, swallowed convulsively again, and mumbled an unintelligible reply.

"Look, Josh, I haven't said anything to anyone, and I won't."

He looked utterly miserable. "Jeez, I'm sorry, I'm really sorry! It's just . . . well, a couple of us were going to a real early preschool practice session at the gym and we were gonna get breakfast first, and we just . . . it was just a . . . a bet. We didn't mean to—"

"Just don't let it ever happen again, that's all," she cut in sternly. "Now, I have a proposition. You work for me for a few weeks to pay for the cost of the repairs to the door, and we'll call it even." He began to nod effusively, the relief apparent in the grateful expression that lit his young face. "Oh, gee, thanks, Mrs. McClellan, thanks a lot! My father'd *kill* me if he—"

"Yes. Well, next time you have a sweet tooth, try the front door," Anne murmured as she turned to leave. "It's a lot less trouble . . . for everyone. I'll give it to you on the house." The last glimpse she had of him before she turned away was the deep scarlet flush staining his cheeks.

By now her head was throbbing. The dull ache in her temples that had resounded all morning had grown to a relentless vibration behind her eyes, and two aspirin and a dark room were beckoning like nirvana. It hadn't been a day she'd anticipated with pleasure, and it was turning out to be even worse than she'd feared. *Damn you, Mike Novak. How'd I let you exert such power over me? I can't enjoy anything anymore because of you!*

"Whoa there, you'll. . . . Oh!" Mike's surprise was almost as great as hers. "Anne."

Damn was exactly the right sentiment! Timing was everything in life, and hers was worse than rotten. A little faster—or slower—and she'd have made it. Instead, she'd managed to walk right into his arms. As if she were destined to be there no matter where she headed.

"Sorry. I'll have to be more careful about where I'm going."

"Are you hurt?"

She stared. Mike flushed a dull red and stepped back hastily.

"Nothing that won't mend, I assure you. I heal fast." *Darn right I do. I'll get over you. I've gotten over other, worse things, Novak. And I sure as hell will get over you.*

She snapped her mouth shut before anything else slipped out. The people he was standing with would soon begin to openly speculate on their relationship—their nonexistent relationship!—and she wasn't about to provide grist for the gossip mills. Anne recognized four of the town's selectmen, along with Mayor Litchfield and Reverend Shaver. How she could have missed seeing them in time to avoid a run-in was a sign of how disturbed she was, Anne thought unhappily. How disturbed Mike made her.

"Well, hi there, Anne." Joe Meacham put his arm on her shoulder and squeezed, holding her inadvertently where she really did not want to stay. She forced a smile and nodded.

"Hi, everyone. Isn't this a wonderful way to end the summer? The weather's so perfect."

"Yeah. Speaking of the end of summer, we were just talking about the election. November's not all that far away, and the primary's just around the corner."

"Let's hear Mrs. McClellan's opinion."

"My opinion about what, Reverend Shaver?" She looked inquiringly around her at the circle of friendly faces.

"It's nothing, Anne. Just foolish pipe dreams," Mike answered abruptly before anyone else could speak.

"No, now wait up there, Mike," Henry Litchfield said. "Anne's a citizen of Whitefield, a business owner. She's no different from a lot of the other voters around here and I'd like to hear what she thinks."

Mike scowled at the cheerful face of his longtime friend. "Look, Henry, it doesn't matter what she—"

"Why doesn't someone tell me what this is all about?" A minute ago she hadn't cared.

But now . . . well, how dare he say her opinion didn't matter. It might matter to *somebody*, even if that somebody wasn't him!

"We've been testing the political wind, so to speak—"

"More like hot air," Mike muttered, annoyed. He'd finally come face to face with Anne, and it had to be under the noses of all these other people. Damn!

"—and we wondered if Mike would consider making a run for our congressional seat. Tom Wilde is retiring and it's up for grabs." Henry Litchfield's face was earnest and enthusiastic, but Mike's was quite the opposite.

Suddenly, Anne glanced to her right. Elliot was standing there—within hearing distance, she realized with dismay, feeling unhappy and embarrassed for him. If her withdrawal had put his nose out of joint, this news might just blast it off his face for good. For one fleeting instant she saw his irritation swell to full-blown rage. Thin lips grew thinner, opaque eyes grew colder. Anne quickly turned away, back to the waiting group.

"Well, I've only been in Whitefield a few months," she hedged, "so I haven't studied the issues and—"

"Well, Mike, did I hear you say you might make a run for Congress?" Elliot had taken a place in the small knot of people, and Anne felt so badly for him she wished she could sink into the ground.

"Hello, Elliot." Mike looked directly at him and the chill in the morning air increased noticeably. "No, I'm not running for Congress or anything else." He glanced at Anne, then at Joe Meacham and the others. "I'm very happy trying to run the Police Department . . . when Ed and Vince let me." He tried to smile and change the subject, hoping they'd lose interest in him and leave. All except Anne. Suddenly, he knew he needed to talk with her. He needed to be with her. He needed . . .

"Oh, I don't blame you," Elliot said. "You've got your hands full from what I hear. Still no luck with the water problem, eh?" His hands rested in his pants pockets and he rocked back on his heels, waiting patiently for Mike's answer. The others followed suit.

"Oh, we'll get them, all right. It's just a matter of time."

"Seems to me you've been saying that for a while now," the mayor said thoughtfully. Elliot looked almost happy at Mike's annoyed expression.

"Won't be long now. We've got a lot of people working on it." Mike shook his head, frustrated. "We've got a plague on our hands in this country, and Coos County isn't immune. We've been a long time recognizing it. I only hope it's not too late."

"I haven't seen any problems around here, Mike," Joe Meacham protested.

"Maybe you haven't looked close enough. Last week we were fishing up on Caroll Creek . . ." He paused for a moment and Anne stiffened, resisting the impulse to turn and flee.

"Well, take my word for it, there's evidence up there. Some dead fish on the banks. The State lab did an analysis and found it was toxic residue from the pulp mills up in Berlin."

"He's right," Anne added impulsively. "Even some of the plant life was affected. And Mike said it wasn't even a massive dose that did it." For a moment she had a vivid recall of the beautiful scene and the negligence and greed that could have spoiled it.

"What the heck do these people want to dump that poison in the water for? There are legitimate, safe ways to get rid of it!" The mayor's round, ruddy face had turned bright red with anger.

"And they're expensive ways, too, Henry," Mike answered. "You're talking big money here. The O.W.M. estimates tens of thousands of dollars. I guess that's enough temptation for a lot of people." Mike had been living with the problem on an intimate level for weeks now and he could view it more pragmatically than they. His temper was no less aroused, just more controlled.

Suddenly, he was fed up to the teeth with it, with everything, with every problem that seemed to hang on and on, no solutions in sight. Well, right now he could try to solve at least one of those problems. And then, if he could get a few restful hours of sleep, he'd begin to tackle the rest.

"Fellas, I hate to break this up, but I've got some business to take care of. And remember, I am *not*, under any circumstances whatsoever, going to run for office. I have absolutely no interest in politics, not now, not ever. Now, is that clear to everyone?"

"Well, Mike," Henry Litchfield laughed, "you really ought to stop beating around the bush and learn to say what you mean!"

They all laughed at that, and the group began to scatter. "By the way, Anne, can I speak to you a minute? It's about that burglary in your shop." For a moment she believed it, recalling her recent talk with Josh, then realized it was his excuse to keep her there when she would have left with the others.

"Very clever, Chief. When it serves your

purpose, you can beat around the bush with the best of them.'' She sighed, staring off in the direction of St. Mary's Church across the square. She couldn't bear to look at him anymore. Her pain threshold was getting lower by the minute. It would soon be nonexistent. "Will this take long? I assume you don't really have anything to tell me about my burglar, since I've already found out who did it and it's been taken care of.''

"You really are an Agatha Christie fan, aren't you?" For a moment he almost smiled, and she almost smiled back. Almost.

Anne jammed her fists into her pockets, desperate to get away before she said or did anything foolish. "Look, Mike, if there's nothing else, I've got a doozy of a headache and I'd really like to get home." Well, it hadn't felt all that much like home lately, but that, too, would pass, she supposed. Patience. Hadn't Caroline recommended it? Maybe that's what she'd meant. You could get over anything with time.

But he blocked her path, as if he meant to say more. At least he'd given her a chance to look at him without seeming too obvious. It was the first straight hard look she'd dared take since she'd walked into his arms.

Boy, he really looked terrible. Her first instinct was to comfort him. Her second was to gloat. Why should she be the only non-sleeper in Whitefield? Good to know her misery had his company. It served him right! A permanent-looking scowl was carved between his eyes, and he had the pasty, drawn appearance of a man who hadn't had a nodding acquaintance with sleep in days.

Well, too darned bad.

Too bad about a lot of things.

"Look, I . . . uh . . . meant to call you." He couldn't count the times his hand had rested on the phone this past week, wanting to call, hesitating, and in the end doing nothing. After what he'd said to her, what other words of his would she even listen to? And what other words had he? He stared down at her face, hungry for the sight. He wanted to bury his face in her hair, to smell that fresh, clean perfume that was so uniquely hers, that clung to his sweater even a week after she'd worn it. He'd kept it in the back of his drawer, hoarding the scent that reminded him constantly of what he'd thrown away.

"I shouldn't have said those things to you. I was out of line."

"Yes, you were. Let me tell you something, *Chief* Novak: I don't want anything from you. And," she paused for a breath, warming to the subject, "it might be a good idea to look up the meaning of the word *friendship*. I didn't ask for, or expect, *ties*. I gave my lo—my affection"—the word sounded inane describing the night they'd had together. "I gave it freely, no strings attached. I don't know what you're used to in your sordid love life—and I use the term loosely—but I am *not* in that category! And *that* is what trust is all about. You'd do well to remember that."

She'd been itching all week for the chance to say that! So, why didn't she feel better now? Because her heart knew it was a lie? Perhaps because he looked so stricken, so much pain moving behind his eyes. Anne knew about pain, all right. She understood it very well, had lived with it longer than she wanted to recall and would now do so again. Because of him.

No. That wasn't fair. He'd promised nothing. She shouldn't have been surprised when that's what he offered. If there was sorrow and disappointment, it lay on her shoulders alone. And she should be glad it had ended so quickly, so cleanly. He was free to live his life any way he chose.

Mike lifted his sunglasses to his eyes, grateful to hide behind the blank concealment they offered. Her words had cut close to the bone and these people around them were old friends . . . too observant, too perceptive, too interested. It was one of the few times in recent years when he envied the faceless anonymity of city life.

"I don't blame you . . ."

"Sorry I can't say the same." Anne frowned. She had to get away before she made a damn fool of herself. She would shed no more tears for Mike Novak. Well, not in public at least. Sweet Expectations was looking more like a sanctuary every second. She glared at him, standing directly in her way, but he took no notice. He seemed reluctant to let her go and she couldn't imagine why. Hadn't they both said all there was to say? How much more damage did they need to inflict on each other?

"Have you seen Aunt Caro today? After all, she's not to blame for. . . . Well, I mean, Helena's seen you at work, but Caroline's been home with a cold all week. I know she'd like to see you."

"Nice to know not all the Novaks share your opinion. Two out of three ain't bad."

His face grew dark for a moment. Why had he said those things to her? She didn't deserve it. She'd done nothing, asked for nothing, promised nothing. She hadn't disappointed or betrayed. But he'd punished her, the only way he knew, for someone else's sins.

And now, here she was in front of him, and all he wanted was to take her in his arms, right there in the middle of the crowd, and hold her, tell her . . . kiss the living daylights out of her! Just the thought of touching her, all warm and happy and giving, all heat and joy and comfort. . . . He wasn't sure he could keep his hands off her. There'd been no refuge anywhere. Even home had become a cheerless destination at day's end, when there was no place else to go and nothing else to occupy his thoughts. All week it had been hell, trying to keep Helena and Caroline at arm's length, avoiding questions, keeping conversation on neutral ground. It was a masquerade that was growing increasingly intolerable, unbearably painful. He couldn't let her go yet. He couldn't.

"Let's see where they've got to? Ah, there's Aunt Caro with the 'nit-pick knitters.' " He smiled and, for a moment, so did Anne.

"Yes, I'll bet they're doing a good job picking on what's new in the Whitefield news."

Their smiles faded self-consciously. Had they been the recent Whitefield news? Were they still? Both took surreptitious measure of the eyes and ears nearby. Fortunately, the pancakes and syrup seemed to be a much more interesting object of attention to the voluble and neighborly gathering than did either of them. Even Elliot, a few feet away, holding forth to a group of would-be constituents, seemed to have forgotten them.

Just then Anne spotted Helena and Josh with their friends on the far side of the gazebo. Mike glanced in the same direction. He muttered something and Anne turned at the sound. Even behind his glasses, she saw the change in his expression.

"What the hell is that Cappello kid doing, hanging all over her? Who does he think he—?" He would have headed straight for the group of teenagers had not Anne, forgetting her own wish for escape, grabbed his arm and held him back. Not so easy to keep a determined Mike Novak from his parental crusade.

"Mike," she whispered urgently, "what are you doing?"

"What do you think I'm doing? I'm not letting my daughter be pawed by—"

"For heaven's sake, he's not pawing. What is it with you? First you practically explode when she dances with a boy. And now this. All he did was put his arm around her shoulder, in full view of the entire town, not to mention the police force," she said tartly.

"I knew the lipstick was a mistake," Mike muttered, eyes still fixed on Helena and Josh across the grass.

"Mike, this is the twentieth century, remember? A tube of lipstick does not a fallen woman make! My God, you've certainly got the heavy-handed father routine down pat!"

"Listen, Anne, I'm raising her to be a good, respectable kid. There's more to life than fun and games, flirting with boys and running around. . . ."

Of course.

It was eminently clear to Anne. Worry more than anger riddled Mike Novak. She worried, too, for a different reason.

"Stop it this instant!"

Mike swung around, stunned, and faced Anne's determined face and glittering eyes. "Just stop it, Mike, and listen to me for one minute, unless you want to cause an embarrassing scene. I know, the last thing you want is to listen to me, but I'm going to say this anyway and I'm not letting go of your arm until I'm through." She stopped for a breath.

"Open your eyes, for heaven's sake. Helena is *Helena*. She is *not* Adrienne!"

Any more than I am, Anne reflected sadly, then put the thought aside.

"You're looking for Adrienne and your

mother in everything Helena does, Mike. You're anticipating it, sure of it, and that's wrong . . . and what's more it's dangerous. Your daughter is a sweet, loving, normal fifteen-year-old, a good, decent girl. But one of these days you could drive her away with this . . . this paranoid distrust of yours. Your suspicions just might force the very thing you dread."

"What do you know about it? Do you do psychological counseling on the side, *Dr. McClellan?*" His voice was hoarse with the strain of whispering. Between Helena and Anne, he'd wind up in the nut house! What had happened to his life lately? Hell, what had happened to *him?*

"I'll tell you what I know about it!" Anne spoke through gritted teeth. "No one wants, or deserves, to be blamed for someone else's past sins. Helena's not Adrienne—" She stopped, then sucked in a deep breath and plunged ahead. "Everyone gets knocked down now and then; you just have to get back up. So you've had a couple of bad breaks. Well, tough rocks!" Her face was red with emotion, her eyes flashing, her tousled hair bouncing in undisciplined agitation.

Mike's mouth dropped open. He stared at her, then he suddenly started to laugh and said the first thing that popped into his mind. *"Tough rocks?"*

"Well, whatever . . ." She smiled wryly, suddenly calm, her abrupt burst of fury deflated. "I know the current thought is that fathers should be interested and involved with their children, but maybe you should be *less* interested. Maybe you need a hobby, some other interest besides Helena's possible fall from grace." He was still gazing steadily at her, an unnerving prospect, she thought, to say the least. "Look, Mike, neither Helena nor I are responsible for the past. It doesn't matter about me, but she deserves better than that from you. And you know it. Helena has to grow up—and you have to let her. Let her love you."

As I would have.

That was it! She couldn't look at him another second without the floodgates opening. Anne turned and hurried away as quickly as she could without attracting any more attention than she already had. She didn't look back to see Mike still staring after her.

Mike spent a rare Sunday afternoon in his office at the station. It was easier than facing the inquisition he'd find at home. Here he could pull down the blinds, shut the door, and be assured none of his staff would dare break his solitude unless Judgment Day was at hand. He couldn't take any more accusing eyes on him . . . not Helena's, not Caroline's. He had enough accusation to face from himself. After all the years of being in control, not needing to answer to anyone, knowing exactly where he was going and why, Anne McClellan had come along and promptly put an end to his nice comfortable existence. And he'd called Elliot Gilcrest smug!

Thank heavens it was a relatively quiet day. Obviously, everyone in Whitefield was too replete from pancakes and syrup to have enough energy for mischief-making. The station was unusually silent. When the phones rang at all, they were muted by the secluded atmosphere of his office.

But there was no silence in his head, his heart. Emptiness, yes. But the memories, the hopes, the glimmerings of once-possible dreams, all clamored noisily inside him. One day, when his job was done—and that wasn't so far off, he admitted—when he was simply too old to continue and retirement was his only option, what then? The simple satisfactions of his planned and pleasant life no longer held meaning. They held, quite simply, nothing. He'd shut the door firmly on the only thing that would have given them meaning.

Anne.

Once the sound of her name had brought knee-jerk annoyance, irritation. Now it brought loneliness—and desire. Emptiness and hunger. He wouldn't, couldn't, say her name aloud. He didn't have to. He heard it in his head, his heart.

The price of everything and the value of nothing. He cursed himself for the fool he knew he was.

Sixteen

"Michael, how in the world can you work in all this mess? This office looks like the Coos County dump."

"Don't start, Aunt Caroline." His temper was on a short leash, even with her. It had been a long time since he'd felt this rotten. Fourteen years, to be exact. Endings, no matter what was ending, weren't easy. The trouble was, he was no longer sure he *wanted* an ending. And of course, an ending meant there had to be a beginning. Just exactly what had begun between him and Anne?

If you don't really want to know the answer, don't ask the question.

"You don't have to bite my head off, young man."

"Sorry. What are you doing in town, anyway?"

"There's a sale at the Yarn Barn." She was ready with her answer. "You need a new sweater but all they had was grey. Is that all right?"

"Mmm-hmm . . . perfect!" He felt grey. Mike dropped his head into his hands, rubbing his temples, his eyes. She knew quite well who that "something" was.

"Michael, dear, what's the matter? Is something bothering you?"

"Nothing's bothering me, not a thing." He dumped a healthy portion of sugar into his coffee. He never used sugar. "Not a thing!" Not those warm gentle eyes. Not that unruly hair, the silver frosted dark waves framing her cheeks. Not the generous smile on soft pink lips . . .

Not a thing!

"Have you got a headache?"

"Like a sonic boom inside my skull," he muttered. "I'll get some aspirin." He started to rise but she pressed him back into his chair.

"Sit. I'll get it for you." Caroline gazed down at him, shaking her head, then walked into the outer office.

"Edwin, have you any aspirin?"

He looked over her shoulder at Mike, through the glass partition. "That has to be the granddaddy of all headaches, the way he's been actin' today, Miss Caroline. Was he out on a tear last night?"

Caroline almost smiled at the exasperation in Ed's voice. "No, I don't think it's that kind of pain." She recalled Mike's silence when he'd walked in the door the night of the fishing trip. When she voiced her concern over Anne's cold-water swim in the river, his terse answer told her she would get no more out of him. In the ensuing two weeks, the power of speech hadn't noticeably increased, either. But that was how he'd always reacted to pain. Bit down hard on his lip, even if he drew blood, and said as little as possible. Boy and man, some things didn't change. Only the depth of the pain.

The deputy handed her a small bottle and took a bite out of the doughnut in his other hand. "Yecch! This stuff from the grocery store tastes like the bottom of a birdcage." His expression was almost forlorn at the thought of the pastries he'd gotten used to in the last few weeks and from which he was now undergoing severe withdrawal. "Guess I'm spoiled by all the good stuff we been eatin' round here lately." He grinned and pointed to a discarded blue box in the wastebasket.

To Caroline, it was mute support for her own theory about Mike's behavior. Silently, she returned and handed him the tablets, waiting while he swallowed. "Now, how about taking an old lady to lunch?"

"Not today, Aunt Caro," he answered shortly. "Got a lot of things piling up here." His hand rested on the morning's O.W.M. report. They— whoever *they* were—seemed to be increasing the amount and frequency of their midnight excursions. Toxicity was up in the small feeder streams and now reports of fish kills were starting to show up closer to town, and closer to the river and the reservoir. But at least he had a good excuse to avoid Caroline's sharp eyes; her incisive third degree for an hour over the lunch table sure wouldn't help him forget the look in Anne's eyes.

"Well, you had your chance, my dear."

He looked up, startled. How could she know?

"Time was, an offer like that would have been snapped up by any man in town." He sagged with relief as she smiled and walked briskly to the door, her back erect, her step as steady as it had ever been, apparently with nothing more on her mind than the problem of filling her stomach.

But her mind, and her eyes, and especially the innate sense of the emotional state of her loved ones provided more than her appetite for Caroline to ponder. Michael was a grown man, a good man, and his life was his own.

She'd always known she could rely on his good judgment and discretion. He certainly didn't need an old spinster busybody overseeing his actions.

But this, she was certain, was very different. These last few weeks, there'd been a new Michael Novak in evidence. And she wasn't the only one to notice. Betty, over at the Yarn Barn, had been fishing for information and not very subtle about it, either the old longnose! Later, when she made the bank deposit, even young Gilcrest had mentioned seeing Anne and Mike together. Couldn't be much going on in Whitefield lately, she thought, if that's all they had on their minds!

She waved goodbye to the office staff and strode down the street toward King's Square, her determined pace and purposeful air belying her years. Without thought, her steps led her in the only direction in which she had any interest. She almost walked right into a tall blond woman coming toward her.

"Oops, I'm so sorry, I didn't . . . oh, Miss Novak! Hello!" She hugged the older woman.

"No harm done . . . why, Harriet Ryan! How are you, dear? You haven't been by for a cup of tea in donkey's years." Caroline smiled at the blonde while she adjusted her scarf and took a firm grip on her plastic bag full of yarn.

"Well, I've been so busy this year. They gave me an extra class in English Lit and I've got my hands full staying one step ahead of my students. They're already convinced they know more than I do; I can't take a chance they'll prove it!" she laughed. "So, what brings you into town?"

"Just saw that nephew of mine. Mean as a bear with a sore foot! Goodness, I can't figure out what's got hold of him." She eyed the younger woman with avid speculation. There would never be a better time than now to find out. "It's been a while since you two have seen each other, hasn't it?"

"Miss Novak, are you fishing?" Harriet laughed. "Nice of you to be so diplomatic, but I think Mike's interests have moved in another direction. Anyway, you know Mike and I were never serious. We've been convenient company for one another, that's all, and good friends far too long to be anything else. It would be like having a romance with my brother, if I had one. And, frankly, since my divorce, I've often thought one trip to the altar was quite enough. I think I'm too independent and ornery to share my space with a man . . . permanently. But, who knows, there's world enough and time for another turn at the marriage lotto." She winked. "Besides, as I said, I think Mike's found someone who interests him a lot more than I ever did."

The grey head and the blond one nodded together without needing any more words. A brisk breeze caught the end of Caroline's scarf, flipping it up and off her shoulder. She shivered. "Weather's changin' mighty fast, isn't it? Let's get in out of the cold. Are you busy, or would you like to join me for a bite of lunch? We can catch up on the news."

"Sounds wonderful. What do you feel like having?"

"I know! Let's try that new shop . . . what's it called . . . ? Oh, yes, Sweet Expectations. I hear they serve lunch now." She smiled innocently at Harriet, who smiled back with perfect understanding.

The two began walking, blond head and grey bent together in eager conversation.

"I've broken the neck on every one of these stupid swans! I never have trouble with this stuff. What is wrong with me today?"

No answer. No answer needed when you talk to yourself, she thought wryly. Disconcerted, Anne stared at the crumbling remains of the choux-dough swan's head in her fingers. Oh well, stainless steel swans couldn't have survived today at her hands. If she kept up at this rate, the special order Swan torte for the Spalding Inn would end up completely un-swanned, and she'd have to resort to plain old chocolate shavings. Swan torte with no swans. Shit. *Well, tough rocks, kiddo . . . you wanted to own a business!*

"Either my biorhythms are low, or today's horoscope was a doozy!" Anne shrugged, her mouth twisted in a sour grimace that imitated a smile.

Anger. Frustration. Hurt. They all vied on twin battlefields of heart and mind. Along with love, the most stubborn adversary of all. No matter what, it resisted banishment in the face of overwhelming provocation. And Mike had certainly done his best to provide that.

Anne winced. Well, really, wasn't it better this way, to know, to see now, rather than to delude herself about him? Perhaps Mike had done her a bigger favor than he knew.

She didn't believe it for a second.

The cheerful jingling of the bell was a welcome interruption to the dismal direction her mind had taken, and Anne hurried from the depths of the kitchen. A smile of genuine delight lit her face and she came round the counter to greet Caroline—and only then spotted her surprise companion, who was just slightly less unwelcome than an invasion of fire ants. Anne's mouth was caught, comically, between delight and dismay.

"Brrr," Caroline shivered delicately, "winter's coming on fast. Hello, Anne dear, we came in for some lunch." She gestured at Harriet. "I understand you know—"

"We've met. Uh . . . Mike introduced us once. . . ."

"Oh, yes, I remember. You're Mac, aren't you?" The blonde's hand hung, lonely, in midair for a fraction of a second, before it was taken by the shop's suddenly silent proprietor in a less than enthusiastic greeting.

"Yes, and you're . . . Honey." There was no coy hint that Anne wasn't completely conscious of who the other woman was.

Honey grinned, and Anne thought spontaneously what a natural and open smile it was. Damn, she might really like this woman if they'd met under other circumstances.

"Can you join us while we eat, dear?" Caroline, taking charge, was steering the other two toward an empty table at the side of the small room. Only one other table was still occupied and the two women there were finishing their meal, making ready to leave.

"Just a minute while I get their check, Caroline," Anne whispered, then turned to the cash register. Caroline looked at Honey and winked. They sat down while the two ladies paid their bill and, with a smile and nod to Caroline, left the shop. For a few moments, at least, the three were alone.

"What would you like to eat? We have pecan chicken salad or I think there's some smoked trout salad still in the fridge. And there's some good hot black bean soup, too." They nodded and made their choices.

Anne was sorely tempted to serve them and retreat to a hiding place in the kitchen. Lots of things to keep her busy there. *Anything* to avoid the discussion she knew was imminent. After all, how was she to avoid Mike's name in a conversation with those two? Damn, just what she needed today—mutilated swans, that call from Sandy Larkin, moldy strawberries, and Mike Novak.

But still he nagged at her! She needed to speak about him, hear about him. It was perverse, she knew, like poking your tongue at a sore tooth. Why would a woman with an iota of self-respect and character have even a speck of interest in a man who had dropped her so precipitately, the way he had? Why indeed? It was obvious she had absolutely no strength of character.

Anne ladled out the soup, pushed through the door with the laden tray, and sat down at the table.

"I'm really glad you came in today, Caroline. I needed the lift. Sandy Larkin called earlier. . . . Jamie's home sick, won't be in today. I'll have to take the deliveries myself after I close." She shook her head and shrugged ruefully. "Boy, that sounds pretty bitchy, doesn't it? Lord, *he's* the one who's sick and I'm complaining. I don't know what's wrong with me. . . . I'm way past using PMS as an excuse." She sighed, giving away more than she knew in that short breath. "Guess it's the weather or something."

Or something. Anne glanced at the women across from her. Surprisingly silent, Caroline sat there smiling down blandly at her folded hands. Honey was grinning directly at her, as if she knew exactly the dilemma Anne was in. Shit, she probably did. She was obviously on intimate terms with the "dilemma."

Anne sighed once more, annoyed with herself, and looked again at Honey, suddenly noting her appearance with a jolt of surprise. Suggestive allure was conspicuous by its absence. Today she was dressed in a demure dark skirt and high-buttoned blouse beneath the bulky winter coat she'd just shed. Her pale lipstick and the large glasses perched atop her sleekly confined blond hairdo made her look about as sexy as a high school English teacher.

"Uh, so, Miss . . . er . . ."

"Oh, it's Ryan," the other woman grinned. "Rotten Ryan or Ryan the Wretched, depending on which of my students you speak to. But please call me Harriet."

"Students?"

"Yes, Freshman English at White Mountain."

Good grief, she *was* a high school English teacher!

"As a matter of fact, Helena would have been in my class but I told them to put her in another class. I'm afraid I'd have been prejudiced about her."

Boy, Anne thought, that's putting it on the line. She and Mike were really close! "Is that like a doctor not treating his family?" she asked, not quite hiding the sarcasm that etched her words.

"Yeah, something like that," Honey laughed back innocently. "You mentioned Sandy and Jamie Larkin; she's one of my students. I just saw her in class this morning. She mentioned her brother's in the hospital."

"The hospital!" Anne stared, concerned. "My God, what's the matter? She never said anything when she called this morning."

"They think it may be appendicitis," Harriet said reassuringly. "They're keeping him under observation until they're sure, doing tests. She said he had really bad stomach pains last night, and it got so bad they finally took him to the emergency room."

"Oh, I hope he'll be all right. Perhaps I'll go see him if he's allowed visitors."

"I'm going over after I finish at the school. I'll let you know what they say. Jamie was one of my students, too, a couple of years ago."

"My son would have sold me into captivity to get a teacher that looks like you."

Honey leaned back, laughing heartily. "Don't you believe it. My kids have never seen my femme fatale getup. I change clothes in a phone booth." She grinned and lifted her spoon to taste the hot soup.

Hell, Anne thought, you couldn't help but like the woman! It really was *not* fair.

"That's some phone booth. May I borrow it sometime? If I could come out looking like that . . ."

"I'm so glad you said that. I've worked hard on that other me! Mike's a dear; he lets me put on the glitz and glamour with him, for practice. 'Till the real thing comes along,' you know?"

Anne's heart jumped. "You and Mike have known each other a long time, hmm?"

"Goodness, since junior high, at least. My Galahad!" She fluttered her eyes, then winked.

"Not exactly the way I'd have described him," Anne answered dryly.

"Ah, well, he never had to rescue you from 'a fate worse than.'" Honey was still smiling, but there was a serious glint in her blue eyes.

Anne looked puzzled.

"You see, Mac—"

"Make it Anne. That's what my adult friends call me."

"Anyway," Honey took a bite of her chicken salad, "I was an early bloomer, so to speak. You might say nature's gifts came to the forefront." She looked down, then up at her two listeners, a conspiratorial grin on her face. "I guess the male teenage libidos were—how should I say it?—ready to explore. But I wasn't. To make a long story short, Mike rescued me from a scary situation with two boys who'd gotten me in an isolated corner. I was scared witless, and he looked like Prince Charming and the Jolly Green Giant all rolled into one heaven-sent package. And from then on, it seemed he was always just . . . there whenever I needed someone. He was one of the few members of the opposite sex who gave me credit for an IQ higher than my bra size. I never had a brother, but I couldn't have had a better one than Mike Novak." Casually, she took another healthy bite while Anne mulled over her words.

Caroline hurried to fill the void while she still had Anne where she wanted her. "Anne, dear, this soup is delicious! Wonderful on a day like today. Especially after the chill I got from Jolly Green Sir Galahad just now." Subtle. Caroline couldn't fiddle around with subtlety; she had to keep the agenda on track. Time was of the essence. She wasn't getting any younger and neither was Michael. She didn't want him to let this one get away!

When Anne didn't immediately pick up the cue, Honey jumped in. "What's wrong with Mike, Caroline? I mean, he wouldn't be angry with *you* if you chopped up his fishing gear for firewood."

"I can't understand it, either." Dear Harriet, she was perfect. Between them, Anne didn't stand a chance. "As a matter of fact, didn't you two go fishing a couple of weeks ago, Anne?"

As if she didn't know. Anne nodded, took a large bite of pita bread and chicken salad, and veered from dangerous ground. "Mmm, this isn't bad, is it? I wasn't sure whether to add a dash of curry or—"

"I remember he came home so late we never got a chance to talk. Did he catch anything? How was his luck?"

Anne choked.

"You must have swallowed the wrong way, dear. Have some water." Butter wouldn't have melted in Caroline's mouth.

Slowly, Anne put her sandwich . . . and her cards . . . on the table. Without all the gory details, though. She needed to preserve her pride, after all.

"We had a . . . very nice day. It wasn't quite as long as he'd planned. We had to cut it short when I filled up with water. My boots, I mean."

"Yes, those things are a bitch to waddle around in, aren't they?" Honey laughed in sympathy.

Anne kept looking at her teacup, running her finger round and round the rim, wishing desperately she could think of a reason to excuse herself from the table. "Anyway, he took me home and we . . . uh . . . talked and it was late so he . . . uh . . . left."

"Oh, gosh, speaking of late!" Honey glanced at her wristwatch, her eyes widening. "My lunch hour's over and I've got to get back. Staff meeting this afternoon and I never did finish my shopping." She put a five-dollar bill on the table and pushed back her chair. As she slipped on her coat, she turned to Caroline. "It was marvelous seeing you again, Miss Novak. As soon as I get myself on schedule, I'll drop over for tea . . . if you promise to have some of that delicious pumpkin bread, too!" She squeezed the older woman's hand, then faced Anne, backing hurriedly toward the door as she spoke.

"I'm so glad we talked and got to know each other a little. It's always nice to make a new friend." She clasped Anne's hand firmly and smiled. "Lunch was delicious, and if I don't leave now, I'll wind up with a box of those fabulous-looking pastries. My hips will kill me if I do!" She grinned, and in a flurry of smiles, waves, and a final wink, she was gone.

"I should have such careful hips!" Anne turned to the table and began gathering the dirty dishes. "She's really very nice, isn't she? I didn't realize . . ."

Caroline's eyebrows rose but Anne deflected any questions with a shrug, busily cleaning the table. "Come on into the kitchen, Caroline. I have some things to finish. And Helena will be here soon since there's no school this afternoon. You want to wait?" She felt as if she were clinging to Caroline, not wanting to break this contact with. . . . No, she was *not* going to think his name again!

Caroline checked her watch. "Yes, I think I will. I'm in no rush. Dinner's all ready and Michael won't be home until after six o'clock." She waited, but Anne was busy ignoring the obvious opening. "I just don't understand what's bothering him lately." Again she waited.

Nothing.

Desperate measures. Caroline sighed, picked up a small paring knife, and started peeling plums, just as Anne was studiously doing. "How many do you need?"

"Just a couple more will be—"

"Hi, Mac. Hey, Aunt Callie! What're you doing here?" Helena burst through the back door, hugged her aunt, waved at Anne, and deposited her jacket on the hook by the door, all in the space of twelve seconds . . . a little slower than usual, Anne thought with a smile.

"Helena, you run on as fast as the express train to Manchester. Can't you try the local for a change?" Caroline smiled at the girl, smoothing the long dark hair with an affectionate gesture.

"I thought I was late. . . . I told Mac I'd be in at lunchtime today, but I was talking to Sandy and then I bumped into Mr. Gilcrest when I got off the school bus and he started talking to me and . . ."

"That's what wristwatches are for, child."

Helena flushed and bit her lip, frowning. "I . . . guess I left it home this morning." Hastily, she tied on a long white apron like Anne's and started washing the bowls and rubber spatulas soaking in the sink.

"So industrious. I'm very impressed, young lady. I've never seen you so diligent at a kitchen sink." Caroline's dry comment brought a smile to Anne's face, a martyred expression to Helena's. "By the way, we just heard about Sandra's brother. Have they found out anything more about Jamie yet?"

Helena shook her head. "No, Sandy says it's probably his appendix."

"Well," Caroline said, "tell her I wish him well. Now I'd better be going. I've a couple of stops to make before I head for home. Anne, come walk me to the door."

Anne wiped her hands on her apron and followed Caroline from the kitchen. She was surprised when the older woman turned, all humor gone from her face, a serious expression in its place.

"The trouble with good advice is it's almost certain to be ignored, but that's no reason not to give it. I know I'm a meddlesome old busybody and it's none of my affair, but before you tell me to mind my own business, I want you to know how fond I am of you. If I didn't care so much about my dolt of a nephew, I wouldn't open my mouth. Please, Anne, be patient with him. For a smart man, he does and says some very stupid things.''

Anne bit her lip and looked away from the sharp grey eyes.

"Yes, I thought so," Caroline murmured. "I'm right, aren't I? Well, you don't have to answer. But I do hope you'll think about it before you send him packing.''

"Uh . . . well, I . . .'' Anne was flustered. She didn't normally indulge the urge to "show and tell,'' but the words just spilled out. "It wasn't I who sent him packing, Caroline. It was the other way around.'' She walked away a few steps, resolute, then turned back. "We did have a lovely day fishing, but I don't think Mike and I will be seeing each other anymore. He seems to think I'm trying to . . . uh . . . get my hooks into him.''

"About time, too.'' Caroline looked distinctly approving.

"I . . . beg your pardon?''

"Mac, I can't find—'' Helena pushed the swinging door open and stopped. "Oh, Aunt Callie, I didn't know you were still here!'' She looked from one to the other. "Uh . . . well, I'll wait till you're through. . . ." She retreated back into the kitchen.

"She likes you very much. And you're quite fond of her, too, aren't you?" Caroline looked from the still-swinging door back to Anne and, not waiting for an answer, took a deep breath. "Look, I'm a plain-speaking woman, Anne dear, and I figure I'm old enough to say what I think without beating around the bush. You don't have to listen, but I'm sure you're too polite to interrupt." She sat heavily at one of the empty tables, her purse and parcels clutched in her lap. Her voice was pensive as she spoke, all the while staring straight at Anne.

"My Michael is a man who is very sure. About everything. He doesn't waver an inch once a decision is made. And he made his decision about women a long time ago." She pursed her lips. "Has he ever said anything to you about his mother and father or about his marriage?"

"He told me what happened with Adrienne."

Caroline sighed deeply. "You may have noticed in some areas my nephew is a cynical man." She smiled ruefully at Anne's snort of agreement.

"Yes, I see you have. Well, you must understand that much if you have any hope of understanding him. He had his first lessons from Dorine—his mother." Caroline's usually controlled voice was suddenly grim, harsh, and unflinchingly icy. "I'll tell you right out, I wasn't any too fond of my late sister-in-law. She was vain, thoughtless, foolish—an almost criminally selfish woman—and although my brother may have asked for that kind of treatment, Michael certainly didn't. He was a good-natured young boy, neglected by both of his parents much of the time and forced to grow up too early, to face harsh reality much too soon. But his memories of his mother were very fertile ground for his early cynicism." She sighed heavily and shook her head. "And, too, he saw what loving her did to Conrad. My brother hadn't that renowned granite backbone we New Englanders pride ourselves on, and Michael had to watch him drown himself in a bottle because of her." Caroline looked up at Anne, a rueful smile on her lips.

"And that awful marriage to Adrienne only confirmed and reinforced that lesson. It's a matter of trust, you see. Michael doesn't trust women."

No kidding. "What about you?"

"My dear," she chuckled, amusement suddenly lightening her features, "Michael doesn't see me as a woman. Steady, dependable, trustworthy Aunt Caroline. Rather like an aging Girl Scout or an old dog." She smiled and Anne smiled back.

"Well. I guess I've had my say. And more." Caroline paused and took a small linen handkerchief from her capacious old leather purse. She touched it to her eyes, looking up at Anne from beneath her lashes. "Please, my dear, indulge a foolish old woman's love for her family. . . ." Her voice quavered just the slightest bit. "Perhaps I had no business telling you all this, but I have a feeling that there's something between you and Michael, something that shouldn't be discarded."

Anne sighed, wishing Caroline hadn't told her all this, not wanting to know so much about Mike Novak, not wanting to feel guilt and pity and sadness and loss—not wanting to *feel* at all. And in the end it couldn't matter anyway. It was not up to her anymore. Mike would have to make the move, not she.

"Forgive me, Anne, if I've overstepped the boundaries, but I wanted you to know. Perhaps it's none of my business and I guess garrulous old busybodies shouldn't be let out in public!" Caroline rose and patted Anne's hand as she turned to leave.

"Caroline?"

"Yes, dear?"

"For an aging Girl Scout, you have a terrific arm."

Caroline stared, uncomprehending.

Anne couldn't hold back a smile. "You can really sling the old baloney."

"What?"

"No matter how you slice it, it's still baloney!" Anne leaned back against the counter, arms folded, grinning hugely. "You almost had me, up until that 'none of my business' stuff. Garrulous old busybody, my foot! That performance deserves an Oscar." Anne laughed aloud. "And I almost fell for that little snow job. 'A foolish old woman. Poor Caroline, poor Helena, poor Mike.' "

Caroline's mouth turned down, and she shrugged and shook her head. "I was afraid I'd overdone it. Ah, well, it was worth a try. You seemed like the type who'd respond to an appeal like that." She looked up at Anne, a smile at the corner of her mouth. "But the rest of it is true, you know. And I did want you to . . . to understand. Don't give up on him. Not yet."

They looked at each other then, and a few moments later when Helena poked her head through the doors again, the two women, tears and smiles mingling, were hugging each other. She gazed up at the ceiling as if to ask "what now," then silently disappeared once more.

"Tell me something, Caroline," Anne finally managed to ask, wiping her eyes with the corner of her apron. "Does Mike fall for that poor-mouth act?"

"Well, every now and then if I'm forced to resort to those tactics to really get his attention . . . yes, though I truly don't do it often. Only when it's something very important and if I know I'm right."

Serious now, Anne looked at her. "And you think this is important."

"And I *know* I'm right."

"How I envy you." Anne folded her hands and studied her fingernails carefully. "Let's face it, Caroline. Mike and I are still getting to know each other." She winced, recalling how well they already *knew* each other. "As you said, he's a grown man, he's been around, and he knows what he wants. That doesn't necessarily mean me."

"The question is: Do you *want* it to mean you?"

Yes, of course, that was the question. Anne rather thought she already knew the answer.

She looked at Caroline and shrugged. "Even if I do—"

"Well, then I'm sure it will all work out." Caroline smiled in benign self-satisfaction, as if she'd already accomplished an exceedingly difficult task.

"Please, Caroline, don't . . . uh . . . don't . . . say anything to him." Anne's cheeks flamed scarlet and her words were barely more than a mumble. "Whatever happens—or doesn't happen—the next move has to be Mike's."

"Oh, my dear, of course. I guess I came across as an interfering old witch. Believe me, Michael and I wouldn't have lasted fourteen days, no less fourteen years, if I hadn't been more discreet and less overbearing than that! Just remember, you and I are friends, and it's not so bad a thing to have a friend in your corner." Then she squeezed Anne's hand and hurried out the door.

Squaring her shoulders and her resolve—there *must* be other things to think about!—Anne walked back to the kitchen.

"Hi, Mac. Aunt Caroline gone? Gee, you two sure were having a long talk."

"Mmmm. Have you seen the flour sifter?" Anne searched, looking everywhere but at Helena.

"So . . . uh . . . maybe you'll come out to the house for dinner again soon?" Helena waited, in vain.

"Mmmm." Anne gave a noncommittal little shrug and smiled. "Sweetie, will you hand me a sheet of parchment paper, please?"

"Uh, she's kinda worried about my dad, I think." Well, at least Mac looked at her that time! "He's acting kind of weird lately. . . ."

"Mmmm." Anne bent her head and began kneading the dough on the table.

"Mac, are you *sure* you weren't born in New Hampshire?"

"Mmmm." Anne looked up. "What?"

Exasperated at the dry well she was digging, Helena looked straight at her. "Aunt Callie says *nobody* can clam up like us granite-heads."

Anne grinned at the girl. "Then clam up! We've got work to do! By the way, what did you want to ask me before?"

"Huh? Oh! I just wondered if you found my—" She stopped, looked down at her hands, then hurriedly put both behind her back. "I mean, I wondered if you wanted me to start some dill pepper rolls! We're almost out."

"Good idea. I'm glad you noticed. I want to finish these miserable, cursed swans. Off with their heads!" Within seconds the air was heavy with flour and more than a few unanswered questions.

Anne chewed her tuna salad and sipped her cup of soup, but she couldn't have said what it was she was eating. Her thoughts were not on the quality of her cuisine. The light from the television screen lit the room and she had absolutely no idea what she'd been watching for the last hour. When the phone rang she jumped, lunging for it, then stopped and made herself wait for a second ring.

"Hello."

"Mom?"

"Oh, hi, Jerry." Her voice was dispirited. He couldn't help but notice.

"Uh . . . something wrong? You sound so . . . funny."

Ho, ho, ho! She didn't feel very funny. "No, dear, everything's fine. How come you're calling tonight? You okay?"

"Oh, yeah. But lately you've been sounding kinda . . . you know . . . strange. And last night, you hardly asked me any questions at all."

She chuckled in spite of herself. "Yes, unheard-of behavior for a mother!" What was she supposed to tell him? "Well, everything's just . . . fine," she answered weakly. Fine. "Really."

"Mmm, this . . . Chief Novak. You . . . you see a lot of him?"

She bit her lips to hold back the ironic laughter in her throat. There'd been one memorable night when she'd sure seen a lot of him!

"Oh, once in a while. It's a small town, of course, and everyone knows everyone else. We're . . . friends." Did that sound as weak to him as it did to her? She wanted to ease his uncertainty. "You know, Jer, I still think about Dad sometimes, and I miss him."

"Yeah, I do too, Mom." He sounded uncomfortable voicing his emotions to her.

"He loved being your father, you know. Don't ever forget that," she said fiercely, recalling Caroline's story of Mike's childhood. "And don't worry, even though he's gone we'll survive"—*I'll survive*—"because we learned how to love each other. That's what he gave us to keep forever." That's what Mike never had.

"Uh, Mom, I thought, maybe . . . what I mean is, I think it's okay if . . . it'd be a good thing for you to . . . uh . . . to go out, you know, on dates and . . . stuff."

Anne smiled. How difficult this was for him. How could you think of your *mother* going out on dates? Do mothers actually do that kind of stuff? "Honey, that's awfully sweet of you. I'm sure I will . . . go on dates. You know, I loved your dad very much. . . ."

"Jeez, Mom, I know that!" Now he sounded embarrassed. "You don't have to explain anything to me. I just figured I ought to let you know—"

"Thank you, honey." Her eyes stung with tears. "I . . . I really do appreciate your concern, and I'm glad you told me how you feel." She sniffled and wiped her eyes on her sleeve. "So, how's school?"

"Mom, you asked me that last night, remember? It hasn't changed much in one day!" He hesitated, then asked, "Hey . . . uh . . . are you crying?"

Anne swallowed quickly and wiped her eyes again. "Of course not. Why would I be crying?"

"Listen, if that Novak guy made you—"

"No, no, he certainly didn't make me cry. Don't be silly. I told you, everything's fine."

"Okay, I'll talk to you Sunday. You sure you're okay?"

"I'm sure. Love you, honey. Bye!"

Anne sat there, eyes closed, tears streaming down her cheeks unchecked. Then she stood abruptly, walked into the bathroom, and splashed her hot face with cold water. She stared into the mirror at the red-eyed apparition facing her, crying over Michael Novak. Why? Why now, why him?

I didn't cry for Paul, did I? Poor Paul, he deserved that; I owed him that. So many tears inside, but they never showed.

Oh no. Uh-uh! Anne blew her nose into a handful of sodden tissue, shaking her head. She was still Anne McClellan, pastry shop owner extraordinaire, successful and smug mother of Jerome Andrew, the world's most perfect son. She lifted her chin. And Paul's widow. Mike Novak wasn't going to make a liar out of her! She'd told Jerry everything was fine. And that's exactly how everything was going to be!

She walked back to the living room with a purposeful step. The last of the tuna tasted delicious, the lukewarm soup absolutely marvelous. And the program she watched was utterly fascinating. By the time the dishes were done and she undressed for bed, she actually believed it. She left the small lamp on and walked into the bedroom.

When she turned off the bedside lamp, the picture frame was still hidden in the drawer.

Seventeen

"I really don't want more lamb chops, Aunt Caro." Mike pushed the food around his plate impatiently, wanting to get finished with dinner so he could escape to his den, with no curious eyes to watch him and no questions to be avoided.

As if he could find a way to avoid his own thoughts. He'd searched, God how he'd searched! And the only enemy he'd found was his own lack of trust. What was that line from the old comic strip? *"We have met the enemy, and he is us!"*

". . . don't know what's gotten into you. Maybe it's all that greasy coffee you drink. Why don't you start drinking some good coffee for a change?"

He looked up and caught the calculating look on Caroline's face before she could camouflage it. "Are you 'managing' again, Aunt Caro? Subtlety's not your strong point."

Startled, she looked down, tightening her

grip on the fork in her hand. He could hear the thought as if she'd spoken: The "boy" was smarter than she'd realized.

"Can't fool you, can I, Michael?" She smiled and he smiled back, the first break in his grim expression in the last eight days.

"If I weren't wise to you after all these years, I'd quit my job and start pumping gas for a living. I sure wouldn't be much of a policeman."

"Helena, dear, will you bring in the sponge cake for dessert?"

"How long do you want me to stay in the kitchen so you can talk?" Helena's face assumed a look of all-knowing superior teen-aged wisdom and the other two stared at her. "Boy, how dumb do you think I am? I've known you guys all my life! Every time you get to the good stuff, I suddenly have 'things to do'!"

Caroline shook her head and rested it in her hands. "After all these years, I've got a revolution on my hands."

"Don't take it so hard, Aunt Caro. We're very happy under your benign dictatorship."

"I don't think you're funny, young man."

"Uh-oh," Mike raised his brows and glanced at Helena, "I'm in trouble when I become 'young man.'"

"Helena, dessert! And, Michael, don't change the subject."

"What subject?" It was hopeless, he knew. Like a dog, she wouldn't let go of this bone until the last bit of meat was disposed of.

"You. You are the subject." Or part of it, the pursed lips told him. "I've never seen you this way."

He crumpled his napkin and tossed it on the table. "Not quite true. About fourteen years ago, I'd say, was the last time."

"Michael!" Disgust was evident in her voice. "When Adrienne walked out fourteen years ago, you came back home from New York with good reason for your anger, your disillusion. But you were an inexperienced boy back then. Have you learned nothing since?" She sat rigid in her chair, eyes focused unrelentingly on Mike's face. "Because you're quite wrong if you equate Anne McClellan with Adrienne . . . or your mother, for that matter."

He looked up at her with a hard stare. "I think I've learned my lesson, Aunt Caro. There are some things . . . and some people . . . you can only depend on for the short term."

Her eyes gentled then. "And there are others that will prove their worth over a lifetime. Are you such a fool you can't tell the difference?"

His mouth opened for a moment, then stubbornly closed again. He rose swiftly from the table, his eyes shuttered. "I don't really want to discuss this with you, Aunt Caro. I love you, almost better than any other human being on earth, but this is not your business."

"Daddy? Mac's a really great person. I thought you—"

Mike turned toward Helena standing in the kitchen door, listening. "Yours, either."

He walked heavily from the room, and Caroline and Helena stared after him, silent. For the first time in as long as she could remember, Caroline felt the sharp sting of tears forming beneath her eyelids. The woman and the girl exchanged sad, worried looks. From the other end of the house, the silence was punctuated by the slam of a door.

Who in the world was banging on the door? It was a little late for company. Anne hurried toward the outside door. She could make out a large figure, presumably male, through the curtained glass.

"Anne? Anne, I know you're there. Open the door."

She closed her mouth and opened the

door, and he stood there staring at her, fist poised in midair, ready to knock again.

For a moment she stared back, absorbing his presence, the oh-so-welcome sight of him. But her voice, cool and quiet, showed nothing of her excited pulse, her pounding heart.

"Why, hello, Mike. This is certainly a surprise." She made no move to usher him in.

"Look, I . . . may I come in, please. It's cold out here."

"Well, you'll find it's still pretty cold in here, too."

"How gracious."

"You want gracious? Go see Miss Manners."

"Annie," he persisted, "I . . . I'd like to talk to you."

She looked at him, brows raised. If it were possible, she decided he looked even worse than he had at the Lions' breakfast yesterday, and that was in broad daylight. He'd aged ten years in the last day. The only way she could describe him tonight was haggard. "Okay, talk. You've got three minutes. That's all I can spare." Now, that sounded good. She was proud of herself. "I want to get to bed early. I need some sleep."

"Yeah, well, so do I. I feel like I haven't slept in days."

Better and better! "Really? Is that my fault?"

Oh, she hoped it was. Just his appearance at the door gave rise to all sorts of hopes.

"Yes, damn it!" He ran his fingers through his hair until it stood in tufts all over his head.

Anne bit her lip to keep from laughing.

He stopped, taking a breath. "I'm doing this all wrong, aren't I? I don't know how . . . what to . . ."

She sighed. "I don't think I can help you, Mike. And you've got about two minutes and ten seconds left."

"Will you stop that? Can't you give me a break?"

She shrugged again, leaning against the door, waiting, content for the moment to fill her hungry eyes with the longed-for sight of him.

But at that instant Mike, finished with waiting, did the only thing he could think of. He pulled her into his arms, kicked the door shut behind him, and covered her mouth with his.

Oh God, she tasted . . . just right. He couldn't get enough of the flavor of her mouth, the weight of her in his arms, the heat of her along the length of his body. He drank of her mouth, touching his tongue to her lips, moistening them with his own. All the while he was sliding his hands over her back, the fleecy cotton of her sweatshirt not enough to bar the heat of her flesh from searing him. He probed her mouth, wanting to drain every last bit of her passion, her warmth.

And Anne almost forgot, almost lost her control completely. It would have been so easy, because this was what she wanted, what she had missed when he walked out the door that last time. And for a moment she let it happen, enjoying the heat of his mouth, the brush of his soft dark moustache against her upper lip, the strength of his arms holding her crushingly close. Holding loneliness at a distance.

But it was Anne who broke away. Her instincts fought for self-preservation and she knew she couldn't allow this to happen again, allow him to hurt her again. Shaking, whether from fear or from passion she couldn't tell, she stepped back, her hands on his chest, keeping a precious few inches between them. That wouldn't stop him if he didn't want to stop. She *couldn't* stop him if he kissed her again. But no matter what Harriet and Caroline had told her, she and Mike had to understand each other—now.

"I think," she whispered breathlessly, "you'd

better tell me why you came. Your time's almost up."

He didn't answer, just stood, staring at her face. "Annie, I've missed you." He held out his arms and she had to fight every instinct in her body to keep from seeking haven there.

"Mike, please." Her voice was low, shaky. "Don't do this to me. We've been through this before and I got your message. Now I want to give you mine. Maybe I . . . misled you, somehow. I don't know, but if I did, I'm sorry." Weary, Anne leaned her head against the cool wood of the door frame. "Look, I enjoyed a long and happy marriage, and it's true, I don't like lying down alone at night and waking up alone every morning. But I'm not willing to grab any offer that comes along. I'm not going to be a convenient roll in the hay for you whenever you feel it's cold out there."

He winced, but she didn't pause.

"I can't change overnight, no matter how much I sometimes wish I could. I guess I'm the kind that goes in for the long haul. I just can't settle for a little intermittent screwing whenever your hormones—or mine—get restless! But I do want to set the record straight about one thing." She took a deep breath. "You must know how I feel; I don't seem to be able to hide it very well. God knows I don't *want* to want you, but I would have been satisfied to be your *friend*. You do know the meaning of that word, don't you?"

He had the grace to look ashamed. Anne knew it was a hollow victory.

"I don't want your friendship, Anne." And he couldn't bring himself to risk asking for more. His eyes closed over the pain, the confusion moving behind them. "I want . . ." He stopped, shaking his head.

"You want . . . but you don't—you *won't*—trust. That's it, isn't it? Oh, it's written all over you. Look, Mike, I'm sorry, but I'm not in the absolution business, so I don't know why you came here. It's late, and we both need some rest." She walked to the door and opened it. "You still can't say what I need to hear. If you ever . . ." She stopped, then shook her head, unutterably weary. "What's the use? Good night, Mike." She touched the sad smile on her lips with trembling fingers, then touched his, and a moment later Anne closed the door behind him.

She made her way to bed, brushing the slow tears from her cheek. Because, despite yesterday's apology for his coldness, his abrupt departure that night two weeks ago, and despite the fleeting passion they'd shared just now in that heart-stealing kiss, nothing had really changed. He still felt the same. He couldn't bring himself to believe in her, to trust in her, in *them* . . . in the future. He wanted, but that was all. And she wanted, but she *needed,* too, and that was worse.

No one could have heard the quiet sobs muffled into the pillow she clutched in her lonely bed. Anne wasn't aware how long Mike stood at the top of her stairs in the unbroken silence of early morning, alone.

The dank chill of an autumn morning seeped beneath the partly open window and covered the sprawling body in the much-rumpled bed. Mike stiffly eased himself into a sitting position and swung his long legs to the floor.

Son of a bitch . . . another wasted night. His head throbbed and his mouth tasted like dirty socks. Hell, if this is what the golden years feel like, who needs 'em!

He yawned, then stretched, wincing at the pain in his skull, and rose slowly, making his way to the bathroom. Maybe a shower would help. The water beating on him would be more merciful than his own thoughts. Mike grimaced. Hell, if he couldn't sleep, he might as well make himself useful someplace. He was persona non grata with Anne, and well on the way to the top of Caroline's shit list as well. Even Helena must be having sour thoughts about him. At least at the office he might be productive. The sun hadn't yet crested the far mountaintops when Mike let himself out of the house.

"*Chief?* What the heck you doin' here so early?" Cully Bryant stared across the desk as Mike closed the door firmly behind him. "Jeez, the day shift don't come on for another hour and a half. Uh, somethin' happenin'?"

"No, Cully," Mike answered tersely. "Just decided to catch up on paperwork." Yeah, sure, the kid'd have to be deaf, dumb, and blind to fall for that. And even *he* was smarter than that! Whether reasonable or not, Mike was self-consciously convinced the entire town of Whitefield had nothing more than Anne and him to occupy their interests. And why not? There wasn't much else going on right now. The Grange had nothing scheduled, the big Lawn Bowling Tournament up at the Spalding Inn was over, the Sunshine Boutique wasn't having a sale, and the Congregational Church's Annual Harvest Country Fair was two weeks off. The most exciting thing happening was the scheduled estate auction over at the old Burns dairy farm. And it would be kind of insulting to think he ranked lower on the town's gossip agenda than a couple of old Ford tractors and a milking machine!

"Cully, get the mayor's office. I want to see him as soon as he's in."

"Uh, Chief . . . ?"

"What? Come on, Cully, spit it out!"

"Well, it's not seven yet. I don't think anyone's there this early."

Mike stopped short, one foot in his office. "Yeah, sure . . . well, call in an hour. Evalyn should be there by then. Tell her to set it up. Any coffee left?" Oh, Christ, that was stupid. There was always coffee on the hot plate. And would that word forever remind him of Anne McClellan?

So, smart ass, what *isn't* a reminder of Anne?

He swore under his breath and went to his desk.

It was a long hour and a half, but Mike congratulated himself on making a dent in the files he'd been neglecting for the past week, finally clearing a square foot of desktop right down to the wood. The sound of Vince knocking on the door startled him back to the present.

"Morning. When'd you come on duty?"

" 'Bout ten minutes ago. Cully knows you

don't like long goodbyes." The gaunt-cheeked deputy's sarcasm was born of a long-time friendship with his chief.

"Very funny. Y'know, I could transfer you to the dog-and-cat rescue squad." They grinned at the old familiar threat, Vince raising his dark brows in the knowledge that he was too good a cop to worry.

"In a town this size, Mike, we're all on the dog-and-cat squad, sooner or later. Anyway, I just wanted to tell you Evalyn called. Said Hiz Honor's in and you can come over anytime. She's got the doughnuts waitin'."

"Nope, gotta cut down." Mike patted his middle, slightly thicker now than it had been a few weeks ago. *Like I said, what isn't a reminder of Anne?* Shit! He grabbed the thick folder on his desk and stomped from the room, leaving Vince staring after him.

It took only a few minutes to cover the distance across the building from police headquarters to the mayor's office. The expression on his face, Mike realized, must be a sight to behold, judging from the speed with which Evalyn Carey moved to usher him through the door and close it behind him. He slowed his steps, taking a deep breath. "Henry."

"Morning, Mike. What's so danged important you had to call me this early? We got trouble?" The mayor held out a box—a blue and cream box, Mike was pained to see—but took it back at the shake of Mike's head, selecting a plump glazed doughnut for himself. He took a bite, smiling contentedly. "Well, what's on your mind?"

"We have to let the town know about this water problem, Henry." The man across the desk stopped chewing and sat up straight. "It's getting worse every day." Mike slapped the folder onto the desktop. "They're dumping that crud more often now, and in larger amounts. The toxicity's building up faster than nature can handle it. People have a right to know what's happening. We can't just keep quiet anymore hoping for the best."

Dropping the partially-eaten doughnut onto the blotter, the portly man across the desk was rapidly losing his aplomb. His face paled and beads of sweat appeared on his forehead; he ran a finger around an apparently too-tight shirt collar. "Now, wait a minute, Mike. Slow down. After all, we can't panic the people. . . ."

"You mean, we can't panic *voters*, don't you, Henry? Why can't you admit in public that this perfect little town may not be quite so perfect after all? You might lose a couple of votes if you come right out and tell them something unpleasant?" He slammed a fist on the arm of his chair. "Shit, how long are you going to bury your head in the sand? This is *happening* . . . it's happening *here* and *now!*"

"Now just a goddamn minute there, Mike! I resent that! You've got no right to talk like that to me. After all, nothing's *happened* here. There's no reason for panic. I think you're overreacting. Just because you haven't been able to catch these people in the act is no reason to drag everyone in town in on this. I mean, what good will it do? You have a police department that's supposed to handle this sort of thing, and the state police are working with you. What could we do that you haven't already done?"

His words stung, because they aroused a feeling Mike had been living with, and resenting, for weeks. Why *hadn't* he nabbed these bastards? Hell, now he wasn't even any good at his work! It was a thought he'd been avoiding but couldn't escape any longer. Or, maybe Henry was right. Maybe he *was* overreacting, trying to use this to fill the gaps that had suddenly appeared in the rest of his life. . . .

"Tell you what, Mike. Why don't we bring it up at the next meeting of the selectmen. We'll discuss it and—"

Mike gestured at the thick sheaf of papers on the desk. "I don't think it can wait. The O.W.M. is ready to post warnings and put it on the air, about the drinking water. People will have to use bottled water for a while, or at least boil the tap water for twenty minutes—" Mike's words were interrupted by the sudden shrill of the telephone.

"Damn, Evalyn, I told her to hold the calls," Henry muttered impatiently. "Yes, what—?" He raised his brows and wordlessly handed the receiver to Mike.

"Novak, here. Yeah, Ed." He listened intently, frowned, then suddenly closed his eyes, his hand gone white where he clutched the phone. "Shit," he whispered, visibly shaken. "Oh shit!" He stared at the mayor, ashen-faced, then abruptly hung up. "The hospital has Jamie Larkin in Emergency. His mother brought him in, unconscious. They think he's been poisoned."

"Poisoned! What are you talking about? How—?"

"You know where the Larkins live, Henry? Do you know *how* they live?" Mike's expression of shock was replaced by one of disgust. "They have an old trailer parked down by the creek, off the shallows where the dead water is. They're not just poor, Henry; they'd need a month of prosperity to get up to 'poor.' Seems they figured on saving the cost of water by plugging directly into the stream. Only now it may cost a lot more than they figured."

"Is he . . . uh . . . will he—?"

"They don't know yet. It'll be a few hours." Mike dropped back into the chair. His strength had finally deserted him and he felt drained. The room was silent for a few seconds.

"Well, Mr. Mayor?" Mike muttered. "It's a little closer to home now, isn't it? Of course, it's just a poor family; they're really nobodies." *Like the Novaks were. "He's you, isn't he, Michael?"* That scene in the kitchen at Helena's party was a vivid image in his mind, Caro's words like sharp steel cutting through his thoughts. The fury and resentment fueled by the memories showed in his cold eyes. "On the other hand, it might happen to one of the 'good' families one of these days. It might even hit a 'voter,' God forbid."

"Mike?" The mayor's voice was shaken, subdued. "That's not fair. You know me better than that. I don't care if it's the Larkins or my own family; we can't tolerate this and we're not taking any more chances." He drew a deep breath and straightened up in his chair, bracing his hands on the edge of the desk. "I had no idea . . . I'll do whatever has to be done."

Mike rose abruptly. "Sorry, Henry. I'm a little overtired. I shouldn't have said that." Henry was right, of course. It hadn't been fair, accusing him of such blatant disregard for the welfare of the Larkins. He was a genuinely kind and decent man—as were most of the people in town, Mike realized, once more aware that the bulk of the self-consciousness and resentment he'd been dragging around most of his life had been of his own making, no one else's.

"Okay," the mayor admitted with weary resignation, "so . . . it's not just a possibility anymore. It's hitting too close to home, and we have to do something. Damn, why didn't I believe you sooner! I could have taken steps . . . maybe this wouldn't have happened." He rubbed his hand distractedly across his forehead. "I'll call an emergency meeting of the Selectmen's Committee, and we can contact the radio and TV stations, and *The Courier* and *The Coos County Democrat*. And with the O.W.M.'s decisions, I don't know what else we can do."

Mike felt the coldness growing inside him. "That's all you *have* to do, Henry. And I assure you, you're not to blame for any of this. This isn't your fault."

No, he knew whose fault it was. Next to the bastards doing the dumping, the blame was his. He'd let things slide, hadn't concentrated enough on his job, had allowed too many distractions. . . . The image of Anne's sad face and empty eyes tore at his heart.

No, close that door. No more impossible, dreamlike distractions. No more what-ifs and maybes, and could-bes. Back to the things he could count on, depend on . . . Helena and Caroline and his job. That's what he knew, that's what he did best.

Oh, God, if that boy died because of him . . .

"The rest of the job is mine, Henry. And this time, they won't get away. . . ."

Eighteen

"Hey, Anne, how're you doing?"

Her foot on the first step of the outside stairway at the side of her building, Anne turned at the sound of her name. Lou Rowan was hurrying from her gift shop down the street, the keys that dangled from her fingers gleaming dully in the light of the street lamp. Anne waited, pulling her coat collar up closer against the chill air, a large bag of groceries cradled in her arm.

"Hi, Lou," she said with a sudden flash of real pleasure. It had been a while since they'd had time for more than a hello-and-goodbye over morning coffee. It was just that Lou had such an unerring nose for news that Anne had opted for the easiest, most cowardly way of avoiding the temptation to, "let it all hang out." Suddenly, though, the lure of a friendly face and the warmth of friendship was stronger than her worry over piquing Whitefield gossip. "What're you doing around here so late? You're usually long gone by now."

"I came back after dinner. I've been up to my ass in that miserable paperwork. Boy, how I hate records and inventories and that stuff. Can you imagine how many trees they'd save if they'd stop sending me invoices? Yuck! Everyone wants to save the owls. How about *me?*" she wailed.

Anne chuckled at Lou's forlorn expression. "Poor baby. Wanna come up and have a cup of tea? I think there may even be some cookies up there," she added, suddenly feeling the need to talk. Lou's direct, no-nonsense approach to life was exactly what she needed just about now, Anne decided as she swung the door open and ushered her friend inside.

"Listen," Lou said, shedding her heavy jacket and taking two mugs from the cupboard, "the reason I was kind of keeping an eye out for you is Carl called and told me he'd heard the latest on Jamie Larkin."

Anne swung around, the box of tea bags clutched in her hands. "How is he? What did Carl say?"

"He's gonna be fine!" Lou beamed at her and Anne sagged with relief against the counter. "Seems he didn't get enough of that stuff in him to do any permanent damage and his folks got him to the hospital in time, thank God."

"Thank God!" Anne echoed fervently. "It was so close. . . ." He'd been unconscious for three days. She shuddered, thinking about what might have happened. "I keep imagining how I'd feel if it had been Jerry."

"Yeah, I know what you mean. Lord, my kids used to swim down there in that river—all the kids around here do that. And that poison's been getting dumped since late summer, hasn't it? It's a miracle no one else has gotten sick or . . ." Her voice trailed off, the thought too terrible to say aloud. "Well, now I know how those poor people on the Love Canal must have felt."

"Yes . . . mad as hell! I hope Mike—" Anne stopped herself, turned away to get out a plate, then spoke again. "I hope the police get whoever's responsible for this. They should be put away for life! How could anyone, no matter how much money is at stake, put innocent children . . . any innocent people . . . at risk? There isn't enough money in the world to excuse that!"

The hissing and spitting of the boiling kettle interrupted and she laughed sheepishly. "See? Not a pulpit or a soapbox in sight, but I still spout off."

"But when you're right, you're right, Anne; sometimes you need a soapbox! Let me tell you, everyone's really up in arms over this. Poor Henry Litchfield, when the voters get this mad, he's in deep shit. I don't remember when people have been so stirred up." She pulled out a stool and arranged her bulk comfortably, resting her elbows on the counter.

"The trouble is," Anne observed, slicing a lemon, "will all that righteous anger last long enough to do any good? People, including me, I'm afraid, forget and let things slide, and then we wring our hands and complain that somebody should have done something."

"I don't think that'll happen this time. Especially after Jamie's experience." Her usually cheerful and animated face became still and thoughtful. "Ya know, Anne, people live up here for a reason. Look at you . . . and me and Carl, for that matter. Either they've resisted the glitz and glamour and stayed on here, or they've chosen to move here because they recognize and want a quality of life they can't find in a big crowded city. And then, when they see someone come along and deliberately despoil it . . . well, that's hitting us where we live . . . literally!"

Anne stared at her with new understanding.

"Lou, I don't think I ever heard you so serious over anything."

Lou looked abashed at Anne's surprise. "Yeah, well, I'm not usually, but every now and then something pushes my buttons. It just frosts me to think how criminally selfish and thoughtless some people can be! You know, Carl has a saying from when he was in the army: You don't shit where you eat. A little crude," she wrinkled her nose, "but it gets the message across. I mean, these lowlifes have absolutely no concept of consideration or concern for anyone else's welfare and, you know, Anne, by this stage of my life, I'm just sick and tired of folks who don't give a damn. There're just too many people on the take!"

"Hear, hear! Hey, Lou, did you ever consider that maybe *you* should run for Congress? You've got my vote," Anne said, reaching over to hold her friend's hand for a moment.

She sat down, pouring the steaming water into their mugs, and then her mouth widened in a sudden smile. "You know, it reminds me of all those John Wayne movies I used to love."

Lou looked up from stirring artificial sweetener into her tea. "Huh?"

"I mean, it's kind of like the code of the

West, you know? The way they used to feel about horse thieves," Anne mused. "When someone comes along and callously steals something that's really a basic necessity of life . . . I mean, they've taken the one thing you need to survive, and that's *life*-threatening and it's unforgivable. And that's just what's happening here, isn't it? Of course people will react."

"Ah, well, I never thought of Mike as the 'Duke,' but now that you mention it, it's not a bad comparison!"

Is that what I did, make Mike my hero? My personal John Wayne? Just shows there are some problems even the "Duke" can't handle—and love and trust are at the top of the list. Well, let him go kiss his horse when he's cold!

". . . and I have a feeling Mike and the state police'll get these scumbags," Lou was rattling on. "In fact, I was talkin' to Sylvie Pritchard yesterday and she said Ed told her Mike's pretty sure it'll be over soon. God, I hope so! We don't want any more close calls like that poor kid Jamie Larkin! Life's tough enough to survive, especially for the Larkins of this world."

"Amen to that! Well," Anne lifted her mug in a toast, "here's to truth, justice, and the American way . . . and survival." Yep, that was the key word: survival. She was still too raw and anything that smacked of Mike Novak hit too close to home. A change of subject was definitely in order.

"Now, let's shovel in some tea and cookies. Since we aren't using sugar, we're entitled to the calories, right?"

"Right!" Lou nodded emphatically. "I've rationalized every single pound on my body. It's nice to know I have an ally!" She took a dainty bite and smiled. "Mmmm! These are great." She swallowed and held up one of Anne's florentine cookies. "How come I never tried these before?" She took a sip of tea and settled back onto the high stool, a contented smile on her round face.

"So many cookies, so little time," Anne observed sagely, and they both burst out laughing.

"Well, you can't say I don't give it a good try!"

"Me, too," Anne chuckled, patting her stomach and hips. "As anyone can plainly see."

"You'll get no sympathy from me, kid. I'd die happy if I could get down to where you are. Oh, well, I, my dear, am an equal opportunity eater." Lou broke off another piece of cookie and popped it into her smiling mouth.

"Well, that's one of the things I like about

you, Lou. You enjoy life—and dessert—and you don't agonize over it. Like they say, let it all hang out."

"Yeah, well, I haven't much choice, have I?" Lou answered, her mouth turning up in a quick smile. "Hey, speaking of dessert—and when aren't I?—I've been meaning to ask you, have you a good recipe for pecan pie? Carl may have lived most of his life up here, but he hasn't forgotten his 'Joh-ja' childhood. He says this year I have to make a pecan pie for Thanksgiving instead of pumpkin. Can you help me out?"

"Thanksgiving? Boy, you sure plan ahead, don't you?" Anne laughed, shaking her head. "It's almost two months 'til then. What's the rush?"

"If I don't ask when I think of it, I'll forget. The memory's the first to go, you know."

Ah, damn. Hadn't she said that herself not too long ago—to Mike? So, how come she couldn't forget *him!* "Sure, I've got a recipe in my file, somewhere . . ." Anne stopped, snapping her fingers at a sudden thought. "Oh, Lou, I've got a great idea! Thanksgiving's always been my favorite holiday, and Jerry's coming home—here—and I'd really love to have you and Carl join us. It's been so long since I did any serious cooking and

I'm itching to go all out with a big spread. Are your kids coming up? They're invited, too!"

Lou shook her head. "Nah, they go to the in-laws this year; they'll come to us for Christmas. It's just Carl and me. And we'd love to come. I'd accept an invitation for gruel and bread if it meant I could avoid the kitchen."

Anne nodded, grinning. She had been slightly depressed at the prospect of the two of them sharing the holiday alone. "I promise I'll do better than gruel and bread. You know what? I think I'll ask the Larkins, too. I couldn't stand the thought of them not having a nice holiday, and they really have a lot to be thankful for now that Jamie's back on his feet. And you can tell Carl I promise he can watch every football game on the tube. I'm used to it after all these years with Jerry. . . ." They shared a grin.

The only cloud on Anne's horizon was the nagging thought of who would *not* be sitting at the table. Until even a couple of weeks ago, there would have been no question about giving thanks with the Novaks. She'd hoped to share Thanksgiving with the people who meant the most to her. But not now. No, not now.

"I'm so glad I thought of it. It'll give me

something that's fun to think about and plan for." Something else besides Mike, she admitted to herself. "My very first Thanksgiving in Whitefield."

At the end of the next day, an exhausted Anne locked the door to the shop, turned off the lights, and had dragged herself half way up the stairs when she heard the familiar chirping sound of the phone. She hurried up the last few steps and into the living room. The phone was still ringing.

"Hello!" she answered breathlessly.

"Oh, Anne, I'm so glad I got you. I honestly didn't know whom else to call!"

"What's wrong, Caroline?" She knew the older woman. If Caroline was as worried as she sounded, something was very wrong.

"Is Helena with you?" Caroline's anxious voice asked.

"Why, no. I haven't seen her since yesterday."

"She missed dinner, and she's not home yet."

"But it's after seven! Where would she go on a school night?"

"That's why I'm so . . . concerned." Fear was not a familiar word in Caroline Novak's vocabulary.

Anne bit her lip, frowning. "Caro, when did you see her last? Didn't she say anything?"

"About four-thirty or so I heard her tearing up her room . . . the whole house if I'd have let her. She seemed so worried, almost scared, and I asked if I could help her find whatever she was looking for. But she just burst into tears, and all I could get out of her was something about her father, and me, and how angry and disappointed we'd be. But why would she think that? We'd never . . ." Caroline's words trailed away, sounding extremely distracted.

"Caroline!"

"What? Oh . . . oh, yes, sorry. I—where was I?"

"You said she was saying you and Mike would be angry . . . ?"

"Yes. Well, she . . . she suddenly stopped crying and let out a yell, then she hugged me and tore out of the house, and that's the l—last I saw of her."

Caroline's voice was tight and controlled, her bone-deep panic barely held at bay.

"Where's Mike?" Anne couldn't imagine him eating dinner with Helena missing.

"He had an emergency meeting with the O.W.M people up at the county seat this afternoon and an appearance in the Littleton District Court. And then he was detoured down to somewhere near Caroll, on Route 3. There was a bad pileup . . . casualties, I think. It was such a crazy day, and . . . he's not back yet and . . ."

The two women were silent with apprehension, then Anne thought of something. "Did Helena take her bike?"

"Oh, dear, I never looked. Just a minute. . . ." Anne paced, gnawing on her lower lip.

"No, her bicycle's still in the shed!"

"Well, then, she's got to be near the house. She certainly wouldn't head for town on foot. Look, how about my coming over. I'll be there in ten minutes." Before Caroline had hung up the phone, Anne was down the stairs. Six and a half minutes later, the sporty black Porsche jerked to a stop in Mike's driveway and Anne was running up the steps to meet a very fearful Caroline.

"Thank you for coming, Anne! I've called everyone I could think of! Lord knows I'm not a worrier, but . . ." She shook her head and they looked at each other, imagining.

Anne shivered, pulling her jacket closer against the rising damp of an insistent night wind. "Caroline, what was she looking for that was so important?"

"I don't know if it was homework . . . well, she wouldn't say." Caroline frowned and closed her eyes, concentrating, remembering. "She just kept pulling out drawers and looking under furniture. She was so frantic and—" Caroline slumped into a straight-backed chair beside the door, frowning, trying to recall every detail of the scene. "She kept rubbing her wrist; I remember noticing how red the skin was. But I—" She stopped and stared at Anne with dawning realization. "Well, of course!"

"I don't—"

"I had asked her what time it was! Don't you see? That's what she was looking for. Her watch! The watch I gave her for her birthday. Oh, Anne, that must be it!"

"Have you notified Mike yet that she's mis— that she's late?"

Suddenly, Caroline let slip her mask, and icy cold fear shone from her eyes, in her voice. "I—I didn't want to get him all upset if it turned out to be nothing. Helena was so agitated; she was afraid we'd be angry."

"Good grief, Mike's no ogre any more than you are, Caroline. You'd both cut off an arm before you'd hurt one hair on her head."

"Of course, but why didn't *she* know that? Dear God, I'll never forgive myself if she . . ."

"Now stop that! She's just an impulsive fifteen-year-old girl, and she can fly off in twelve different directions at once! But that still doesn't tell us where she's gone. Now, who lives near enough? Where would she be likely to go?"

"No, I called all the neighbors already. But, Anne, she's always going off on her own. I think she's got a favorite place somewhere, but—"

"Oh, good heavens, Caroline. I'm so stupid. I know where she went . . . I'll bet money on it. The cave."

"But isn't that close enough for her to be back by now?"

They read the same thought in each other's eyes. *If she's all right.*

Anne looked up at the night sky pressing black and ominous against the brightly lit windows. "Look, I'll go after her—I'm sure that's where she's gone—and you wait here in case she comes back or calls. But I'll bet I meet her on her way back!" she reassured Caroline, hugging the older woman, her hands tightening on the fragile bones sharply defined beneath the thin wool sweater.

"Wait, Anne." Caroline went to a table in the hall and took a large flashlight from the drawer, a twin to the one Mike carried. It helped conjure up his image, for an instant, large and comforting and safe, that night of the storm. For one moment Anne's heart filled with warmth, before the anxiety resurfaced.

"You don't think I'm a foolish old worrywart?" Caroline couldn't force even the shadow of a smile to her pinched mouth. She looked, at that moment, every one of her seventy-three years.

"Well, then, I guess that's two of us." The strained optimism on Anne's face vanished the moment the door closed behind her. She ran across the back yard to the top of the downward path, moving as quickly as she dared, more quickly than she'd have thought possible. After a second's hesitation, she plunged through the dry thicket and prickly underbrush that pulled at her clothing with sharp greedy fingers to hold her back.

The police car, sirens silent now, headed back down the long road toward town. The wreckers had hauled away the twisted metal, the ambulances had screamed off with the injured, and Mike could finally go home. Well, after he'd done the reports. Damn, it had been a hellish day.

He should have known: that call from the O.W.M., the waste management people. All they ever had to give him lately was bad news.

Then that meeting with the mayor. That's why he'd driven over to Lancaster, to see the people in charge. He'd outlined his theory and they'd listened . . . listened because they were all fresh out of plans. If he were right, they were within inches of nailing the bastards. If he were wrong . . . they were looking at full-blown disaster along a large portion of the northeastern watershed.

Mike rubbed the back of his neck tiredly. He'd been convinced nothing on his schedule was more important than that. Nothing. But earlier in the afternoon, driving back from the meeting, she was there, still clutching at the edges of his mind—Anne. He couldn't evade it any longer. Truth was a relentless prod; it was time to give in, to admit it. He'd call her . . . better yet, he'd go see her. And this time he'd make her listen, make her understand, because now, at last, *he* understood. The thought had brought immeasurable relief, and he'd grinned to himself: How the mighty are fallen! Well, not as mighty as he'd like to believe or like others to believe. But loneliness was too high a price to pay for an image. Yes, when this current job was all cleared up, he'd go to Anne, tell her, explain . . .

And then, just when he'd thought he had a firm grip on all his plans and was headed back home, the radio call had come through about the accident outside of Caroll. It was a bad one. Bad enough to need help from every P.D. in the area. It was a miracle there were no fatalities. At least not yet. He'd call the hospital later to see about the couple in the sports car. He found himself praying they'd make it, that life lay ahead for them, that it hadn't been cut short in a moment of senseless tragedy.

That sports car. An involuntary shudder snaked down his spine and cold sweat filmed his body at the vivid picture imprinted on his mind. He knew what had shaken him even more than the horrendous sight of the accident. The small black sports car crumpled beneath the weight of a huge commercial auto hauler . . . for that split second all he could think of was Anne's black Porsche. If he'd lost her . . . ! Even now his fingers clutched the steering wheel and the sickness in the pit of his stomach churned again.

That moment had told him all he needed to know: Life could offer a lot, but it didn't come with guarantees. So when you knew the value of something, or someone, you had to try, had to believe. Anne was worth taking a chance on and she had nothing to prove to him. But he had something to prove to her, all right. Trust. How had Caroline put it? Some people will prove their worth over a lifetime. She'd called him a fool for not recognizing that. And she'd been right. He had been a blind fool before, but no more. His eyes were open now, and so was his heart. And nothing took precedence.

He couldn't remember ever experiencing the sense of complete joy he felt at that moment, as if he were making some fantastic discovery. And he was. He was discovering himself, emotions he'd believed he would never feel for a woman, emotions he'd always secretly suspected didn't really exist. How wrong could he be? He smiled wryly to himself. He'd learned lately he could be wrong quite a lot! He'd go to Anne, hold her, beg her if he must, tell her . . . tell her how very much he loved her.

Mike took a deep breath, bracing his arms against the steering wheel. Loved her. Hmm. Loved her! Now, that wasn't so bad, was it? No, not so bad.

He grinned, thinking ahead to their reunion. How would she look when he told her? Would her dark eyes take on that sleepy inviting look, her mouth open with a moist welcome, her arms reach to embrace him? His body tightened, his heart skidding at the thought of holding her in his arms, sliding his hands along the soft skin of her shoulders, then cupping her full heavy breasts in a loving caress, feeling her passion answering his, her nipples beading in arousal under his loving hands, his lips. . . . As if a millstone had been dissolved from around his neck, Mike sat straighter, smiling behind the wheel as the car erased the miles between him and Anne and their lifetime together.

His happy anticipation was interrupted by the harsh squawk of the radio. "Yeah, Vince, what's up?" No more emergencies, please!

"Mike, you've got a call from Miss Caroline. . . ."

"Well? What is it?" He frowned, puzzled. Caroline never called him when he was on duty. "C'mon Vince, what did she want?"

"Mike, she . . . she said . . . uh . . . she said it's about Helena . . ."

"Helena!" God, no! "What's wrong with Helena?"

"Jeez, Mike, I . . . she . . . uh . . . she's missing."

Anne could taste frustration and rising fear the farther she went. Peering ahead, she prayed for Helena's face to appear in the light's beam, prayed for the heavy dread to become a foolish memory. But there was nothing . . . nothing but the snapping of brush and twigs in her wake, the loud chitter of night birds and animals, angry at this unnatural disturbance of their domain. Anne ploughed through the obstacles in her path, heedless now of distance or fatigue or cold, intent only on moving ahead—quickly, quickly!

She shivered. It was so eerie out here at night. The pleasant serenity and seclusion of daylight assumed an ominous alien air; every shadow hid a danger, every crackling twig a threat. The sharp bright beam of her light suddenly caught a pair of pine martens darting from under a clump of fireweed and mountain laurel, out on a foraging expedition. Their frenzied dash for cover only emphasized the imminent danger that might lurk beyond, in the black night.

She'd been here only that one time, with Helena, walking the lovely tree- and boulder-studded ravine beside the swift brook that rushed to empty itself into the Connecticut River. So different now! Perhaps fear had a tangible smell, not the clean, fresh forest scent of a green-gold sunlit afternoon, the sharp, sweet tang of wild grapes and chokecherry, sweet fern and raspberries; those had succumbed to a faintly disagreeable odor that permeated this remote stretch of the night-shrouded creek bed.

Anne moved faster now, over the level path along the bank. She had to concentrate here to stay on the right path. Was this where they'd veered off, an experienced Helena in the lead, to begin the climb upward along the slanting face of the wildflower-studded ever-rising hillside? By this point they'd been out of sight and sound of the house or, indeed, any other overt signs of civilization. Anne was uncomfortably aware of the isolation now.

She stopped abruptly. Oh, God, what was that? The noise sounded different somehow. Louder, heavier, and she sensed a stealth, a furtiveness to the movement.

"H—Helena, is that you?" Anne's voice quavered slightly in the utter silence. There was no answer, and yet she knew she was not alone in the densely wooded darkness. But what, or who, was her companion?

C'mon now, Annie, you're too old to be afraid of things that go bump in the night.

She took a deep shuddering breath . . . and wrinkled her nose in distaste. Had something chosen this stretch of riverbank to come and die? The air had grown noticeably more foul during her short journey, and a rank odor of death and decay hung oppressively in the trees. Everything seemed to contribute to an increase of her worry, and she swung the flashlight around to push back the unseen, unknown anxieties. The glint of light on metal caught her eye and she looked closer, staring until she made out the semi-hidden shape of a car concealed in the dark shadow of a thick clump of aspen.

For a moment, sheer surprise pushed aside Anne's worry. Whose car was it, and why was it down here, of all places? It certainly wasn't the most accessible spot in the area, although amorous teenagers might be persistent enough to try it. But somehow she doubted it. Pulse pounding, breath fearful and labored, she took a step toward the car.

"Anne."

Her heart stopped and she felt as if she'd jumped at least a foot. Her head jerked around, in the same direction as the bobbling beam of her flashlight.

"Elliot?" Shock and relief flooded through her. "You scared the wits out of me! Thank heavens it's you! What in the world are you doing out here?" She started toward him, but his answer stopped her in her tracks.

"I've been waiting for you."

"Waiting . . . *for me?*"

"Yes, my dear." His voice sounded weary, resigned. "At least, for someone. I was rather hoping it would be you."

"But . . . look, Elliot, I don't understand what you're talking about, but I haven't time now." Anne peered past him, up the dark mass of the steep hillside. "Helena's missing, and Caroline and I thought she might have come here, to the little cave up on the ridge." Her beam of light searched hopefully along the shadowed reaches of the upward path.

"Oh, she did."

Anne swung the light back to him, her eyes wide. And then she saw the gleam of light on the metallic object he held in his hand. He raised it and she realized he was pointing a gun, a mean-looking little snub-nosed pistol, the small hole in its barrel aimed directly at her chest.

She stared, incredulous. This was crazy. *Elliot*? Elliot Gilcrest, threatening her with a *gun*? His hand trembled slightly, but the expression on his face, the set mouth, suddenly told her he wouldn't hesitate to pull the trigger.

"Are you *mad*? What's going on here, Elliot?"

"I suppose it can't hurt to tell you now." He shrugged, then gestured up the path, indicating she should precede him. He deftly removed the flashlight from her hand as she passed and they began to walk. "The moment you told me about that afternoon, out here with that girl, I was afraid it might come to this."

"Come to *what*? What's this all about?" Anne glanced back, stumbling on an unseen rock in her path.

"Careful, you'll hurt yourself."

The irony of it almost brought a laugh to Anne's lips. He was pointing a gun at her, and he was worried she might hurt herself? She looked at him. "Chivalry lives."

He flinched at the unconcealed angry sneer in her voice.

"You said Helena is here. Where is she? What have you done with her?"

"She's fine. She's . . . resting, up there in the cave. I'm not going to do anything to her . . . to either of you." His words were labored, his breath coming in quick gasps. Elliot was not used to any terrain rougher than paved sidewalks or the bank's marble floors.

They reached the crest of the hill, shrouded thickly with trees standing guard over the undisturbed wilderness. Partway along the broad ledge, the narrow opening to the cave was a dark gaping mouth in the lighter black of the cliff face. Nervously, Anne peered around them.

"All right, Elliot, where is she? I'm warning you, if you've done anything to that girl . . ."

"That's rich! Look who's giving warnings!"

Startled, Anne swung around as a dark shadow detached itself from the blackness of the mouth of the cave. In the illumination of the flashlight, it assumed the shape of a man. He was almost totally bald, only a drift of grey fringe above his ears, a bit shorter than Elliot and perhaps fifteen years older. The open front zipper of his white coverall revealed a dark suit, white shirt, and tie beneath. His feet were hidden inside high rubber boots and in one well-manicured hand he held a pair of heavy work gloves. In the other was a menacing length of wood, a short stubby limb from one of the many trees surrounding them. He tapped it impatiently against his leg and swung around to face Elliot.

"For God's sake, Gilcrest, what took you so long!" he hissed in what was obviously a rhetorical question, because he continued immediately. "Let's get on with it. We haven't got all night!"

"Get on with what? Elliot, what the hell is going on here?"

"I . . . I'm really sorry about this, Anne. I wish—"

"If you can't manage this, I'll do it myself!"

"All right, Martin, all right. Anne, please go inside." He started to take her arm, but she pulled back.

"Wait a minute . . ." It all began to come together in that instant. The foul odor along the river, the gun, Elliot's bizarre behavior, the casually brutal tone of this stranger. "This has something to do with the chemical dumpings in the river, doesn't it?"

"So clever of you, Mrs. McClellan." The older man grinned, the upward-shining light endowing his sarcastic smile with an even more sinister cast than it already had. "Too bad the girl had to come along, tonight of all nights. This would have been our last time around here, and nobody would have been hurt."

"Hurt?" She swung back to Elliot. "You said you wouldn't do anything to her!"

He shrugged. "I won't. It will be . . . an unfortunate accident." Anne stared at him with growing horror.

"Well, I couldn't let her go after she'd seen us here, could I?" he asked quite reasonably. "And we knew, eventually, someone would come looking for her. We had to wait until now so we could empty the trucks without any further interruptions." He seemed perplexed that she didn't understand the logic of his reasoning.

"Sorry we ruined your schedule!"

"Let's cut the talk and get on with it! Someone else could come up here at any time." The man named Martin prodded Anne with the wooden stick and pushed her toward the cave.

"Don't you touch me, you son of a bitch!" Anne pushed the stick aside and walked stiffly to the cave entrance. At the opening to the gaping black void, she froze, fear rising in her throat like a stone, choking her. Before he could push her again, the sound of a muffled groan from the darkness was enough to break through her panic.

"Helena? *Helena, where are you?*" She whirled on Elliot. "What have you done to her? My God, she's a child! How could you!"

"She recognized me. I couldn't let her tell anyone." His words were dispassionate, brooking no argument she might put forth. "Anyway, she's all right. She just bumped her head. Get inside please, Anne. We have to hurry."

"Elliot, are you crazy? You'll never get away with this! Why, Mike's probably on his way here already. He'll be here any minute!"

"No, Anne, I think not. There's a very bad wreck up on the highway, quite a long way from here. I happen to know Novak is over there, probably for quite a while. Such a conscientious public servant," he sneered. "It's rather like . . . destiny, don't you think? That accident coming along just when I needed it."

That he could interpret the death or maiming of others as a good omen for his viciousness. . . . She stared, horrified.

"My God, you're truly despicable! How could I have ever called you my friend?"

"You could have been much more!" Raw hatred suddenly shone in his face. "You made your choice, now live with it!" He laughed, a harsh chilling sound. "For as long as you can. Get in there—now!"

"Do it, Mrs. McClellan. I'm not nearly as concerned about manners as my partner is."

Anne turned to the other man. His face was blank, cold. "No, I'm sure you're not." She looked back at the mouth of the cave, gritting her teeth, and took a step inside. As she moved forward, she heard a whoosh of air behind her. Something slammed into the back of her skull and she pitched forward into total blackness.

Nineteen

Dark. Nothing but cold and the dark!

Anne closed her eyes, clinging with desperation to a shred of reason, praying she would see *something* when she opened them. But she saw nothing, nothing at all. Cold sweat beaded on her forehead, bathing her face in a humid mask. Nausea swelled in the pit of her stomach, threatening to overwhelm her. *No-no-no-no-no, please, God, no!* Wracking sobs filled her chest, choking her, suffocating her. Were the walls closing in? And the ceiling, pressing the air away by inexorable inches, until there was no oxygen to drag into tortured lungs? Huddled on the cold, hard surface of dirt and stone, she lay frozen, the sour taste of panic clutching her throat.

All alone, with impatient death her only companion.

But she wasn't alone.

From somewhere to her left, she heard the faint irregular sound of harsh labored breathing. With a desperate focus of her waning strength, Anne broke the paralysis of fear and panic. Dizzy and disoriented, she pushed herself up to a sitting position, every movement setting off a bright explosion of fireworks behind her eyelids, her head throbbing with painful agony. This fetid smell of damp air and impenetrable blackness was too reminiscent of . . .

She choked back the bile that rose in her throat. Concentrate. She must concentrate!

"H—Helena?" It was a hoarse whisper, absorbed by the black vacuum around her. "Helena! W—where are you?"

"Ma—ac!" The voice was more of a whimper than an actual sound. "Is that . . . really you?" A faint cough. "I'm . . . here . . ."

"Where?" The weakness of Helena's voice crystallized the awful terror of their situation. "Honey, keep t—talking, so I can tell where you . . . are."

Totally disoriented, Anne moved her hands through the space surrounding her and, when her fingertips brushed a solid form, tried to inch herself in a painful sideways crawl to her left, until her shoulder bumped the cold damp granite of the cave wall. When she managed to control her breathing she rose stiffly, painfully, to her knees, fighting off, with sheer determination, the blinding agony in her skull and the threatening faintness. For a moment, she rested her forehead against the damp stone, then bracing herself, she rose on unsteady feet, biting her lips tightly to still the nausea and dizziness.

"Talk to me, honey. Are you h—hurt?" she gasped. "What did they d—do to you?" The chattering of her teeth was beyond control in the dank, frigid air of the cave.

"I c—can't find it, Mac. My watch . . . I came to find my . . . my watch, the one Aunt Caro gave me. I was scared I'd lost it, and I didn't want them to think I was c—careless and b—be mad . . ." The small voice trailed off on a sob.

Following the sound, Anne suddenly stumbled on Helena's outstretched legs. She fell to her knees beside the prostrate figure of the frightened girl. They clutched each other and sat huddled together, both shaking uncontrollably with cold and fear.

"Oh, Mac, I . . . I'm so glad you're h—here. I want to go home!" She sobbed uncontrollably, her shivering form burrowing into Anne's welcoming embrace. *"I want to go home!"*

"Shh, I know, honey, I know. Me, too! It'll be okay. Don't worry, we'll be fine." Fine?

Would they? Anne hoped she sounded surer than she felt. She strained to see something, anything, but the darkness was unrelieved.

Anne stroked Helena's head, and her hand came away sticky. Oh God! "Helena, you're hurt! What happened to your head?" She held the girl close.

"I don't know. . . . I was kneeling down . . . looking for . . . my watch and I heard . . . a noise and I turned around and . . . Mr. Gilcrest was there and he . . ." She shuddered. "He said something about . . . too bad the Novaks didn't know their place or something . . ." She sniffled back her tears. "Then this other man came in, too, a— and when I tried to get outside, he . . ." The tears came afresh, and she leaned against Anne's shoulder. ". . . he slapped me and I fell and . . . well, that's all I can remember. I guess . . . I hit my head on the stones. Oh, Mac, it hurts! Can't we get out now? Aunt Callie'll be worried, and Daddy, and . . . Mac, I think I'm going to be sick!" She leaned away from Anne, retching in the blackness, the sour smell rising and mingling with the dank odor of moldy earth and fear. "I want to go home!"

She began to sob silent tears and Anne almost joined her. She was so afraid, so deathly afraid they'd never get out of here. How could they? My God, what irony, that she should end up dying the same death as Paul. *Oh, Jerry, I love you, sweetheart. I never got to say goodbye. And Mike. I never told you . . . I never said how much I love you! Why do we always wait until it's too late? Why don't we learn?* No matter what he'd said that last night, she should have understood, should have heard the plea beneath the words, should have known. Should have. . . . And she'd thought she'd begun a new life, with no regrets and no might have beens and should haves! Now she and Helena were trapped here in the dark, maybe forever.

Forever.

No! She wouldn't accept that! Anne tried to sort out everything that had happened in the last . . . how long had she been in here! She moved her arm, trying to focus on the wristwatch she held up before her face. Bless the man who'd invented the luminous dial! It was at least a tiny point of light to cling to in the unrelieved blackness. She calculated roughly the time that had elapsed since she'd left Caroline. Only little more than an hour. But in that short time it had gotten uncomfortably colder and she shivered, huddling close to Helena, trying to warm the girl's chilled body with her own.

"Wait a minute, hon, let me get this jacket off." Helena had taken impulsive flight without donning anything warmer than her sweatshirt. It was no match for a wintry White Mountain cold front sweeping down from the north. Exposure would make Helena's weakened condition even more dangerous. Anne wrapped the girl's slight, limp form in the heavy wool, knowing how inadequate it was in this weather. She had to get them out of here. And she had to do it fast.

"You didn't happen to bring a flashlight, did you?" She had little hope, but still . . . "Helena?"

She mustn't fall asleep! Anne knew that was dangerous after a head wound, especially in extreme cold.

"Wake up, Helena! Oh, honey, keep talking. Don't fall asleep!"

"Huh? . . . 'kay, Mac, I'll tryyy . . ." Her words were barely intelligible.

"I just hoped you might have brought a flashlight."

"Noooo . . ." Helena's voice faltered and Anne felt her body begin to droop again. ". . . think . . . might be . . . matches."

"You have matches! Oh, I love you. You're

wonderful!" She had to keep her talking. The girl's words were beginning to sound slurred, and in the dark there was no way of knowing how badly she'd been injured. Anne had another insistent flash of memory, of she and Paul, trapped in the isolated darkness of their Mexican hotel. She fought another wave of immobilizing panic that swept over her as she felt the blackness pressing against them.

No!

Dear God, you can't let Helena die. Help me!

This time help me to do something.

"Where are they, honey? The matches! Where?"

"Hmm? Oh, uhm . . . pocket . . ."

She felt among the girl's pockets, willing herself to be calm, not to fumble.

"So, tell me about your biology paper. How did you do?" Keep her talking! Helena's mumbled words were a comforting backdrop to the forbidding black chill. And then Anne's hands discerned something in one of the jeans pockets. She felt a packet of facial tissues, a lipstick and . . . a book of matches!

The dim light of the match was as welcome as a brace of floodlights. In the flickering glow she took a quick survey and saw, rather than the dark cave of her imaginings, a shallow cleft in the face of the ledge, a space so small Elliot and his partner hadn't needed to do much to seal the opening. She also noted there were only two more matches before the flame nipped her finger and she dropped it in the dirt.

"Honey, I have to look at your head. I'll try not to hurt you, but . . ." She helped the girl sit upright and lit one more of the precious matches, setting the package of tissues aflame. In the sudden bright flare of light, her fears were confirmed. The scalp was badly gouged, the swollen flesh looking angry, and the heavy flow of blood was steady, pooling and seeping into the dirt where her head had rested. Loss of blood was something Helena could not afford at this point.

The flame flared and went out. Anne tore a strip from the bottom of her shirt, making a thick wad of the fabric, then tore another piece into a long strip. Feeling as gently as she could with increasingly numb fingers, Anne pressed the wad against the open wound, flinching at the girl's sudden gasp of pain, and tied the strip around Helena's head to hold the pressure pad in place. She hoped it would be enough to stop the blood or at least slow it. Then she scrabbled back to the opening and, oblivious to the numbing cold and her torn, bloodied hands, began to dig.

She would never know how long it took before the sudden rush of cold wind told her she'd broken through the great mound of rocks between them and freedom. Thank heavens Elliot had been so inept in his planning, their makeshift tomb had been less secure than he'd thought. Pushing and prying and kicking at the heavy stones with a strength born of desperation, Anne managed finally to open a space large enough to allow her and Helena to wriggle out. The girl had been silent for many minutes, she realized. Anne prayed as hard as she'd ever prayed in her life while she felt for a pulse, thanking heaven when she heard Helena's ragged breathing. She pulled the semi-conscious girl to her feet.

"Hang on, baby. Just a little longer. Hang on!"

Anne struggled to pull the almost-comatose girl through the small opening and then, supporting Helena's dead weight, they took their first tentative steps into the now-angry winter night. Feet slithering and slipping on the damp rotting leaves coating the narrow path, they began to make their tortuous way back down the twisting trail. At first Anne heard nothing except the chattering of her own teeth in the sudden blast of cold wind, the furious pounding of her own heart.

Suddenly, from far below, the night exploded with strobelike flashes of light and the unexpected staccato sound of fireworks. Who would be shooting off fireworks now?

Whoever it was, it meant help was near! She tried to hurry their pace, but by now Helena was almost a completely dead weight on Anne's fast-flagging strength. Anne bit her lips in concentration and despair, with one thought in mind: Get down to those fireworks, those people. To find help.

Oh, dear God! She stopped dead in her tracks. That wasn't fireworks. Elliot was down there somewhere, with a gun.

Mike. He was shooting at Mike!

Her head whirling with indecision—what to do, which direction to turn, how to protect Helena, how to help Mike—Anne looked around wildly and, in the dim light from the cloud-mottled sky, saw the heavy stick lying abandoned beside the path. The last time she'd seen it it had been in the hands of the man, Martin, Elliot's nasty-tempered accomplice. She bent to grab it, wishing she could plant it firmly on their skulls. She was seething with a fury that desperately needed an outlet. How dare they hurt Helena and try to kill them both. And Mike! Dear heavens, *what had they done to him!*

Stumbling as fast as she could, Anne half dragged, half carried Helena down the sloping path, quietly sobbing with anger and frustration and utter exhaustion. It seemed much steeper under her burden, in the dark. She tried to go as quietly as she could manage, listening fearfully in the suddenly eerie and ominous silence for some indication of what was going on down below at the water's edge.

Suddenly, Anne froze, then pulled Helena off the path into the shelter of the thick underbrush. Heavy footsteps were advancing up the path. She pushed Helena down beneath the bushes, holding her fingers over the girl's lips. "Be very still!" she hissed into Helena's ear, not even sure her words would be heard. Clutching the heavy stick, Anne stood and slipped into the shadow of a thick tree trunk beside the trail . . . and waited.

She saw the flashlight beam first and raised her makeshift weapon above her head. The light swung steadily from side to side as the figure moved rapidly upward toward her, and Anne began to lift the stick up and forward. It caught for a moment on a low branch and the slight crackling sound was like a clap of thunder. The beam of light swung around and caught her, crouched in readiness for an attack.

"*Anne!*"

"Mike?" It came out more as a sob than as a recognizable word. "Oh, Mike, thank God it's you!"

Mike stared, stunned. In that split second his brain registered the sight of Anne . . . an Anne he'd never seen, never imagined. The hands that gripped a large tree branch at the ready were scraped raw, blackened and bleeding, her hair was in matted and tangled disarray, her eyes wild with an animal fury, her face streaked with dirt and tears and blood.

"Annie!" He held her fiercely, gratefully. "Thank God you're safe! Where's Helena! Did you find her? Is she—?"

"She's here, Mike. She's hurt, but I think she'll be okay once we get her to the doctor."

"Oh God!" He ran to where she pointed. "Helena, baby, answer me. It's Daddy, honey. Are you okay?" He lifted her in his arms, but there was no response save for a muted whimper. He turned and headed as fast as he dared down to the waiting police cars, an exhausted, shivering Anne trailing after him. When they reached the busy riverbank, he realized she wasn't wearing a jacket.

"Damnit, Annie, you're freezing! Here, put

this on." He slipped his heavy leather jacket around her, hugging her for a second, then slid behind the wheel. Seconds later, with sirens blaring, lights flashing, the police car streaked for the hospital emergency room. The last thing Anne saw as she looked back were the ashen faces of Elliot and his partner in the eerie blue-red flashing lights, handcuffed together, being shoved none too gently by two of Mike's men into a waiting police car.

She felt older than Caroline right now. But it was amazing what hot water and soap could do for you. Had anyone ever written a scientific study on the therapeutic effects of bubble bath? She yawned and pulled the warm robe closer around her old and battered body. Probably. There was nothing new under the sun. Hadn't someone once said that? Probably. She was repeating herself.

Maybe it was delirium. The doctor had discharged her, disinfected, swabbed, bandaged, and non-concussed, so it must be merely fatigue. Merely. Well, fatigue might not be so bad. It would help her not think about . . . uh-uh. . . . She wasn't going to think about what's his name. The large gentleman behind the badge. The thief of her sleep for the last few days, the intruder in her life for the last few weeks. After all, she and her problems were not unique. Everyone had some kind of cross to bear in this world.

Why does mine have to be six feet tall and two hundred twenty pounds?

Ah, but he's not mine.

Her last sight of him had been his white-faced, tense figure relentlessly prowling the confines of the waiting room. Afraid to think, she'd huddled in a corner of the worn brown leather sofa, studying the frayed seams, the cigarette-scorched cushions permanently indented by how many hundreds of other agonized souls, waiting to hear the fate of loved ones. What was the percentage, she wondered, of good news to bad? Anne shuddered. Keeping her mind occupied with innocuous details was the only thing between her and whimpering hysteria as they'd waited those interminable minutes, until they knew Helena was all right. A slight concussion and some loss of blood, a broken arm, a touch of incipient pneumonia that would respond to antibiotics. Fortunately, the exposure hadn't been long enough to do any real damage to her healthy young body.

Relief had washed over Anne and the adrenaline had suddenly drained from her system, leaving her as limp as yesterday's spaghetti. When the doctor summoned Mike to Helena's bedside, Anne had taken the opportunity to slip away unnoticed, after calling Caroline to reassure her. Ed had been outside in his car, waiting to find out about Helena, and he'd been kind enough to drive her back to her apartment.

Well, now what? The sudden letdown felt anticlimactic. She looked around for a moment and the familiar room now appeared . . . boring? She had a hysterical urge to laugh, realizing the rest of this day had been anything but dull! What sane person would want more of that kind of excitement in her life? Oh, she knew what kind of excitement she was missing. But she couldn't go through another go-round with him. She just couldn't. Not when she knew in advance what the end would be.

When Anne heard the firm but quiet knock on the door it might have been *déjà vu*, except the last time the knocking had been loud, demanding. But the man at the door was the same. Her heart jumped, then she groaned. No, no more. She wasn't strong enough to face him again, not now.

As before, Mike stood in the same spot,

hand upraised to knock, and they looked at each other in silence. She would have been content, she admitted to herself, to be able to look at him for the next eternity or two. How wonderful to be wrapped inside those strong arms, to be held and stroked and caressed, as she remembered his caresses. To be kissed and aroused, as she so clearly felt the memory of his kisses, his touch. It was a pain she couldn't bear.

"Hello, Anne." Mike hesitated, suddenly awkward, unsure. "May I . . . please come in. It's cold out here."

Déjà vu. They both thought of it . . . that last time. Her mind worked slower tonight, and defeated, she gestured him inside.

Her small bandaged hand on the doorknob shook visibly when she closed the door, and she couldn't take her eyes off him as he moved across the room. His mere presence made it his domain; he took charge just as he seemed able to take charge of her senses whenever she was near him.

I'm like some damned sixteen-year-old . . . except my boobs are bigger and my skin is clearer!

"Is Helena all right?" She knew the answer, but she had to say something to restore reality to herself. Because she was losing touch, drifting into fantasy again, and she couldn't afford that. Not anymore.

"She'll be fine. Thanks to you. I . . . we owe you everything."

"You owe me nothing, Mike. I did what anyone would have done." Not gratitude, please. Not from him. Better nothing. Better a polite little note of thanks if he had to discharge his obligation some way. But she couldn't stand here and watch him and listen to him and know gratitude was all there was.

"No. Not anyone. You. And it's strange, isn't it, that I wasn't surprised when Caroline told me it was you she called. I knew you'd be there when we needed you . . . when I needed you." He stared at her, saying things with his eyes that words couldn't tell her nearly as well. "Are you, Annie?" His voice seemed to crack. "Are you here for me now when I need you?"

Something was wrong. She couldn't see him suddenly, and then she backhanded the tears from her eyes, the gauze on her hands absorbing the moisture. He reached for her and she came into Mike's waiting arms.

His mouth claimed hers, gently, softly, not invading and taking, but offering, seeking, asking. His lips touched and caressed, his tongue tenderly meeting and tasting hers, the sweetness of all she had to offer. And then their mouths fused in greedy desire, released and unrestrained. Mike explored again every tiny crevice, every ridge and whorl and hidden source of pleasure, and knew he would be eternally grateful for this second chance. His tongue danced maddeningly across the surface of hers, touching and teasing in a sensuous exchange of pleasures.

It was a kiss filled with all joy and passion, all bright promise and unexplored future, all of themselves that had waited for this perfect moment. As if the world had been re-created especially for them. A kiss filled with love.

Love. Mike pulled back slowly, reluctant to allow even a breath of air to separate him from Anne. He hadn't wanted to think of love. And now he could think of nothing else. But there were things to be settled, things he had to tell her. If she would only listen . . .

"M—Mike?" Anne leaned back against the wall, eyes closed, still in the circle of his arms. She tried to catch her breath, the breath he'd stolen with his kiss. "Wow! I think you just melted the fillings in my teeth!"

"Annie, I . . . I want to talk to you."

"Well," she gasped, rearranging her robe, "you sure have a way with words!"

"God, I hope so!"

She looked at him through eyes misty with newly awakened passion, and Anne knew the center of her life rested here, in the arms of this gentle giant of a man. How very odd that this man, whom she'd once thought so hard, so harsh, so unyielding, should prove to be the source of such indescribable beauty, such intense, exquisite delight . . . such incredible joy! She leaned toward him again.

"No, wait, Annie. We have to talk. Please, let me say this." He held her at arm's length. She couldn't know what that gesture cost him.

"Okay." She touched his cheek, smoothing his moustache with her fingers, rubbing her thumb along his lower lip, wanting . . . "Come on and sit down. Why don't I make us some coffee?" She walked to the stove, turning as he started to chuckle.

He fell onto the couch, shaking his head ruefully and laughing. "My God, don't ever tell Caroline you said that or I'll never hear the end of it. She told me the trouble with me lately is I should start drinking some good coffee for a change." He sat back, looking at her with a gentle smile. "You're a hell of a lot better looking than Juan Valdez!"

"My, my, you'll turn my head! You sure know how to dish out the compliments."

He grinned and watched while she finished

up in the kitchen, content to see the way she moved, the lovely expression that serenity and happiness brought to her face. He wanted to watch her, to love her, to wake up beside her for the rest of his life.

She brought two steaming mugs back and sat down beside him, an unspoken need to be close. "You know, Mike, I never heard the whole story about tonight. What was it all about? Why would Elliot, of all people, get involved in something as despicable as that? What possible reason could he have?"

"Elliot isn't—never was—the businessman his father was, I guess. Too many bad investments and he wound up 'borrowing' from some of his accounts. And he came damn close to getting away with it. His secretary, Janine Murray, is engaged to Cully Bryant, one of my men . . . the one with the big mouth," he said with barely controlled anger. "It wasn't hard for Elliot to pump enough information from Janine to figure out where we'd be staked out. It'll be a long time before Cully forgets when and where to keep his mouth shut!"

Mike sighed, leaned back, and took a healthy swallow of the hot brew. "Mmm, good! Anyway, the auditors are due in three days and he was desperate for money. And he didn't particularly care how he got it. I never liked him, but I didn't realize what a vicious streak he has in him." His mouth tightened. He looked very dangerous just then. "I think if he'd done anything to . . ." He closed his eyes and reached with his free hand for Anne's. He winced at the sight of the gauze and clasped it very gently, lifting it to his lips to press a kiss to the bandages.

"For the first time I think I understand what the term temporary insanity means. I think I went nuts there for a minute when I got my hands on him. If Ed and Tim hadn't pulled me off him, I don't know what I . . ." He put the mug on the table and pulled Anne into his arms; he needed to feel her, the reality of her body close to him, her warmth mingling with his. He needed to know she was really safe, here with him, and would always.

"Poor Elliot." She rested her head on Mike's shoulder, stroking the back of his neck, enjoying from memory the feel of his skin, sliding her wrapped hand over his thick, unkempt silvered hair. "Now that it's all over, I can almost feel sorry for him."

"Well, you're a hell of a lot more charitable than I am. I won't complain if he rots in a cell forever! After what he did to you and Helena . . ."

"I remember reading something once, I think it was from Winston Churchill: 'You can measure a man's character by the choice he makes under pressure.' If he's earned our hatred, he's also earned our pity."

Mike looked down at her, his heart spilling from his eyes, and placed a gentle kiss on her tousled head. "Caroline was, as usual, absolutely right. You are a nice girl. His expression sobered again and he sat up on the edge of the couch, separating himself from her. He clasped his hands between his knees. "Look, Anne, that night after we . . . after we made love I . . . I made a real ass of myself."

"Yes."

"You've become so agreeable." He sighed. "I said some stupid things to you and you didn't deserve them. I know that, I knew it then, but I . . . I was . . . please don't laugh, but I was afraid." He stared down at the floor, reluctant to face her. "You scare me, lady. I had everything figured, all arranged in neat little labeled compartments of my life."

"It's right there on your badge, isn't it, Mike?" He looked puzzled and she grinned at him. "The state motto: 'Live free or die.' "

He made a sour grimace with his mouth. His hands flexed into hard fists, then opened again, resting on his knees. "When every idea you've built on and lived by for a lifetime is suddenly turned upside down, you don't know what to believe in anymore. It was so easy to decide the trouble was you, not my way of thinking or my judgments, but you."

He lifted his eyes finally and looked at Anne. "Because I had a couple of . . . bad experiences, I shut myself away from believing in any other kind." He lowered his head, holding it between his hands, staring down at the floor. "I've never wanted anything in my whole miserable life as much as I wanted to erase that night when I walked out of here and left you like that."

He sat silent, tense, waiting before he finally looked up . . . and thought he could happily drown in the smile that curved her lovely mouth. As if someone somewhere had kept a promise.

"I hope you don't want to forget *everything* about that night."

Mike stared at her. "No," he breathed hoarsely, "no, there are some things I'll never forget."

They both stood, and she held out her

hands to welcome him back. "Oh, Annie, sweetheart, you don't know what it was like—"

"Oh, don't I?" she murmured against his chest, holding him closer, tighter, afraid she'd wake up in her cold, empty bed and find it had all been a taunting dream. "If I'd known you were such a pushover for a good cup of coffee, I'd have started a delivery service." She pushed his jacket down his arms and he let it drop to the floor. The sleeve flipped over the empty mug, toppling it off the table. It bounced against the leg of the couch and came to rest by his foot. He bent and put it back on the table.

"I've learned a lot of things are tougher than they look."

"See," Anne mumbled against the furred contour of his wide chest, "who said you're a dumb cop?"

"You know," he whispered against her ear, the soft breath sending shivers down her spine, "I owe Caroline and Helena a helluva lot for rattling my cage." His mouth savored the taste of the soft flesh along her jaw and down her throat.

"Mmmm, keep talking." Anne tilted her head back, offering a clear field for his kisses. She shivered despite the delicious heat of his arms imprisoning her so tightly. "Guess I'm your prisoner, Chief. Held by the long arm of the law." She ran her tongue across his chest and he groaned.

"Who's got who?" he murmured, sliding his hands down over her hot skin.

"I'm telling you right now . . . aah, that's nice! . . . you'd better not be here just because of Caroline and . . . oh, *Mike* . . . and Helena." She said the last word with hesitation, still needing a final bit of reassurance.

He stood back as she made an attempt on the buttons of his shirt. "Damn," she muttered, frustrated, holding up her hands. "Me and my gauze paws."

He laughed and gently lifted the mittened hands, then pulled his shirt off. Her robe joined the shirt. Mike's hands slipped beneath the straps of her nightgown and pulled them off her shoulders. His mouth followed the same path, leaving a warm, glowing trail along her flesh. He pressed her back against the wall, allowing the full weight of his taut arousal to slide against her. "For now, let's forget Caroline and Helena. Only you and I matter right now. How much evidence do you need?"

"Mike, it's just so hard—"

"Yes, I know!" he groaned.

"Stop that! You know what I mean," she

laughed, and he felt the sound inside his heart.

"I'm trying to say it's hard to believe you'd want me. You could have anyone . . . the youngest, most beautiful . . ."

"I don't want the youngest, most beautiful, I want you!"

"Gee, thanks a lot!" she mumbled. "I know, I know, I'm better looking than Juan Valdez."

He stood there, holding her close, grinning.

"I just . . . look, Mike, please don't play with me. I'm not in your league. I'm not . . . built for speed." She blushed, and he thought he'd never seen anything so appealing in his life.

"No, Annie love, you're not built for speed. You're built for comfort . . . and, as you once said yourself, 'the long haul.' " He smiled, a lazy, confident smile, as if he knew a joke he hadn't yet shared with her. "Hell, I'm not a kid anymore. I know what I want, and if you're honest with yourself, you know it, too. Come on, Annie, what are you afraid of?"

"You." He might have missed her whisper entirely if he hadn't been concentrating so hard. "I'm afraid of you." Afraid of loving too much. Afraid of maybe losing too much.

His eyes widened, his nostrils flared slightly with the sudden intensity of the moment.

"That's funny. Until now that was my line. We both have to take a chance, Annie. I had to learn that, too, to get over the fear. I guess that's why I wanted you to think there were other women, to keep you at a distance. You know, Honey was the only one, and even she wasn't—"

"Oh, I know about Honey. We had lunch the other day, and we talked about you . . . a lot."

"Oh, hell, that's all I needed, you two to gang up against me!" He laughed, shaking his head. "I wanted so much that night to prove to you—no, maybe I wanted to prove it to *me*—that I didn't need you, didn't love you, and I—"

"Did you say . . . ?"

"What? Did I say what?"

"Love."

He just stood, looking at her, his steady gaze never wavering.

"Listen, Novak, I distinctly heard that word . . . right out of your mouth. You don't think I'm gonna let you take it back, do you?" She smiled a contented smile and ran her hand down the length of his spine.

Mike tightened his arms around her, lifting her off the floor. "I learned something very precious tonight, something some men aren't fortunate enough to ever know. I learned the meaning of the word *trust.*" Anne swallowed a sudden lump, wiped a couple of tears on the gauze, and said a quiet prayer of gratitude. "That makes this important enough to fight for. So, I couldn't take it back even if you said no." He nibbled on her lower lip and she reacted just the way he'd hoped. "Mmm, that felt very nice."

"Uh . . . said no to what?" Anne raised her arms and wrapped them tightly around his neck.

"I'm too old and stiff—"

"So you are, so you are!" She began to kiss him, nipping at the lobe of his ear, teasing with her tongue in the sensitive crevices, letting him know exactly what she was thinking about.

"—to get down on my knees, but I'm telling—*asking*—you to marry me, Annie. Marry me and lie beside me and make love with me, and grow older and greyer, and see the seasons change, for all the years we're lucky enough to have."

Anne smiled through eyes heavy with rising passion. "Yes, oh yes, my darling Michael Novak, I most definitely say yes! Oh!" She looked at him suddenly, eyes wide. "We'll have to call Jerry and tell him you're making an honest woman of his mother."

Mike pulled her into his body, settling her even more firmly against him. His hands slid up from her waist until his thumbs found the rigid mounds of her breasts. He bent his head, nuzzling the tender flesh, then gently placed his mouth on one swollen nipple, rolling it between his teeth and his tongue.

"Oh, Mi-i-ike." The sob was torn from her throat with a passion she couldn't hold back. "All . . . right, all right, we'll call . . . later!"

"Caroline's been letting me know for years she thought I should find a good woman to settle down with." He grinned and murmured against her parted lips. "Let's see how good you are!"

Anne arched her brows, a wicked smile turning up the corners of her mouth. "Oh, I'm very, very good. And when I'm bad, I'm even better!"

Mike's eyes glowed with a new tenderness and passion, and a lazy smile curved beneath his moustache. He held her close to his heart. "Ah, Annie, you're not so bad. You're not so bad at all!"

Epilogue

"Anne, unless you have elastic under the plasterboard, I still don't see how we're all going to fit."

Laura stuck a carrot stick between her teeth and, chewing studiously, studied the small apartment.

Anne looked up from the stove, where she was giving a final stir to a saucepan of deep brown gravy, and made a face at her friend. "Oh, ye of little faith. There's plenty of room, don't worry."

"You know me, I never worry. But you could've made it easier on yourself by doing this at Mike's. After all, tomorrow it'll be your home, too."

They'd waited until the Thanksgiving weekend for the wedding so Jerry could be there. Tomorrow they'd gather in Mike's living room for the ceremony, surrounded by the friends and family who mattered most to them, and Jerry would give his mother's hand to the man with whom she would share the rest of her life.

"You could even have done it downstairs, that big kitchen, and there's plenty of seating room."

"No, Laura," Anne murmured, looking around the room with affection, running her hand over the countertop and the wooden cupboard. "That's too much like a restaurant. This is home, where I started my new life; it's where all the good things began, where Mike and I met, and Helena. It's a special Thanksgiving for me and the last time here." She shook her head, smiling. "No, this is the place to be."

"Well, okay, give me the plates and I'll set 'em out. By the way, when are they all going to be here? The food's all ready, isn't it?"

"As soon as the football game's over. They're at the Rowans'. Carl got this huge new TV screen and he asked them all to come watch at his place, thank goodness. Can you imagine stepping over all those legs while we set the table and get ready? Like a scene from the Marx Brothers."

Laura gathered the silver Anne had lying on the counter and carried everything into the larger room. "So, how many are coming? Lord, you've been here . . . what . . . five months? And already you've got half the town coming for Thanksgiving dinner. Of course, the room's so small it only *seems* like half the town." She picked up the list Anne had prepared, which included the names of her guests and the menu for the day.

"I see you've started to do this, too, huh? I always thought you worked off the top of your head."

"Yeah, sure," Anne laughed, turning down the oven temperature to warm. The mashed and sweet potatoes and the stuffing were cooked; they just had to stay hot. The broccoli and carrots were steaming on top of the stove, and the turkey, all twenty-two brown and fragrant pounds of it, was sliced and keeping hot on a platter in the lower oven. Dessert was being provided today by the guests.

"The ol' memory's been on vacation for quite a while now, Laura. I'm pretty good if I fooled you all this time, but that list is all that stands between us and starvation today. Without it, I'd have forgotten to buy the cider or peel the potatoes or take the cranberry sauce out of the freezer. So just thank your lucky stars for that list."

"Nice to see you're human, too, sweetie. So you're not really Wonder Woman after all, hmm?" She grinned, then consulted the paper again. "Let's see, how many—? Anne, you've got *thirteen people coming?*"

"Yes, why? Oh, Laura, no, I don't believe it! You're not superstitious, are you? I've known you forever and I never—!"

"Well," Laura shrugged sheepishly, "I'm not *really* superstitious. It's just . . . just that . . . well, you know, *thirteen* . . . it just kind of startled me and . . ."

Anne walked around the counter and hugged her friend. "Oh, Laura, the people at this table today couldn't be anything but *good* luck! I'm surer of that than of my own name."

"Well, don't forget, tomorrow that'll change, too."

Anne nodded, grinning, and Laura had never seen her happier. "I'm so happy for you, Annie. If anyone deserves a second time around, it's you. I told Mike he better be good to you or I'll go after his knees with a baseball bat!"

"You didn't!" Anne cracked up and collapsed onto a stool, laughing aloud at the image of a vengeful Laura chasing after Mike through the streets of Whitefield.

It wasn't a problem she'd have to worry too much about, she thought, smiling fondly at the other woman. Last night they'd all gotten together, straight from the airport over in Montpelier across the state line in Vermont, Laura and Jim and especially Jerry, to meet Mike and Helena and Caroline. Mike had taken them to dinner at the Spalding Inn— Anne smiled, recalling the night she'd met him with Honey—and afterward they'd gone back to his house . . . their house, Anne thought with a deep sense of wonder and joy. Their house. *Their home.* She hadn't realized how tense she'd been over that meeting, not until Mike had brought them back here, she and Jerry. He'd bedded down on the sofa, but first they'd sat up talking, catching up.

"I really like him, Mom. He's okay. As long as you're happy and you're sure . . ." She'd heaved a sigh of relief at Jerry's thumbs up. He'd also appreciated Caroline's dry sense of humor and preened like a peacock at Helena's open hero worship. A college man, after all! Laura and Jim had approved, too. *Well, what's not to approve.* Mike could hold his own with anyone, anywhere, and it had been a wonderful evening. For sure, somebody up there liked her, Anne thought gratefully.

"Seriously," Laura was saying, "I do like your Mike. He loves you, and for me, Annie, that's all that matters."

"Yes, he's quite a guy."

"Not to mention sexy as hell!"

"Well, yeah, that, too," Anne said with fervor, her cheeks flushing noticeably.

"Good for you, Annie!" Anne stared, and Laura hugged her. "You're rotten at keeping secrets from me, you should know that by now. I told you I can read you like a book, and right now it's the *Kama Sutra*, I bet. A little try before you buy?"

"Laura!" Anne looked around guiltily as if expecting to find an audience hanging on their words. "Don't you dare say anything in front of Jerry."

"Oh, come on, Anne," Laura couldn't contain her amusement, "give me some credit, please! I raised three kids, and they don't think Jim and I 'do it,' either. They think I found them under a rose petal, for God's sake. Although if you think Jerry would be surprised, you're crazy. He's a healthy male, and they recognize each other, believe it! He might not want to actually hear it from you or admit it, but he knows. Oh yeah, I'll just bet he knows!"

She was still chuckling to herself, setting knives and forks in place, when Caroline and Helena knocked at the door, with Sandy Larkin in tow.

"We picked up Sandy on the way over. Whoa,

boy, it is *freeeeezing* out there. Brrr!" Helena and Sandy unzipped their parkas and dropped them on the couch. Caroline unbuttoned her coat after first depositing a large sweet-smelling pan on the counter. "Your favorite, Anne, apple grunt. Kind of figured it might have some sentimental appeal." She winked at Anne as Laura sniffed appreciatively and examined the dish.

"Grunt? What's—"

"Don't ask. I'll tell you some other time. For now, just think delicious or maybe sinfully delicious." Anne grinned at Caroline and took her coat. "Girls, could you please put your jackets in the closet, okay? We need every bit of space."

Helena's grin stretched her cold-reddened cheeks. "Jeez, Sandy, they aren't even married yet, and already I'm taking orders from the wicked stepmother. Oh, all right, just kidding!" Anne and Caroline smiled at each other.

Just then they were interrupted by the loud rumble and thundering vibrations of heavy male footsteps ascending the outside stairs. "Ah, the thundering herd approaches," Laura observed, and swung the door open before they could splinter the wood. The sudden arrival of six male bodies seemed to shrink the room. They were all grinning, laughing aloud, and it was obvious that the New England Patriots had been victorious.

"Hey, Mom, guess what? The Lions won, too! Yahoooo!" Jerry punched the air with a fist and gave Anne a high-five before giving her a quick hug. Then he and Jamie Larkin who had formed an immediate alliance, made a calculated detour toward the small bowl on top of the TV. They each took a handful of cashews and fell back under a female barrage of "you'll spoil your appetites" and "dinner's ready!"

"Boy," Jerry grumbled good-naturedly, "one of you is bad enough, but that's not fair . . . it's seven against two!" Jamie, not a talkative boy under the best of circumstances wisely said nothing, opting instead to hastily swallow the offending nuts.

Jerry edged around the table to the chair nearest the TV. "Anyway, I swear nothing ever spoils my appetite! So, when do we eat?"

"Right now!"

Caroline and Cora Larkin helped set everything on the table, which, with the strategic addition of a couple of card tables, stretched the length of the living room. It was admittedly a little crowded, but there was such good feeling in the air no one could have cared less. Nothing could spoil this day.

"Well," Anne stood at the end of the table, Jerry on her left, Mike on her right at the head of the table, "if I started listing all the things I personally feel thankful for, we might never get to eat dinner." She bent and kissed her son's head, and he winked and grinned up at her. She looked at Mike, not caring in that instant if anyone could see the emotion written on her face. "I can only say, I'm so very grateful for all of you and for everything good that's happened in my life in this last year."

Jerry, who could stand only so much of this, finally coughed and said plaintively, "I'm starving!"

Anne laughed, shaking her head. "He said it; nothing spoils his appetite. I hope that goes for everyone else. So, let's just remember what this day stands for and how much we have to be grateful for. Okay, that's it, sermon's over. Go on, dig in!"

"Before you sit, I want to give you something." Mike's words were low, unheard by the others who were busy demolishing days of cooking in the space of three minutes. Puzzled, Anne let him steer her toward the bedroom. He closed the door behind him and immediately pulled her into his arms. It was a few minutes before they came up for air, and Anne linked her hands behind his neck, gazing up into his eyes, wrapped in a warm sensation of home and joy and love.

I've been more lucky in my life than any woman could hope for. I've had the love of two very special men, and there's nothing more in this world I could ever want. Thank you, God. Thank you!

"I couldn't wait one more minute to kiss you. Do you realize that's the first time today?" Mike was gazing intently at her face, as if memorizing every feature, making sure she was real, making sure she was *there*. He'd begun to believe that tomorrow wouldn't ever arrive, that something would happen to snatch away the future they'd begun to plan.

Every day since that hellish night when he'd waited at the hospital for news of Helena, Anne had been in his thoughts, in his heart. He'd think of her and marvel all over again at how incredibly lucky he was to have found her. He'd been a man without trust for most of his adult life and even before, and it had been the one thing he'd vowed never to do . . . to allow someone inside those walls he'd built. But Anne, with her simple honesty, her warmth, her love, had made it impossible for him to keep her out.

And he should get down on his knees every day for the rest of his life in gratitude.

"If you don't stop looking at me like that, Novak," she sighed, her hands sliding over his back, down his spine, "I'll lock the door and we'll miss out on all the turkey." She moved against him, slowly, trailing small kisses along his neck, murmuring, "Don't you want to taste my . . . stuffing . . . maybe a little nibble on my . . . wishbone. And I have these . . . mmm . . . cranberries . . . to die for," she whispered huskily.

"Enough. You trying to kill me?" He smiled down at her and hugged her as tightly as he could. "Although I guess that'd be something to be thankful for, wouldn't it? What a way to go!"

Anne kissed him once more, quickly, then, hips swaying side to side, she started for the door, caroling, "Not until you taste my *sweeet* potatoes!"

"I've already tasted your *sweeet* potatoes, that's why I'm marrying you . . . so I can have seconds any time I want." He leered at her and wiggled his brows, and they both started laughing, covering their mouths quickly so those in the other room wouldn't hear.

"Wait, I almost forgot . . . I wanted to give

you something—no, not *that*. My, my, you are one dirty-minded woman!"

"Well, if not *that*, then what?"

He retrieved two gift-wrapped boxes he'd had stashed behind the bed. "This is a little pre-wedding gift."

"Two?"

"One's for you, the other's for Laura."

"*Laura?* What in the world . . . ?"

"You'd better open yours in here." His mouth was turned up in a half-smile and Anne laughed with delight. "I love surprises!" She slid the ribbon off, and when she looked inside her eyes opened wide. Then she began to laugh. "You don't forget a thing, do you?"

She held up the black satin sheets and the subscription blank for the Sunday *New York Times*. "I'd love to have been a fly on the wall when you asked for satin sheets—*black* satin sheets. Did you keep a straight face? Did the saleswoman keep a straight face?" She put her arms around him. "I think I'm gonna like hanging out with you, Chief Novak."

"I figured I might as well eliminate at least one problem ahead of time." He kissed her gently, then took her hand and sat on the edge of the bed, pulling her down onto his knees.

"Anne, I want to tell you this and I won't have another chance before tomorrow." He looked very earnest and very uncomfortable. "I'm not a poetic man, I'm not great with words, but I have to tell you this . . . and maybe I won't ever say it again, but always remember it." He closed his eyes for a moment, then looked straight into her eyes, her heart.

"It took me a long time to learn how to trust, to even know the meaning of the word. You taught it to me, and I think maybe I knew almost from the first time we met. I love you, Anne, and I trust you, with everything that's dearest to me. That night, when you overcame your worst terrors to save Helena, I was forced to admit what I'd been too stubborn and too proud to see. Annie, you're the best thing that could ever happen to me and . . . and I know how precious you are."

Tears glistened in her eyes, and Anne couldn't see him clearly. She didn't have to. With her heart, she saw what he was, and in that moment she loved him more than she'd believed possible. When she was with him, he filled her with rainbows. "Oh, Mike, we're so lucky to have this second chance. I think we've both learned how to trust . . . ourselves and each other. We each took a chance and it worked . . . we made it. Second chances are too precious to ignore."

At that moment, the door thudded with a heavy fist from the other side. "Are you two ever coming out, or can we have your share, too?"

"We're coming, Jim, just a minute." Anne stood, pulling Mike up with her. "I love you, Chief Novak, you can't know how much, and I'll always remember this moment. Some things are too important even for *me* to forget." They smiled at each other, then turned to the door.

"Oh yeah, Laura's gift." Mike picked up the other box from the bed and they went in to the others.

"Hello, young lovers," Jim teased them.

"Boy, you two can't even wait until tomorrow? Tsk, tsk, such scandalous behavior!" Carl Rowan laughed so hard his chins were in constant motion. Lou jabbed her elbow into his prominent stomach, shushing him, and passed the bowl of stuffing to Emil Larkin on her left. "So, Mr. Larkin, I hear you're moving into those new garden apartments on the other side of the park. If you need any help, Carl and I'll be glad to lend a hand."

"Thanks a lot, Mrs. Rowan—"

"Oh, come on, just call me Lou."

"Well, thanks, Lou. Since they straightened out my workman's comp, it's made a big difference for us. And soon as my therapy's finished, I might be able to go back to work. Then maybe Cora will get to stay home a little more. That'll be another Thanksgiving day for me, I can tell you." He smiled diffidently at her.

"We have an awful lot to be thankful for right now, Emil," Cora Larkin murmured from across the table. "Thank God we got Jamie. And, I don't know if he told you, Chief Novak, one of the people at the College Fair and Career Night over at White Mountain High told him she'll help him apply for a loan and a scholarship. Jamie's gonna go to college next September! Can you believe it? He's going to college."

"Chief Novak, I really appreciate how much you've helped me. The job's a real lifesaver, and they'd never have given me the chance if it wasn't for you." A look of understanding and recognition passed between them.

"What job, Jamie?" Helena asked between bites of turkey and gravy.

"I'm going to be working full-time over at the police department! Your dad got them to train me to be the dispatcher." He turned to Anne. "I was going to tell you, Mrs. McClellan. Isn't that great? The chief said he worked that job when he was my age, too. Kind of a coincidence, isn't it?"

He grinned at them, having just spoken the longest string of consecutive words Anne had ever heard from him. It was like watching the birth of a new, relaxed, self-confident human being, and she looked over at Mike just as he looked up at her. She smiled, recalling the night of Helena's birthday. When she looked at Caroline, she knew that the memory was in her mind, also. They shared a quick grin and a nod.

"Anne, what's in the box?" Laura was staring at the long, gaily wrapped gift box Mike had brought out of the bedroom.

"I don't know. Well, Mike, you gonna end the suspense?" They all waited while he stood and carried the box around to Laura. She stared in surprise as he handed it to her. "A token of my sincerity and friendship"—he looked at Anne, and winked—"and *trust!*"

Laura was busy pulling the wrappings away, and when she finally lifted the lid there was a moment of silence. Her mouth began to open, her lips twitched a little, and then she fell back in her chair, howling with laughter. "Well, it'd be pretty hard not to believe you now!" She told everyone at the table about her conversation and promise to Mike the night before, then held up the gift for all to see—a beautiful, brand-new ash wood, tape-handled major league baseball bat. Her name was inscribed across the "sweet spot." "I will treasure this always, Mike." She looked at him with mock severity. "And don't you forget it!"

After the laughter had died down somewhat and before the next round of football games kicked off, Anne remembered a bit of news she wanted to give them. "By the way, every-one, I just got a letter yesterday, from Ilse Kolchak! She's a born-again New Mexican now. And guess what? She's getting married! Isn't that great?"

"See, us men know a good thing when we find it," Mike drawled. "A woman who's a good baker doesn't get left alone for long!" He took Anne's hand and they sat there gazing at each other, foolish smiles pasted on their mouths.

"Well, then," Helena chimed in, "we'll have to see about fixing Aunt Caro up with some-one. How 'bout Mr. Capers, over at the post office? He could use a little fattening up."

"Well, now, I don't know about that," Anne warned. She tipped her head and looked at Mike, a frown between her eyes but a smile twitching on her lips. "I agreed to marry you, but after all, I thought Caroline was part of the deal. Now . . . well, I don't know . . . maybe I'd better think it over."

"Yeah, you think it over, Annie." Mike leaned over and took her face between his large hands. His dark eyes were shining and the mouth beneath that luxuriant slash of moustache was smiling happily. "I'll give you about thirty or forty years to make up your mind." And then he leaned over, utterly oblivious to the other eleven people avidly watching, and kissed the living daylights out of her. It was a very convincing argument.

About the Author

Joan and Norm, her patient and proud husband, live just outside of Detroit, Michigan. Past-President of the Greater Detroit Romance Writers of America, in her spare time she crosses her fingers and still buckles on her skis (at least for now!), loves to read and is a part-time librarian and mother of three grown children: Bob, Larry and Helene, who are now *True Believers!*

HELLO, LOVE, March, '93, was followed by "The Eighth Candle" in the '93 Holiday Anthology, MERRY CHRISTMAS, MY LOVE. In October look for "Dori's Miracle" in Zebra's To Love Again 1994 Holiday Anthology. If you look close you'll see black and blue marks where Joan's still pinching herself: WOW! describes her state of euphoria! *Please* write: P.O. Box 250105, Franklin, MI, 48025.

Coming next month
from *To Love Again:*

HURRICANE HERO, by Martha Gross

TRUE TEXAS LOVE, by Thelma Alexander